THE
TRIALS OF
ZION

BOOKS BY ALAN DERSHOWITZ

The Case For Moral Clarity: Israel, Hamas and Gaza

The Case Against Israel's Enemies: Exposing Jimmy Carter and Others Who Stand in the Way of Peace

Is There a Right to Remain Silent? Coercive Interrogation and the Fifth Amendment after 9/11

Finding Jefferson: A Lost Letter, a Remarkable Discovery, and the First Amendment in an Age of Terrorism

Blasphemy: How the Religious Right Is Hijacking Our Declaration of Independence

Preemption: A Knife That Cuts Both Ways

What Israel Means to Me: By 80 Prominent Writers, Performers, Scholars, Politicians, and Journalists

Rights from Wrongs: A Secular Theory of the Origins of Rights

America on Trial: Inside the Legal Battles That Transformed Our Nation

The Case for Peace: How the Arab-Israeli Conflict Can Be Resolved

The Case for Israel

America Declares Independence

Why Terrorism Works: Understanding the Threat, Responding to the Challenge

Shouting Fire: Civil Liberties in a Turbulent Age

Letters to a Young Lawyer

Supreme Injustice: How the High Court Hijacked Election 2000

Genesis of Justice: Ten Stories of Biblical Injustice That Led to the Ten Commandments and Modern Law

Just Revenge

Sexual McCarthyism: Clinton, Starr, and the Emerging Constitutional Crisis

The Vanishing American Jew: In Search of Jewish Identity for the Next Century

Reasonable Doubts: The Criminal Justice System and the O.J. Simpson Case

The Abuse Excuse: And Other Cop-Outs, Sob Stories, and Evasions of Responsibility

The Advocate's Devil

Contrary to Popular Opinion

Chutzpah

Taking Liberties: A Decade of Hard Cases, Bad Laws, and Bum Raps

Reversal of Fortune: Inside the von Bülow Case

The Best Defense

Criminal Law: Theory and Process

Psychoanalysis: Psychiatry and Law

THE TRIALS OF ZION

===== A NOVEL =====

ALAN M. DERSHOWITZ

GRAND CENTRAL
PUBLISHING

New York   Boston

Grand Central Publishing
Hachette Book Group
237 Park Avenue
New York, NY 10017

www.HachetteBookGroup.com

Printed in the United States of America

First Edition: October 2010
10 9 8 7 6 5 4 3 2 1

Grand Central Publishing is a division of Hachette Book Group, Inc.
The Grand Central Publishing name and logo is a trademark of Hachette Book Group, Inc.

Library of Congress Cataloging-in-Publication Data
Dershowitz, Alan M.
   The trials of Zion / Alan M. Dershowitz. — 1st ed.
      p. cm.
   Summary: "A novel of Israel today, a place where warring factions from within and outside the Middle East continue to battle for the soul of a land they all regard as holy" — Provided by publisher.
      ISBN 978-0-446-57673-4 (regular ed.) — ISBN 978-0-446-50542-0 (large print ed.)
   1. Israel — Fiction.   2. Jewish-Arab relations — Fiction.   I. Title.
   PS3554.E77T75 2010
   813'.54 — dc22
                                                                    2009049546

This book is lovingly dedicated to the memory of my mother, Claire Dershowitz, who died in 2008 at the age of ninety-five. She always encouraged and defended me. She would have liked this book.

THE
TRIALS OF
ZION

American Colony Hotel

East Jerusalem, Sometime in the Not-Too-Distant Future

PRESIDENT BILL MOORE was a man of many talents, but choreography was not one of them. Yet the entire enterprise on which he had staked his presidency, along with the credibility of the United States, could now be threatened by his inability to choreograph the dance between two reluctant suitors, Prime Minister Amnon Ezratti of Israel and Mahmud Yassin, the Hamas leader who would soon become president of the newly established Palestinian state. Ezratti was willing to shake hands with Yassin, but his government could not survive the traditional Arab kiss on the cheek from a man widely regarded by Israelis as a mass murderer. Last-minute intelligence had alerted Ezratti to Yassin's carefully designed plan to kiss him precisely in order to embarrass and perhaps topple his government.

Moore, who towered above Ezratti and Yassin, had assured his old friend Amnon that he would position himself so as to prevent a kiss, even if it took a not-so-gentle shove. "Remember, I played hockey at Dartmouth," Moore whispered to the Harvard-educated Ezratti. The Israeli prime minister offered a subdued chuckle in recognition of Moore's expectation that those around him would always laugh at his often lame attempts at humor. That's what people do when presidents tell bad jokes.

Yassin huddled with his acting prime minister, Suri Chalaba, the leader of Fatah. Yassin had beaten Chalaba decisively in the last election, and there was no love lost between them. Chalaba had been appointed to his position as a symbol of unity, but it was expected that he would soon be replaced by a Yassin loyalist. The two men stayed in close proximity at public events in order to reduce the risk of an assassination attempt by supporters of the other.

"So this is what it comes down to," Ezratti mused to Moore. "After so many thousands killed, peace depends on your ability to stop that son of a bitch from planting his big Arab lips on my pockmarked Jewish chin."

"They don't write about this kind of stuff in the history books," Moore said with a look of solemnity returning to his handsome face. Ezratti forced a smile, masking his apprehension over the future.

"Okay. Let's do it. The world is waiting," Moore announced, adjusting Ezratti's tie, then Chalaba's, and finally his own, as the robed Yassin looked on with bemusement.

"This is a historic moment," Yassin said. "The end of a long journey and the beginning of an even longer one."

Ezratti didn't like the last part, interpreting it—as many doubting Israelis did—as a way for Yassin to preserve the option of destroying the Jewish state, either demographically or violently. Many Palestinians were equally doubtful, believing that Ezratti would never dismantle the remaining Jewish settlements that still dotted the Palestinian state-to-be or end the targeted assassinations of suspected terrorists.

"Friends don't need peace treaties," President Moore reminded the old adversaries. "Enemies do." Moore was well known for his unsentimental pragmatism — surprising to some from a man of such deep religious beliefs. "Let's sign and see if time, and a few well-placed American soldiers, can't turn you from hot enemies into cold enemies. And then, maybe, by the end of our lifetimes, into decent neighbors."

"And don't forget a few well-placed American dollars," Yassin quipped, reminding the president of his pledge to give the new Palestinian state $35 billion to resettle the refugees.

"You won't let me forget," Moore replied. "So let's get on with the most expensive handshake in history."

President Moore paused for a moment, crossed himself solemnly, and whispered a prayer. Ezratti, who was agnostic, looked on a bit awkwardly, while Yassin and Chalaba turned away.

The four men, with their small entourages and security details, proceeded to walk, almost march, through large doors in the west wing of the American Colony Hotel in East Jerusalem. Entering a poorly air-cooled courtyard, they made their way to the cordoned-off podium area. Chalaba stood directly behind Yassin, watching his every move. The audience, sweating profusely in the early-summer heat, consisted of cabinet members, diplomats who had been instrumental in bringing the parties together, and media representatives from around the world. TV cameras transmitted live images to millions of viewers. The public had been excluded for security reasons, despite President Moore's request to invite some important donors and political friends. When it came to security, the president had a vote but the Secret Service held the veto.

President Moore, with his patented toothy smile, briefly introduced the two signatories, placing his large arms around their shoulders. "Now for the handshake that seals the deal," Moore said out loud. "And don't even think about kissing him or I'll knock you on your ass," he whispered to Yassin without moving his lips.

Yassin smiled. He had a plan of his own. Like an anxious lover calculating a conquest, he knew that any attempt to kiss his enemy now would be thwarted. But later, at the reception... He had already alerted an Al Jazeera cameraman to be poised.

Yassin thrust his hand forward, tossing a head fake at the same time to disarm Ezratti, who stepped back nervously. Moore took Amnon's hand and brought it toward Yassin's. At the precise moment their hands touched, a massive explosion rocked the entire area. Everyone near the podium was killed instantly along with several people in the audience. The blast was seen and heard on television screens throughout the world, just before everything went black.

It was not the worst terrorist attack in history. Thirty-one people were killed and more than a hundred injured—a fraction of the casualties suffered on September 11, 2001. But it was certainly the worst political assassination in history. Never before had so many heads of state and leading officials been murdered at the same time.

The Martyrs of Jihad, a small offshoot of Hamas with close connections to Iranian religious figures, immediately claimed credit, but both the CIA and the Mossad were skeptical, because fringe groups frequently claim credit for terrorist acts in order to raise their profiles and gain new recruits. Within hours a young Muslim radical named Faisal Husseini was seen videotaping the crime scene from the roof of a nearby building. He was arrested by the Israeli police and accused of being a member of the Martyrs of Jihad. He was also suspected of being one of those responsible for the attack. After less than an hour of interrogation by the Shin Bet—the Israeli security service—Husseini confessed to having planted the bomb on behalf of the Martyrs of Jihad, who believed that all of Palestine, including what was now Israel, was holy Muslim land and that the two-state solution was heresy.

Habash Ein, a Christian Arab graduate of Hebrew University Law School with a master's from Yale Law School, was appointed to represent Husseini. This was done to mollify the Palestinians, who were furious that the case was being tried in an Israeli court, despite the fact that the American Colony was in the part of Jerusalem slated to become the capital of the new Palestinian state. The explosion had put everything on hold — including Palestinian statehood.

The arrest of Husseini did not slow down the investigations being conducted by the Israeli Mossad, or by the American CIA, FBI, and Secret Service. Both Israel and the United States claimed jurisdiction over the horrible crime that had killed their leaders. They were determined to solve it and to prosecute those responsible. The United States did not seek to extradite Husseini for trial in America — at least not yet. Their investigation was far from complete. Let Israel take the first shot at bringing Husseini to trial, the Americans reasoned. A rush to judgment — especially in such emotionally laden cases — often produced the wrong result. If the Israelis got it right, the Americans could always bring him to the United States later and execute him — assuming the Israelis didn't execute him first, under a rarely used law that authorized capital punishment in extraordinary terrorism cases involving multiple victims.

The new president of the United States, former vice president Christine Randall, declared a week of mourning and solemn prayer, while at the same time raising the terror-alert level to red. The acting prime minister of Israel, former minister of justice Tal Bar-Lev, asked his people to "sit shiva" in memory of the murder victims, while sealing the borders with Palestine and placing its air force on the highest level of preparedness. The Palestinian parliament could not agree on a new president or prime minister, but the spiritual leader of Hamas called for jihad, which he said involved purification through vengeance. The supreme leader of Iran characterized the deaths as "Allah's revenge" against infidels who would give sacred Islamic land to "Zionist crusaders," while demanding that Russia bolster Iranian air defenses against a possible Zionist attack.

I

Decision

Cambridge, Massachusetts, a Few Days Later

D AD! I've got incredible news!"
Abe Ringel's quiet morning was interrupted by the exuberant appearance of his twenty-six-year-old daughter, Emma. She'd only recently moved back to Cambridge after finishing law school at Yale, and Abe still hadn't gotten used to her being home. In fact, while he read the morning newspaper, still filled with accounts of the devastation in Jerusalem and its political aftermath around the world, and drank his single cup of decaf—he was hyper enough without caffeine—he'd almost forgotten she was in the house. There was no forgetting her now. Her energy was palpable. Before he had a chance to ask what the news was, she'd begun speaking in rapid-fire sentences.

"I'm going to the Mideast. I've gotten a job with a Palestinian human-rights group," Emma Ringel gushed, thrusting a printed-out e-mail into the lap of her father. Her words tumbled out breathlessly. "Remember my friend Habash from Yale? He hired me!"

"Habash Ein?" Abe set his paper on the kitchen table and retrieved the e-mail from his lap. As he read, a look of recognition passed over his face. "You used to bring him by for dinner, didn't you? Isn't he the guy they appointed to represent the guy who bombed the American Colony?"

"Yeah! It's so exciting!" Emma threw herself into a chair and grabbed the e-mail back from Abe. Since she'd finished school, the number-one topic of conversation in the Ringel household had been what her first job should be following her clerkship. She'd had offers—quality offers—thanks to her great grades and good, if controversial, pedigree. The daughter of Abe Ringel, famous defense attorney, part-time Harvard Law teacher, and celebrity in his own right ("TV ham" according to Emma), was sought after by law firms, corporations, and various do-gooder organizations around the country. But she'd turned down each job offer, much to Abe's confusion. She told him she was waiting for the *perfect* job. It hadn't occurred to Abe that she might leave the country. And now that the topic of going to Israel was raised, his stomach was uneasy.

"Habash needs help with the Husseini case." She misconstrued the look on Abe's face. "Jealous, Daddy? It's your kind of case. But don't try to horn in on me if I get to do it."

Abe didn't take the bait. "No way you're going to the Mideast now," he replied reflexively. Forty years of defending people in courts around the world made it hard for Abe to announce a decision without providing a detailed explanation. "It's a tinderbox over there, especially with the leadership all dead. At least we have a vice president to take over for Moore. The Israelis have an interim prime minister, but the Palestinians have nobody.

There's going to be civil war on top of the existing war. Maybe two civil wars."

His words hadn't done a thing to dampen Emma's determination. In fact, a smile lit up that face that looked so like her mother's, with her brown eyes and long black hair. "It's the perfect time. It's so exciting. I can make a difference."

"You've already accepted a clerkship with Judge Wolf. You can make a difference working with him." When Emma didn't say anything, Abe continued, "You can't just pick yourself up and go to a battle zone! You have a commitment to the judge."

She smiled, about to play her trump card. "That's the beauty of it. Judge Wolf agrees. He's holding the clerkship for me for a year."

Abe was rarely outmaneuvered, and he didn't like the feeling. Especially at the hands of his own daughter. "You told him first, before me!"

"I had to find out whether he would hold it before I told you."

"Asked me, you mean."

"No, Daddy, told you." Emma crossed her arms over her chest, and her chin tilted in a display of stubbornness. She got that streak from him. "I'm an adult. I don't need to ask you anymore, but I would love your approval."

Abe glanced at his baby, now a beautiful young woman. As Emma unconsciously tossed her long black hair, Abe found himself thinking about her late mother, who had been killed in an automobile accident years earlier. Emma had the same remarkable combination of sweetness and — Abe hesitated even to think this — sexiness. Having lost one love of his life, it was easy for him to imagine losing another.

"Emma, be reasonable. Put yourself in my place. You're my only child. I couldn't go on without you. Please stay here. Do your clerkship. There'll always be opportunities to do good."

Emma nodded, and the tone of her voice softened. "Now's the opportunity. I don't want to go through life regretting blown chances."

"But you do want to go through life! You're too young to put yourself at such risk."

"I'm going, Daddy. You just have to accept it. I'll be safe. I'm smart, remember?"

"Lots of smart people get blown up by dumb bombs, Emma. Think of Yarden."

Emma flinched. This was a direct hit from her father, and Abe felt momentarily sorry for saying it. Yet it was important to him that Emma think through the possibilities, and what better example than Yarden Golani, an Israeli woman who had been Emma's bunkmate at Camp Ramah in the Berkshire Mountains when they were both in their early teens.

Yarden had become a jewelry maker and was engaged to a young Israeli archaeology student named Ram Arad. Yarden and Ram had visited Emma several months earlier, in Boston, where they'd had a great time planning their wedding. Emma then traveled to Israel to be one of Yarden's bridesmaids. On the night before the wedding, Yarden and her father, a Holocaust survivor and emergency-room doctor, had gone to a café on Emek Refaim in Jerusalem for a celebratory drink. A Hamas suicide bomber blew himself up right next to them, killing them both. Yarden's wedding day became her burial day. Emma, wearing her bridesmaid dress and with a face streaming with tears, was a pallbearer at Yarden's funeral.

Tears came to Emma's eyes again as she remembered her friend. "I'm going to the Mideast for Yarden, Daddy." Her voice was now unsteady, woeful. "There have been too many Yardens on both sides. Too many funerals of young people. I want to help stop this."

"Believe me. I understand why you want to do this. We all want the violence there to end, so that the Yardens of the world can lead happy lives. But what can *you,* Emma Ringel, a young American, do? You're a lawyer, and, need I remind you, not a very experienced one."

"Experience is just repeating old mistakes."

Emma looked so sure of herself. Abe knew that this argument was one he'd lose; she was too young, too idealistic, too naïve about the situation in Israel to listen to her father's wise words.

"Emma, you don't know what you're getting yourself into. The hostilities in the Middle East go back generations. Everyone living there has a personal history tied to the conflict." Abe paused, leaning over to touch Emma's hand. "Even our family has suffered from the violence. Over there, experience is *everything.*"

Emma shook her head. "They need fresh eyes. Young people who aren't locked into the mistakes of the past."

Abe exhaled, and his shoulders sagged just slightly. His posture signaled to Emma that he was resigned to the loss of this argument.

"Don't ruin it for me by worrying all the time. How will I be able to enjoy myself if I'm worried about you worrying?"

Abe looked deeply into his daughter's eyes. "I may not be able to stop you from going, Emma. I wish I could," he said wistfully. "But you can't stop me from worrying. It's a father's prerogative."

Emma smiled at him. "Deal, Daddy. I go. You worry. And then I come back with the Nobel Peace Prize. Okay?"

"Not okay, but what can I do?"

Emma sprang from her side of the table and threw her arms around her father.

"When are you planning to leave?" he asked as he hugged his daughter, disappointment audible in his voice.

"In a week," Emma said, smiling.

"A week!" Abe ran a hand through his hair. There'd be no time to talk her out of it.

She shrugged her shoulders. "I'd go tomorrow if I could, but I need clothing and stuff."

"That's Rendi's department," Abe said, referring to his wife and Emma's stepmother.

"I know. Rendi's on board. We're going to Banana Republic this afternoon."

"You told Rendi before me, too?"

"Of course. I needed her advice on how to make my case to you. She's my dad coach. She has you down pat."

Abe groaned. "'Patsy' may be a better description."

"Seriously, Dad, Rendi understands Israel. She knows the Israelis and the Palestinians. I figured I could pick her brain while we shopped." Rendi had been born in Algeria and had worked for Israeli intelligence before coming to America. Emma had often tried to coax her to tell stories of this time in her life, but she wouldn't. She would purse her lips and change the topic. But now Emma hoped Rendi would tell her secrets, especially since Emma was going to be in the middle of the action.

"That was years ago, Emma. You need more current information, too. I'll call my cousin Shimshon. You remember him?"

Emma nodded. She had met Shimshon Regel when she was thirteen and in Israel for her bat mitzvah. That branch of the family had changed their name, but there were still ties and shared family traits. Shimshon was also a lawyer, but a career prosecutor. Abe liked to call him "the black sheep in our family of defense attorneys."

"He's a wonderful man," Abe said. "I'll arrange it so that you stay with him."

Before Emma could protest, Abe continued, "No, it'll make

me feel better to know you're with family. And you'll need Shimshon: He can tell you about the conflict between Israelis and Palestinians in a way that newspapers and reporters' accounts never could. He can tell you the personal stories."

"Okay, Daddy," Emma said, kissing his cheek.

"The Regel family helped to establish Israel more than a century ago," Abe said with pride. "We have deep roots over there, Emma. And Shimshon takes this genealogy stuff very seriously, so he can tell you about it. He not only plants orange trees in his spare time, he constructs family trees."

"I promise, Daddy, I'll dig into the family history. I hope I don't find too many skeletons," she joked.

"There are always skeletons. That's why we have closets," Abe said, with a knowing look designed to pique his daughter's curiosity.

II

Habash Ein

In and Near the Offices of Pal-Watch, Israel

Emma hadn't told Abe all her reasons for wanting to go to Israel.

Everything she *had* told him was true: She wanted to make a difference, and she believed that her unbiased opinions would help mend fences.

But there was something else. Some*one* else.

Habash Ein.

Habash Ein was a Christian Arab, a demographic that Abe said was part of a shrinking minority in the West Bank and even more so in the Gaza Strip, where Hamas had made the lives of non-Muslims difficult. After graduating from Yale a year before Emma, Habash had returned to East Jerusalem and opened up a law practice specializing in human rights — the Palestinian Human Rights Watch, or "Pal-Watch." Emma had followed his work through newspaper accounts and updates from Yale colleagues. Unlike other so-called human-rights lawyers, who represented only "their side" against "the other side," Ein had Palestinian *and* Israeli clients. He also challenged both the Israeli government and the Palestinian Authority. Consequently he had few friends, since he took no side other than that of human rights.

At Yale Law School, Emma and Habash had both been part of a human-rights reading group. Emma was the "fox" and Habash the "hedgehog" among the group. (Isaiah Berlin had borrowed this distinction from the Greek poet Archilochus, who observed that "the fox knows many things, but the hedge-hog knows one big thing.") Emma was something of a dilettante who dabbled in many subjects, while Habash focused exclusively on human rights in one small part of the world. She had grown infatuated with his intellect, as well as his olive skin and chis-eled good looks, so she asked him out on a date. Habash apolo-getically declined, giving no reason. Yet they remained platonic buddies during their years at Yale, and he would often go to her house for dinners with Abe (his blatant admiration for the man, bordering on sycophancy, amused Emma). She always won-dered why he had resisted her romantic overture. She never saw him with another woman — or man. He was a mystery that she wanted to solve.

She hadn't told her father about her "other" reason for accept-ing the job with Pal-Watch. She worried that he might doubt her sincerity in wanting to make a difference. She also wondered whether he would approve of a relationship — if one were to develop — between her and an Arab man. Abe had never given her "the lecture" about how important it was for her to marry a Jew and raise her children Jewish. He was too egalitarian for that, and too smart to think it would work on Emma, but he was always more relaxed around her Jewish boyfriends than around her non-Jewish ones. In that and other ways — often less subtle

than he intended—he conveyed to Emma his true, if unconscious, feelings about intermarriage. Of course she told Rendi
about *her* feelings for Habash but swore her to secrecy. She told
Rendi everything.

And now—after a long flight in the middle seat of a crowded
El Al plane, a chatter-filled ride home with her cousin Shimshon
Regel, and a very pleasant evening spent with him and his wife,
Hanna, and their two children—she was on her way to her first
day of work with Habash, more impressed with his goodness
than ever. Here was a man purposely defending the most hated
man in the Western world—Faisal Husseini, a self-confessed
mass murderer! Her father, Abe, was the only other person
she'd ever met who had the strength of character to do something like that.

She checked the tourist map she held in her hands and crossed
into East Jerusalem on foot—she'd promised Abe no buses
because of his fear of suicide bombers. There were no borders or
barriers, but everything was suddenly different. The sights, the
sounds, the smells—all were more exotic. She had felt at home
in Jewish West Jerusalem, in her cousin Shimshon and Hanna's
comfortable three-bedroom apartment. Now she felt like an
outsider. And then, suddenly, Emma heard a voice calling out
across the humid, busy streets of East Jerusalem. "Hey, Emma,
over here!"

She lifted a damp handful of hair from her neck and adjusted
her backpack. It was Habash, looking just as handsome as she
remembered. He stood in front of a run-down house and waved
at her. *That is how to look good in this heat,* she thought, admiring
the crisp blue jacket that covered his tight frame. His dark hair
was just as it had been back at Yale: wavy and thick. His smile
was warm; he looked very happy to see her.

She moved toward him, crossing the street and nearly getting hit by a fast-moving car honking its horn. "Hey, Habash," she called out. "I expected to see you wearing a caftan instead of that Brooks Brothers blazer you never took off at Yale."

"Old habits die hard," Habash replied, hugging her. She noted that he squeezed her tightly if briefly. It was a heartfelt embrace. "You may notice that the blazer is a bit tighter than it used to be."

"Too much falafel?" Emma quipped, patting his stomach.

"I wish," Habash said seriously. "I could always get rid of a few extra kilos. I don't think I'll ever be able to stop wearing the bulletproof vest." He opened his shirt to display the cobalt-colored protective garment.

"My God," Emma replied, instinctively moving away from her friend.

"Not to worry, Emma. They're only after me."

"A bomb can't tell the difference," she said, remembering Yarden.

"I'm not important enough for them to waste a suicide bomber on. I'm a candidate for a cheap, well-aimed bullet in the back."

"I'll remember not to dance with you," Emma joked half-heartedly. "Is this it?" She pointed at the building behind him.

"Yes. This beautiful building serves as the base for Pal-Watch and also as my home. I sleep in the attic, and the rest of the house is full of files, computers, volunteer research assistants, and him." Habash pointed at a large, dark-haired man dressed in a black suit who lingered just inside the doorway.

"Who is that?" Emma asked.

"That would be Jamal. He keeps me alive."

"Armed guard?"

"It's necessary."

Emma looked at him, recalling Abe's worried warnings in the days before she left Boston. Habash was a target, he'd said, high on the hit lists of both Islamic and Jewish extremists. Now the danger she was putting herself in seemed real.

As if sensing Emma's thoughts, Habash placed his hand on her back and steered her away from Pal-Watch, toward the opposite side of the street. "I wasn't sure you'd come, Emma. This is a dangerous time and place."

"You mean you thought my dad wouldn't let me come."

"Your old man is a powerhouse. I figured he'd get your passport revoked." There was a teasing tone to his voice.

"He would have if he could have, but I'm my own person," Emma insisted, raising her head a bit and twisting her hair.

"You don't have to tell me that," Habash said. "You proved it in the pages of the *New York Times*." He was referring to Emma's very public dispute with her father about whether torture should ever be authorized to prevent terrorism. Abe had written an op-ed piece arguing that since the United States was in fact using torture to obtain information from captured terrorists, it would be better to bring the practice out into the open and regulate it. Emma wrote a letter to the editor arguing that her father's proposal would lend legitimacy to a barbaric practice that should never be tolerated. It had been the talk of Yale and the subject of much discussion at the occasional Ringel Friday-night dinners, which always included several other "FOEs" and "FOAs" (friends of Emma and Abe), as they were called by Rendi.

Habash stopped walking when he came to a large building whose beautiful façade had been defaced by an explosion. There were police barricades erected between the sidewalk and the entryway to the structure, but because of the damage, Emma could see the interior. It looked untouched.

"Is this the crime scene?" she asked, excitement gathering in her words.

"Yes, this is the American Colony Hotel."

Emma took in the scene before speaking. "I thought the damage to the building would be much worse, considering the number of people killed and injured."

"The explosive was concentrated. It was designed to destroy lives, not buildings."

"It sounds as if those who did it knew what they were doing."

Habash pointed at her. "Exactly. They weren't amateurs— remember that when you meet our client Faisal. The attack was clearly designed to accomplish big things."

The two of them stood in silence for a minute as Emma focused on Habash's characterization of Faisal as "our client." It made her feel good to be part of the team.

"I'm ready to go to work," she said as Habash began to walk them back to Pal-Watch. "How is it going with Husseini's defense?"

A troubled look passed over Habash's face. "I was appointed by the court, but there's a problem. Husseini doesn't trust me. He'll barely speak. I don't think he did it. I don't think his group was even involved, but they're claiming credit. The prison authorities even have him on tape bragging of his guilt to the other prison inmates."

"Prisoners always brag about high-profile crimes they didn't commit. My dad had a client who went around telling everyone he was involved in the murder of Martin Luther King Jr. He figured that this would ingratiate him with the Aryan Brotherhood and frighten the black prisoners. You can't believe jailhouse brags," Emma said proudly, eager to show she had something to contribute to the case.

"I think the prison authorities here know that, but in any event they moved him to solitary confinement for his protection."

Emma slowed her steps and peered up at Habash, who was at least a half foot taller than she. "But just because he's bragging, doesn't prove he's not guilty," she said softly. "Maybe he did it."

Habash smiled. "No. This holds with what we know about him. In the past he volunteered to be a suicide bomber. There's no reason to believe he wouldn't volunteer to be a suicide defendant. If he is convicted and executed, his group would gain credibility—maybe even electability. The more we investigate, the less cooperative Husseini becomes. If we can prove that his group had nothing to do with it, they're finished."

"I thought Israel didn't have the death penalty," Emma said, arching her brow.

"They don't, except for genocidal acts of the kind Eichmann was hanged for, and terrorist acts that cause multiple deaths."

"Like this one."

"Yes, like this one. If Faisal is convicted of killing so many heads of state, there will be great pressure on Israel to execute him."

"Which is what he wants, right?"

"Precisely."

"Can I meet him?" Emma asked eagerly.

Habash's smile told her that he appreciated her enthusiasm. "I'm trying to arrange something for today. I would value your outsider's perspective on whether he's being truthful. But I warn you, I'm having enough trouble getting him to open up to a fellow Arab who speaks his language. And with you there, a Jewish woman, I wouldn't expect him to talk, or even be civil. You'll have to be patient."

"It's among the qualities I lack," Emma admitted.

"I know. It's one of your most appealing traits."

She smiled at Habash's ability to turn what she regarded as a flaw into a virtue.

By this time they'd arrived back at Pal-Watch, and he led her into a large open room that looked like a mini-UN, with young men and women of all colors and shades sitting at or standing near the dozen desks. There were Muslim Arabs, Christian Arabs, Druzes, Kurds, Bahais, Sephardic and Ashkenazi Jews, and even one coal-black Ethiopian Jew. The amazing thing to Emma was that you could hear a pin drop. They were all working on their computers. No one was talking.

"What's the matter with these guys? Don't they get along with one another?" Emma whispered.

"They get along fine. There's plenty of time for chitchat after hours. During the day it's all work, no play. Sorry, Emma. I know you're used to a more lively work setting."

"I love it, especially the diversity."

"We needed a little affirmative action," Habash teased. "That's why we hired a WASH like you." At Emma's puzzled expression, he explained, "A White Anglo-Saxon Hebrew — in other words an American Jew."

"Our classmates at Yale would be surprised to hear this descendant of Polish Jews referred to as Anglo-Saxon."

"Here you're as close to Anglo-Saxon as they come. It's all a matter of perspective."

Habash led Emma through a maze of desks until they came to a small corner of the office. A bare desk sat beneath a small window. She placed her backpack on the chair and asked, "Where do I start? What's my first assignment?"

"Your job is to come up with alternative suspects. You were infamous at Yale for your wild imagination. Now put it to good use. Explore, speculate, go with your imagination — who else had motive, means, and opportunity?"

"Wow. That's quite an assignment."

Habash sat on the corner of her new desk. "Let's start with the obvious. Muslim extremists. But that one category includes several subgroups. There are Palestinians: Hamas, Islamic Jihad, al-Aqsa Martyrs' Brigades." With each group he extended a finger, counting them off on his hand. "Then there are the non-Palestinians."

"I know about them," Emma said, pulling a notebook from her backpack and jotting down a list. "There's Hezbollah, al-Qaeda, who knows what else."

"And then of course there's Iran, who pulls the strings of Hamas and Hezbollah. The Mossad is investigating any possible Iranian connection — direct or indirect — to the American Colony. There is a rumor circulating that the Mossad found some kind of match between the explosives used at the American Colony and a lab in Tehran that is experimenting with explosives that could serve as a nuclear trigger. Nothing solid. Certainly not enough for an accusation. But Iran is definitely on the list of Islamic extremists with motives.

"Also, Emma, not only are there Muslim extremists who don't want a two-state solution, but there are Jewish extremists who don't see that as an acceptable solution."

Emma looked up at this, surprised to hear mention of Jews as suspects. "Have any Jewish groups done something like this?"

"I'm sure you've heard of the King David Hotel back in the 1940s. More people were killed in that attack than in the American Colony. And that was pulled off by Jews. Don't ignore the possibility that Jewish extremists did this."

Emma made a note. "Who else?" she asked.

"The Popular Front, old-line communists, most of whom are secular Christian internationalists, who still think they're doing the bidding of the Soviet Union. Remember Dr. George Habash. Those awful airplane hijackings. Some of the old KGB agents are still doing their mischief here. They're waiting for the second coming of Stalin. Ironically, one of their leaders is Faisal Husseini's older brother, Rashid."

Emma looked at the very long list of groups and wondered what she'd gotten herself into. "So how do we begin our investigation?"

"By learning everything we can about every one of these groups: their history, their grievances, their agenda, their alliances, their finances, their modi operandi."

"I'll get online."

"Online you'll learn what they want you to know. There's a better way, but it's more dangerous."

"As long as you don't tell my father."

Habash shook his head. "He doesn't have to worry. It's not that dangerous for you."

"What do you mean?"

"We have operatives of our own who go to recruitment sessions. I'll put you in touch with some of them so that you can pick their brains. You have to be careful where you meet them. If you blow their cover, they're dead—and you could be at risk as well."

Emma's eyes widened as the full scope of her task became evident.

Habash smiled. "And at least you won't be alone. Every Israeli and Arab is playing the same game of 'guess who might have done it.' But you're doing it professionally, as part of a court-appointed legal team. Your only competition is the CIA, the Secret Service, Mossad, Shin Bet, and Palestinian intelligence."

Emma suddenly felt overwhelmed, and it must have shown on her face, because Habash smiled broadly and said, "Welcome to the Mideast.

"We have one big advantage over everyone else. We have access to the man who has already been charged with the crime—limited access to be sure, but at least no one else can get to him where he is."

"Where is he?"

"At a secure location, with instructions to speak to no one but us."

"According to you, he's talking to everyone but his lawyer."

"Let's see if we can change that."

III

Faisal Husseini

Gar Prison, Jerusalem

FAISAL HUSSEINI DID NOT MIND solitary confinement. Before, in the main block where all the prisoners were held, he couldn't breathe. The air stank with sweat and fear and desperation, and he couldn't pray in peace. He hated sharing space with criminals, hated the taunts that filled the air whenever he bowed his body toward Mecca.

It had been his duty to tell his fellow inmates why he was there, his obligation to stir up unrest. It was the only way to bring his plight into focus, to make sure the guards and criminal Jewish lawmakers knew that he was serious, that the Martyrs of Jihad were not men to be trifled with. It was providence that the reward was this nice, quiet cell, where he could think, read the Koran, and pray in peace.

Most prisoners hated solitary, but for him it wasn't so bad. He had a cot and a sink and a toilet. It didn't seem much smaller than the one-room house he'd grown up in, that he'd had to share with his father and mother and brother Rashid.

The steel door to his cell swung open, and the close-cropped head of an Israeli soldier appeared. Faisal instinctively spit onto the ground and swore at him. It didn't matter that the soldier didn't understand him, didn't matter that the soldier was younger than him by nearly half a dozen years. Every Israeli soldier reminded Faisal of the death of his father, killed by shrapnel from the explosion of an Arab-owned car. The Israeli government had claimed they'd targeted and killed the driver because he was a terrorist, but what of the three passersby who'd been killed that day? What of Faisal's father?

This was why the American Colony bombing had been necessary. This is why Faisal would do everything over again, exactly the same.

The soldier cursed at Faisal in Hebrew and kicked the leg of the cot until the flimsy metal frame rattled against the wall. From Faisal's seat on the floor, he saw the soldier open the door wide and usher in two people, a foreign woman with long dark hair and his traitorous so-called lawyer, Habash Ein.

Habash sat on the cot and peered at Faisal. Habash was entirely too well fed for a Palestinian. Faisal's older brother, Rashid, had taught him never to trust a man with a soft belly. Habash had never been hungry, obviously. He didn't understand what it was like to grow up in a refugee camp, scrounging for food, scared that each day might be your last.

Faisal turned his face to the wall. Habash spoke, in Arabic: "Faisal, I'm here to introduce you to Emma Ringel, the newest member of your legal team."

The woman strode forward and extended her hand. Faisal didn't move his gaze from the wall. He merely shifted his legs, drawing them into his body so as to not touch any part of her.

The woman looked confusedly at Habash, who merely sighed. She spoke slowly in her native tongue, drawing out her words as one does to someone who speaks a different language. "Faisal, we're here to help you."

Faisal responded in broken English. "I don't talk to Jews."

The woman, Emma, inhaled sharply, as if she'd been slapped. Faisal grinned at her then and hugged his legs into his body.

"You might not talk to me, but I'm sworn to defend you, even if you want to die here," she said, her voice cracking with nervousness.

Faisal narrowed his eyes into slits and sneered, "I killed those people. I wish more Jews like you had died, too. Soon Iran will have an atomic bomb, and they will drop it on the Jews. The days of you Zionists are numbered."

Habash stood and reached for Emma, whose face had gone pale. "That's enough for today." He rapped on the cell door, and the soldier opened it. As they left his cell, Habash turned to Faisal and said, "We don't think you did it, and we will do everything we can to free you if you are innocent."

Faisal shouted back, "If I am released, I will kill hundreds more!"

He saw Emma's fists clench as she walked away. Just as every Israeli soldier reminded Faisal of his murdered father, every accused Palestinian terrorist reminded Emma of her murdered friend Yarden. This was going to be a lot harder than she'd expected.

Emma's thoughts immediately turned to her father. Abe Ringel was famous for accepting only hard cases, unwinnable trials, unpopular clients. "I didn't work so hard to get where I am in order to win the easy ones," he would say. But Emma wondered whether her father had ever taken a case as hard as this one, with a client as eager to die—and kill—as Faisal Husseini, and with no apparent leads to other suspects.

IV

The Investigation Begins

ABE HAD ONCE TOLD EMMA, only partly in jest, that if he were ever murdered, they would never solve the crime. "I'd become a cold case, because there would be too many suspects—too many people with motives: every paroled murderer whose case I had lost, the relatives of every murder victim whose killer I had defended, every cop I destroyed on the witness stand, every nut I offended on TV. And on and on."

As she sat in her corner of the large, open room on the first floor of Pal-Watch, Emma wondered if Abe had ever defended a man so violently full of hatred for him. Faisal's animosity had lodged itself in her breast, like an itch that couldn't be scratched. He didn't even *know* her, she thought angrily as she watched page after page tumble from the tiny printer that Habash had set up on her desk.

After leaving the prison, Emma demanded to know why Habash thought Faisal was innocent. And so he'd brought her back here and given her all the information the Pal-Watch team had on him.

The first item in the Husseini folder was a picture of a teenage Faisal standing in a dusty street, arm in arm with a similar-looking boy, perhaps a year or two older—this was his brother, Rashid. Behind them stood a tall man, who from the looks of him was clearly their father. The Faisal in this photo was nothing like the mangy, angry man she'd just met. This boy was happy, hopeful, and clearly he hadn't suffered much. Yet.

According to the file, after the death of his father, Faisal, who had always been more religious than his brother, turned to radical Islam for solace. Conversely, Rashid lost all faith in religion and turned to Marxism. Faisal became devoted to his imam, who preached violence. Soon after this, Faisal's name began turning up in police reports of anti-Jewish vandalism—burning a synagogue in a West Bank settlement, attacking an Israeli checkpoint with rocks and other objects, planning the bombing of a discotheque, and trying to kill a Palestinian who had collaborated with Israeli intelligence. He had a history of violence dating back a decade to the time of his father's death.

Most of this information, along with transcriptions of Faisal's statements at meetings conducted by his imam, had been supplied by an operative working with Habash, a man named Adam. According to Adam's accounts, Faisal became a strong believer in and practitioner of violence as the only way to liberate Palestine from the "Crusaders." His hero was Mahmoud Ahmadinejad, president of Iran.

Currently Adam was working on getting financial information about the Martyrs of Jihad. Because even though Faisal had a personality fitting the description of a mass murderer, his group had to have had the means and the access to the American Colony in order to perpetrate such a crime. And Habash was convinced that they had neither; his belief in Faisal's innocence hinged on this.

In just one afternoon, Emma found plenty of groups who had motive. It was surprisingly easy to get access to the sermons of radical imams. A website called Memory.org monitored many mosques, whose sermons they posted, with translations. Habash's undercover operative, Adam, had managed to record sermons in those mosques that Memory.org could not infiltrate. All the sermons sounded the same, full of violent rhetoric and praises for *shuhada* — martyrs.

In this part of the world, it seemed that forgetting the past, especially perceived indignities and injustices, was a grievous sin. "Remember Amalek," the Jewish Bible commanded, referring to the nation that had attacked Jewish women, children, and elderly during the exodus from Egypt. "There is no statute of limitations on Amalek," Emma's Hebrew-school teacher had insisted. "In every generation there arises a new Amalek. He who forgets the past is destined to repeat it." The teacher believed he was quoting a Jewish sage, rather than paraphrasing George Santayana, a twentieth-century philosopher (who himself was paraphrasing a Jewish sage).

Jews had pogroms, the Holocaust, and the Arab attacks on the Jewish state to fuel their animosity.

Muslims, too, had long memories. The word *nakba* was repeated over and over in the preachings Emma had read and listened to. *Nakba* referred to the "catastrophe" of the establishment of Israel, the failed attack on the new Jewish state by the neighboring Arab states, and the resulting displacement of so many Arabs to the refugee camps, which remained a daily reminder of their plight.

But the bombing of the American Colony seemed designed more to stop the future than avenge the past. The two-state solution that was being implemented at the moment of the blast was heresy to Islamic extremists. They regarded Israel as part of Palestine and demanded control over the entire area. It was a religious obligation to prevent Jewish control over Muslim land.

But not only Muslim extremists were upset about it. Emma had found leaflets from Jewish extremists decrying the two-state solution as well. They regarded the West Bank — which they called by its biblical names, Judea and Samaria — as a God-given part of Israel. For them it was a religious obligation to prevent Muslim control over what they regarded as Jewish land. Emma had been vaguely aware of these polar positions, but being so close to those who would kill and die for them brought home to her the reality that for extremists of both religions this, was a zero-sum game, and the compromise of two-states was religiously forbidden.

Emma turned first to the Islamic extremists, focusing on Faisal's group. After hours of reading about the Martyrs of Jihad and their admiration for the Iranian leadership, Emma stretched her hands over her head and yawned.

"It's tiring work." Habash spoke suddenly in front of her desk. He'd been careful around her since their meeting with Faisal, as if he were responsible for the hateful words the man had spewed at her.

"I need to turn my chair so that I can see people coming!" Emma said sweetly.

"Soon enough you'll develop eyes in back of your head. It's a necessary skill here," Habash said.

She smiled. "I suppose so. What can I do for you, boss?"

Habash's complexion changed ever so slightly and he shoved his hands in his pockets. "We're closing for the afternoon. I wondered" — he looked anxiously over his shoulder, stepped closer to Emma's desk, and spoke a bit more softly — "if you might want to get a coffee with me."

It took her all of two seconds to leap to her feet, grab her bag, and follow him out the door. Emma had promised Shimshon that she would pick up some sweet wine for the upcoming Shabbat dinner on her way home from work, but the wine could wait until tomorrow, Friday. Coffee with Habash was now. *Here's some real promise,* she said to herself. Habash had finally asked her out. She'd endure a hundred belligerent meetings with Faisal if they resulted in a coffee date with Habash Ein.

V

Shimshon Regel

Shimshon and Hanna Regel's Apartment

S HALOM ALEICHEM," sang the Regel family in unison. The words were a comforting bit of familiarity to Emma. She'd been in Israel for two days, two days struggling with the heat, the unfamiliar city, and the prejudice and anger of her client. But there had been good moments, too. Her coffee date with Habash had gone well, she thought. No hint of any romantic interest on his part, but he seemed to be comfortable with her, chatting about their time together at Yale and her upcoming clerkship. He had even walked her home and kissed her cheek. It was a promising start.

Now it was Friday night, what should have been her second day of work, and the offices of Pal-Watch had been closed for the Muslim holy day. Habash told Emma that he'd considered opening up three offices: one in East Jerusalem that would close on Friday and be open the rest of the week, another in West Jerusalem that would close only on Saturday, and a third in the Christian Quarter that would close only on Sunday. "That way we could work seven days a week," he'd said. "But we couldn't afford the rent."

Perhaps it was just as well. The day had given her a chance to relax a bit, to distance herself from work and even from Habash, to reacquaint herself with her cousin Shimshon and his wife, Hanna. Emma had met the whole family during her first trip to Israel, when she'd been thirteen. She had gone for her bat mitzvah, which Abe fought to have at the Western Wall, a site Orthodox Jews regarded as a synagogue where men and women had to pray separately and women could not read from the Torah. It had caused an international sensation, resulting in her bat mitzvah's being televised. But because of Abe's battle, girls were now allowed to celebrate this milestone at an isolated section of the Western Wall.

What she remembered most about Shimshon was his penchant for conversation — especially about politics and family. He and Abe sat up late into the evenings arguing and sharing stories during that trip. He was kind, too, fond of his family and proud of his heritage. And then there was the matter of his past as an intelligence officer in the army. Abe and Rendi had refused to divulge too much information about this, and so of course Emma had become hell-bent on learning the truth.

As for Hanna, she had been plump and cheery before but now she was rail thin and reserved. In the years since Emma had seen her, she'd lost one of her three sisters to a suicide bombing at a market in downtown Jerusalem. She was still as openhearted and welcoming as Emma remembered, but there was a spark of life that was definitely gone. Emma noticed a nervous shaking in Hanna's leg, and her mind kept returning to Faisal Husseini's threat, that he'd kill more people if he were released. How many more women like Hanna and Yarden's mother would lose loved ones if that happened? Would Emma be responsible if she helped free him? She tried to hear Habash's voice in her head, resolutely sure that Faisal was mostly bluster. But the man she'd met—pale, skinny, feral—seemed entirely capable of murder.

Emma was determined to enjoy the day and to put thoughts of Faisal out of her mind. She had bought wine at a little boutique that specialized in small-batch Israeli vintages, challah at a local bakery, and chocolate-covered lemon peels—her father's favorite indulgence.

One thing that hadn't changed about Hanna was her ability to cook. The Shabbat dinner she'd made the family was incredible: two types of chicken, boiled flanken, gefilte fish, roasted potatoes, Emma's challah, greens, and fresh oranges from the trees Shimshon had planted. And now, as Emma sat in her chair in the blue-painted dining room, she was happy to sing along with Shimshon and his children the traditional song welcoming the "queen" of the Sabbath. Emma knew the song from her summers at Camp Ramah as well as from the Shabbat meals she'd had with her father.

When the song was completed and the kiddush recited over the wine Emma had bought, Shimshon, a tall, thin man with hair that covered his forehead in a salt-and-pepper arc, asked everyone at the table to mention something for which he or she was thankful. The youngest, seven-year-old Mars, a round-faced boy with brown hair that stuck out in all directions, began. "I am thankful that the Maccabi Tel Aviv basketball team won the European championship, because I bet ten shekels on them with my friend Yoni."

"It has to be something personal or political, Mars," Hanna admonished, passing Emma a platter teeming with potatoes.

Shimshon interjected, "It *is* political. The point guard on the team is an Israeli Arab. The victory was an important unifying event," he said to Emma.

35

"Okay, okay, it counts," Hanna conceded. "How about you, Zara?" she asked, pointing to the ten-year-old girl sitting next to Emma.

"I am thankful Emma is here." The little girl looked at Emma with wonder. "I heard all about her bat mitzvah. I want to follow in her footsteps and have mine at the Kotel," she said, using the Hebrew name for the Western Wall.

"When you have your bat mitzvah, I will be there to see it!" Emma patted the girl's knee.

Zara beamed at her. "It's your turn."

Emma took a deep breath and looked around the table. "I'm thankful for having a job with Pal-Watch and my old friend Habash. I love to be in the middle of the action."

"Hanna, my dear, you're next." Shimshon looked at her expectantly.

"I'm thankful our children have the chance of maybe growing up without war or terrorism. Maybe. Maybe." A tear of memory formed in her eye.

"I guess it's my turn," said Shimshon, standing. "I'm grateful to Avraham Ringel, Emma's great-great-great-uncle, for leaving Poland in 1884 and coming to this godforsaken desert. If he had not left, we"—he pointed to his children—"would not be alive today," he said, pausing for emphasis as he looked deeply into his children's eyes. Then he continued, "Now I want to tell you his story."

Emma laughed as Zara and Mars groaned. "Again!" Zara complained.

Shimshon said, "Emma hasn't heard it! She needs to know the story for her work."

"But how many times do *we* have to sit through this?" Zara complained.

"Until you know it well enough to tell it to your children, but don't worry—I'm only going to tell the beginning tonight," Shimshon said, turning to the account of how his great-great-grandfather Abraham Ringel had made aliyah to Israel more than a century and a quarter before.

VI

History Will Solve the Mystery

Rzeszów, Poland, 1884

S HIMSHON RECOUNTED how the Enlightenment had largely
bypassed the small Polish town the Jews called Raisha. It was
not quite a shtetel, nor was it a full-fledged city. Its population of
fourteen thousand in the mid-1880s comprised eight thousand
Poles and six thousand Jews. It was a place where superstitions,
omens, curses, and talismans held a higher status than reason,
science, or liberal education. These primitive beliefs, with slightly
different contents, were among the few factors that united the
Jews with their Polish Catholic neighbors.

A handful of men and women rejected the old ways, and
most of them became outcasts and left for Kraków, Warsaw, or
Prague, where reason and secularism were more respected.

The Jews of Raisha spoke Yiddish, though most could read the
Hebrew of the prayer book and the Bible. Many spoke a smatter-
ing of Polish—enough for them to do business with their Polish
neighbors. Jewish men were tailors, goldsmiths, tavern keepers,

hatmakers, teachers, furriers, musicians, butchers, and tile makers. Some were beggars, and a few were rabbis.

Shimshon described the Jewish women of Raisha as *balabustas* — keepers of the home. This elicited a whispered retort from Emma: "Not to be confused with the modern term 'ballbusters.'"

Shimshon whispered back, "I bet some were both." He then continued to explain how their teenage marriages were arranged by their parents and that their primary responsibility was to give birth to and raise as many Jewish children — preferably boys — as possible. This, too, drew a snicker from Emma.

Shimshon told them that in the early years of the eighteenth century the body of a murdered Christian child had been found and the Jews of the area were accused of killing Christian children and using their blood for religious rituals. A Jewish woman was convicted and sentenced to death. She was offered her freedom if she agreed to convert to Christianity. She refused and was executed. Emma gasped, "Oh my God," as Shimshon continued.

The Jews of Raisha, it seems, were always on trial for something. At the core was the old accusation: They had killed Christ. It was especially dangerous around Easter time. The local Catholic bishop had issued a decree forbidding the Jews to leave their homes during Easter week. It was unclear whether this was intended to protect or to punish them.

It was during the Easter week of 1884 that Blima's son ignored the decree. "Where is Avrumi?" shouted the forty-two-year-old Blima, who looked twice her age. "Avrumi" was the family nickname for Avraham Mordechai Ringel, the elder of Blima's two sons. "He shouldn't be out this late on Easter Sunday."

Naftuli, her younger and better-behaved son, tried to calm his frightened mother. "Avrumi can take care of himself," he said with pride.

"Then you tell that to a crowd of drunken men who think that he killed their God. Remember what they did to Duvid last year on Easter Sunday. Remember what Father Glemp had preached that morning."

"Last year was different, Mama. After Duvid was killed, they promised to tone down the sermons. And we organized our self-defense group, the Shomrim. Nobody is going to pick on Jews this year."

"From your mouth to God's ears, Naftuli."

"I'll go find him. I know where he hangs around."

Before Naftuli could leave, the door flew open and Avrumi walked in, holding a book as if it were a small treasure.

"Where have you been? Hanging around? With who?" Blima demanded.

"With the BILU guys." Avrumi playfully punched his younger brother in the arm.

"BILU? Is that some sort of gang?" she demanded of her son.

Avrumi laughed. "Yeah, Mom, it's a gang. It stands for 'Beit Yakov Lechu Ve-nelcha'—'House of Jacob, let us go up.'" Blima looked to Naftuli to see if that made any sense to him. Avrumi explained, "It's a quote from the Bible."

"Up to where?" Blima asked, confused.

"To Eretz Yisrael. The land of Israel. We were reading this book by Leo Pinsker," he said, showing it off proudly. "They let me take it home to finish."

"Who?"

"A guy from Russia who wants Jews to get the hell out of Russia and Poland and go to Eretz Yisrael." Avrumi sat at the kitchen table and leaned forward with enthusiasm. "He says only we can free ourselves from these prisons."

Blima threw her hands up in disgust. "What kind of talk is

that? We've lived in Poland for hundreds of years. This is our home. There are no Jews in Eretz Yisrael. Arabs live there."

"You're wrong, Mama. Thousands of Jews live there. Jerusalem has more Jews than Arabs. Tzvat, Hebron, Jaffa, Ashkelon—all have Jews. They've lived there longer than we've lived in Poland."

"So how come I never heard about them?" Blima asked skeptically.

"Because they're mostly Sephardim, not Ashkenazim like us. But the Sephardim are our cousins. They have the same religion as we do. They just look a little different."

Blima had heard enough. "How do you know how they look?" she asked, turning her back on her son and proceeding to begin preparations for their dinner.

"We saw pictures. They're beautiful and dark. You should see the women," he whispered to Naftuli, making the universal gesture for a shapely woman.

"They're not going to like you, gingy," Naftuli quipped, referring to Avrumi's curly red hair.

Suddenly there was a scream from outside. Avrumi ran through the door, quickly followed by Naftuli. A large figure lay on the ground, blood pouring from a gaping wound in his neck. It was Yankel Ringel, their father. He was gasping for breath. *Vey iz mir!* he cried as life slipped away from him.

Naftuli tried to revive his father as Avrumi took off after the assailants. He tackled one of them as the other fled. "Get your damned Yid paws off me!" the large blond man yelled as he drew the bloody knife from his waistband. Avrumi was on top of his father's killer, grabbing with his powerful left arm for the hand that held the weapon. As the killer tried to break free, Avrumi picked up a rock with his right hand and brought it crashing down on the killer's face. The rock hit him squarely on the bridge, and his nose splattered blood. With his right arm, the killer aimed the knife at Avrumi's neck.

Avrumi smashed the rock into the side of the killer's head, rendering him unconscious. Then he took the knife from the killer's limp hand and ran back to Naftuli. A small crowd had gathered. It was obvious to all but Naftuli that Yankel Ringel was dead.

Avrumi went back to the house to try to comfort his hysterical mother, who was standing in the doorway with her head in her hands. This was not the time for him to tell her of the decision he had reached at the moment he saw the blood flowing from his father's neck. Avrumi Ringel would not live out his life in Poland, as the Ringels before him had done for generations. He would go to Eretz Yisrael.

A week after sitting shiva for his father, Avrumi boarded a train for Odessa. He took with him one change of clothing, the Pinsker book, some photographs of his family, and the knife that had killed his father. He left behind his tallith, tefillin, and other religious items. He also left behind a criminal charge of assault. From Odessa he went by boat to Jaffa, the historic port city from which Jonah had begun his ill-fated biblical journey.

On the boat Avrumi decided to shorten his first name to Avi and to hebraize his last name to Regel, which means "foot." The new name represented the spontaneity with which he had decided to make aliyah: *al regel achat* — while standing on one foot — which was a symbolic reference to a traditional Jewish story of a challenge issued to the great Rabbi Hillel to summarize the entire Torah while standing on one foot. Hillel responded, "Love your neighbor as yourself. All the rest is commentary." Avi Regel's "Torah" could also be summarized while standing on one foot: "Go to Eretz Yisrael. The rest is detail." But there were to be many devils in the details of Avi's life-altering decision.

The strapping twenty-year-old man who stepped ashore at Jaffa was now Avi Regel, *chalutz* — or "pioneer." His passage had been arranged by the BILU group, whose parting gift to him was their bible — namely Pinsker's book *Auto-Emancipation*. An earlier *chalutz* named Akiba Gibor — changed from Asher Gibrovsky — waited for Avi at the dock.

"Shalom aleichem, welcome to your new home," Akiba said in Yiddish. He was a short, stocky man with a bulging belly, a warm demeanor, and a friendly, open face. "This is the last time I will speak to you in the language of the oppressed. Here you will need to learn two new languages — first Hebrew, which we speak, and then Arabic, which they speak." Akiba pointed to the many dark-skinned and robed men milling around the dock area. "*Shalom* and *salaam* are a good beginning."

"Wow. I didn't know my great-great-great-grandfather was murdered. Dad never told me that. Do you think *he* knows?" Emma wondered.

"Of course he does. He's been at this table. He's heard the family history here, if not from his own parents," Shimshon insisted.

Zara had curled up into Emma's lap, and Emma was stroking the little girl's hair as she asked, "How did my branch of the family get to America?"

Shimshon helped himself to another portion of Hanna's dessert. "Five years after Avi left for Israel, Blima and Naftuli also gave up on Poland. They settled in the Dorchester section of Boston because they had *lantslaite* there — people from the same town. Naftuli was your great-great-great-grandfather, Emma."

"My father has told me our family history in America. Poor Jew gets off the boat with a dollar. Three generations later his great-grandson is a big-shot criminal lawyer. Every Jewish family I know has its own version of the same story."

43

"From the International Ladies' Garment Workers' Union to the American Psychiatric Association in one generation, and from the president of the shul to the president of Yale in two," Shimshon quipped.

"Boring," Emma insisted. "But ours actually starts with a murder. Not boring. So he leaves the best part out. Why?"

"Probably because he didn't want you to feel like a victim," Shimshon suggested. "All storytellers have to decide on a starting point. It's never accidental. Where you begin determines where you come out."

"So why does the Israeli branch of the family begin its story in Europe, with murders, pogroms, and discrimination?" Emma asked.

"Because that's how modern Zionism began — as an antidote to persecution. I will tell you more about Avi's adventures here another time. It's important for you to know where you come from, where we come from. It will help you with your work: History may help solve the mystery," Shimshon said with a knowing smile.

"In the meantime, eat," Hanna said, in her best Jewish-mother voice.

As Emma slurped Hanna's delicious chicken soup, her mind was already turned to the field assignment Habash had given her for Sunday — to go to the movies with a man named Adam.

VII

Flix Movie Theater
Adam

RENDI WOULD BE PROUD, Emma thought. And Abe would be appalled.

As Emma walked down the aisle of the Flix movie theater, situated in the heart of the Jaffa Road district in West Jerusalem, she counted off the rows. Row eleven. Then she counted the seats. Nine. She slouched into the seat she had been specifically directed to occupy. Her heart beat wildly as she looked around. There were mostly teenagers in the darkened theater, which featured kung fu and other action films needing little in the way of translation.

She hadn't chosen the movie or the seat.

Adam had.

Adam, Habash's one-named contact, had told Habash that he had vital information about the case that he must pass on immediately. He'd been putting together a financial paper trail for the Martyrs of Jihad, and Habash was desperate to get his hands on

45

Adam's findings. Emma begged Habash to let her take the meeting. She wanted to impress him with her dedication, but also she thought it'd be fun to participate in a clandestine meeting with an undercover agent. Habash had reluctantly agreed. "Don't get your hopes up," he'd cautioned. "My contacts rarely hear about operations or specific plans. Usually it's just sermons or general ideology. Maybe financial data or names of contributors. But we sometimes get leads. Be careful not to blow his cover. And *don't ever* tell your father I let you do this."

More than half an hour of intolerable hand-to-hand combat later, Emma was beginning to think that this Adam wasn't going to show. Then, as two men were beating each other senseless with nunchucks, a young man sat down one seat away from her. She glanced at him, expecting him to be surprised at seeing her instead of Habash in the designated seat, but he did not seem at all surprised. She did as Habash instructed: She pretended to yawn, covered her face, and then pulled on her earlobe three times. It was a signal that Adam understood, for he slunk down in his seat and began to watch the movie.

It was dark, but she could make out a few of his features—he was curly-haired and olive-skinned. She'd been told he was a Sephardic Jew from Tunisia who made a living masquerading as a devout Muslim. He spoke perfect Arabic and looked and sounded the part. Habash had warned Emma to be careful not to do anything that might expose his cover, because he was a valuable asset to Pal-Watch, and if he were exposed as a Jewish plant, he would be abducted, tortured, and beheaded. That's what they do to informers. His profile was strong, and Emma was psyched by the scene she was participating in, meeting a good-looking spy to obtain top-secret information.

For another quarter hour, Adam made no effort to communicate with her. Then he placed his jumbo popcorn container on the seat between them and quickly left, as if the bathroom beckoned. But he never returned, and Emma waited what seemed like an eternity before casually reaching for the container. She put her hand in the remaining popcorn and retrieved a small, flat envelope. It reminded her of the toy on the bottom of the Cracker Jack box that her father used to buy her when they visited Franklin Park Zoo. She put the tiny treasure in her pocket, finished the popcorn, and sat through the remainder of the terrible movie, so as not to generate suspicion. When she got outside the theater, she walked directly home to Shimshon's. She did not notice the man who was discreetly following her from a distance.

Back at the apartment, she locked herself in the attic room that was hers while she was in Jerusalem. Hanna had furnished it comfortably, with a soft-mattressed bed, a solid pine desk and chair, and a window seat that looked out onto the busy street below. Emma stood in the middle of the room, opened the envelope, and inspected the contents, anxious to see if the Martyrs of Jihad had the money to pull off the American Colony bombing.

Inside the envelope was a small negative, the size of a dental X-ray, and a many-times-folded paper that had writing on both sides. The negative she set aside, but the paper she read with anticipation. There was nothing on it about Faisal or his group. Instead Emma found herself reading a short dossier about an American Jew named Dov Kahane who divided his time between New York and the West Bank Jewish settlement of Kiryat Arba. The dossier strongly implied that Kahane was implicated in the bombing of the American Colony Hotel. She stared blankly into the mirror Hanna had hung above her desk. The name Dov Kahane seemed familiar. Suddenly she remembered.

He'd been one of her father's clients.

VIII

TNT

Boston, Massachusetts

"E MMA! You haven't called enough!"
Abe was sitting in his kitchen in Cambridge, the *New York Times* spread before him. Its front page had three stories related to the bombing. The first was about the growing risk of civil war between Hamas and the Palestinian Authority. The second was about the ongoing investigation of Faisal Husseini. The third was about the political turmoil in Israel, as politicians jockeyed to fill the power vacuum. Emma's voice was such a welcome surprise that he tipped his cup of coffee over onto the paper. Since Emma had left, his nerves had been on edge. He followed the events in the Mideast with more than professional interest. Only Rendi had kept him from pestering Emma with phone calls. "You have to let her live her life!" Still he called Shimshon frequently to keep up with Emma's comings and goings.

The spreading coffee forgotten, he leaped to his feet and began to pace while peppering his daughter with questions. "How's the case? What's Husseini like? And Habash? How's he? Have you gotten the family history from Shimshon like you promised?"

Emma's giggle stopped Abe's questioning. "Daddy, slow down." She quickly caught him up to speed on the basic facts of the case and then surprised him with the following: "Tell me everything you know about Dov Kahane."

If Abe hadn't already spilled his coffee, he would've then. Never in a million years did he expect to hear that name from his daughter's mouth. Abe had once represented Dov Kahane, the American founder of an offshoot of the Jewish Defense League in Brooklyn, provocatively named TNT. It was an acronym for the Hebrew "Terror Neged Terror," which meant "Terror Against Terror," but the initials also described the group's modus operandi: It responded to Palestinian suicide bombings by detonating explosives in Palestinian offices.

Abe had been careful to keep Emma from the details of the case. Kahane was suspected of involvement in a car bomb that had blown off the legs of a radical West Bank mayor. Abe had persuaded the United States Attorney that there was insufficient evidence to proceed, but Abe, too, was suspicious of Kahane's role in the bombing. All Emma had known at the time was that Dov was allegedly connected to a shadowy organization that operated in Israel. She had been applying to colleges during that period and hadn't paid as much attention as she usually did. And Abe had been glad. He didn't want her poking her nose around where Dov was concerned. Dov was charismatic — especially to Jewish adolescents — and extremely dangerous. Apparently he was even more dangerous now.

"Why do you want to know about *him*?" Abe demanded. "What are you involved in?" As he was speaking, Rendi walked into the kitchen. She'd been at the gym and was wearing a pair of black spandex pants and an old Harvard T-shirt.

Dark-skinned and dark-haired, with prominent features, Rendi spoke with an ever-so-slight accent of indeterminate origin. She'd been born in Algeria of Jewish parents, had moved to Israel as a child and then to America to attend school. She looked European to Americans, North African to Israelis, and American to Europeans. She was universally regarded as beautiful, sultry, and mysterious. Though she was now in her forties or fifties—no one knew for sure—she still turned heads. Her boss at the Mossad had once told her, "The only characteristic of a good spy you lack is not being noticed." Rendi was always noticed. Rendi immediately heard the alarm in Abe's voice and went stock-still, not budging until he motioned for her to sit down at the table. She moved silently, stealthily, her years as a spy manifesting themselves as she focused all her energy on listening to Abe's side of the conversation.

"I'm not involved in anything," Emma said to Abe. "I'm investigating. My role here is to come up with alternative suspects."

Abe knew she wasn't telling the whole truth. Call it a father's intuition or the gut feeling of a defense attorney used to evasive clients, but he could hear it in her tone. "And you think TNT is an alternative suspect?" At the mention of the group, Rendi's brows shot up. Instinctively she fetched her cell phone from the backpack she held on her lap.

"Maybe," Emma replied coyly, casually. "Just tell me what you know about them."

Abe took a deep breath, unable to quell a feeling of concern. "They were founded by Meir Kahane, before he was murdered by an Arab terrorist. They are technically an Israeli group, but Dov Kahane, Meir's nephew, who now is the leader, spends a lot of his time here in the States, fund-raising and recruiting."

"Do they have any kind of political clout?"

"Not among mainstream Jews, but they appeal to disaffected Jewish kids—and to some extreme-right-wing adults," he replied, loosely gripping the back of a kitchen chair and meeting Rendi's eyes. Without tearing her gaze from his, she punched a number into her phone. Abe continued, "They have small cells all over the world—America, South Africa, France. They have a few wealthy contributors. And they have a lobbying wing in Washington, too, but it doesn't do much. They're vehemently opposed to any two-state solution that would end the settlements in the West Bank, where most of them live."

"So they have some political connections. And they have money."

Abe understood that Emma was thinking out loud, and the conclusions she was drawing worried him. "Some. They're considered a noble enterprise by a small number of extremist Jewish right-wingers, but they're despised by the mainstream. Emma, they have a dark underbelly. They are allegedly responsible for some gruesome retaliatory attacks against Arabs. When I worked with Dov, my students investigated and turned up connections to some attempted murders, maimings, you name it. What they lack in size and widespread support, they make up for in zeal and ruthlessness." His voice was getting loud.

But instead of understanding the risk, Emma only seemed excited. "This is great, Daddy."

"Great? It's dangerous!" Abe thundered. He could hear Rendi whispering a message into her phone, "Dennis? It's me. I need to know what the Secret Service has turned up on TNT. In relation to the American Colony bombing."

Abe returned his attention to his own phone call. Emma was now laughing. "See, Daddy? This is why I haven't called. Why should I, if you're only going to get more worried about me?"

"Here I am hoping you're keeping your head down, and you call and ask about TNT! Promise me your investigations are done in the office only."

"I promise, Daddy." She spoke calmly and sweetly. Abe knew she was lying.

After they'd exchanged I-love-yous, he hung up and looked helplessly at his wife. "You called Dennis?" he asked her, and she nodded.

Dennis Savage was one of Rendi's oldest friends from her time as a spy for the Mossad, and he was currently somewhere in the Mideast, learning what he could about the American Colony bombing for various agencies. He was a true American hero—a Boston-born, Irish kid from humble beginnings who'd worked his way up through the ranks of the Secret Service. He'd taken a bullet once for the vice president and had landed squarely on tabloid covers and in American hearts as the United States' most eligible bachelor. He was a blond, blue-eyed, honest-to-God patriot, and he was also a little bit in love with Rendi. Or so Abe and Emma teased her after he came to one of the Ringels' Shabbat dinners and seemed to have eyes only for her. The truth was that Abe and Emma didn't understand the nature of their friendship. When they'd first met, Dennis was accustomed to women falling into his arms and his bed. Despite some initial sexual attraction toward him, it had soon become clear to Rendi that they weren't meant to be more than friends. They were extremely close in every other way, though; when Rendi examined their relationship, she thought they were like old war buddies. They'd gotten each other through a few tight spots and tough scrapes, and in the course of those escapades they'd discovered things about each other that nobody else would ever know. He was the first person Rendi would call in a situation like this, and she trusted him implicitly.

Dennis was now officially "retired" from the government and working freelance as a "consultant," but Rendi knew that he still had connections to the American intelligence community. He always turned up where the action was, and there was no doubt where the action was now.

"If TNT's involved and the American government knows about it, Dennis will tell me," Rendi soothed. "And if he's over there, I'll have him keep an eye on Emma." She stood and placed a hand on Abe's back. "Don't worry, she'll be fine."

Abe shook his head. "I don't have a good feeling about this" was all he said before he left Rendi standing in the kitchen alone.

IX

The Dossier

At the Home of Shimshon Regel, Israel

S HIMSHON REGEL WAS A PROSECUTOR now, but in his
younger days he'd worked for army intelligence and then
briefly the Shin Bet. Shimshon had been particularly skilled at cat
burglaries. Most of his missions involved breaking in to a secure
location and taking pictures with a tiny camera that was sometimes fitted into a special pen. Then he'd develop the pictures in a
darkroom he'd installed in the basement of his and Hanna's home.
With the advent of digital photography, Shimshon rarely used his
darkroom. His children had pleaded with him to turn it into a
game room, but Shimshon loved the old-fashioned Hollywood spy
stuff and insisted on keeping his anachronistic developing lab as
a reminder of what he used to do back in the day. Now, with the
dental-size negative that Emma had gotten from Adam, the darkroom would come in handy. Hanna had cautioned Emma not to
mention anything in front of their children. So she waited until
they'd gone to bed before handing him Adam's envelope.

54

While Shimshon worked with the negative in his darkroom, Emma waited for Habash, who'd given her the okay to hand the evidence over to Shimshon. Habash didn't want to wait until morning to learn what Adam had given them, so Emma invited him to come over and wait with her. When he entered the Regels' modest kitchen, Hanna's eyes went wide, and she made a face of approval in Emma's direction. Emma stifled a giggle. Habash, though not tall, was an imposing, handsome man, and Hanna's reaction to him amused her.

Hanna made tea while Emma recounted her evening to Habash and showed him the dossier Adam had handed over to her.

It contained excerpts from Israeli and American intelligence and police reports about a group of men and some women so ruthless that they would stop at nothing to kill their way to their goals, which centered on retaining "all of Israel," especially the biblical parts of the West Bank. They also sought political power, and some of them seemed interested in financial self-enrichment. Habash told Emma that Adam had been hanging around TNT for several months, passing as a fanatically religious Jew who would do anything to prevent Israel from giving up the West Bank. He played the part well, even though he was secular. Because he could pass for an Arab, he also attended several radical mosques, surreptitiously recording sermons. Habash had nicknamed him "Chameleon" because of his remarkable ability to take on radical Arab characteristics when he went to mosques and radical Jewish characteristics when he went to TNT meetings. Adam had reported several planned activities to Habash over the span of that time, including planting a bomb in a Palestinian official's home — a scheme that never got off the ground — and the Islamic suicide bombing of a Jewish market — that plot was thwarted by the Shin Bet. Where he had gotten these confidential intel documents was anyone's guess, but Adam had his sources and Habash had learned not to ask too many questions.

After Hanna had produced freshly baked cookies and refilled their teacups, Shimshon emerged from the basement holding a shiny new photograph. His smile froze when he saw that there was company.

"Shimshon, this is my boss, Habash Ein," Emma said, confused by the expression on her cousin's face.

Shimshon quickly recovered and stepped forward. "Welcome, Mr. Ein. I see that my wife has already begun to feed you."

Hanna shushed Shimshon from her station at the stove, and Habash stood to shake his hand.

"Thank you, sir. Emma has told me about your darkroom. What have you got for us?"

Shimshon sat at the table and placed the photograph in front of them. "I've blown it up to eight times the size of the small negative."

Emma peered at it. The photograph was an aerial shot of the American Colony Hotel in the aftermath of the explosion. Smoke still filled the air, and rubble was still smoldering. Emma looked to Habash to see what he made of it, because to her it looked like a crime-scene photo and nothing more. Clearly Habash thought the same thing, since after he'd reached for the photo and held it close to his face, he put it down and shrugged his shoulders.

"Did Adam say anything to you? Anything at all about how this connects to TNT?" he asked her.

Emma shook her head. "He didn't utter a word."

Shimshon, who watched Habash carefully, asked, "If he has evidence about the bombing, why doesn't your friend go to the authorities?"

Habash sat back and crossed his arms contemplatively. "He's

embedded deeply in many groups. He doesn't want to lose his position. He distrusts the police. He's often given me information like this." He rubbed the bridge of his nose. "Cryptic things that don't immediately appear to mean anything."

"Why all the cloak-and-dagger stuff?" Shimshon continued. "He could have left this envelope at the Pal-Watch offices and nobody would have been the wiser."

"He is under orders from me never to come near Pal-Watch. We don't want anyone to suspect a connection," Habash said curtly as Shimshon held the picture up to the kitchen chandelier.

Emma hoped that Shimshon, with his prior experience, could decipher the meaning of the photo. "Can you make heads or tails of this, cousin? What do you think we're supposed to take from this photograph?"

Shimshon shrugged and put the photo down, while Habash began to think out loud. "TNT has been around for a long time," he mused. "And when they pull off something — an attack, an assassination, anything — they tend to leave a calling card."

"What do you mean?" Emma asked. Abe hadn't mentioned anything about a calling card.

"I mean, Dov Kahane is very clever. He's never gotten caught doing anything illegal, but it's common knowledge among Arabs that he's masterminded all kinds of attacks on radical Muslims here and abroad."

Shimshon shifted uncomfortably in his chair. "Knowledge or prejudice?" he asked, a bit defensively. Emma was surprised at the tone in his voice.

Habash didn't seem to react to any hostility, though. He said politely, "Every bombing that TNT's been responsible for, he's let us know."

"Us?" Shimshon prodded.

"Yes, us. Arabs." Habash answered him directly. "They want

us to fear them. They want us to be deterred by the fear of retaliation. TNT — Terror Neged Terror! Terror Against Terror! Tit for tat! That's their style. Their name itself is a double entendre. They leave a calling card, something so that we know they did it but that's subtle enough so it wouldn't stand up in court." Habash raised his teacup in the air. "Once it was two tea bags."

"How was that a clue?" Emma asked, confused.

"Tea and tea — TNT." Shimshon snorted, and Habash nodded in his direction. "Exactly. Nothing certain, but enough for us to get the message. They even have a sense of humor, macabre as it is."

Emma shrugged. "Now the tea bags, *that's* a stretch. And I'm the one who believes too easily!" She playfully nudged Habash in the shoulder. He granted her one of his devastating smiles, and she quickly looked at the photo to hide the blush she felt creeping across her face. When she raised her head, she found Shimshon's stern face gazing at her.

She swallowed, puzzled at the unspoken emotions filling the room. "A calling card, huh?" she asked, to keep the conversation going. She took the photo from Shimshon and looked at it again — this time for any telltale hint of a calling card. "All I see is a smoke-filled crime scene with debris neatly placed in piles, I'm guessing for forensic analysis."

"No tea bags there," Habash joked quietly.

Shimshon folded his hands, placed them on the table, and sighed. "The Kahanes have a long history with the Regels, Emma," he said, always anxious to find some reason for resuming his account of Avi Regel's role in the early history of Israel.

She looked sharply at Shimshon. "How?"

He smiled ruefully. "It started in Rishon L'Zion, and it had to do with Avi. It's important for Habash to hear, too, because it involves his people as well as ours. There are devils on both sides."

X

Rishon L'Zion

Jerusalem/Rishon L'Zion

Shimshon pulled out a map of Israel and pointed to Rishon L'Zion, explaining that it means "First to Zion." It was the earliest European Jewish settlement in Eretz Yisrael. Located south of Jaffa, it had been established in 1882 by a group of Jews from Khirkov, Russia, who'd bought the land from an Arab real-estate speculator.

Shimshon described a visit Avi and Akiba had made to an adjoining Arab village and some of the difficulties they had experienced in adapting to the very different climatic conditions of this new country.

"You have to drink all day, Avi. This is dehydration country. Europeans drop dead all the time from not drinking enough," Akiba said as he handed Avi a clay jug.

Avi took a long drink and immediately spit it out. "This is terrible water. It's warm and dusty."

"Aha!" Akiba exclaimed, his broad smile infectious. "Now

you're learning. The trick is not to quench your thirst. That way you drink more. A quenched thirst is the enemy of hydration. The Bedouins have a proverb: 'When a camel stops being thirsty, it dies.' The last thing we need around here is dead camels. Always be thirsty."

Akiba handed Avi a hat next. "The second thing," he said, somewhat pedantically, "is to cover your freckled Ashkenazi face. This part of the world was made for dark-skinned people, not for ghosts like us. We don't tan. We stroke. So wear a hat."

Avi took the hat somewhat reluctantly. "I thought I was leaving my hat in Poland," he joked, referring to the Jewish religious obligation to keep one's head covered.

"Maybe God purposely made his Holy Land sun-scorched so that even *apikorsim* like you" — Akiba joked, using the Talmudic word for a religious skeptic — "will have to keep their heads covered. Here you can eat without a yarmulke, but you can't work without a *kova,* which is the Hebrew word for 'hat.'"

They continued their journey along the dirt road until they arrived at a squat house made of clay bricks.

"Say salaam to Ali Barakit," Akiba commanded Avi, putting his arm around the man's shoulders. "He's our manager, friend, and connection to the land."

"Salaam," Avi said, extending a hand.

Ali replied, "And shalom to you."

"Ali's family moved here last year from Ramallah. He speaks better Hebrew than you do."

"There's no work in Ramallah," Ali interjected. "Only olive trees that need very little tending. Akiba wants to make wine, and I know about grapes. Grapes take real work, every day. So we moved here where my wife has some family. Now I have a good job."

"How do you plan to make money from wine when so much

of the population is Muslim?" Avi asked. "I thought they don't drink alcohol."

"In theory, in theory," Ali chimed in. "You can make a lot of money on the alcohol our Muslims don't drink in theory."

"They're not our market," Akiba insisted. "We don't want to make any problems with the imams."

"You make it sound like the relationship between Jews and Arabs was idyllic back then," Emma interjected, leaning her head on her hands.

"Certainly not idyllic, Emma, but a lot better than now," Shimshon replied.

"Why has it gotten so much worse?"

"One word," Habash said.

"And what word is that?"

"Religion. Until the 1920s, this wasn't seen as a religious conflict to most Arabs and Jews. But then the British appointed Hajj al-Husayni to become the grand mufti, and Husayni turned it into a religious conflict over whom God gave this land to."

"But there were agitators even before Husayni," Shimshon interjected. "People who weren't ready to accept new settlers. Let me tell you about one that our relatives had trouble with, and that will lead us to the Kahanes."

"Ali had a brother-in-law, Mustafa, who belonged to a small mosque whose imam preached violence against the Jewish interlopers. Mustafa's imam ordered his followers to attack them wherever they were vulnerable. Mustafa decided to ambush a convoy of camels that were carrying water from Jaffa to Rishon L'Zion. Several Jews, including Akiba, were injured and their water jugs stolen."

"How does this involve the Kahanes?" Emma wondered.

"I'll tell you," Shimshon continued, shifting to his story-telling mode.

* * *

Gershon Kahana was the town butcher and a physically powerful man in his early thirties, widely looked upon by the citizens of Rishon L'Zion as a leader. He was incensed when the Jewish men wandered into town, bruised, limping, and without water. Gershon proposed a plan that would teach the assailants a lesson.

The following week Avi and Akiba were once again sent to Jaffa to fetch water. Near the same dune where the first assault took place, Mustafa's men attacked again, but this time ten Rishon men, following surreptitiously behind the camel, jumped them. A fight ensued, with the Rishon men giving the Arabs a good beating. "Next time it will be much worse!" Kahana shouted in Arabic as they chased the bloodied thugs over the dune.

A few weeks later, word reached Rishon L'Zion that two Muslim men had killed a Jewish merchant in Jaffa, shouting, *"Allahu Akbar! Al mawt al Yahud!"* God is great! Death to the Jews!

A meeting of the Rishon L'Zion community was organized. Gershon Kahana insisted, "We Jews must retaliate. We should kill two Arabs. We have to show them that Jewish blood isn't cheap. This can't become another Poland, with pogroms and no retaliations. Two eyes for an eye. Two lives for a life."

Avi replied angrily, "An eye for an eye and a life for a life refers to the killer, not to some innocent person who happens to be an Arab. That's barbaric. It's precisely the improvement the Bible made over the Code of Hammurabi, which allowed the killing of the murderer's innocent children. Our Bible forbids the revenge killing of the innocent."

"Didn't you want to take revenge when that Polack bastard murdered your father?" Gershon asked rhetorically.

Avi blinked. He hadn't known that this tale had followed him from Europe. "Of course I did," he admitted, recovering himself. "And I took revenge—on my father's murderer, not on some random Polish peasant. And I'll tell you the truth, it didn't feel so good, and it certainly didn't bring my father back. That's one of the reasons I got out of there so quickly."

"Well, we can't get out of here," Gershon insisted, preaching to the many people crowded around Avi. "If anyone's going to leave, it's gonna be them, not us."

"Then what *should* we do?" Akiba asked.

Avi was ready with an answer. "Create a police force. Protect ourselves. Arm ourselves. Create an intelligence unit. Take action before it's too late."

"That's not enough!" Gershon screamed. "Blood for blood!"

A vote was taken. It was decided to initiate a meeting of all the local Jewish settlements with the goal of creating a police force, and Akiba was told to ask Ali if he knew the identities of the two killers.

But Akiba's requests to Ali for information were met with silence.

"I cannot tell you anything, my friend" was all that Ali would say.

Akiba felt that he didn't know anything, but Gershon became gripped by the notion that Ali did know but was protecting his people.

So one morning while Avi and Akiba slept, Gershon went to Beit Dijan, snuck up behind Ali while he was busy planting a tree, and hit him in the head with a shovel.

His young son Khamil found Ali's dead body the next morning.

Gershon fled eastward to Hebron, where he had a sister and a brother-in-law. He knew that the Arabs of Beit Dijan would never find him but that Jews like Akiba and Avi, men who cared about their neighbors more than their own people, would. And within three days, Avi, Akiba, and a small gang of men from Rishon L'Zion were on the road to Hebron.

With the help of his brother-in-law, Reb Shlomo, Gershon snuck into the Tomb of the Patriarchs, one of Judaism's holiest sites. When Reb Shlomo saw the two pistols in Gershon's possession, he sadly uttered, "So now Jews must kill Jews. The rabbis back in Poland said it would come to this if the Zionists tried to create a Jewish nation before the Messiah came."

A bit of investigation quickly led the Rishon men to Gershon's hiding place. Akiba's anger became even more acute. "That bastard! To hide in a holy place, a sanctuary, where there are people praying! Rabbis, kids, women. We can't just barge in and grab him, much as I'd like to."

"He's playing us for fools, Akiba," Avi said. "He doesn't believe in that sanctuary crap any more than we do."

"But *they* do!" Akiba shouted, pointing to the praying crowds.

"How are we going to get him out of there?" Avi wondered.

Akiba thought for a moment and then said, "We go into the tomb to pray."

Avi laughed. "And how's that gonna help? God will deliver him?"

"The people inside will. We go inside and befriend some of those who are praying. Then we tell them that a murderer is hiding among them — that he's creating impurity in that holy place. Remember, the idea of a sanctuary for murderers is not a Jewish idea. It is Christian. The Torah provides sanctuaries *only for accidental killers.*"

Avi grinned broadly. "Brilliant, Akiba. Why didn't I think of that?"

"Because you didn't pay attention in yeshiva," Akiba joked.

It wasn't long before Akiba, who was always good at making

friends, befriended two rabbis inside. When the rabbis were told about Gershon's presence, they found him and made him leave. Akiba and Avi had left two men outside the tomb, and it was these men who overpowered Gershon, took his guns, and tied him up.

They took him to Jerusalem and turned him over to the Ottomans. But Gershon's sister, Sarah, soon raised money from some Jewish zealots and bribed the Ottoman authorities to deport Gershon instead of prosecuting him. They put him on a ship to Cyprus, from where he went to America, where he continued to rabble-rouse in favor of expelling all Arabs from biblical Eretz Yisrael.

When Mustafa learned that Gershon had been freed by Jewish bribe money, he and his gang went on a rampage, attacking several Jewish merchants in Jaffa and elsewhere. The cycle of violence had begun in earnest.

By the time Shimshon finished his tale, it was late. Hanna had gone to bed, and the long day was beginning to show on Emma and Habash. He was slumped in his chair, and she rested her head on her hand. "And Dov Kahane is a direct descendant of Gershon Kahana?" she asked as brightly as she could, considering her weariness.

"Yes," Shimshon replied. He looked no worse for the late hour. "The olive apparently doesn't fall that far from the branch, even if it's from an old olive tree."

Emma's enthusiasm suddenly dimmed, though, and her face contorted. "But that doesn't mean Dov Kahane was responsible for the American Colony attack. Why would he launch an attack that would kill so many Jews?"

"The camel and the scorpion," Habash said, reluctantly.

"What camel and scorpion?" Emma asked.

"You don't know the story?" Shimshon asked in surprise. "You can't understand the region without understanding the story. Why don't you tell her, Habash?"

Habash stretched and sat up. "There was this scorpion that needed to cross the Jordan River to get home, but he couldn't swim. He saw a camel about to cross and asked him for a ride. 'But you might sting me,' the camel replied. 'If I stung you, both of us would die—you from the sting and me from drowning. It is in my interest for you to make it across the river,' the scorpion assured the camel. Thus persuaded, the camel agreed, and the scorpion climbed on his back. At the midpoint of the raging river, the scorpion stung the camel. As they both began to drown, the camel asked the scorpion, 'Why did you sting me? Now you will die, too. It isn't logical.'

"The scorpion replied, 'What does logic have to do with it? This is the Mideast.'"

Habash smiled, and Shimshon chuckled. Emma sat still, trying to figure out the punch line.

"In this part of the world, scorpions sting whether it serves their interests or not," Habash mused, rising from his chair.

"Instinct, revenge, honor—these are more important than logic or even self-interest," Shimshon added. "It's in the nature of things."

Emma smiled. "You both agree with me, then, that although there is no hard evidence that Dov Kahane bombed the American Colony, he remains a possible suspect."

But there was no time for the two men to agree or disagree with her, for as Shimshon walked Habash to the door, the night was interrupted by Habash's ringing cell phone. The sound made Emma jump; it was nearly two in the morning.

Shimshon and Emma looked at each other nervously. No good news came at that hour.

Habash's face went pale as he listened to the person on the other end of the line. "Oh, no! How? Who did it?"

"What happened?" Emma whispered harshly.

Habash looked at her with a grave expression. "They poisoned our client," he said, placing a hand over the mouthpiece as he listened for details.

"Well?" Emma hounded after he ended the call.

"All I know for sure is that Faisal Husseini has been poisoned," he said, passing a hand over his eyes. Suddenly he looked ten years older. "He was given his dinner, by the same attendant who serves him every day, and two hours later he was in cardiac arrest. Fortunately, the jail had a defibrillator. He's critical, but at least he's alive."

"This was an attempted assassination," Shimshon said.

"Why?" Emma was confused. In all the years she'd lived with Abe, nobody had ever tried to kill one of his clients, and he'd represented men and women who inspired fervent anger in those who believed in their guilt. This was uncharted territory for Emma, but Habash seemed unsurprised. Worried and thoughtful, but unsurprised.

It was Shimshon who answered Emma's question. "To keep him quiet. He knows whether his group is responsible or not. And somebody was afraid he might talk."

"So somebody else—whoever poisoned him—also believes that he didn't do it," Habash said with an air of vindication.

"Not necessarily," Shimshon said, thinking as he spoke. "Whoever tried to kill him might know he did it but might be afraid that he would deny it when the reality of execution or long-term imprisonment hit home. Dead men don't change their stories."

"It could still be TNT," Emma insisted. "To throw everyone off the track. Remember, they don't want to be caught. They want the Arabs, but not the authorities, to believe they were responsible."

"And then there is the scorpion," Habash said with resignation.

"Again with the scorpion," Emma said with frustration. "What do you mean?"

"We're thinking rationally about who would have a motive. It could be an entirely irrational act by someone *without* a clear motive."

"In other words" — Emma sighed, shaking her head — "we're no closer to solving the bombing than we were before our client was poisoned."

"Maybe we can learn something from the medical report," Habash said, grasping for something positive.

XI

Poison

The Offices of Pal-Watch, Jerusalem

A HALLUCINOGEN?" Emma asked. It was the next day, and she was in Habash's office at Pal-Watch. Both of them were bleary-eyed and on edge. Habash's mood only worsened as he read aloud from a file that had been delivered first thing that morning.

"Yes, in addition to a drug that stops the heart," he replied.

Emma sat in the chair directly across from his desk. "How could the Martyrs of Jihad or TNT or another group get access to both these drugs—and access to his food?"

"The medical report doesn't answer hows or whys, only whats," Habash said, still reading.

"So what happened?"

"All we know is that he didn't finish his meal. It was a sort of goulash, and it spilled, apparently accidentally, after he swallowed a few spoonfuls, or maybe he tasted something funny and threw it down. We don't know. What we do know is that if he

69

had finished it, he would be dead. According to the tests they ran, there was enough in it to kill a sumo wrestler. When the guard found him, he was in cardiac arrest and most of his meal was spilled across the cell floor. Even with what little he ate, his bloodstream was loaded with drugs."

Emma took the paper from Habash so that she could read it herself. But seeing the words on the page didn't make anything clearer for her. "Could he have somehow given *himself* the drugs? So that he could die as a martyr?"

"No way. Martyrs don't poison themselves. It's a dishonorable way to die. They must die by the hand of the infidel," Habash insisted.

Emma thought about that. "You think somebody paid a guard or the cook to poison his meal?"

"Could be," Habash said, throwing up his arms. "All we can be sure of is that it was someone who wanted him dead before any trial."

"So we're back where we started. Whoever wanted him dead had him poisoned. But why? Because he was guilty or because he *wasn't*?"

"Precisely."

"So who did it?"

"Whoever wanted him dead."

"Habash, this is beginning to sound like the Abbott and Costello routine my dad thinks is so funny."

"Who's on First?" He stopped her dead with a dazzling smile.

Emma smiled back at him. He was proving to be full of surprises. "Yeah, how did you know?"

"You played it for me at Yale. Don't you remember? That night we were exchanging jokes."

Again a surprise—surprise that he remembered so much

70

about their time together at Yale. He was always so serious back then; Emma thought he had only tolerated her attempts to distract him from work with "real life." Or that he was hoping that spending time with her would lead to meeting Abe. Though he *had* eventually met Abe and still would occasionally spend time with her.

However, now was not the time to work on solving the riddle of Habash Ein, so she quickly returned her thoughts to the matter at hand. "But this is no joke. Who wanted Husseini dead?"

"There is one clue, but it could be a false clue," Habash said cautiously.

"What is it?"

"The use of hallucinogens. It's a CIA specialty."

Emma was shocked at the suggestion he was offering. "You've got to be kidding, Habash. There's no way the CIA killed our president."

"Two possibilities," Habash replied in a somewhat didactic manner. "One," he said, holding up his index finger, "some rogue CIA operative or former operative with a weird agenda."

"Are you watching American television when you're supposed to be working? That's something that would only happen on TV," Emma teased. "What's two?"

"Two," he replied, sticking up a second finger, "someone wants us to *think* that the CIA was involved."

"I've got three," Emma chimed in, holding up three fingers.

"What's your three?"

"If the CIA had really done it, they would have used a hallucinogen that isn't detectable. I learned that from Daddy, who won a case involving a sophisticated drug that left no traces."

Habash thought for a moment. "Good, but that's really not three. It's two A, because it helps to prove that the CIA wasn't involved."

"Okay, okay. Then I have four, or at least three A, but I don't believe it."

Habash smiled at how elaborate their counting system was becoming. "What do you have?"

"In theory at least, the CIA could have done it deliberately using a detectable hallucinogen, so that smart people like us would think that they weren't involved."

"Now you're beginning to use Mideast logic."

She narrowed her eyes at him. "Yeah, crazy. We know the CIA didn't do it and yet Mideast logic makes us keep them on the list."

"At this point *everyone's* on the list, with the exception of you and me—and I'm not so sure about you," Habash said with a smile.

"I have an alibi. I was seven thousand miles away. Where were you, Mr. Wise Guy?"

He pointed out the window, to where there was a glimpse of the hotel. "Just a few hundred yards away. I guess that makes me a suspect," he said, smiling some more.

"I have five," Emma said, looking up from the computer she had been accessing. "It turns out that Iranian intelligence also uses primitive hallucinogens to interrogate dissidents—and theirs are detectable. Isn't Google wonderful!"

Habash's mood was now deadly serious. "We have to find out who had access to his cell or his food. He's still our client, even if he's unconscious. We have to find out what happened and investigate whoever set him up."

"You think they'll hand over that information?"

"Of course not. Not only will they want to protect themselves, but I have a feeling the Shin Bet and the CIA and Mossad and who knows what other agencies are already there, creating their own version of what happened."

Emma was more confused than ever. "So what's *our* version?"

"Look, we're the only team with no agenda but to find out the truth. That's what the court said when they appointed me."

"So our client is *the truth*."

"It's a rare luxury for a lawyer to be retained to learn the truth, wherever it may be buried."

"As long as we don't end up being buried ourselves," Emma replied absently, thinking of Adam and the photo he had given her of the piles of rubble.

"We're not important enough."

"Unless we learn the truth," she said ominously.

XII

The Van

Jerusalem

EVEN AT SIX-THIRTY on a Sunday morning, the hot Israeli air was oppressive. Emma and Habash had spent a sleepless night in the offices of Pal-Watch, manning the phones in a vain effort to try to get themselves cleared to see Faisal in the prison hospital. She'd fallen asleep at her desk at three in the morning, left for Shimshon's and a change of clothes at five, and now found herself on her way back to work to meet with her stepmother's friend and contact, Dennis Savage.

Rendi had called him about TNT and given him Emma's cell-phone number, on which he left a message. Emma also wanted to ask him about hallucinogens and which intel agencies used them. He confirmed that the CIA used sophisticated and unde-tectable drugs that had a hallucinogenic effect and that Iranian interrogators also were known to employ hallucinogens. Feeling uncomfortably warm, Emma slipped off her light jacket and headed out in the direction of Jaffa Road to an all-night coffee shop where Savage would be waiting.

It was shaping up to be a long day. After her meeting with Savage, she and Habash were going to the prison hospital and weren't leaving until they were allowed in. They knew by now that their client was conscious and able to talk, and Emma hoped that his brush with assassination would influence him to trust his lawyers.

Faisal was likely to have some suspicions about who had attacked him. And she hoped that this would give them some clue as to who might have been involved in the bombing. Habash warned her that there were no tidy endings to cases like these, that it was just as probable that two separate groups were responsible for the two separate attacks, both with different motives.

Hopefully, Dennis could help with this problem, too. He had access to information that the American government wasn't likely to share with the Israeli authorities—or with Habash. But Dennis was an old family friend. Emma still suspected that he harbored a bit of a crush on Rendi, despite Rendi's dismissive denials of any such notion. Emma smiled as she thought of how Abe became a little louder, a little taller, and a little more apt to brag when Dennis was around. Of course, everyone knew that Rendi only had eyes for Abe, but it was amusing to see his feathers get ruffled. Dennis had told Rendi about the CIA and the Iranian use of hallucinogens. Emma hoped he would provide her with other useful information.

As she passed by a park and crossed the street, Emma thought that this was precisely the moment in a case when some sort of miracle clue would land in Abe's lap. She hoped she had some of her father's luck. She knew she had his determination.

And that's when she saw him: Adam, Habash's contact. He was walking toward her.

"What are you doing? I didn't think you were allowed out in the light of day," Emma said jokingly as he pointed to a park bench a few feet in front of them.

"I've been following you," Adam said without a hint of apology. "We need to talk — privately."

Emma hid her annoyance at being followed. He must have a good reason, she thought.

Adam ran a hand through his hair and shifted his weight. "Faisal Husseini was poisoned," he said, clearly upset.

Emma was taken aback. "How did you know that?"

Adam seemed agitated, and he looked over his shoulder.

His behavior made Emma worry a bit about being alone with him. "Why don't we walk to my apartment? We can have coffee," she said, beginning to stand up.

Adam shook his head, his jaw set in an angry line. "It's too late for that," he said, grabbing her arm, stopping her from getting up.

Emma opened her mouth to say something, but she didn't know how to respond. All she felt was confused by the difference in his demeanor. He had been so dashing and helpful the night of the popcorn exchange. But maybe that was merely her fantasy. After all, he hadn't spoken a word to her that night.

That was Emma's last thought before a white van came screeching to a halt in front of their park bench.

Three men jumped out of the back of the van. Their heads and faces were covered in black scarves. They were holding machine guns.

Emma leaped up from the bench, but the men were coming right for them. Adam once again grabbed her arm.

"Run!" she shouted to Adam, trying to push him away. Emma was convinced that she had blown his cover and that the Arab groups he had infiltrated were coming to get him. She was worried more about his safety than her own. "Get out of here, run!" she urged him. But Adam didn't move. His grip on her tightened, and that was when one of the gunmen clamped down on her other arm and started speaking quickly in a stream of mostly incomprehensible language. Emma had taken two semesters of Arabic in college, thinking that her Hebrew-school knowledge would give her a leg up on another Semitic language. She got B+'s but was far from fluent, especially in the street jargon these guys were mumbling and shouting.

Adam didn't loosen his hold on her arm. He responded to the men in kind. In Arabic. Quickly it hit her. They were not after Adam. They were after her. And Adam was one of them! Emma turned to him and studied his face. It was olive-skinned, and he had curly black hair. Before she could process what she suddenly understood, the two of them lifted Emma and began moving.

"No! No! No!" she screamed. "Let me go!"

Adam didn't answer. Her feet were off the ground, and while the two extra men stood guard, she was carried to the back of the van.

By this time there were people crowded around the scene: dog walkers, mothers taking their children to school, men rushing to work. They were Emma's only hope. "I'm being kidnapped!" she screamed at the top of her lungs as Adam tried to place his hand over her mouth. She still managed to yell, "Please help me! My name is Emma Ringel! I work for Pal-Watch!"

But nobody dared move, for fear of being shot.

And then she was thrown into the black depths of the van. She tried to scramble toward the open door, but Adam caught her and pushed her roughly toward the far wall of the vehicle. The three gunmen jumped into the van, and the door was shut, and she was suddenly plunged into darkness.

The van windows had been tinted. Her eyes couldn't adjust to the lack of light quickly enough, and the only sound she could hear was her own breathing coming faster and faster. She felt around her new environment with her hands. The floor of the van was covered in rough carpet. The walls were also covered; the scratchy material scraped the back of her neck. Everything was covered. Nobody would hear her if she screamed.

The first thing she was able to see was a man handing Adam a small handgun. None of the men spoke.

Finally Adam moved so that he was closer to her. "Just sit back, and don't cry." The contradiction between his looks and voice and his current actions made her stomach lurch.

"You're a double agent!" she spit at him.

"Stay calm. Be good." He leaned in toward her, ignoring her accusation. "Or we will have to restrain you."

She didn't know if he was trying to get her to cooperate or to warn her. Then the driver spoke. His voice, higher-pitched, mean-sounding, called from the front in a rapid stream of lilting language she didn't understand.

Adam responded to the driver, and the sound reverberated through her. He'd been able to pass for an Arab or a Jew, Habash had said, but he was secular. The truth, though, was that Adam had been playing Habash. She studied his face. He looked Jewish. He spoke English with very little accent. She had never suspected that he was anything other than what Habash said he was.

She locked eyes with him. "Who are you? What do you want with me?"

Adam reached into his pocket. He withdrew something and reached for her.

She recoiled in fear until she saw that it was only a veil.

XIII

Kidnapped

WHEN DENNIS SAVAGE APPEARED at Pal-Watch looking for Emma because she hadn't shown up to their meeting at a local coffee shop, Habash knew that something was wrong.

"Maybe she got a more important lead." Dennis sat in Habash's office while Habash paced back and forth. Habash had seen pictures of Dennis online, after he took the bullet for the American vice president and became a national hero, and he'd heard him mentioned at Abe and Rendi's house but hadn't met him until now. He was an impressive-looking man — tall, broad-shouldered, blond, and blue-eyed. His demeanor was deceptively casual. Habash noticed that he wore loafers without socks. He lounged in a chair, yet Habash could tell that he was acutely aware of everything and everyone around them.

"No. She would have let me know," Habash said, pulling his phone from his pocket. He called her cell phone but got her voice mail. Then, reluctantly, he dialed Shimshon's, and Hanna answered.

"Emma? No, she's not here," she said, alarm in her voice. "She left an hour and a half ago!"

"She did?" He immediately regretted calling and worrying Hanna.

"Yes, she ran in and then ran right back out. Something about an important meeting."

After promising to call the minute that Emma walked through the door, Habash hung up. He felt helpless. He stood in the middle of his office, not moving and not knowing what to do next.

Dennis Savage sat in the chair that Emma usually occupied, fingers steepled, a frown on his face. "If you want an old Secret Service man's advice, I think you should trace her steps."

Habash nodded his head as the man stood. Dennis's cell phone rang, and he looked at the panel while being careful to keep it from Habash's view. For some reason this spylike maneuver made Habash's heart sink. "I'd go now," Dennis commanded. "And you need to be the one to call Abe," he said, pointing his finger at him.

With that, Dennis walked hurriedly from the room and out the front door of the Pal-Watch offices. Habash stood stunned for a moment, knowing that something very bad had happened yet still unsure of what. But it was clear that the American agencies were already contacting their people.

Trace her steps, Habash repeated silently. He shook himself from his inertia, grabbed a jacket, and ran as fast as he could toward Shimshon's house. His mind was a tangle of thoughts, both professional and personal.

From the first time that they met, Habash had had complicated feelings for Emma. He'd invited her to join Faisal's legal team because he thought she'd be a good fit, but he also wanted to see her again. Now, as Habash crossed the main road where the office was and veered to the left to get to the side street that Emma often took to work, he was reminded why he never indulged in romantic encounters. Because of the anxiety and concern that came with them. And because anyone close to him could become a target.

He quickly decided that blaming himself for Emma's disappearance was far-fetched and a bit self-referential. She was, after all, an American Jew, with a prominent and controversial father, who was snooping around the most dangerous investigation in Israeli history. There were plenty of reasons Emma could get into trouble — if she even *was* in trouble, rather than simply out of touch following another dead-end lead.

He walked on, scanning the people on the streets for a glimpse of her. The sun pounded down on the pavement, and he began to sweat. There was no sign of her. His cell phone rang. It was Hanna. He couldn't bring himself to answer it. When the alarm announcing a new voice mail sounded, he opened the phone and then called Emma's cell again. This time it didn't ring; her voice came immediately over the line and then went to voice mail.

"Emma, I'm getting worried. Please call me and let me know where you are."

He stared at the phone for a moment before continuing his journey. He ran across the path of oncoming traffic, ignoring blasting horns, and turned the corner. The minute he did, he saw a large gathering of people milling around the entrance to a park. There were three parked police cars. Detectives and policemen were interviewing bystanders. He ran to the scene, and when he was close enough to the crowd, he grabbed a woman by her arm. "What's happened here?"

"A kidnapping," the woman whispered. "Of an American girl. The kidnappers were *Arabs*."

Habash's worst fears were confirmed. As he strode forward to find the detective in charge, he pulled out his cell phone and dialed Hanna.

Habash sat on a bench outside the entrance to the park. He'd approached a plainclothes policeman and had told him who he was. The policeman had looked at him with the usual suspicious eyes and told him to sit and wait for the lead detective.

The detective stood above him now, and the other plain-clothesman took out a little notebook and dabbed the tip of his pen on his tongue.

"You are ...?" the detective asked.

"I am Habash Ein," he said, rising and extending his hand to shake. The detective wrote down his name without extending his own hand, and Habash was too shell-shocked to remove it quickly. He stood there foolishly with his hand raised, waiting to be told what had happened. "I am Emma's boss," he said, knowing that the word "boss" didn't scratch the surface of what he was to her. "I came looking for her when she didn't get to work right away."

"Her boss." The policeman scribbled something on his pad.

The detective merely looked at him. Habash knew that the detective was remaining silent so that he'd spill his guts, and it worked. He was too upset and worried to keep his head.

"I run Pal-Watch. She is here assisting me on a case."

"You're the people trying to tell everyone that Faisal Husseini is innocent," the policeman said with an accusatory tone. The lead detective was clearly not pleased with the officer spouting his personal opinions. He took the notebook and pen from him and ordered him to go question other witnesses.

The lead detective sat down. "I am Detective Tamir. I'll need to ask you about what she was working on, whether there were any threats made on her life or any other suspicious events."

Habash nodded.

"Does she have family we can call?"

"Yes, her cousins are on their way. I called them when I heard what happened." Habash stared at his hands. "And we have to call her father." It was a call he dreaded making.

XIV

The Trip

EMMA'S ELBOWS WERE GETTING BRUISED. With every bounce and oddly executed turn of the van, her limbs jammed against its side. She'd managed to maneuver her body to keep her head from slamming against the ceiling, but just barely.

Her eyes had adjusted to the darkness by now, and she was very aware of the men sitting across from her. Especially Adam, or whatever his name was. Every time the van passed over a bump in the poorly cared-for roads they were traveling over, his feet kicked her knees. She had drawn them in as far as she could.

After the first fifteen minutes of travel, they exchanged vehicles with another pair of Arabic-speaking men. She knew that this was because the witnesses to the kidnapping had seen the big white van. She was quickly transferred to a smaller black van.

It was after the new van had taken off that she realized how angry she was. She felt anger like none she'd ever known. To think that this man had been submitting reports to Habash for years! And the photo that allegedly would incriminate TNT — what had been the purpose of delivering that to her? And why was he abducting her now? And who the hell did he work with?

But anger wouldn't get her out of the back of the van, so she focused her energy on keeping track of the car's turns. She counted rights and lefts, but that didn't help. All she could tell was that they were traveling far from Jerusalem. The moment the road had gone from smooth pavement to rough dirt, she'd felt it. They'd been driving unpaved streets for some time now. They could be taking her anywhere, and she knew that her chances of escaping in a small desert town were much less than if she were in the bustling city.

Desert or no, she would make a run for it when the van came to a stop. And it had to stop sometime, right? Well, when it did, she'd be ready. She had decided that there was no way this could continue. To be a victim of kidnapping? That was not why she came here to Israel.

And she also wanted to free herself before her father could find out.

Abe. The thought of her father caused a lump to form in her throat, and unknowingly she let out a strangled sob.

Adam shifted his gun from one side of his lap to the other. She pressed herself into the wall of the van and brought a hand to her face to clear it of tears.

"What's your real name?" she asked.

She was surprised when he met her gaze simply and said, "Mohammed."

His direct answer made her feel bold, but before she could ask any other questions, the truck came to a lurching stop. Her head hit the roof with a resounding thud.

"Ow!" She slipped her hand beneath the veil that covered

her hair to check for lumps, but Adam-whose-real-name-was-Mohammed pulled her arm away. Then he grabbed at her wrists roughly.

"No!"

"Don't struggle, it won't hurt, I promise." He laid a finger across her wrist gently, as if to reassure her. She had no reason to believe a word he said, and yet she had no choice. He produced a pair of old-fashioned handcuffs from a bag that one of the gunmen handed him.

Her heart sank at the sight of them. "No," she implored, pulling her hands away.

"They won't be on long."

Before he locked them into place, he pulled the fabric of her veil so that it covered her wrists and put the cuffs over that.

"That won't work, you know," she said matter-of-factly. "The fabric will slip and it'll chafe my skin anyway. Just do it the right way." And with that she shook the fabric from her arms.

He snapped them into place. Once she was cuffed, the other men sprang into action. Opening the back door of the van, they jumped easily onto the ground and turned to await Emma's descent.

Emma wondered how she could run for it with four men so close to her and also how she would get the cuffs off her hands once she had made her breakaway. And then Mohammed pulled a large black hood from the bag.

"No!" She scrambled away from him, but he caught her arm and held it tightly. "You didn't blindfold me up to now. Please don't. It frightens me."

"Up until now you could not see anything outside of the van. Now we are taking you to a house. It's better that you don't know exactly where it is." Mohammed slipped the hood over her head. Her heart broke. This had been her only chance, and now she was bound and blindfolded. Her chest constricted, and her eyes filled with tears. He easily lifted her and handed her to the men on the ground. Emma could tell that she was now in sunlight, though she couldn't see a thing.

Initially she thrust her weight downward, trying to immobilize herself. But then one of her captors poked her in the ribs.

"Just walk. It will be okay. We're taking you somewhere safe," Mohammed spoke quietly.

Safe. Safe was the last thing she was.

"Keep walking forward. Almost there. There's a set of stairs in two paces. Five steps. Here we go." Mohammed helped her navigate the stairs, with one hand in hers and one around her waist.

"Stop now." He held her tightly to keep her from moving. She assumed she was on a landing of some sort. The voices of the other three men began to speak over one another, and then there was the call of a new voice, a female voice, and the ungreased squeak of a door.

The woman grabbed hold of her arms and corralled her into what Emma assumed was the house.

The environment instantly changed. The weight of heat in her lungs lifted, and her skin tingled with swirling cool air. The change in temperature was so dramatic that it gave her a chill. It was central air? She shook her head within the hood to dismiss her stray, bizarre thoughts; she should be concentrating on where she might be and how she might escape and how tall she thought her kidnappers were, not worrying about creature comforts like air-conditioning.

"Emma, you will be hungry by now." The woman leaned in and spoke to her gently.

This was not what Emma expected to hear, and almost involuntarily she shook her head no.

"Of course you are." The woman took her hand and led her forward. "You should always eat when you can. Especially here."

Especially here? What did that mean? Were they going to starve her? Beat her? Make a video and then behead her? As she imagined her heartbroken father watching the videotape, tears fell down her cheeks, dampening the hood.

The woman clutched her hand. "Don't be frightened."

Emma didn't know what to make of this new captor. She spoke English without a trace of accent, unlike the men, with the exception of Mohammed, whose tones were thick with their country. "Where are the others?" Emma asked, gathering her courage.

The woman's hand moved from Emma's hand to her shoulders. She propelled her forward. "They'll be back after we eat." With that, the hood came off and Emma was blinded by bright white light. She raised her hands to her eyes but saw only the woman whose voice was so comforting. They could have been sisters. They were the same age, same build, even with similar hair. Only the woman's traditional Arab clothing distinguished her.

"Those won't do," she clucked. She took Emma's hands and called out in Arabic. Mohammed appeared.

"Of course," he said as he removed a small key from his jeans pocket and unlocked the handcuffs.

Emma whirled around to face him, rubbing her raw, red wrists. "Why have you done this? What was the point of giving me that file? How could you betray Habash like this? You have to let me go!"

Mohammed didn't answer. Instead he looked at the woman, nodded, and headed back out the door.

"He's not going to tell you anything," the woman chided, her gaze warm and her posture relaxed. It was as if she were talking about the weather.

"Then *you* tell me," Emma demanded.

The woman's face didn't change expression, and Emma wondered what, if anything, she knew. "Come. Let's wash you up," the woman said. "Ah! And I didn't introduce myself, did I? My name is Nawal."

Emma was baffled by Nawal's friendly demeanor, but it did the trick. Emma followed her without resistance into a large white room decorated with potted plants and wicker furniture. There were sea blue and green pillows thrown everywhere, on chairs and love seats and the floor. Emma had never seen a room like this in her time in Israel. It was like a room in a beach house on Nantucket, or from the pages of a Pottery Barn catalog. She eyed her captor suspiciously.

The woman crossed the room to the far wall, where she opened floor-to-ceiling curtains that revealed two glass doors. Emma gasped. The view was incredible, a large garden of orange and lemon trees with a green clearing only feet from the door. In the background was the panorama of a town set between two hills, with gleaming white houses and full green trees and cars in parking lots.

"Where are we?" Emma asked, not moving forward, staring at the view. She couldn't help asking.

"Don't you recognize it? This is Jericho, the famous city in the Bible." The woman Nawal stood on the other side of the doors, beckoning to her.

Jericho, Emma thought dejectedly. Jericho was miles from Jerusalem, a town under Palestinian control. What she knew of Jericho was the walls, of course, and that there was a casino in the town. She also knew that Jericho was a middle-class city and that because it was mostly a peaceful place there wasn't any significant Israeli presence. A perfect location to hide a prisoner.

Then another realization set in. Why had Nawal told her

where they were, especially after her captors had taken such precautions to keep her from seeing their route? Did Nawal know something the others didn't know — that it didn't matter whether Emma knew their location? She'd never be able to tell anyone, because she wouldn't leave there alive! She shuddered with fear as she took in the surroundings.

On the other side of the glass doors was a patio of white stone. To the left, where the woman stood, was a broad table, with a sink and a spigot. It was an outdoor washroom. Emma looked around at the view again.

"How do you have all this?" She gestured back at the house, then to the view and the wash area. Shimshon and Hanna were well-off, and their apartment was tiny compared to this place.

"We are very fortunate. And while you are here, you will be treated as a guest."

Emma snorted. A guest would be allowed to *leave*.

The woman smiled. "A guest with restrictions." She handed Emma a white towel and washcloth, then turned the spigot until a rush of water filled the basin. "Look how dusty you are from the trip! Wash, and then we'll eat."

Emma dipped the cloth into the water and dabbed the dirt away from her face, slipping it beneath the fold of the veil that remained in place around her hair. As she did so, she could hear birds twittering in the trees and smell the hint of oranges on the breeze that blew through her head scarf.

She couldn't fathom what kidnappers were doing in a house like this.

When Emma had finished washing, the woman led her through a wide courtyard and into a spacious dining room. Nawal pulled a chair away from a large oak table and gestured for her to sit.

Emma's mind hadn't caught up to the events of the day yet.

And the sight on the table added to her confusion. There were two bowls full of dates, figs, and oranges and a platter heaped high with couscous dotted with slivers of almonds and chunks of fig. A dish of hummus sat nearby, next to a plate of steaming falafel. There was enough food on the table for Shimshon's family.

"You need bread," Nawal called out in a loud, vibrant tone, and soon enough a tall, reedy girl with almond-brown eyes and long black hair rushed through a swinging door at the far side of the room. She was holding a large basket full of pita. "My sister. Always forgetful."

The tall girl sneered at her sister, then pulled a chair out and sat down opposite Emma. Nawal pulled a chair next to their "guest." Salma selected a piece of bread from the basket before placing it in front of Emma. "So you're the daughter of the famous American lawyer, eh?" she sneered in heavily accented English.

"Salma!" Nawal admonished.

The girl called Salma popped a fig into her mouth and made an incredulous face at her sister. "What?"

Nawal was visibly angry. "It is not for you to be talking so freely!"

Salma rolled her eyes and shook her head, dismissing her sister.

Emma sat there, not filling her plate and not talking. Her heart had sped up at the mention of her father. *Abe.* They had kidnapped her because of Abe.

She picked up a fork and absentmindedly began to fiddle with it. "I was taken because of my father?" She asked the question pointedly of Nawal, who didn't meet her gaze.

"Of course you were!" the girl called Salma answered. "Do you think we'd go to this trouble" — she gestured at the food on the table — "for any old rights worker?"

"Salma, Rashid wants to handle this!"

Emma's sharp intake of breath drew the two women's eyes. Rashid. *Rashid*. Emma instantly visualized the stack of papers Habash had handed her on her first day of work, the information compiled about Faisal Husseini. How after his father's death he'd turned to religion. And how his brother had turned to communism. His brother *Rashid*.

Emma wasn't so shocked by this revelation that she didn't notice that the mere mention of Rashid's name had caused the girl Salma to quiet immediately.

Nawal turned to Emma. "We know who you are, and that is why you are with us. If my sister says anything else, she will be cleaning the house for one whole month. Now, eat." Nawal reached for Emma's plate and piled food on it.

Emma had no appetite but remembered what Nawal had said about eating when she could. She stabbed a fork into her falafel, her mind desperately jumping from thought to thought as she tried to figure out the answers to her questions. Did they take her because of Abe? If so, why? How was Adam/Mohammed connected with Rashid Husseini? Mohammed had referenced Faisal's poisoning before they'd nabbed her — were they the people responsible for the attack on Faisal? Had his own brother poisoned him? But, more important, what were they planning to do with her?

"It's not poisoned, you know," Salma spit out at her, as if reading her thoughts.

Emma raised her eyes to Salma and decided that she didn't like her one bit. "I have some questions."

Nawal and Salma looked at each other; Salma's expression was one of delight, and Nawal's was one of dread.

"I think it's the least I'm owed here."

"In Palestine we are all owed, and none of us ever get our due," Nawal replied evenly.

"Why me? I came here to help you," Emma pressed on.

Salma snorted. "You're all alike, you Western snobs. No idea about what life is like here."

Nawal spread a thin layer of hummus over her pita. "We will answer everything in time, Emma. For now, eat—and try to ignore my sister. That is what I am going to do, and that is what I want you to do, too."

Salma collected two figs and pushed away from the table. "I'm done here." And with that she got up and walked back through the door from which she had entered.

After lunch Nawal led Emma back through the section of the house she had already seen. "I'm taking you to your room now."

At the top of a grand, ornately decorated staircase, Nawal drew a key from her pocket and opened a door to her right.

"You'll be spending much of your time here," she said. Emma walked into a large room, with a double bed covered in a hand-made linen bedsheet. There were tapestries on the wall and urns of dried flowers on the floor, and a small, windowless, doorless bathroom stood off to the left. Also, there was an expansive picture window next to the bed, and the view was as breathtaking as the one she'd seen from the wash area. "We will come for you in the morning, and you can walk with me in the garden."

"Walk?"

"Yes, walk. We are not tormentors, Emma."

"I didn't mean—" But she cut herself off. She was about to say that she hadn't meant anything insulting by her words before remembering that she had every reason to insult her new "hostess."

"At mealtimes I will escort you to the kitchen or bring you

a tray. I'll try to keep Salma from bothering you, but you have seen how headstrong she is. And you can visit the library as you wish."

"The library?"

"It is down the hall, the next door to your left."

Emma turned to the door, looking toward the hall in confusion. "I'll be able to go to the library when I want?"

Nawal sat on the bed, smoothing out the linens as she did. When she spoke, her voice held a determined, deadly seriousness, one that Emma hadn't yet heard. "Emma, while you are here, you can go to the library, you can walk with me, you can eat. If you try to leave the house, you will discover that you will not be able to, and then Mohammed will restrict your movements. We want to be courteous and to treat you better than we'd be treated by your kind, were the situation reversed."

The phrase "your kind" hit Emma like a slap to the face. She was so taken aback by the steely sound to Nawal's voice that she didn't know what to say or do.

"Do you have any questions before I leave?"

It wasn't until Nawal had risen and passed Emma on her way out of the room that Emma found her voice. "Yes. Why? Why did you do this? And why did Salma mention my father?"

Nawal raised an eyebrow. Her voice was again the pleasant one of a normal young woman. "You will know soon, Emma. Be patient." And with that she walked out the door.

XV

Abe Ringel

I N THE END IT WAS SHIMSHON who phoned Abe. And he and Rendi had been having such a lovely morning, too. They had risen with the sun for their early-morning jog. Afterward they bought croissants and coffee at the Hi-Rise bakery down the street. They ate in their kitchen, lounging and debating the merits of the Red Sox trading a young starting pitcher for a veteran reliever to help the team down the pennant stretch.

And then the call came through. Rendi had never seen Abe look so white-faced, nor had she known him to be so silent. He barely spoke, just grunted short, one-word responses to Shimshon. And then Rendi's phone rang. She picked up the call because it was Dennis Savage.

"Have you heard?" His voice was tight, terse.

"I think we just did," she responded in shock, still unsure of what had happened.

"It was a straightforward kidnapping," Dennis continued. His

95

words would have filled any other stepmother with dread, but all Rendi felt was an acute alertness, as if each of her senses were sharpened and suddenly stronger. Part of her was also grateful that Dennis was already involving himself. "Plenty of witnesses, Israeli police on the case. Rendi, the CIA alerted me almost immediately, so they're on top of it." When she didn't respond, Dennis lowered his tone. "We'll find her," he said gently.

Rendi mumbled her thanks and said they'd be in touch once they landed in Israel. She left Abe sitting distraught in the kitchen while she packed two bags. By the time they got to Logan Airport, she realized that she hadn't packed any toiletries.

In the airplane Rendi held Abe's hand as he stared out the window. She could only imagine what he was thinking — this had been his greatest fear about Emma's job with Pal-Watch, that something "political" would happen to her. Rendi's own thoughts were of desperate hope. She hoped that Emma had had the good sense to keep her head down, to do whatever she was told to do. Emma, a chip off the old block, could be opinionated. Rendi hoped she could for once keep her thoughts to herself.

Abe shifted in his seat. "I should have forbidden her to go," he said.

"You couldn't forbid Emma anything," Rendi replied, squeezing his hand in response. "That would only have sent her to Israel faster."

"I should have locked her in her room," he said emotionally.

"She's not a child. You can't keep her from living her life."

"And look where it's gotten her!" he exclaimed, to the evident annoyance of the person sitting in front of him.

"These things generally work out. We'll get there and see." Rendi believed what she was saying. Sometimes a hostage was just a means to an end; sometimes the abductors would hold them until their demands were met. Rendi's instincts were honed after a lifetime in espionage. And her gut was telling her that there was a reason that Emma alone had been chosen among all Habash's multinational employees. She was American, with a famous father. That had to have been the reason she'd been targeted.

And if Dennis already knew about the kidnapping, that meant American agencies were working toward a resolution even now. The last thing they would want would be the death of Abe Ringel's daughter at the hands of terrorists. The play this would get in the press would whip up even more bellicose sentiment, and if there was one thing American agencies wanted to keep in check, it was that.

When they landed at Ben Gurion International Airport, Shimshon was standing at the gate, his face, drawn and tight-looking, half hidden beneath a battered Boston Celtics cap. Rendi hadn't seen him in several years, since Abe's last visit to Israel. Shimshon grabbed Abe by the shoulders and hugged him forcefully. He looked into his face and began to speak but became emotional. He lowered his head.

Rendi stepped in to take charge. "Has there been more news?"

Having a direct question to answer seemed to untie Shimshon's tongue. "Nothing new. I'll take you right to Pal-Watch. The detectives are there with Habash Ein now, going over the evidence they'd collected in the Husseini case."

Abe asked, "Do they think there's a connection?"

Shimshon reached for Rendi's bag and led the two of them through the airport to the baggage claim. "They're starting there, obviously. She'd been talking to people, different informants. They're looking at everybody."

"What was she doing, dealing with informants?" Abe thundered. "She should have been behind a desk!"

Shimshon shook his head. "This wouldn't have happened if she'd been working for an Israeli firm, a nice, safe firm in Jerusalem. It's Habash Ein's fault. There are all sorts of questionable characters in and out of the Pal-Watch doors. Who can guess what criminals she's met with?"

Rendi ignored Shimshon's allegation and placed a cooling hand on Abe's back. "She was doing her job, researching. She was doing exactly what you would."

"But I'm a sixty-year-old man! Not a young girl alone in a foreign country!"

Rendi turned to Shimshon. "Have they heard from the kidnappers yet?"

Abe mopped the sweat from his brow with a handkerchief as Shimshon shook his head in the negative.

Rendi smiled ruefully. If Emma's abduction were related to the Husseini case, surely the people holding her would call with demands. This would mean that Emma was still alive. "We will. I'm sure of it."

XVI

Hostage

WHEN SHE WOKE the next morning, Emma didn't remember where she was. But it all came rushing back as soon as she opened her eyes. *Kidnapped.* Kidnapped and, she noticed as she peered around her room, kept in better condition than she kept herself. This was not the typical sleeping arrangement for a hostage. She thought of the footage shown on YouTube.com and other sites of abductees sitting on floors, wrapped in flags of countries not their own, looking scared and underfed and threatened, surrounded by men whose faces were covered in scarves.

But this was different. There was a breeze flowing through the window. She'd slept on a comfortable bed and then eaten a plateful of dates that had been placed on the dresser. Emma walked to the closed door. She knocked on it twice, and a man she didn't recognize opened it. His face was pockmarked and pinched, and he was tall, skinny, and mean-looking. And he was holding a machine gun.

He pointed it at her violently, and Emma grew instantly afraid. She slammed the door shut as the man screamed in Arabic. She sat on the bed, shaking, for several moments, and then the door reopened. Emma was paralyzed with fear even when she saw Nawal's friendly, open face. "Ready for your exercise?" Nawal asked cheerily.

Emma could barely shake her head yes or no. Nawal followed her gaze to the man with the machine gun. "Don't worry, he won't shoot," she teased. Emma's eyes filled with tears.

Nawal took a deep breath. "Sorry. Bad joke."

She led Emma from her room through the house and outside into a large grove of trees. The man followed them silently, the gun slung behind his back.

As they wandered down a paved path, Nawal chattered on about the time she'd spent in America as a student at USC. Before that she had been educated in schools for children of American diplomats. This explained her perfect English. Emma had two friends from law school who'd gone to USC for undergrad, and soon Nawal and Emma discovered they had a common acquaintance, a radically obnoxious boy Emma had known in law school, named Elmer Jones. Nawal, too, had disliked Jones, despite his obsequious support for all things anti-Israel and anti-American. "He put the moves on me," Nawal confided. "He thought I owed him, on account of his support for our cause. He said he'd always fantasized about deflowering a virgin. What a jerk."

"He put the moves on me, too, even without the cause and fantasy BS," Emma said, pleased that they had something in common. They both laughed, making her forget for just a second that this was not simply a case of two girls engaged in boy talk.

She quickly remembered that they were being followed by a man with a gun. But she was intrigued by Nawal, who spoke of the beach, of learning to surf, of her taste for hamburgers. Her mood was easygoing and carefree. She plucked an orange from a tree, peeled and ate it, offering Emma sections as they walked. She didn't seem politically inclined *at all*. And, most important to Emma, they didn't seem all that different from each other. So what could have persuaded a young woman like this to get caught up in something as dangerous and illegal as the kidnapping of an American citizen?

After their walk, Nawal brought her back to her room. Emma used the solitude to sort through what she knew. "Adam" had given her information on TNT. Then "Mohammed" had kidnapped her. It didn't make sense. Were these people framing the members of TNT? Were they themselves the perpetrators of the bombing at the American Colony? She didn't think so. They seemed too educated for mass murder. The minute she thought that, she realized how snobby she was being. Remembering the 9/11 terrorists, she knew that educated people could murder just as easily as uneducated ones.

Emma stared out the window, the view transforming from gorgeous to oppressive as the hours ticked by. She walked the perimeter of her room for what seemed a thousand times. She counted the number of planks in the floor, she sang herself little songs. Finally she couldn't take it anymore and remembered that Nawal had told her she was free to visit the library. It took another hour for her to summon her courage — she knew that on the other side of her door was the gunman.

Once she was brave enough to knock, the door opened and the man looked in on her.

"Library?" She spoke timidly, pointing in its direction.

The man grunted and waved the gun to the left to show she was free to walk.

Emma took a deep breath and left her room. She wasn't

surprised when the man followed her. He kept a yard behind her at all times, even when she slowed or sped up her steps.

The library was impressive—a wide, long room, darkened by thick linen curtains hung over floor-to-ceiling windows. The sheer number of books took her breath away. Shakespeare, Milton, Fitzgerald, and Hemingway in English; Molière and Dumas in French; Márquez, Neruda, and Cervantes in Spanish. There were also rows of leather-bound books in Arabic, books that Emma held and opened and returned to the shelves with wonder.

There were also shelves and shelves of nonfiction organized by topic. There were histories, biographies, philosophy, even psychology books by Freud and Jung. Emma wandered the aisles of these books, growing more and more confused with each topic. What kind of people were these? Learned, educated, and obviously wealthy. Again, not how she would profile a band of kidnappers.

She learned something else about her captors, too. At least one of them came from family money. Some of these books were decades old, some dusty and rarely opened, some had pages that were worn and ink that had faded with time. On the inside cover of several of them was an elegant bookplate with a family crest and a name in beautiful Arabic calligraphy. She could not recognize the name, but it was clear that this was a cultured and influential family.

She walked the center aisle until she came to a set of large oak double doors, looming and ominous, with bas-relief scenes carved into twelve sets of panels. They were battle scenes, scenes of martyrs from the time of the Crusades. She recognized the wide cross of the Knights Templar and the tunics of the Muslim soldiers. Rendered in wood, these characters seemed to have color to them, life. The wood was smooth as chocolate when she ran her hand over it. Then she wondered whether the same sorts of carvings were on the other side of the door. She didn't even think twice before turning the knob and peering around to see what was on the back side.

There was more carving, but Emma no longer cared. For coming from the other side of an open door, ahead and to the left of where she stood, was the sound of angry voices arguing above the sound of a news broadcast. She looked over her shoulder—her escort was at least fifty feet from where she stood and thumbing through a newspaper. He wasn't even looking at her. So, without considering the consequences of what she was doing, she moved quickly through the dark hallway, heading as quietly as she could for the beckoning sounds.

As she approached, the arguing voices became louder and she recognized Adam's—or Mohammed's. She still had to remind herself of his real name.

She pressed her ear against the open door and kept watch behind her for the gunman, her heart pounding. She couldn't understand every word, but the thrust of the argument was clear even to her relatively untutored ear. Thank goodness for her decision to take those two semesters of Arabic, she thought.

"—said from the beginning. It is not wise to keep her here!"

"You are bloodthirsty, Yassir."

Emma shifted her weight so that she stood as close as possible to the door.

"He insults me, Rashid!"

Then a third voice spoke—Emma could tell that it was a new person because it came from another part of the room. "Shhh, Yassir, Mohammed means no insult. We are having a healthy debate."

"A healthy deb— There is nothing to debate! While we are wasting time, the Mossad is probably planning to attack! Do you really think they will let us get away with this? The teams are on their way, probably, just like in the Nachshon Wachsman case when they fired indiscriminately, killing everyone."

"Your emotions are getting the better of you."

"If you say one more condescending thing, Mohammed, I am going to punch you."

The third voice again intoned, plainly trying to keep peace. "There will be no violence! We stick to the plan."

Emma held her breath, hoping against hope the third voice would reveal what "the plan" was—and that she could understand it if they did.

But the first speaker was more irate than ever. "I am telling you, we should take video of her and then kill her. We need to kill her today. This very moment, and then get away from here."

As several other voices, new voices, sounded their support for this idea, Emma gasped and sobbed out loud.

It was a huge mistake. The door suddenly swung open, hitting her in the head and knocking her back. A large, heavyset man with a dark beard and sweaty hands grabbed her violently beneath the arms, bruising her skin as he dragged her into the room. Men brandishing guns leaped toward her. They yelled at each other in Arabic. Emma reached for the man holding her, attempting to loosen his grip on her shoulders. He screamed, "Do you see? Do you see what trouble we have brought upon ourselves? Kill her *now*!"

"No! Please! I'm so sorry!" she sputtered in her broken Arabic, her body suspended in the air by the man's strong grasp. He shook her a bit, and then Mohammed lunged for him, pushing him hard. Emma fell to the floor in agony.

Suddenly she heard the third voice from before shout in command, "That is *enough*!" He was clearly the leader, for everybody froze. Everybody but Mohammed, who crouched near Emma, lifted her to a sitting position, brushed her hair from her face, and asked gently in accented English, "Are you hurt?"

She shook her head, tears spilling down her face. Her nose was running, and she'd never been so scared in her life. As Mohammed sat there with her, Emma looked past him and for the first time noticed the interior of the dark room she'd been dragged into. There were two leather couches and several reclining chairs. Sadly, she was reminded of her father's study. And then she actually saw her father's face.

He was on the television in the corner, on the local news. He was in Israel. She tried to read the caption, which was in Arabic, but it sped by too quickly. She did recognize her own name printed among the writing. A small boy saw her gazing at the TV and shut it off.

There were about a dozen men in the room, all in various stages of alert, most holding guns. But there was one man who sat calmly in an overstuffed leather chair, fingers folded on his lap, eyes pensive. She raised her hands in the air, the way criminals did on cop shows. "I didn't mean...I'm so sorry...." she said pleadingly in her limited Arabic, to this man, for he was clearly in charge.

The sound of her voice alarmed everyone all over again. Several men spoke angrily, and one pointed a gun in her face. Mohammed swatted it away from her and bitingly spit out a stream of Arabic.

She was frozen, unable to move. The gunman continued to shout what she assumed were curses, then lowered the gun.

"That's enough, everybody," the man in the chair intoned in Arabic. Instantly everyone fell silent and stepped away from Emma—all except for Mohammed, who helped her to her feet and handed her a small white piece of cloth.

She wiped her tears as the man in the chair snapped his

fingers toward the television. The young boy who'd turned it off now turned it back on.

"Come," he said, speaking in English and raising a beckoning hand. "Come, Emma."

Mohammed nudged her forward; she staggered, only because she wasn't expecting it. In truth the man's use of English calmed her a bit.

"Relax." The man in the chair spoke soothingly. "Yassir is sorry for hurting you, aren't you, Yassir?" he called to the heavyset man who'd dragged her into the room.

The heavyset man cursed in both English and Arabic, his face reddening. It was only when the man in the chair turned his body toward him that he capitulated and muttered in accented English, "I'm sorry."

Emma didn't know what to make of this apology. "That's all right," she said, without conviction.

Mohammed steered her until she stood directly in front of the man in the center of the room. With a hammering heart and tears threatening to spill again, she took the man in. He had small brown eyes, a stern mouth, thick wavy hair, and a thoughtful expression. He looked nothing like the slight, teenage boy he'd been in the photo in Faisal's file. Now Rashid Husseini was a man, filled out and weathered. Though he was youthful, there were worry lines around his eyes.

He seemed to understand all that she had learned with just a look. "You know who I am?"

She mumbled, "Yes," immediately regretting that she had.

He nodded in confirmation and smiled. Then he waved his hand at Mohammed, who in response pushed Emma into the chair next to him, which happened to be right in front of the television. Then the boy turned the volume knob on the television, and soon Emma's tears fell again.

What they were watching was indeed news footage of Abe, walking into the King David Hotel. His eyes were red and surrounded by dark circles. His hair hadn't been combed properly, so that a small thatch of curls stuck out awkwardly from the side of his head. His clothes were rumpled, and his face was drawn. He marched through the entrance without looking at the cameras. Rendi clutched his arm. She wore a sharp blue suit with a starched white cotton button-down shirt underneath. Emma knew this outfit—she herself had bought it for Rendi as a going-away present. They'd laughed together as Rendi scolded that it was *Emma* who should be getting the going-away gift. Now the entire memory caused Emma's heart to clench, but part of her wondered if Rendi had worn it on purpose, in the hopes that Emma would see her in it. She wondered if Rendi was giving her a sign that everything would be all right.

Following slightly behind them was Habash. He looked as if he hadn't slept in a month. His face was stricken. His steps were robotic, as if he were walking in a dense fog, propelled forward not by his own volition. Just before disappearing into the hotel, he cast a pleading glance at the cameras.

"This is your family?" Rashid asked her, bringing her back to this scary reality.

"Yes," she choked out. "My family."

"Except for Mr. Ein, the great hope of Palestine and Israel," he said, without a trace of sarcasm in his voice, though the comment clearly intended it.

"He is trying to help," she said. Her own voice sounded small. She was aware of the dozen men standing around her in a circle. The gunman who'd been guarding her in the library was now in the room, looking a bit sheepish. All the men appeared ready to spring to action should they need to, as if Emma's proximity to the man in the chair were a dangerous thing.

Rashid turned toward her. "Your father is a good lawyer." His tone was steady, betraying none of his motives.

Emma couldn't speak. She only nodded.

"A man like that believes he can defend anybody." His gaze didn't waver.

She felt as if his brown eyes missed nothing. She knew she'd better be brave. "He can. And he has."

The man nodded. "You think he can do better than you and your Christian boyfriend, then."

Emma swallowed hard.

The man continued and shifted in his chair so that he faced her. "Emma, your father is to defend my brother. And he's to get him acquitted."

"Faisal has lawyers already," she said, shaking her head.

The man spoke evenly. "We want your father to take over."

Emma drew a deep breath. With honesty in her voice, she said, "It doesn't matter who defends him. Faisal won't let anybody help him."

The sitting man seemed worried by Emma's remark. This was the first moment that any emotion had passed over his face.

"Your father can defend *anybody,* yes? Even those who do not want to be found innocent?"

Emma countered, "Is Faisal innocent?"

"Of course he is."

His calm demeanor gave Emma a false sense of security. "Did you poison him?"

"Of course not." He looked at her condescendingly. "He is my brother."

"Then who tried to kill him?"

"We believe it was his own radical Islamic group. They are crazed. They do not value human life, even of their own people. They are tools of the Persian zealots who want to turn the entire Middle East into an Islamic caliphate. They hate us even more than they hate the Jews and the Americans. They want to take credit for the American Colony explosion. They were afraid he would crack under pressure. Dead men don't crack, and his death would have closed the case, with everyone believing he was guilty on account of his confession. His life remains in danger. That is why your father must free him, so that we can protect him. We will then talk sense into him about the group that tried to make him a martyr."

Emma sat back in her chair, her mind working feverishly. It had been obvious to her that she'd been taken because of the case. But she hadn't truly believed Faisal could be affiliated with these people, mostly because they were so well educated, well spoken and respectful. Faisal was rude and insulting and bigoted. Rashid wasn't like him at all. How could two brothers be so different from each other?

But no matter how different they were, Emma realized she had been kidnapped because Rashid was desperate to help Faisal, whether or not he wanted to be helped and whether or not Rashid's group had planted the bomb. "Then who *is* guilty?" she asked, wondering if she'd actually get an answer.

At this, Rashid smiled, a small, tight smile that made Emma's skin crawl. "It was not Faisal. That is all that matters for now, because your father is going to defend him and win him his freedom. And if he does not, he'll lose his daughter." Though he had barely shifted in his chair, though his posture was completely casual, though his face was smiling, at that moment Rashid seemed to Emma the scariest, deadliest, most calculating man she had ever come across.

Rashid, without lifting his eyes from her, signaled to Mohammed that the conversation was at an end. Emma was abruptly lifted by the elbow and marched through the room and out the door, the dozen men parting like the Red Sea to let her pass by.

She was suddenly furious, and she couldn't exactly pinpoint why. She twisted in Mohammed's grasp and sneered at him. "You *killed* the president of the United States!"

They were now in the library. Mohammed yanked a wooden chair away from a table and deposited Emma into it roughly. "What in the world is wrong with you? You eavesdrop on your kidnappers? Of all the arrogant, brazen...Do you have any idea how much danger you're in? I'm doing everything I can to keep you alive, and then you go and *spy on us*?"

Emma was flabbergasted by his anger. He was red-faced and pacing. "Do you know how close some of the men in that room are to killing you? Yassir barely needs an excuse, and then you tumble into Rashid's study!"

"I...I'm sorry," she babbled.

"Sorry! You're sorry!" He finally ceased pacing and ran a hand over his face. He exhaled deeply.

Emma's shock at his outburst abated, and in its place her anger returned. "How long had you planned this?"

Mohammed answered immediately, as if he were tired of keeping secrets. "Rashid decided that taking you was a perfect backup plan as soon as we knew you were here."

Emma shifted in her seat to more fully face him. "And you knew I was here —"

"When you showed up at Pal-Watch. We have our sources, too."

"When did you decide to frame the Jews by pointing us in the direction of TNT?" she asked boldly.

Mohammed approached her and leaned his hands on the back of the empty chair next to her. "We've been trying to point Mr. Ein in the direction of other suspects."

Emma snorted. "You have some work to do. A photo that shows nothing? No wonder Rashid got so desperate."

Mohammed looked at her thoughtfully. "That photo showed proof of TNT's hand in the bombing. It's too bad that neither you nor Habash Ein was *clever* enough to see the clue I gave you." This was the first time Emma heard real contempt in his voice.

"What clue?"

From a desk in the corner of the library, Mohammed took out a copy of the photo he'd given Emma and placed it in front of her.

"Look carefully."

She studied the photo and stared at him blankly.

He shook his head as if in disappointment. "Your father would have seen the clue."

She hated the implication that she wasn't as capable as Abe. "What clue?" she challenged him, turning the picture and holding it close to her eyes. She, Habash, and Shimshon had stared at this picture for hours. There was absolutely no clue in the photograph.

Mohammed exhaled in annoyance. "Look." He grabbed the photo from her and pointed. "The piles of debris have been neatly arranged by the Israeli authorities who were examining the crime scene."

Emma took the photograph from him to see what he was talking about.

"Now connect the dots," he commanded.

"What dots?"

"The twelve piles," Mohammed said in frustration, running his index finger over the photo, which had been shot from above.

Suddenly she saw a pattern that she hadn't noticed before.

"Oh, my God!" Emma exclaimed. "If you drew a line from pile to pile, the lines would form the Star of David!"

"A TNT signature," Mohammed insisted. "They always leave a calling card."

Emma stared at him. It was just what Habash had said about them. Now she was confused. "But how did they manage to arrange the debris in that configuration?"

Mohammed shrugged. "Someone in the Israeli investigative squad must be involved with TNT. He arranged the debris so that we would know who caused the explosion, but without enough evidence to tie it to any individual or to prove it in court. I was hoping you would see it and use it to help defend Faisal, but I apparently overestimated your perceptiveness and subtlety."

He was irritating her. Emma threw the photo down on the table. "How do you know someone else didn't arrange the debris so as to frame TNT? Maybe you did it."

Mohammed shook his head. "We have no access to the crime scene."

There was a moment where neither of them spoke. Emma's head was spinning. "So you really believe TNT killed all those people?"

"We don't really care who did it," Mohammed said dismissively, reaching for the photograph and dusting it off. "Certainly TNT has done things in the past that they should be punished for anyway. We just wanted you to get Faisal off."

Emma slowly began to understand. "And then he was poisoned by his own group."

Mohammed nodded. "We don't have time for Pal-Watch to flounder around. We needed to use our backup plan. That's when Rashid ordered us to take you."

Emma desperately wished she could get some of this information to her father and Habash. After a moment, sensing that

Mohammed's mood was returning to something approaching calm, she mused, "So everyone here is a communist?" Habash had told her that Faisal's brother was a member of the Popular Front, that he'd turned to communism.

Mohammed nodded.

"For communists, you sure live like capitalists," Emma said, quickly regretting that she had not censored the thought.

"We make no apologies for this house," Mohammed replied evenly. "It was left to me by a wealthy uncle whose family made their money off the sweat of Palestinian workers. Now we are using it in the interests of these workers."

"So you . . . you're one of George Habash's followers, too?"

George Habash had been the founder of the Popular Front for the Liberation of Palestine, a group that was Marxist-Leninist in its leanings and aimed to unite the Arab world. He also wanted a one-state solution in Israel and conducted terrorist attacks in the 1960s in an effort to wipe the Jewish state off the map.

"In philosophy, maybe," Mohammed responded to her question. "When George died, Rashid formed his own group. Welcome to the headquarters of the Palestinian Marxist Liberation Front." And he bowed his head slightly. "Although my name is Mohammed, I'm a heretic, a disbeliever in all religions."

"But you're a Palestinian, not a Jew, as you duped Habash into believing."

Again he nodded, this time smiling proudly at his ability to fool even his most perceptive enemies.

Emma looked around the room. Her curious side was eagerly digesting this information. But her rational side was panicking. The more Mohammed told her, the less likely it was that she would ever walk out of here alive.

Once again Mohammed seemed to read her mind. "We don't believe in killing innocent civilians, even American ones." His tone meant his words to come across as lighthearted, but Emma's wariness grew stronger. "If your father gets Faisal off, you'll be free to go, no harm done."

Emma decided quickly that she had to improve her chances by making a promise of her own. "I promise you that if you let me go, I will never disclose your whereabouts or testify against you or Rashid. You have my word."

"We don't need your word. Our plan does not require your death if your father succeeds. We believed you would recognize the city we are in, and we have made plans to move us all to a different safe house in a different part of the country, if there is an acquittal. We love this house, but Faisal's life is worth more than a house, even one as beautiful as this one. We will have to keep our word if your father fails. Your life is entirely in his capable hands."

"Then why did you blindfold me?"

"To keep you from foolishly trying to escape. They would have shot you in an instant. It was for your own protection."

"George Habash, the founder of your movement, was infamous. He killed many people."

"Rashid is a bit more pragmatic than George. He doesn't believe in losing Palestinian lives. And this attack, this was far beyond anything we could have accomplished. We wouldn't even have been able to get into the room."

Emma doubted that her captor's humility was genuine here. "I have a feeling you could do whatever Rashid set your mind to. You took me, after all."

"You weren't that hard to take. A young American girl, wide-eyed and idealistic, eager to trust people and meet with spies and run around town."

Emma's face went hot. She didn't like hearing herself described that way.

Mohammed smiled and sat on a corner of a table. "There are some in Palestine who envision a holy state, a country ruled by Islam. We do not agree. We want a secular, socialist, Arab state, a place where Christian Arabs and even heretics like me can live peacefully among their Muslim brothers."

Emma understood what he was saying to her. "So none of your followers choose martyrdom?"

Mohammed nodded. "Precisely. Our goals are achieved through military actions. Sometimes guerrilla, but never through suicide. Rashid believes—as do I—that suicide is a waste of precious Palestinian lives."

Emma had a realization. "So if you believe that Faisal is innocent, Rashid must be livid that he's willing to die for his cause."

"It is simply a matter of an older brother trying to protect the younger brother he loves, despite their differences."

"My father can get him acquitted, I am sure of it. But won't the people he works for try to kill him again?"

Mohammed stood. "We will protect him once the Israelis free him. Your father's job is to get him acquitted. We will do the rest."

XVII

The Photo

ABE'S SUITE IN THE KING DAVID HOTEL was opulent. There were sofas and two chaises covered in lush, jewel-toned materials, there were high ceilings and cushioned carpeting, the bathroom contained a Jacuzzi-style tub, and the service in the hotel was world-renowned. But Abe could concentrate on only one detail of the room: a small black box that sat on the desk. The box had a single button, and the Israeli counterterrorism police had instructed Abe to press it if either his daughter or the kidnappers called. The box would instantly trace their location.

Abe was familiar with this kind of technology. A similar black box, also developed by the Israelis, had been used by the Colombian authorities to help rescue American and French hostages who'd been held by rebels for more than five years.

As it happened, Abe and Rendi already knew where Emma was and who had taken her, but they kept the information from the Israeli authorities. On their first full day in Jerusalem, Dennis

Savage had visited. He was cleared by the Israeli guard stationed outside Abe's door, though had they suspected what Dennis smuggled into the room, they would've detained him.

Dennis brought a grainy photograph of a young woman standing at a window in a large home. Despite his retirement, it was obvious that Savage still had connections with the Company. The CIA wouldn't confirm for Dennis who was in the photo or where it had been taken. But as soon as Abe saw the picture, he knew it was Emma. Dennis told Abe and Rendi that the photo was probably taken from a spy plane that morning; it seemed that Rashid Husseini was on the CIA's terrorist watch list and they'd been routinely photographing several of his safe houses. Dennis also told them about the group — that they were secular communists who would likely act more rationally than Islamic zealots. Unfortunately, the American authorities could do little with this knowledge. They were not about to try a rescue operation in the West Bank, and they didn't want to share this particular bit of intelligence with the Israelis, lest *they* try to rescue the American hostage. Dennis brought the picture to them at considerable risk; Rendi was thrilled, Abe pessimistic.

"Look at her, Abe! She's doing just fine!" Rendi insisted, trying to bolster his spirits.

"Yesterday. Yesterday she was just fine," Abe said morosely.

Now, two days later, they still hadn't heard from the kidnappers, and Abe hadn't slept more than a few minutes at a time. Rendi, when she wasn't pacing the floor talking on her cell phone with every contact she could think of, kept pleading with him to get some sleep. He refused. He was afraid he would miss a crucial phone call or breaking news. And yet there was no news, no ransom note, no claim of responsibility. Dennis visited each day but was able to obtain only the one picture, and precious little information was trickling down through the American intelligence agencies. The Israeli news organizations were reporting that Emma had been kidnapped, with no allusion to who the kidnappers might be or what their motive was. Of course, everyone working the case had a theory, but not knowing *why* was beginning to drive Abe a little crazy.

He had checked into the King David Hotel because he believed that if the kidnappers were trying to reach him, they might try Jerusalem's most famous tourist hotel, smack in the middle of the city. He purposely allowed himself to be televised entering the hotel for the same reason. Now he was waiting for the phone to ring, but he dreaded it as well. It could be proof of life — or of death.

Rendi had persuaded Abe that Emma, an American human-rights worker who supported Palestinian rights, was far more valuable to her captors alive than dead — if her captors behaved rationally. And knowing that she was likely being held by Faisal Husseini's brother convinced Abe that some sort of terms would be offered. He spent the waiting hours racking his brain as to what they might be.

Abe always tried to anticipate every opportunity or risk.

He first considered the possibility that they would ask for money — a lot of it. He was prepared to pay whatever it took. He recalled an acquaintance of his — a Las Vegas entrepreneur — whose daughter had been kidnapped several years earlier. The kidnappers, who were simply in it for the money, had called Abe's acquaintance and asked for $1 million in ransom. He responded by upping the ante: He offered $2 million for the safe return of his daughter but warned them that if she were not returned alive, he would give $5 million to the Mafia to track, torture, and murder each of the kidnappers and their immediate family. He also told the kidnappers that he had no interest in prosecuting them if his daughter was returned safely and they were caught.

He did not want his daughter to have to go through a trial. He also told them that this was the last negotiation he would have with them: "Take it or leave it." Within hours his daughter was returned in exchange for the $2 million, and, true to his word, he never called the authorities or tried to track the kidnappers down. Abe was ready to offer the same sort of deal.

Abe also thought about the possibility that a prisoner exchange would be offered, and he had already contacted influential friends in Israel and the United States to put pressure on the Israeli government to release any number of prisoners to save his daughter's life. The problem was that years earlier he had written an article urging the United States and Israel never to negotiate with terrorists and never to participate in prisoner exchanges with them. *So what!* he now thought. *Let them call me a hypocrite.* He was reminded of one of his law professors who was arguing a case in the Supreme Court and taking a position entirely contrary to what he had previously written in an authoritative book on the subject. The chief justice confronted him with the contradiction, to which the professor responded, "I think better when I'm paid more." Abe realized that he, too, thought more clearly when the stakes were even higher than money or professional reputation. Abe thought of Samuel Johnson's observation that "when a man knows he is to be hanged in a fortnight, it concentrates his mind wonderfully." Having a daughter held by terrorists focused the mind even more clearly.

XVIII

Double Cross

THIS MORNING Faisal Husseini was able to sit up. The nurses in the prison hospital acted as if he'd just traveled to Mecca on foot. Such joy over his progress. They were idiots, marking each day since his poisoning on a large paper calendar they'd hung on his wall.

Why were they trying to make him better? If their roles were reversed, he would be doing everything in his power to kill them. Maybe they *were* trying to kill him.

He'd lost weight in the days since the poisoning. He could feel his own ribs through the hospital gown. He refused to eat or drink, and so he had been hooked up to an IV. They were force-feeding him, thinking that his inability to take nourishment was a result of the poisoning.

It was because of the humiliation.

To be killed in such a way would have been a disgrace to his cause, to his mother, to Allah. He wanted to die a martyr. He wanted to stand trial, be put to death by the Israelis, and get to heaven a hero. But to be taken down in such a way? Poisoned food? There was no honor in that.

"Faisal, you have a visitor!" His least favorite nurse, the loudest, nicest Israeli in the whole prison, bustled into his room. He turned his face to the wall and grunted.

The nurse replaced his IV bag, adjusted his blanket, and patted his feet before two policemen opened his door and ushered her out. In walked Habash Ein.

Habash Ein looked different. His hair was limp, his face gray, his jaw clenched. His clothes looked like they'd been slept in — his shirt was misbuttoned, and his body was several pounds lighter than the previous time they'd seen each other.

Faisal had been surprised that Habash hadn't come to him earlier; he'd have guessed that a poisoning was a big event to his lawyer, that he'd want to *check* on him, see if the attack had changed his mind about his defense or about telling what he knew.

He'd be wrong about that. Faisal had adopted a no-talking policy, and he wasn't about to break it now.

Habash waited for the policemen to leave the room and shut the door. Then he walked to the side of Faisal's bed, grabbed him by the front of his hospital dress, and shook him violently. "Where is she? Damn it! Tell me where she is!"

Faisal tried to push him away, but his grip was too tight and Faisal was weakened by the poison. He pulled at Habash's hands, but that did nothing to stop him from shaking Faisal until his brain was slamming against the inside of his skull.

A look passed over Habash's face, the realization of what he was doing. He released Faisal violently and without warning. Faisal crashed against the pillow, his head pounding, his neck smarting from where the hospital gown's fabric had dug into his flesh.

Habash sank into a nearby chair and bowed his head. A deep purple blush climbed up the side of his neck. Faisal smiled to see it. Mr. Ein was too soft to handle any kind of violence, even that of his own doing.

This spurred on Faisal's curiosity, if nothing else. "What happened?"

Habash lifted his head in surprise, shocked to hear Faisal's voice. "Your brother kidnapped Emma Ringel. And I think it's my fault."

Faisal said nothing else. He couldn't even if he wished to; he was consumed with fury. *Rashid*. Damn him. Always meddling. Always sticking his nose where it wasn't wanted. No doubt he was cooking up some sort of scheme to free Faisal, to end his bid for martyrdom.

Faisal didn't know what his older brother was up to, but how dare he! Whatever Rashid was doing, Faisal was sure he was trying to ruin his plans. It would not work. Faisal was destined for paradise, and no one could interfere with destiny. He couldn't care less about Emma Ringel.

XIX

The Deal

A BE TURNED UP the volume on the news and stretched out on a chaise, his head resting on an overstuffed pillow and his cell phone just inches away. As he was drifting off to sleep, the phone rang. At first he wasn't sure it was real, because on several prior occasions he'd been shaken out of the beginnings of a slumber by what he thought was a ringing phone only to realize he was dreaming. Rendi stopped her frantic pacing, hung up her own cell phone, and stared at Abe's. This time it was real. He cautiously picked up the phone and pressed the "talk" button.

"Hello?" he asked tentatively.

"Hi, Daddy. It's Emma."

Abe immediately sat up in his chair and snapped his fingers toward Rendi. She came running from the other side of the room and grabbed the black box from the table. Abe waved it away.

"Oh, my God, are you okay?" he gushed.

"I'm fine, Daddy, at least physically, but I'm scared." It was as if she were calling from college just to say hello. Her tone of voice was typical Emma.

"Are you sure you're okay?"

"Daddy, I'm okay. Everything is copacetic."

Abe took a deep breath and relaxed a bit into his chair.

Years earlier he and Emma had agreed on code words that would signify she was telling the truth in the event she was ever in a situation like this. Emma loved the word "copacetic." She had picked it up while working on a kibbutz during the summer of her bat mitzvah. She had actually written a term paper on the origin of that strange word, tracing it to Cajun French, American slang, and even Hebrew. On the kibbutz it was used interchangeably with the Hebrew phrase *hakol b'seder*—"everything is in order." Abe decided it was a good code word to signify that everything was fine. They also had a second code word, as a backup in case her captors wouldn't let her use the word "copacetic." This one was even simpler. If she wanted Abe to know she was not telling him the truth, she would call him "Father" instead of her normal "Daddy."

Abe heaved a silent sigh of relief as he heard Emma say both of the positive words. She really was okay. She was telling the truth. "What do your kidnappers want?" Abe asked anxiously.

"Daddy, they want you to defend Faisal Husseini."

This was the last thing that Abe was expecting to hear. He had money and political favors lined up, ready to be cashed in. It hadn't occurred to him that the kidnappers would want *him*. "But Pal-Watch is defending him," he said, as if the request were an impossibility.

"I know."

Abe's mind quickly began working over possible connections between the kidnappers and Faisal Husseini. "Listen, Emma," he whispered, "we know *who* took you. Is Faisal part of their group?"

"No. Husseini is as radical a Muslim as they come. Habash will tell you that he always talks about getting to paradise as a martyr and rails against Israel. The guys holding me — including his brother — are Marxist, an offshoot of the Popular Front for the Liberation of Palestine."

Abe knew that from Dennis, but didn't say anything, fearful that Emma's kidnappers, who were surely listening to the call, might move their location if they were aware they were being watched. He slowly passed a hand over his face. Trying to disentangle the kidnappers' motives suddenly seemed unimportant. Abe looked at Rendi as he asked, "And if I defend him, they will release you?"

Emma didn't answer right away. There was a long pause at the other end of the phone. "It's not as simple as that. Here comes the challenging part. They said they would release me only if you win the case."

Now Abe became angry. He stood from his chair suddenly, the pillow falling to the floor as he did. Rendi stood, too, though she didn't know why he was upset. Abe spoke slowly, assuming that Emma's captors were listening to every word. "I can't control the outcome of a trial! I can do my damnedest, but I can't promise them I'll win."

Now was the first time that Emma's voice broke, her calm demeanor betrayed by a sense of urgent fear. "You have to win, Daddy. They'll kill me if you lose. I know they will. I'm sure of it."

The sound of her voice and what she said shocked Abe into stillness. He stared at himself in the mirror as he spoke. "How can you be sure they'll actually release you, even if I win?"

Emma had, of course, thought of that frightening prospect. Indeed, the snippets of argument she'd overheard — the repeated juxtaposition of her name with the Arabic word for death—had brought it chillingly home to her. She decided to address it directly.

"They'd kill me, Daddy, without a second thought, if they believed that killing me would help their cause, so I decided to make them a promise. I told them that if they released me, you would agree to defend any of their members who get caught in the future. That way they have an incentive to keep their promise. Will you agree?"

"Yes, of course. I agree."

"I also promised that we wouldn't help the Israelis find or prosecute them. And I'm going to keep my promise."

"You did right. You can tell them that I, too, promise we won't help the Israelis if they free you."

There was an uneasy silence, and then Emma said, "Daddy, I don't know what you know about the case. But do you think you can win it?"

For a moment she sounded like a little girl. "If your life depends on it, I will win—whatever it takes." Abe paused and repeated for emphasis, "Whatever it takes." There was nothing he wouldn't do to save Emma's life. Nothing!

Abe had not pressed the button on the black box. He knew that if the precise location of Emma's kidnappers were found by the Israeli authorities, they would probably try a rescue operation. The last time such an operation was tried, for a hostage named Nachshon Wachsman, the operation succeeded but the patient died: All the kidnappers were killed, but so was the hostage. Abe wanted none of that. Nor did he tell the authorities that the man who had ordered the kidnapping was Faisal's brother. That piece of information might also lead them to the location where Emma was being held. Had Emma not used the agreed-upon code words to signify that she was okay, or had she told him that there were some among her captors who wanted to kill her no matter what, Abe might have decided to take a chance on a rescue effort, but he preferred to know that his daughter's life would be in *his* hands, not in the hands of some soldiers or prisoner-exchange negotiators. For that, he was relieved. In his wildest dreams or nightmares—and he had many, starting from the day he learned of Emma's kidnapping—he could never have imagined that his daughter's life would depend on the deal described over the phone. Now he had to figure out a way to assure an acquittal in the Husseini case.

XX

The Stakes

THE STAKES HAD BEEN HIGH for Abe in other cases. His clients had faced the death penalty. He had faced discipline, even disbarment, for questioning the integrity of judges and prosecutors. He had been indicted for criminal defamation by an Italian prosecutor for criticizing an Italian judge who had freed some terrorists because she thought they were "freedom fighters." Once, when he was about to cross-examine a mob boss, his own life had been threatened. But all these paled in comparison with the stakes he now confronted: win an acquittal for a probably guilty mass murderer or lose his beloved daughter.

Abe had also been criticized — sometimes savagely — for his choice of clients. This time it was far worse. Both the American and Israeli media attacked him for defending the man who killed their leaders. The Israeli press also berated him for taking a case instead of trying to retrieve his daughter. As usual, Abe ignored the criticism.

Abe rarely experienced nervousness or self-doubt before a big case. He loved the challenge — the harder the better. He was like a great brain surgeon who relished high-risk operations, but this was different. Emma's life hung in the balance. If he lost, she would die. He knew they meant it. It was as if that brain surgeon were operating on his own child. No surgeon would ever do that. But Abe had no choice.

He considered telling the judge, in secret, about the dilemma. But the kidnappers had been clear. Five minutes after Emma had hung up the phone with Abe, he'd gotten another call, this time from one of her abductors, a man Habash Ein had known as Adam. If Abe told anyone about their deal, he said, Emma would be killed. The kidnappers knew that if Abe told the judge, or the prosecutors, they might issue a fake acquittal and then retry the defendant as soon as Emma was released. But if Abe won, fair and square, the defendant could never be retried. He had to win, and he had to win without the thumb of a hostage release on the scales of justice.

But *could* he win? In Israel there was no jury and therefore no chance of any emotional defense or appeal to the prejudices of the jurors, as there often is in an American courtroom. Here the judge would decide, and the judge selected to preside over Israel's trial of the new century was Dan Shamgar, one of the country's most distinguished jurists, a former attorney general and law professor. Shamgar was a no-nonsense judge with a reputation for calling it straight and never being swayed by emotional appeals. "Just the facts," he would say, paraphrasing the American TV show *Dragnet,* which had become a popular rerun in Israel.

Abe admired Shamgar and liked his approach. But he worried that in this case "just the facts" pointed in only one direction — to his client's guilt.

It had been easy enough to get assigned as one of Faisal's

lawyers. Since Pal-Watch was already defending him, Habash simply appointed Abe as Pal-Watch's lawyer. The one good thing Abe had going for him was the strength of the work that Habash had already done: There were pages and pages of evidence suggesting that Faisal might not have done it, that he hadn't had the wherewithal to get into the American Colony Hotel to plant the bomb. In fact, though his group, the Martyrs of Jihad, claimed responsibility, Habash's team had amassed substantial reports on their financial backing and political connections. Habash believed that this particular group might have had the resources to successfully carry out an attack of this magnitude but certainly didn't have the opportunity.

It was a start, but it wasn't enough to assure an acquittal. Abe knew that in a high-profile case — and there was none with a higher profile than this one — it would not be enough simply to cast some doubt on his client's guilt. He would have to prove that his client didn't do it.

Abe read over all the evidence, looking for something, anything that he could latch onto and use as evidence that Faisal was innocent. But it seemed to him that for every argument Pal-Watch was prepared to make, the prosecutors had ammunition with which to prove Faisal was guilty.

Abe's task was made more difficult by his client's adamant refusal to talk to him about the case. When Habash had first brought him to meet with Faisal and had explained that Abe would now be the primary lawyer, all Faisal said was "I don't trust Jews." Abe's decision to retain Habash Ein as his co-counsel didn't help. "I don't trust Arabs who collaborate with Jews," Faisal would say whenever Habash tried to elicit information from him.

"He's been saying this to me since I first started meeting with him," Habash confided in Abe.

"We're on our own here," Abe told Habash, who was the only person, other than Rendi, with whom he shared the details of the desperate deal he'd been forced to make with Emma's kid-nappers. This did nothing to help Habash's mood. Abe remem-bered him from his Yale days as a vibrant, passionate advocate of human rights. His mind was quick and his demeanor admirable. But since Abe and Rendi had arrived in Jerusalem, Habash had been despondent. Abe noticed daily changes in him. Habash was growing thin, terse, and irritable. While his files were helpful, Abe had trouble engaging him in conversation about the case. He'd stare off into space or lose his train of thought. Rendi thought his guilt was eating him up. Habash had alluded to feeling that way only once, when Abe had caught him one day at Emma's desk. Habash shook his head, his voice breaking. "It is my fault. Adam was *my* contact, and I should have seen through him."

Abe didn't try to comfort him, because he agreed. It *was* Habash's fault. His fault for inviting Emma to Israel, his fault for encouraging her boldness, his fault for not keeping her out of harm's way. But Abe promised Rendi he wouldn't make accu-sations that would damage their relationship, since they had to work together to get Faisal acquitted.

So they soldiered on, presenting a united front to the general public. Abe called a press conference the day after the kidnap-pers contacted him and announced that he had agreed to step in for his kidnapped daughter on Faisal's legal team because that is what she would want him to do.

The stakes were high indeed as Abe walked into the small Israeli courtroom on Weizman Street in Tel Aviv, where the pre-liminary phase of the trial would be conducted.

Unlike in the United States, where courtroom backups cause trials to be delayed for months, criminal trials in Israel — especially ones involving terrorism — tend to be placed on a fast track. In this case Abe had demanded a speedy trial for his con-fined client, and his motion had been granted.

Abe was accustomed to grand American courtrooms, with high ceilings, portraits of judges adorning the white walls, and majestic desks from behind which the judges presided with mahogany gavels. Not so in Israel. Courtroom Gimel, the Hebrew equivalent of three, looked more like a small classroom in an underfunded American public high school. Everything was functional, including the folding chairs and the mismatched tables from which the prosecution and defense argued their cases. The judge, too, sat behind a single table in front of a black-and-white photograph of Israel's president and a small blue-and-white Israeli flag. There were three rows of seats for the press, as well as a pressroom on the floor below, which carried the proceedings via video hookup. There were two rows of seats for spectators—Habash pointed out Faisal's mother, who sat draped in yards of black fabric, holding a picture of her son. Several other Palestinian Arabs sat near her. At the back of the room, nowhere near Faisal's mother, was a man who looked like an Israeli businessman. Habash whispered that this was Rashid Husseini, the defendant's brother, in disguise. As he did so, Abe noticed that Habash's hands balled into fists.

Abe was both pleased and angry. He was pleased because Rashid would see how hard Abe worked to get his brother's acquittal, but he was angry because the man who might kill his daughter was sitting free in an Israeli courtroom. For a moment he thought of approaching Rashid and asking about Emma, but he knew he couldn't do that. What if Rashid were identified and arrested? Then Emma's life would be in danger. Abe simply had to act as if Rashid weren't there. He told Habash as much and made him promise to keep his head.

The windows opened to the busy street two floors below, and the constant honking of car horns punctuated the words of the soft-spoken judge. "Since everyone here, including the defendant, speaks English, and since Mr. Ringel does not speak Hebrew, I propose that the trial be conducted in English, unless there is any objection."

Abe looked to where the prosecution sat and saw that they posed no objection. The lead prosecutor nodded his head at Abe, and as Abe was about to speak, Faisal rose.

Faisal was shaky on his feet; the poison had left him unable to stand without aid. But the cane he'd been using clattered to the floor, lending a dramatic flair to his actions.

"What are you doi——" Abe began to ask him.

Faisal shouted in Arabic, pounding his hand on the table in front of him.

Abe looked to Habash for translation. "He wants the proceedings to go on in Arabic," Habash explained grimly. At Abe's blank expression, he continued, "He's technically allowed to request this, as Arabic is one of Israel's two official languages."

"Can you explain to him that I don't speak Arabic?"

As Habash spoke rapidly in Arabic to their client, Judge Shamgar calmly asked Abe to restrain Faisal. "We will not tolerate outbursts in this courtroom, Mr. Ringel."

"I understand, Your Honor," Abe replied. He noticed that the prosecuting attorneys sat quietly, with their hands folded in their laps and amusement in their eyes. Abe realized that they thought this case would be easy to win. They had no idea how motivated their opposing lawyer was and that he would stop at nothing to beat them.

Finally Habash got Faisal to sit, not with logic and words but by reaching out to touch his shoulder. Faisal, avoiding Habash's grip, fell into his chair, whispering in Arabic. He turned his face away from the judge and from Abe in disgust. He pushed his hands through his unkempt long hair and sat stoically.

"Well?" Abe asked Habash under his breath.

"He talked himself out of the request," Habash whispered

in response. "He decided that if his demand were agreed to, it would lend an air of legitimacy to what he calls 'an entirely illegitimate proceeding.'"

Abe turned to the judge and spoke clearly. "My client has withdrawn his objection to conducting the trial in English, sir."

"Very well. My clerk is fluent in Arabic as well as Hebrew and English, and so if anyone does not understand a word or phrase, she will be available to translate. Does anyone have anything to add before we proceed?"

Abe quickly rose, his "robe" draped so casually around his shoulders that it rode down his jacket sleeve. Although everything else about the courtroom was far more casual than its American counterpart, Israeli lawyers were required to wear robes — a throwback to the days when Palestine was part of the British mandate. But true to Israeli style, the robes — dismissively referred to by Israeli lawyers as *shmattas* (Yiddish for "rags") — had themselves become more informal over the years, to the point that they were more like scarves or shawls than the full-body robes worn by British barristers.

"Your Honor," Abe began, "the charge against my client is that he was part of a large conspiracy to carry out the awful bombing at the American Colony Hotel, in which several heads of state were killed, but the indictment fails to include any other alleged conspirators. How does the government propose to prove a conspiracy without conspirators?"

"Good question, Mr. Ringel. I'm sure the prosecution has an equally good answer. Does it?" The judge turned his gaze upon the prosecutors.

"I hope so, Your Honor," said Yehuda Arad, the state attorney, a man with salt-and-pepper hair and a large gut. "Though I'm sure my answer will disappoint some. We will prove that there were at least three and probably many more conspirators, but we are unable to name them at this time."

There was an audible groan from the media representatives, who were hoping for names.

Abe rose again. "Unable or unwilling?" he insisted, hoping for a legal issue.

Mr. Arad also rose. He was a theatrical man, an attorney who loved being a part of prominent cases. When he spoke, it was with the voice of an actor, loud and pronounced. "I'm sorry to disappoint you, Mr. Ringel, but we simply don't know their names. I'm fairly sure, however, that your client does. Perhaps he is willing to share them with you"—here he paused for effect before continuing—"and with us."

For the first time since arriving in Israel, Abe was completely comfortable. He shook his arm with a small flourish and said, "My client refuses to speak to me. He will not tell me anything about what he did or didn't do—or whom he did it with or didn't do it with. But the burden of proof is on the prosecution, not on us. They have to prove he conspired, and if they can't name his alleged co-conspirators, I will be free to argue that there was no conspiracy or, if there was one, Faisal Husseini was not part of it." He tipped his head toward Mr. Arad.

"We still have a week before trial," the prosecutor replied. "We have overwhelming evidence of a conspiracy, but we currently lack the names of other conspirators. We expect to have more evidence by then."

"As the defense rightly says, it is your burden," the judge said. "Mr. Ringel has no burden to produce anything."

"We understand our burden and expect to carry it," the prosecutor insisted.

"Is there anything further?" Judge Shamgar asked. When both

lawyers said nothing, the judge continued, speaking to Abe. "I'm troubled by your lack of communication with your client, Mr. Ringel. If you want to raise any legal issue concerning that, please do it now. I don't want to go through an entire trial and then have you file a complaint that your client was incompetent to stand trial."

Abe gestured to Faisal, who had continued to focus on the empty wall to his left throughout the entire exchange between lawyers. "My client is completely competent. He simply regards himself as a prisoner of war and a political prisoner." At this, Faisal finally shook off his statuelike pose. He glanced briefly at Abe, narrowing his eyes. "Faisal Husseini does not recognize the authority of this court and refuses to lend it any legitimacy by participating in the proceeding." Abe looked at Faisal for confirmation, and as if he realized that he was cooperating with his lawyer, Faisal looked away contemptuously. But Abe felt for a moment that there *had* been a very brief thawing in Faisal's feelings toward him.

"That's his choice," the judge replied. "As long as he's making it competently."

"He is, Your Honor," Abe assured the judge. For all that Faisal knew, Abe had been faithfully articulating his position. But Abe couldn't have cared less about what Faisal wanted or what political messages he wanted to send. All he knew was that every day the trial lasted was one more day that Emma must endure horrible imprisonment.

"The trial will begin next Sunday," the judge said as he got up and exited the courtroom.

Abe watched him go. He wondered how he'd be able to wait an entire week before beginning.

XXI

The Tactic

ABE FOLLOWED FAISAL to the small cell in the basement of the courthouse, where he would await transportation to the secret location in which he was being held pending trial. After the attempt on his life, the Israelis had assigned twenty-four-hour guards to Faisal, and they'd moved him to a cell that was virtually underground. They wouldn't even let Abe come to see him without several days' worth of planning. So he knew it was now or never. Abe would have only fifteen minutes during which to try to persuade Faisal to accept the only tactic that Abe believed could save his daughter, without compromising his obligation to his client.

The holding cell was barely large enough to fit Faisal, and he was as small as a person could be. Though he'd survived his poison attack, his flesh still had a wasted appearance. Sitting on the metal wall seat, he looked malnourished and gaunt and unsteady.

Faisal crossed his arms when Abe entered the cell but didn't turn his face away. Abe knelt on the floor so that he could look into his client's face as they — or rather he — talked.

"Listen, I know that you know about the case against you. Habash has been thorough."

Faisal said nothing, so Abe continued. "The evidence against you is all circumstantial. I've been reading the notes on the case and reading the newspapers. There are doubting Thomases among your people, Palestinians who don't think you had the brains or guts to do this." Abe noticed a tic in Faisal's jaw when he said this. Abe had been hoping that Faisal was aware that some thought he hadn't the strength or wherewithal to carry out such an attack. Judging from the mounting tension in the cell, Abe could tell that it made Faisal angry. He played on these feelings. "There's only one way to convince them."

Silence. But Abe knew he was getting to Faisal, and he wasn't going to stop now. "The only way to convince them is for you to testify."

Abe couldn't believe he was saying this to his client. Although the client has the right — at least in theory — to make the final decision whether to take the stand, Abe had spent a professional lifetime trying to persuade arrogant, know-it-all clients *not* to testify on their own behalf. Usually he succeeded, but sometimes the client insisted — almost always with disastrous results. As Abe had learned over the years, they did fine on direct examination from their own lawyer. But then would come cross-examination by the prosecutor, and boom — the whole case would blow up. There would invariably be damaging facts the defendant hadn't told his lawyer, because he was sure the prosecutor wouldn't find them. But good prosecutors always did, and then the defendant would try to lie his way around them, and the trap would be sprung. Checkmate! Time for sentencing.

Now Abe was doing his damnedest to persuade his client to

take the stand—in order to prove his own guilt! Everybody said the Middle East was a topsy-turvy world, but this was even more than Abe could have anticipated. He'd never needed so desperate a tactic before, and he'd never had a less cooperative client.

He looked deeply into Faisal's eyes. They were surrounded by dark circles, aftermath of the wasting poison. But there was intelligence in them, too, and Abe could almost see his wheels turning. Faisal looked away. He didn't want to look into Abe's eyes. He didn't want to make a connection. But Abe's argument resonated with him. He remembered the taunting he had received from some of his Palestinian cellmates before he was placed in solitary. They didn't believe his claim that it was he who had planted the deadly bomb. How many others had similar doubts? Faisal wondered. After what seemed like many minutes, he spoke.

"I will tell the truth—a deeper truth than you can understand. I will testify. The world must know that it was I and my holy group who killed the infidels. There must be no doubt."

"That's good. We all want to hear the truth," Abe assured him, reaching out a hand to touch Faisal but quickly withdrawing it. Their interaction was over, at least for now.

XXII

Yassir

P LEASE, CAN I PLEASE SEE the television?" Emma stood in
her room, half dressed. On the bed beside her lay a pile of
new dresses, dresses that were demure and long-sleeved.

Nawal stood by the door, arms crossed. "Try the purple. It
will look nice on you."

Emma ignored her, crossing her own arms. Nawal had
brought her new clothes, but that wasn't what she wanted. She'd
been held prisoner for days now, spending her time walking in
the garden, reading books from the library, and eating. Each day
Nawal made sure there was food for her, just as she'd made sure
there were fresh clothes. She'd been wearing dresses of Salma's
since she'd arrived. But Emma was aware that today was the first
day of the trial, and she was desperate for news, for a glimpse
of Abe and Rendi and Habash. She was certain that the Israeli
news services would at least show footage of them walking into

the courtroom. "What's the big deal? I just want to know about Faisal's case. Don't you?"

Nawal pursed her lips, a mark of sudden tension. "That is not my concern. What happens will happen. Here, try the purple." She took the dress from the pile of clothes and held it up for Emma.

"Fine." Emma capitulated. She put on the dress. "Let's go."

Her only hope now was to endure her daily walk with Nawal—and then perhaps she could elude her guard during her library visit. She'd go to the room with the television by herself. It was a risky thing to do, but she was fairly certain that nothing would happen to her even if she got caught. Adam—Mohammed—would protect her, at least until the trial was over.

Nawal zipped up the back of the dress and led her into the hall. The ever-present gunman followed. Emma walked steadily so as not to betray her thoughts.

The house held nearly a dozen men plus Nawal and Salma, and yet it was always quiet. There was hardly ever a sound—it was so large that people in other rooms seemed to not be there. But now, as they walked, Emma heard a low, angry voice, speaking rapidly and intensely. Beside her, Nawal's face tightened.

They turned a corner, the gunman striding past them, his weapon raised. Nawal also sped up. The gunman suddenly stopped in his tracks, and Nawal pushed past him, her voice rising in Arabic.

The object of her anger was the heavyset man who'd dragged Emma into the room when she'd met Rashid—she remembered that his name was Yassir. Now he was wildly gesticulating to the person he was talking to, a person who was backed up against the corner of the hallway. It was Salma. Emma could tell they were conspiring about something.

"You shouldn't be here, Salma!"

Salma scurried away before Nawal could get to her.

Yassir stared at Nawal in a way that made Emma's skin crawl. "*You* shouldn't be here," he sneered. Nawal stopped in her tracks. She was afraid of him, and this terrified Emma.

"Come, Emma, let's go." Nawal laid a gentle hand on Emma's arm and nudged her toward the exit to the garden.

But as she walked away, Yassir called after her, "American girl!" When Emma turned to him, he smiled a menacing smile, pointed at her, and then drew a finger across his neck. "I'll see you soon, American girl."

XXIII

The Question

THE TRIAL ITSELF — the taking of testimony as opposed
to the preliminary legal maneuvering — was to be held
in Jerusalem's largest public auditorium, the Binyanei Ha'uma,
where trials of great public interest, such as those of Adolf Eichmann and John ("Ivan the Terrible") Demjanjuk, had been
conducted. It would also be carried live on television around
the world. The auditorium, though spacious, was sparse and functional. The stage had been converted into a makeshift courtroom. Judge Shamgar sat in a high-backed leather chair behind
a simple oak desk. Habash and Abe sat on two folding chairs
behind a large pine table. There were many people behind the
prosecutor's table: Mr. Arad and his two legal aides plus Dr. Shai
Avigdor, a well-known forensics expert who'd spent years working with the Shin Bet and, before that, Mossad.

In the audience sat Faisal's mother, and sitting at the back, as
he had during the preliminary hearing, was a disguised Rashid.

Considering the enormous magnitude of the crime, the trial proceedings would be a relatively low-key event—at least in the courtroom itself. Outside, the entire world would be watching and waiting to decide whether the Israelis had caught the right person from the right group.

Because there was no jury and the judge was entirely familiar with the prosecution's evidence, there would be no lengthy opening statements from the lawyers, as there normally was in the United States. The trial would begin with the evidence.

"Please introduce your evidence, Mr. Arad," the judge said to the prosecutor.

Habash took a deep breath, and Abe attempted to give him a reassuring smile. The young lawyer didn't return the gesture, and Abe noticed that his clothes weren't pressed. This was unlike Habash, who was typically fastidious.

Abe's attention shifted to the prosecutor. Yehuda Arad stood up and spoke directly to the judge. "Our first item of evidence is a videotape. Please lower the lights."

There was a murmuring among the spectators as two court officers dimmed the lights and a large white screen was wheeled in from a side entrance. After a few minutes of preparations, the prosecutor clicked a remote control, and suddenly a familiar, indeed iconic, image flashed on the screen. There was the smiling late president of the United States, surrounded by the late prime minister of Israel and the late prime minister and president of the Palestinian Authority. Everyone in the courtroom knew that within seconds they would all be blown to smithereens by the bomb that Faisal Husseini was accused of planting. Everyone in the courtroom had seen these disturbing images dozens of times on television, but there was something different about seeing them on a giant screen in a courtroom in the presence of the man accused of planting the deadly bomb.

Abe had been prepared for the emotion of this moment, but even he was moved by the horror of what was about to happen. Next to him Habash shook his head sadly. Whether it was because of the explosion or because of the impact on the outcome of the case, Abe wasn't sure.

The two-minute segment was played first at ordinary speed. After it was done, Abe waited for Mr. Arad's next move. It was to play the tape again, this time in slow motion.

Abe glanced at his client to glean any reaction — nothing. Faisal sat on the other side of Habash impassively, his face pale and his body slight. There was no emotion in his face at all, especially not, Abe noted, *pride*.

When the playing of the footage was finished, the prosecutor announced, "That, Your Honor, is the corpus delicti, the body of the crime."

Abe rose. "The defense concedes the corpus delicti and stipulates that this grievous crime in fact occurred. Now all they need to do is prove that my client, Faisal Husseini, had anything to do with it, other than observe it on video, as we all did, and perhaps try to videotape the crime scene, which is not a crime. The videotape we just saw does not connect my client to the crime in any way."

Mr. Arad nodded his head in a mock show of deference to Abe. Arad was nothing if not theatrical. "That is the next phase of our case, and we call as our first witness the defendant himself, Faisal Husseini, who knows better than anyone that it was he who planted the bomb."

In an American court, it would be improper for the prosecutor to call a defendant as a witness, because the defendant has a privilege against self-incrimination and the jury may not hold it against a defendant that he refused to testify. In contrast, under Israeli law a judge is allowed to consider the defendant's refusal to testify. Therefore, prosecutors routinely call the defendant as a witness so that the judge will see him refuse to testify and count it against him.

There was a silence in the courtroom—a rarity in Israel. Nobody but Abe expected Faisal to testify as a witness, and all eyes turned first to the defendant, who sat stone-faced, and then to Abe himself, who slowly rose to speak. Habash stared straight ahead, not moving, careful not to give away what was about to happen. For everyone in the courtroom expected Abe to assert his client's refusal to testify, as he was entitled to do under Israeli law, even though it could hurt Faisal in the eyes of the judge.

Instead Abe turned to Faisal and directed a simple question to him. "Do you wish to testify?"

Without saying a word, Faisal stood up, slowly walked to the witness box with the aid of his cane, raised his right hand, and, in accented English, said, "I shall tell the deep truth."

It was the first time Faisal had spoken in public since his arrest, and the crowd burst into a collective commotion. Habash, for the first time that morning, looked interested in what was about to happen. Abe could hear the sounds of Faisal's mother wailing and the fervent murmuring of the reporters. Faisal seemed unaffected by the reaction his unexpected decision had elicited, and Abe thought what a composed client he was. He couldn't recall having a client he felt surer of being able to withstand a prosecutor's tricks.

Abe allowed himself a moment of enjoyment at the look of shock on Arad's face. It was clear that Arad hadn't prepared for Faisal to testify. When he asked, "Will you please tell the court your name and address," it was clearly to buy himself time. Habash actually smiled, so impressed was he by Abe's simple victory here.

Faisal's back was straight and his voice was calm when he

answered. "You know my name and address. That is not what you need me to tell you."

Arad was thrown off his game. When a second question didn't come right away, Faisal spoke in a clear, steady tone, the tone of a cleric or an esteemed teacher. "What you need me to tell you is that I placed the bomb that killed the presidents and prime ministers at the American Colony Hotel, and I am so proud of having done so. I am sad that other people, some of them innocent, had to die, but that is the way of war, and we are at war with anyone who would recognize a Jewish state on Muslim land, or a Western colonial state on Arab land."

The length of Faisal's speech allowed Arad a moment to compose himself. When it was his turn to speak, he did so loudly. Gesticulating wildly, he intoned, "Did you work together with others to plant the bomb?"

"Of course. One person alone could not have accomplished this monumental achievement."

"Who else did you work with?" It was clear to both Habash and Abe that Arad expected Faisal to answer everything as openly as he'd answered the first question.

"That I will not tell you."

"Why not?"

"Because they are my brothers and sisters, and they must remain free to complete their work, while I am privileged to die as a martyr." Faisal raised his eyes to the crowd and spoke not to the prosecutor but to the room. Abe sensed that he was speaking directly to his brother.

His words stopped Arad in his tracks. Eventually Arad said, "But, Mr. Husseini, how do you know you will die? Did your jailers not save you after an attempt on your life?"

"They did what they did for their own reasons. But it is no matter, for I am already dead. Rotting in an Israeli prison, isolated from my brothers and sisters, is death. All that is missing is paradise, but I shall be there before too long."

Arad took a moment to collect his thoughts, looked ever so briefly at Abe, and then consulted a notepad that rested on his desk. His demeanor seemed to change, and Abe expected that his next line of questioning would be designed so that Faisal's answers laid bare the conspiracy. Habash squirmed in his chair. Abe placed a hand on his shoulder, to remind him to retain his composure.

The prosecutor then began to lob a barrage of questions at Faisal. "How did you get around the security measures that were in place to protect the dignitaries that day?"

"That is our secret. If we reveal it, we will not be able to use it again."

Abe was impressed with Faisal's clever response but worried that it would work against his acquittal. And with each question Arad's voice grew louder, and large beads of perspiration gathered on his forehead.

"Where did you obtain the bomb?"

"I will not tell you that."

"Who taught you to detonate it?"

"I will not tell you that."

"Do you plan additional bombings and assassinations?"

"We will kill anyone who collaborates with the Zionist entity or recognizes it."

"Including Arabs and Muslims?"

"Especially Arabs and Muslims."

"Do you plan to refuse to answer all further questions from me, inquiring about the details of the crime?"

"That depends on the question. I will tell you nothing that hurts our cause or helps yours. But I will tell the truth about

THE TRIALS OF ZION

everything else. I want the world to know what I did, what my holy group did, and why we did it."

The prosecutor turned to the judge and said, "I have no other questions, but I need no more questions or answers. The defendant has admitted in open court, voluntarily and without coercion, that he planted the fatal bomb and that he worked with others to do so. That testimony, coupled with the video, satisfies our burden of proving the murders, the conspiracy to murder, and the defendant's involvement in this conspiracy. The prosecution rests."

Abe jumped to his feet. "Not so fast, Mr. Prosecutor." There was an audible reaction from the crowd; nobody knew what Abe was going to do. Even experienced courtroom observers, and the press, did not know what to expect. Abe walked to the middle of the courtroom, speaking as he went. "Direct examination cannot be considered, under Israeli law, until the opposing side has had a full and fair opportunity to cross-examine the witness. Faisal, though my client, was called as a prosecution witness. Now I must be given the opportunity to cross-examine him."

Mr. Arad sprang into action. "But he's your client. You can't cross-examine your own client!"

"Where is that written?" Abe replied, retrieving an Israeli law book from Habash. "It says here that 'the direct testimony of a witness shall be struck if the witness refuses to answer relevant questions on cross-examination.' The prosecution called my client on direct, and now I insist on my right to cross-examine him."

The judge interceded before the prosecutor could object. "Why don't we dispense with labels here and just say that Mr. Ringel should be allowed to conduct further examination of his client. He can ask him relevant questions. Let's see if we need to decide whether to consider it cross-examination or a variation on direct or redirect examination."

Arad was clearly annoyed as he returned to his seat. Abe took a deep breath, rearranged his legal robes, and stepped forward. Habash sat straight in his chair.

"Mr. Husseini," Abe began respectfully, approaching the man, "you understand, do you not, that you must answer all relevant questions I ask you that pertain to the testimony you gave on direct examination by the prosecutor, and that if you do not answer my questions, your direct testimony will be struck from the record and disregarded? You do understand that, right?"

Faisal, as he had done throughout the proceedings, remained still. "I am a simple man, unlearned in the law. If you tell me that is the law, I understand. I have told the deep truth. I will continue to tell the truth about everything that neither hurts my holy group nor helps my unholy enemies. I am speaking the truth."

Abe nodded. "That is for the judge to decide. You understand that?"

"If you say so."

"You have told the court that you planted the bomb, correct?"

"Yes, I did place it where it exploded."

Abe was hoping that this would be his answer. "Now," he said, pitching his voice so that the entire room could hear him, "you have sworn to tell the truth about everything that does not hurt your case or help your enemy, right?"

"That is right. I have nothing to hide, except secrets that help the Jews."

"Okay," Abe continued, "the Israeli forensic investigators know precisely where the bomb was planted. They have kept that information secret in order to help their cause. So you would not be revealing any secret information to your enemies if you provide that information to the court. In fact, you would be hurting your enemies' cause." He spun around and walked purposefully to Faisal. "So please tell the court precisely where you placed the bomb." Abe paused for a second, and then, in a firm stage whisper directed at Husseini, he added, "If you know."

The last three words conveyed, in a not-so-subtle way, the essence of Abe's direct challenge to his own client. The Israeli authorities had withheld two crucial pieces of forensic information about the bombing: The first was the nature of the bomb — its components, the type of explosives used, the triggering mechanism. Second was the bomb's precise location when it exploded — whether it was under the stage, in a vehicle, in a briefcase, et cetera. They withheld this information in order to be able to test the truthfulness of any confession or claim of responsibility. This was particularly important in this kind of case because there would likely be numerous confessions and claims of responsibility. The person who actually planted the bomb might not know its precise nature, but he would surely know where he planted it. If Faisal Husseini did not know precisely where the bomb was when it exploded, then he was not the person who planted it and he was lying when he claimed responsibility for that criminal act.

Faisal Husseini's calm demeanor finally slipped. He shifted in his seat, moving forward. He looked angrily at Abe. Then he turned his face away from his lawyer and said to no one in particular, "What else can one expect of a Jewish lawyer? Trickery, deception, disloyalty, perversion of trust, sneakiness, dishonesty — you are trying to lay a trap for your own client. You are a Judas, without even the excuse of the coins." By the end of his speech, his voice was loud and his face red.

Despite the charged atmosphere in the air — everyone in the room waited to hear what Abe's response to this sort of slander would be——he responded calmly. "Please answer the question." He leaned on the defense table and crossed his arms casually. "It is a simple one. The person who actually planted the bomb would know where he placed it. A person who falsely claimed to plant the bomb, and had nothing to do with it, would not know where another person, with whom he did not conspire, had placed it. Which person are you?"

There was a palpable tension in the room by now. Everyone was straining forward, desperate to hear what Faisal would say, including the prosecution and Habash.

Out of the corner of his eye, Abe saw Rashid smiling at Abe's clever tactic. Abe suppressed his own smile.

Husseini turned to the judge and asked, "Do I have to answer that question?"

Judge Shamgar replied in a steady voice, "No, you do not. But if you do not, I will be required under law to strike and disregard your direct testimony."

Mr. Arad could no longer stand it. The prosecutor rose to his feet, nearly shouting, "This is a setup. Mr. Ringel arranged this entire charade. Mr. Husseini knows where the bomb was planted, because he planted it. But Mr. Ringel told him not to answer the question so that his direct testimony would be struck and we would be left with only a circumstantial case. It's utterly transparent."

At this there was a rumbling among the viewers. Abe turned to Arad, raising his arms in a gesture of innocence. But before he could defend his tactics, the judge demanded, "Mr. Arad, you are making a serious charge against a well-known lawyer. You'll be required to prove it."

"I can prove it, Your Honor. Mr. Ringel's reputation precedes him. He's known in the United States as a tricky lawyer who has pulled similar deceptive tricks, such as putting a defendant's identical twin on the stand and having the victim identify the wrong person. In Israel lawyers don't do such things."

Abe stood quietly as the prosecutor attacked him, but Habash looked ready to leap to his feet to defend him. Abe gently shook his head, and Habash settled down. Abe had been through this before, and he knew that the best response to such personal attacks was no response at all. Let the judge deal with it.

Judge Shamgar looked sternly at the prosecutor. "I hate to make comparisons, but you're sounding a bit like the defendant in your accusations against Mr. Ringel—'tricky,' 'deceptive.' In my courtroom not only are the defendants presumed inno-cent, so are the lawyers. Therefore, unless you can back up your charge, I will ignore it and ask you to apologize to Mr. Ringel, who is a guest in our country."

The prosecutor sat down, sheepishly whispering, "*Slicha*"— Hebrew for "I'm sorry"—in Abe's direction.

"Then let's get back to the business at hand," the judge ordered. "Mr. Husseini, it is your choice. Will you answer Mr. Ringel's question?"

Now Abe himself was straining forward, anxious to hear his client's answer. He knew very well that Husseini wasn't stupid, and he knew that he'd do everything he could to one-up Abe. And Abe was right, for now it was Husseini's turn to be tricky. "I will need to confer with my lawyer before I decide whether to answer that question," he said, glaring at Abe.

XXIV

The Button

N AWAL WASN'T HER USUAL cheery self on their walk. In
fact, after ten minutes of wandering through the garden,
she retrieved a cell phone from her pocket and placed a call.
Then she took Emma by the arm and practically ran with her
to the other side of the garden, a spot where there were paths
cut through a grove of orange trees. The gunman followed at a
leisurely pace.

"Sit here!" Nawal thrust Emma onto a wrought-iron seat and
paced frantically for five minutes until Mohammed showed up.
He barked an order at the gunman, who shrugged lazily and
left.

Nawal drew Mohammed twenty or so feet away from her.
The two of them conversed in Arabic, low and intensely, just as
Salma and Yassir had in the hallway.

Emma nervously toyed with a fraying edge in her new purple

dress, trying desperately to pick out words she understood and to guess at the meaning of their conversation.

It wasn't hard to figure out that there were those among her captors who didn't want her alive. Nawal's eyes were wide as she gestured toward Emma. Mohammed glanced at Emma briefly before returning his focus to Nawal, nodding tightly. Then the two of them approached her.

"Nawal said you requested a television," Mohammed said to her.

Emma responded, "That's right. The trial began today."

Nawal appeared more nervous than Mohammed. She watched him with darting eyes as he nodded his head. "Yes, it did. But they aren't showing it," he lied.

Emma bit her lip. "Even so, is there footage of my father at all?" She hated the sound of her own voice. It sounded young and feeble and *terrified*.

Mohammed inhaled sharply. "Yes, but you can't see it. I'll make you a deal." Emma ignored the irony in those words. "I'll bring you the newspaper in the library each day. Starting tomorrow."

Emma looked back and forth between them, suspiciously. "What's my part of the deal?"

Nawal held her breath as Mohammed withdrew something from his pocket and pressed it into Emma's hand. It looked like a remote device to open a locked car door. "If anyone other than Nawal or me tries to take you from your room, you press this button." He showed her where it was on the device. "And I'll come for you."

Now Emma was really frightened.

XXV

The Meeting

THEY WERE USHERED by court officers into a basement closet that could barely pass as a room. There were no windows, chairs, or tables, and the air was dead. Faisal walked slowly, led by the arms, and Abe and Habash followed him.

The court officers turned to the two lawyers, and one of them barked out an order. Abe and Habash hurried to the closet where they'd deposited Faisal, and Habash knelt down in front of him, speaking in a low voice a language that Abe couldn't understand.

Faisal knew what Habash was doing. He was hoping to engender trust by speaking to him in his mother tongue. But Faisal didn't trust him. He didn't trust anyone who worked with Jews. While Habash spoke to him, Faisal eyed Abe, who stood in the corner with his arms crossed. Faisal thought that Rashid must have been involved in the hiring of the American lawyer. It was no coincidence that Habash had accused Rashid of kidnapping Emma Ringel and then suddenly her father was on his legal team. His brother's group had a rich supporter, and he thought they must be paying the Jew lawyer. *He's doing it for the money,* Faisal concluded. And Rashid was holding Ringel's daughter as some sort of collateral. That made sense. Maybe he would be paid more if he secured an acquittal. He really was Judas, coins and all! Faisal's contempt for his lawyer grew.

He felt some regret that the poison had not worked. He would have preferred to be stabbed or shot — more honorable deaths than by poisoning — but he wanted desperately to be a *shahid,* a martyr, to bring pride to his mother and to his community. Now his only hope was to be convicted and executed. But his own lawyer was ruining it for him. If he was acquitted, he would be humiliated — like a suicide bomber who couldn't press the button.

Finally, after what seemed an endless stream of words, Habash finished his explanation of why Faisal must answer Abe's question. Faisal could barely contain the contempt he felt for Habash — a betrayer of his own people. "I am guilty, and I must be convicted," he spit at him in English.

"We are your lawyers. Our job is to defend you, to help you and try to prevent your conviction."

Faisal smiled a sad smile. "Being acquitted will not help me."

"Under the law it will."

"Perhaps under the law of the Jews. But I must live by a deeper law."

"The only law that applies in that courtroom is Israeli law," Habash insisted.

"I don't care about Israeli law or Mr. Ringel. He is *my* lawyer, and I insist that he follow my wishes. My wishes are for him to withdraw his question. He must obey my instruction. You must tell that to the judge."

A worried look came over Abe's face. He was not so much concerned that Faisal might be right as a matter of legal ethics. Ethics be damned, Abe thought. His mind was only on his daughter's safety. He was worried that Judge Shamgar might agree with Faisal and rule that the question — which was Abe's only real weapon — had to be withdrawn.

XXVI

The Answer

A BE DIDN'T SPEAK to Habash during the entire walk back to the courtroom, nor did he speak as the officers ushered Faisal back to his seat on the witness stand. He had to make sure that Faisal's testimony proved that he did not plant the bomb, or else his daughter would die. But here he was under direct orders from his own client to withdraw the crucial question — the only question that could prove that his client didn't do it. He had just a precious few moments to come up with a plan that would not only disprove Faisal's guilt but save his daughter's life.

Judge Shamgar arrived and took his seat, and Abe rose to address him. Every person in the courtroom listened attentively. This was the best legal theater these courts had ever seen. Even Habash, who'd spent years reading up on Abe's notorious maneuvers, was on the edge of his seat, anxious to know how he would get them out of this fix.

"I have been instructed by my client to withdraw my question,"

Abe pronounced. There was a ripple of conversation among the observers in the room, and the judge brought his gavel down hard to silence them. Abe acknowledged all the people in the audience with a sweeping look before continuing grandly. "With respect, Your Honor, I refuse to do so. My client wants to be convicted, but I believe he is innocent. I must do everything I can do to secure his acquittal. That is my job."

Mr. Arad leaped to his feet, his belly brushing the side of the prosecutor's table. "If Mr. Ringel has *facts* proving innocence, let him present them instead of engaging in his trickery."

Abe directed his reply to the judge. "The fact that proves my client's innocence is that he doesn't know where the real bomb planter put the bomb. If he did, he would surely say so and prove his guilt, because we all know he wants to be convicted."

Yehuda Arad refused to back down. If Abe successfully won this battle, Arad could lose his case. "But maybe he does know and is withholding that information to secure an acquittal — with or without his lawyer's knowledge."

Abe strode forward, ready to continue engaging in this legal argument, but at this point Judge Shamgar banged his gavel. "I've heard enough. I've seen enough. It is pretty clear to me what is going on. I believe — and so rule — that the defendant wants to be convicted. It also seems possible — although this is less certain and hasn't been proven by either of you — that he is trying to take the blame for doing something that someone else did. Unless he can tell the court where the bomb was planted, I will have no choice but to reject his direct testimony." The judge then stood up and looked straight at Faisal.

"You have instructed your lawyer to withdraw his question because you want to be convicted and executed." The judge paused and stared the defendant in the eye. "I will not let you use this court to commit legal suicide. In this court we convict only the guilty. We do not allow suicide terrorists to abuse our legal system. If you are truly guilty, you should have no problem answering the question. If you refuse, or answer wrongly, that will be evidence that you are a suicide defendant, whose job is to be convicted regardless of whether you are guilty or innocent. The question therefore is relevant to my judgment. You must answer the question, or your direct testimony will be struck."

Faisal felt trapped. Rashid, sitting in the last row of the courtroom, smiled. This time Faisal saw the smile and became even angrier. He turned to their mother, sitting behind the prosecution and clutching the same framed photo of her son that she'd brought to every legal session. She rocked back and forth, a handkerchief poised at her mouth. Faisal knew that she was confused by the attitudes of her two sons and that she wanted Faisal to live but not to be shamed. If he did not answer, he could be acquitted and humiliated. It would be worse than death.

Faisal thought for a moment, peered around the courtroom, then looked squarely at the judge and said, "You have given me no choice. I will answer my lawyer's question."

Abe spun on his heel and faced Husseini. This was the last thing he expected. After decades of defending clients, he thought he knew them fairly well: knew when they were lying and when they were telling the truth, knew often when they were or weren't guilty. He'd bet *everything* — his own daughter's life — on the fact that Faisal was a patsy. But now he began to panic. What if he'd been wrong? What if Faisal really had planted the bomb? What if he were to give the correct answer? There would be nothing Abe could then do to prevent a conviction. Emma would be killed. Had his tactic doomed his daughter?

But if Faisal really had placed the bomb, why did he not

answer immediately? By delaying, he had planted the seed of his possible innocence in the mind of the judge. But now, by agreeing to answer, he had unplanted that seed.

Abe had learned in law school never to ask a question to which he did not know the answer. At an American trial, the defense attorney would have learned during discovery where the bomb had been planted. But Israeli security had kept that important fact from being discovered. Abe was in the dark when he asked the critical question.

Suddenly Abe realized what he had to do. It was risky, but it was the best chance he had. He faced his client and asked the question, this time most pointedly. "Tell the court precisely where you claim you planted the bomb—*if you know.*"

Faisal looked into Abe's eyes and responded, "I placed the bomb in the briefcase of the secretary of state of the Palestinian Authority, who stood directly behind the Palestinian prime minister."

There was silence in the courtroom as all eyes turned to Dr. Shai Avigdor, the Israeli forensics expert seated next to the prosecutor. He was the man who had conducted the investigation of the bomb—its components and its exact placement. Abe looked at Dr. Avigdor in an effort to discern a reaction. Was he surprised? Did he shake his head? Nothing! An absolute poker face. Abe would have to await his testimony to learn the results of Dr. Avigdor's investigation—and his daughter's fate.

Habash had briefed Abe on Dr. Avigdor's history. In the Mossad he had famously designed the first cell-phone bomb that exploded when an incoming call from a specified number was answered. It killed a terrorist in Lebanon. When he retired from the Mossad, he joined the Shin Bet as a consultant specializing in foreign-made bombs. He had been assigned by the state to reconstruct the explosion at the American Colony and determine the precise nature and location of the bomb, which he had done. Here was the part that Habash was furious about: Dr. Avigdor had shared his conclusions with no one outside of the Shin Bet except the new prime minister of Israel. The Americans had their own expert, as did the Palestinians, but little information had been shared among them. Habash, too, was in the dark, though it was his opinion that the Shin Bet had authorized Dr. Avigdor to confirm or deny the testimony of Husseini. Habash doubted that the prosecutor knew where the bomb had been planted.

Faisal was dismissed from the stand, and Dr. Avigdor stood up, took an oath to tell the truth, and listened as Judge Shamgar addressed him. "Dr. Avigdor, in your expert opinion, was the bomb planted in the secretary of state's briefcase?"

Dr. Avigdor looked at Abe and then at Husseini before turning to the judge and saying in a matter-of-fact way, "My investigation established with relative scientific certainty that the bomb had been placed in the briefcase of the man standing behind the Palestinian prime minister. As we saw in the playing of the video, that man was the Palestinian secretary of state. Mr. Husseini's answer is correct."

Abe felt as if he'd been punched in the stomach. He stood in the center of the courtroom, a still eye in a storm of pandemonium. Only the person who planted the bomb would know precisely where it had been planted. Abe himself had said that. Now he was trapped in his own net. His client would be convicted. His daughter would be killed. And it was his fault.

Abe caught Habash's eye then, expecting to see defeat. But Habash didn't look down, he looked dubious. Abe suddenly remembered what Habash had said about not trusting the Shin Bet.

The judge banged his gavel to quiet everyone. "Well, Mr. Ringel, what's your next move?"

Abe breathed deeply and said, "I'd like to replay the video of the explosion." Even as he requested it, he wasn't sure what he was looking for. But it was a good way to gain some time so that he could decide how to undo the damage to the defense's case that Dr. Avigdor had just done.

Once again the lights were dimmed and the video flickered to life. Every eye was on the screen as the three dignitaries once again walked to their death. Behind the Palestinian prime minister, a short, balding man could be seen carrying a thick leather briefcase. Habash whispered to Abe, "That is the Palestinian secretary of state."

Then came the explosion. It was impossible to tell from the video the direction or source of the blast, since it happened so quickly, but Abe demanded that it be replayed at the slowest possible speed and that all other videos and films of the explosion be brought to the courtroom.

"What is your point, Mr. Ringel?" the judge asked. "Are you challenging Dr. Avigdor's truthfulness?"

"With respect, Your Honor, I am. He is a Shin Bet doctor, who worked for the Mossad. His first allegiance is not to the truth. It is to the protection of Israel. The Shin Bet and the Mossad have licenses to lie, when necessary, to protect the state. Remember the Landau Report."

The judge remembered the Landau Report. He had served on the Landau Commission, which had investigated charges that the Shin Bet had tortured some terrorist suspects and then lied about it. The Shin Bet had claimed a license to lie in the national interest. Although the Landau Commission had concluded that there was no such license, there were widespread accounts of continued lying by Israeli intelligence agencies, as well as other intelligence agencies throughout the world.

Judge Shamgar looked angrily at Abe and said in a stern voice,

"I'm fully aware of our report, but it did not cover Dr. Avigdor or the current leadership of the Shin Bet. Now it is you, Mr. Ringel, who are making a serious accusation against a distinguished professional. You are charging him with perjury—a serious crime. Can you back it up?"

Abe knew he was upsetting the judge by his as-yet-unfounded accusation of perjury, but the judge was not his only audience. He was speaking as well to Emma's kidnappers, a representative of whom was in the courtroom. If Dr. Avigdor's answer were to dash their hopes of an acquittal, they might decide to kill their hostage. Abe had to raise their hopes for an acquittal, even if it meant temporarily offending the judge.

"Yes, I can. But I will need a few days to examine the videos and films. I will also need a subpoena for Dr. Avigdor's work product, including his lab reports and any fragments of the bomb and the briefcase in which it was allegedly planted. Then I will place Dr. Avigdor under oath once again and cross-examine him. May these requests be granted, Your Honor?"

"Any objection from the prosecution?"

"Yes," Arad countered. "Plenty. There are state secrets involved."

"There are no secrets from me," the judge insisted. "The matter will be considered in camera—that is, by me alone, with only the lawyers present—to the extent it involves state secrets. Mr. Ringel's requests are granted. You had better be right, Mr. Ringel," the judge insisted, not realizing how high the stakes really were. "The court is in recess."

XXVII

The Threat

EMMA WAS VORACIOUSLY DEVOURING the newspaper while sitting in her room. She had never been an avid newspaper reader. Like many in her generation, she got her news from the Internet—and from comedy programs like *The Daily Show with Jon Stewart*. But this time her life depended on what the newspaper reported, even if it was always a day behind. Emma had read of her father's dramatic question—and the equally dramatic answer his client had given.

In between newspapers she'd been spending time in the library with Mohammed. After she'd pore over the accounts of the trial, they would talk about books and popular culture, staying as far away as possible from the conflict in the Middle East.

For a kidnapper and double-crosser, Mohammed wasn't that bad, Emma thought.

Each day he asked how she was doing, and each day she said

that she wanted to go home. But she understood that he was really asking if any of his co-conspirators had given her any trouble. Knowing that he was concerned about her welfare made her both scared and relieved. Scared that there were people in the house who wanted to act against her, but somewhat relieved that Mohammed was looking out for her well-being.

Emma was growing restless. She tried not to think of the status of the trial, because she would only worry. Sure, it seemed dire, since Faisal had apparently identified the placement of the bomb. But they were in recess, which meant that Abe was doing everything he could to counter his client's damaging words. She knew her father. He'd find a way to make Faisal look like an innocent liar, rather than a truth-telling mass murderer. She was more confident in her father's keeping his part of the deal than in her captors' keeping theirs.

A knock sounded at her door. She folded the paper, set it aside, and rose from the bed, expecting Nawal and her lunch tray.

But when the door opened, it wasn't Nawal.

It was Yassir.

His bulk filled the doorway, and his meaty hands gripped the tray in a way that made Emma think he could snap it in two if he wanted. Over his shoulder the gunman peered in nervously. He spoke in Arabic. Yassir responded with a sneer and kicked the door shut with his booted foot.

Before she could think, Emma backed up as far as possible, until she was pressed against the windowpane.

This delighted the man. He put the tray down on her dresser right next to Mohammed's beeper, which Emma had carelessly left there when she'd gone to bed the previous night.

Inwardly she cursed herself for not keeping it with her at all times, as Mohammed had urged her to.

She was sweating as she watched Yassir take in every detail

of the little room: the dresser, the newspaper folded on the bed, the row of dresses hanging on a portable rack in the corner. She didn't want to look at the beeper, hoping against hope that he wouldn't see it.

He stepped toward her then, filling the room with dread. "To keep you like this. Like you're on vacation. It's disgusting. They treat you better than they treat us."

Emma gulped and pressed into the window, but he kept walking toward her slowly. She became aware of how small she was. He could do anything to her at all, and she'd have little chance of fighting him off. Her only option was to run for the beeper.

"For what?" he continued. "An American brat. You shouldn't be here, but your Jew-loving friends Mohammed and Nawal don't listen to me. Do you know what Israelis do to kidnappers?"

Emma stood silently, too afraid to speak.

He clapped his hands, and she jumped. "Answer me!" he barked.

She couldn't help it. A tear slid down her cheek and she stuttered, "N-n-n-ooo."

He pulled the waistband of his pants over his large belly, and her stomach pitched. "They send in the army. They send in the heavy artillery. Nobody survives. Nobody. But does Rashid listen to me?"

When he paused, it was evident to Emma that she should answer. "N-n-no?"

"He's thinking with his heart." Yassir was standing a foot from her now, and she tried to judge the distance to the dresser and the beeper but was too afraid to manage it. "I think I know what part Mohammed is thinking with." He lifted a finger and drew it down Emma's cheek. She recoiled with revulsion, and he laughed. It was the worst sound she'd ever heard.

"Doesn't matter anyway. That sham of a trial will end, Faisal will be put to death, and then so will you. Let's just hope the Israeli army doesn't find us first, right, American girl? Because if they do, you will be the first to die." He braced his arm against the wall near Emma's head, towering over her.

"My father will win the case. I know it. He doesn't need the Israeli army. Your leader promised to free me if my father wins."

"We will see," Yassir said with a smirk. "Sometimes accidents happen. Sometimes promises must be broken. Sometimes hostages try to escape. We will see. Your fate is not entirely in the hands of your father. If he loses, you will surely die. If he wins, we will see. We will see."

He licked his lips and left. Emma ran to the dresser and clutched the beeper tightly, then collapsed on the bed and tried to control her crying.

XXVIII

Rendi

H<small>E'D HAD THREE DRINKS</small>, and still Habash felt miserable. Wasn't scotch supposed to dull your pain?

The bartender at the small club at the top floor of the newly reopened American Colony Hotel took Habash's empty glass and refilled it. When Habash had arrived at the bar after escorting Abe home, he placed a two-hundred-shekel note on the counter and told the bartender that he'd be there awhile. His plan was to stay until the image of Emma tied up in a dingy cell was erased from his mind.

He was going to be at the bar a long, long time.

The moment the trial recessed, Abe and Habash had run back to Pal-Watch and begun amassing a crew to help them examine the video footage. The two men never mentioned what they both feared to be true: that by gambling on Dr. Avigdor's having lied to the judge, they were grasping at a straw that wasn't there. But Abe was determined to pore over that footage and to find somebody—*anybody*—to dispute their client's testimony about where the bomb was placed.

Habash downed his fourth drink in one gulp and watched the rattling ice cubes slip around the glass. He had no doubt that Dr. Avigdor was lying. He'd encountered this sort of roadblock before. Government agencies were notoriously uninterested in truth and justice. They often decided who they wanted to pay for a crime, then put all their energies into making sure that person looked guilty.

He was becoming jaded.

"Penny for your thoughts." A cool hand placed on Habash's back made him jump. Rendi slid onto the barstool next to him and signaled her drink order to the bartender. "Bulletproof vest, eh?"

Habash only nodded.

"I never pegged you for a big drinker," she said evenly as the bartender served her a Diet Coke.

"I never was," Habash grumbled. He wished he could disappear. Emma's stepmother was beautiful. But worse, her eyes were wise and calculating. Habash felt as if she could read his mind. She must have been a hell of a spy in her day.

"Does Emma know how you feel?" she asked quietly.

"What?" Habash again jumped.

Rendi assessed him, staring at him for a long, silent moment. Then she smiled. "Of course she doesn't. *You* don't know how you feel."

Habash wanted to walk away, but he had never been a disrespectful person. Still, he couldn't think of what to say to her. "It is my fault that she is going through this."

Rendi swirled the liquid in her glass. "It's not. She's the daughter of a very famous man. And she's been interested in the Middle East for a long time. She lost a friend here, and since then she's wanted to help. So she would've found a way here, with you or without you."

Rendi leaned forward and squeezed his arm. "I know you feel guilty, Habash. But when Emma comes home — and she will come home — be sure to tell her what she means to you."

She left without tasting her drink. Habash watched her go, and for the first time since the days together at Yale, he admitted to himself that he had strong feelings for Emma. Or was it guilt? He knew that his feelings toward her went beyond friendship or professional respect. They were stronger than he had ever acknowledged. But what exactly were they? Could he actually be in love with a Jewish woman who would want to live her life in America? His mind was a jumble. He couldn't think clearly about Emma until and unless she was returned safely. Not only had he placed a friend in danger, but he'd also never had the courage to return Emma's feelings. And now he might never have the chance.

XXIX

The Photographer

R UN IT AGAIN — this time more slowly."
  For three days Abe holed up in the lab of Danny Grossman, who had previously held Shai Avigdor's position with the
Shin Bet as chief forensic scientist for bombs and explosives but
was now in private practice as a consultant. Rendi knew Grossman by reputation and recommended that Abe and Habash hire
him. They quickly learned to respect Grossman's attention to
detail and his allegiance to nothing but the truth of what he saw.
He might have loyalties to one side or the other, but Abe hadn't
detected them yet.

The room, in a shabby, run-down building in the business
district, was a cross between a movie-viewing room and a science
lab. Its walls were lined in floor-to-ceiling equipment: sound
analyzers, analog transfer machines, and computers.

Habash was in charge of keeping Abe fully loaded with coffee as Grossman and he worked around the clock. Habash drank lots of coffee, too. The first day of work, it was to combat the headache he had from his long night of drinking. By the second and third days, he drank coffee to keep alert.

At the moment they were viewing the two seconds' worth of footage that contained the march to the stage by the three heads of state. "Now compare it to the next angle," Abe ordered Grossman's film technician.

Abe, Habash, and Danny Grossman had now watched three sets of video, each shot from different places. Most of the hotel's surveillance video had been destroyed in the explosion, but there had been two handheld camcorders retrieved from the debris that contained viable footage. The major source of video evidence came from a camera that had transmitted directly to an Israeli television studio. Although the camera had been destroyed and the cameraman killed, a studio video showed the instant of the explosion before going dark. According to Grossman, this footage seemed to confirm the source of the explosion as being behind the dignitaries.

But this didn't prove Faisal's guilt. The videos showed several people standing in a row behind the heads of state, and Faisal Husseini, like everyone else, had seen the videos over and over again. If he were simply guessing about where the bomb had been planted, it was a smart bet that it had come from behind the dignitaries. It was also a smart bet, especially from someone as suspicious of Israelis as Faisal, that if his guess were plausible, it would be backed up by the Israeli "expert." But Husseini had gone a step further and claimed that it had been placed in the briefcase of a specific person. Was it a guess? Or did he know because he put it in there?

Husseini's guilt or innocence would turn on the answer to

that question—and so would Emma's life. But how could Abe prove that Husseini was guessing, and guessing wrong?

After hours of watching the same two seconds and comparing the differences between the three sets of video, Grossman pushed his chair away from the desk that contained the playback machinery and pinched the bridge of his nose in frustration.

Abe asked, "What's wrong?"

Grossman replied, "The problem is that to prove where the bomb was planted, you're going to have to get access to certain pieces of evidence. Evidence that is in the custody of governments who aren't going to give it to you."

Grossman wasn't saying anything that Abe hadn't suspected. Habash, who was pouring himself a cup of coffee from the plug-in pot on the floor, asked Danny, "What kind of evidence?"

Grossman swiveled in his chair to face him. "To discover where a bomb has been planted, there are certain steps you have to take. First, you examine the videos, if there are any, to give you a rough sense of the location of the bomb." He gestured to the large white screen at the opposite end of the room. "We've done that. If there is no video evidence or if the videos are inconclusive, you have to rely on eyewitnesses, who are often wrong."

Habash walked to where the two men sat. "Arad claims he's given us all the eyewitness accounts. In the preparation phase of the case, my investigators canvassed as many of the people who survived as they could, and we have accounts that aren't in the public record. But nothing is conclusive."

Grossman continued, "In that case you'd look at the point of impact of the explosion—the dead bodies, the damaged buildings. You look for telltale fragments, as well as physical evidence of direction of the impact."

"Fragments," Abe repeated, staring at the screen and thinking aloud. "If the bomb had been in the secretary of state's briefcase, there would be fragments of that briefcase — bits of leather — in the bodies of some of those killed. Right?"

"Probably. More likely in those very close to the impact."

Abe now turned to Habash. "After the explosion what happened to the bodies of the president and the prime minister?"

Habash sat in a chair next to Grossman. "The United States government immediately took control over the recovery operation for the president's body. They flew it to a military hospital in Germany for autopsy and then to Arlington for burial."

Abe fired questions at Habash and Grossman as he worked out his next move. "Well, we can't get our hands on the president's actual body. Would the autopsy result show the source of the explosion?"

Habash shook his head. "Pal-Watch tried to get the autopsy report. We can't. The only people who have it, besides the CIA and the FBI, are the pathologists in Berlin who prepared it, and they weren't exactly willing to share. But, Abe! The Secret Service probably has it, too."

Abe reached for his cell phone, which was in the pocket of his briefcase. "I'll have Rendi call Dennis Savage. See what he can do for us. As for the reports on the bodies of the Palestinian president or prime minister, I think I know a way to get a copy of some of those, too."

Habash was about to ask Abe how he could possibly get access to those — Shin Bet and Mossad probably had them, but they were as uncooperative as the Americans. However, as Abe held the phone in his hand, it began to ring. Habash jumped in his seat. The two men both hoped it was Emma but were careful not to say anything to that effect in front of Grossman.

"Hello?" Abe asked cautiously. Habash slid his chair closer to him.

A voice came over the line — a man's voice. "Mr. Ringel. My name is Tom Ashe. I'm an American." Abe shook his head to let Habash know that it wasn't Emma. Habash's face crumpled in disappointment.

The caller continued, "I know you from television. I may have something that could help you."

XXX

The Confetti

Tom Ashe was an American photographer living in Israel. When he knocked on the door of Danny Grossman's facility, both Abe and Habash felt a mixture of hope and fear. People were always volunteering information during a case like this — Habash had an entire team of legal students sorting through false claims. Since Abe Ringel had joined the case, the number of "firsthand" accounts had nearly tripled. But Tom Ashe got Abe's private number from a mutual friend — a video technician for a Boston TV station — and that was how he found himself sitting in the darkened viewing room mere hours after Abe had answered his call.

"It's good to meet you," Abe said, shaking the forty-something man's hand. "Let's see what you've got."

Tom lifted a large leather case onto the table and retrieved three photos. "I was photographing some goats not far from the American Colony Hotel at the time of the explosion. As soon as

I heard the blast, I started clicking away. Smoke, debris, I even managed to shoot a piece of wood flying through the air. I was uploading the photos the other day and thought you would be interested in something I found." He spread the three photos on the table. "Do you see this?" Tom pointed to one of the pictures; a black-and-white that looked as if it was covered with tiny pieces of torn paper.

"Looks like confetti from a parade," Habash said.

"That's what it looks like to me, too," Abe agreed. "But it's the confetti of death — the residue of the worst terrorist bombing in our history."

Tom returned to his leather portfolio and took out three more pictures. "I enlarged them — as big as I could. It's a technique I often use for dramatic effect. But when I did it to these, I noticed something. Look. The confetti has print on it. English letters, but I can't read all of them, because the more I enlarge it, the blurrier they get. The first letter is an *o,* then a *d.* But I can't make sense of it."

Abe took the enlarged photos from Tom and placed them next to an empty pad. "Let's try," he said. He wrote down the letters he could read: *od cr.* Grossman took a magnifying glass out of his jacket pocket and added a couple more: *t, e.* All four men stared at the paper for several minutes, puzzling over what the letters might mean.

Suddenly Abe shouted, "I think I've got it! Thank God for Hebrew school. It's the first page of the Bible! 'In the beginning God created the heavens and the earth.' It's small fragments of a Bible." Abe looked to Habash, to see if he understood and agreed.

Habash ripped a page from the pad and wrote down the letters in his own hand. Adding in the missing letters to make up the text, he decided that Abe was right. The confetti was made from a Bible.

After Abe and Habash thanked Tom and gave him their

word that they wouldn't sell the photos to any media outlet, Abe sat down with Grossman and Habash. Grossman, upon Abe's declaration that the fragments were biblical, told them that this evidence suggested the bomb was probably in the same case as the Bible.

"Was the secretary of state a Muslim or a Christian?" Abe asked Habash.

"A Muslim and a very religious one. He would not be carrying a Christian or Jewish Bible in his briefcase."

Grossman paused the video on a frame that showed all the people who were standing on the stage the day of the bombing. "Who would be carrying a Bible, from among those behind the dignitaries?" Abe wondered. "Maybe the president's minister? Where was he? I don't see him there."

Habash said, "He survived the explosion, so he must have been at the back of the crowd."

Abe walked toward the screen, so that he could get a better view of the men. "What about the president himself?"

Grossman said, "He's not holding anything, look. And I doubt he carried a full-size Bible in his pocket."

They proceeded to identify everyone who was in proximity and behind the dignitaries. None of the men had anything in their hands. In the back of the picture, though, stood a tall, blond man wearing an earpiece.

"Who's he?" Abe asked, pointing to the man, who stood off to the side of the second row.

"Secret Service," Habash replied. "What's that in his hand?"

"*That* is the football," Abe said excitedly. "The box with the nuclear codes. It's always near the president in case he has to authorize a nuclear attack."

Habash looked at him, surprised.

Abe shrugged his shoulders. "What can I say? I've been

to parties with a few presidents. I know about the football."
He turned to Grossman. "Can you get some footage of earlier
presidents — Clinton, Bush, Obama — and their footballs?"

"Sure, but why?" Grossman wondered.

"I have an idea, probably far-fetched, but let's see."

"Far-fetched" was one of Abe's favorite words. It sounded
almost like Yiddish and reminded him of his maternal grandmother, who would use words like *farklempt, farbissen, far-
shvitzed, farblondzhet,* or *farshluggeneh.* Abe never understood
the precise meanings of these alien words, but they sounded so
quintessentially Yiddish that it brought back warm memories.
For the first time in many days, he smiled. Habash noted that he
paced excitedly while Grossman brought up photos of presidential footballs on the Internet, and this made Habash feel hopeful
that maybe this wasn't a losing effort. Maybe Emma would be
saved, and he'd have a chance at something with her.

The three men leaned over the computer screen, staring at
the footballs, comparing and contrasting them. "The one in the
video just before the explosion looks bigger than these, doesn't
it?" Abe said, peering closely at the images. He was speaking
quickly and a little loudly.

"Seems that way," Grossman agreed, "though it's hard to compare sizes in different photos."

Habash interjected. "But President Moore's football seems to
be in a significantly larger box. What does that mean?"

Abe again began moving in circles around the room. Habash
could tell that an idea was clicking into place for him. With a
furrowed brow, Abe spoke. "It's only a surmise, but hear me out.
President Moore was an evangelical Christian. He was also a
strong opponent of nuclear weapons. Remember, he wrote a college paper in favor of nuclear disarmament, and he campaigned
in favor of ending nuclear proliferation. He famously prayed

for the day when the United States could give up its nuclear arsenal."

"And it almost cost him the election," Habash observed. "I remember. I was in America at the time."

Abe continued to pace. "Yet he knew that as commander in chief he might someday have to press the nuclear button and kill millions of people."

"He promised he would if it were essential to the security of the world," Habash added, trying desperately to catch on to Abe's line of thought.

Now Abe stopped his pacing and spoke to Habash and Grossman as if they were two of his students. "What would an evangelical Christian who hated nuclear weapons want at his side when he had to press the button?"

Grossman jumped at the chance to answer Abe correctly. "The Bible, of course," Grossman said proudly. "That's why the football is bigger. It has room for a Bible next to the nuclear codes."

Abe was grinning now. He moved in a feverish circle. "Can we prove it? 'Cause if we can, we can prove that the bomb wasn't planted in the briefcase of the Palestinian secretary of state, but rather somewhere right next to the president's Bible," Abe said triumphantly, continuing. "We *can* prove it, and we will, no matter what it takes."

Habash, who was used to being in charge, asked, "So what do we do?"

In a gentle but firm voice, Abe began to hand out assignments. "Habash, first call Tom Ashe. Ask him to go through every one of his photographs and enlarge any of them that contain confetti fragments. I'm not only looking for letters. I'm looking for shapes as well. Grossman, I need you to get some of your people to comb the area and see if you can find any remaining fragments that the intelligence agencies didn't sweep up."

"I think they did a pretty thorough job of gathering up everything," Grossman said. "They were there for days with little vacuum devices and other high-tech gizmos. I don't think they could have missed much."

Abe shook his head. "All they had to do was miss one piece. If they did, we have to find it. Remember, it's paper, and Jerusalem can sometimes be a windy city. There must be a fragment somewhere waiting to be found."

"I'll give it my best shot, but I'm not hopeful."

Abe then turned to Habash and said, "After you speak with Tom, you have to go to all your sources. Dig really deep. Where do the Palestinian security forces think the bomb was planted? They must know about the Bible fragments — maybe they even have some in their possession. How did they explain them?" Then, turning back to Grossman, he said, "The Shin Bet has to know about the Bible fragments as well. Why did Avigdor lie? What are they hiding? Who are they protecting? What's going on here?"

Habash, who was getting caught up in Abe's excitement and by the fact that they finally had a concrete break in the case, asked, "What about the Americans? They have to know about the Bible fragments, too. I want to know why everyone is so eager to let Faisal Husseini take the rap."

Abe replied, "Look, there are two issues. The first and the only one I care about now is, did Faisal Husseini plant the bomb? It really is seeming now like he didn't. If we can prove that, we win the case. That's my job. That's my only job. Once Husseini is acquitted, everybody will be asking the next question: If Husseini didn't plant the bomb, who did? And if Husseini didn't plant the bomb, why is the Shin Bet so anxious for the court to conclude that he did? That's the big question for someone else to answer. Maybe you, Habash, once I'm safely home in Boston." Habash knew that what Abe meant to say was "Once *Emma* and I are safely home in Boston."

Abe continued, rallying his troops so that they could get to work. "But we can't get ahead of ourselves. We don't even get to the second question until we answer the first one definitively. And we're awfully close to doing that now. So let's not take our eye off the ball — the football — even for a minute."

They all shook their heads in apparent agreement as Abe began to leave the room.

"What's your task?" Habash asked Abe.

"I'll tell you when I complete it," Abe said mysteriously as he hurriedly left the room.

He went straight to his cousin's house, hoping to find Shimshon Regel at home.

It was ten o'clock at night when Abe knocked on the front door of his cousin's apartment. A lone bulb hanging above the doorway suddenly filled with light, and Shimshon appeared wearing a robe and sweatpants. He opened the door, speaking worriedly. "Any word about Emma?" He took Abe's coat and ushered him inside.

Abe shrugged. "Nothing, but I think she's safe for the time being." He stepped from the foyer into the main room and peered through the doorway that led to the kitchen. "Is Hanna here?"

Shimshon shook his head. "She's upstairs putting the children to bed. Since the kidnapping they're having a hard time falling asleep." His face was drawn and pale.

Abe stepped toward him and dropped his voice into a whisper. "I need your help."

The urgency with which his cousin spoke signaled to Shimshon that Abe was asking for a *special* kind of favor. "To get her back or to help that guilty bastard you're defending?" He made sure to speak in a low tone, so that his voice wouldn't carry up the stairs to his wife and children.

Abe sat on the arm of a stuffed chair. "I can't give you details, but it will help get Emma back."

Shimshon took a deep breath. Abe hadn't told his cousins of the deal he'd made with Emma's kidnappers, so they hadn't been able to understand why he had taken over as Faisal's lawyer. In fact, they'd argued about it, Shimshon demanding to know why Abe would waste any time in Israel when he should be searching for Emma. But now, in the dark of night, seeing the determined look on Abe's face, Shimshon had confidence that Abe knew what he was doing.

Shimshon was decisive. "I'm in. What can I do?"

"I need someone I can trust to do some dirty work."

Shimshon was intrigued and sat next to Abe. "How dirty?"

"Not very. A two on a scale of ten. But if you get caught, it could be serious."

Shimshon joked a bit. "It's always serious if you get caught. As long as I don't have to hurt anybody."

Abe waved his hands in reassurance, and leaned forward. "No way. Just a small black-bag job."

"Like in the old days."

Regel had worked as a contract agent for the Mossad when he got out of the army. His specialty was cat break-ins—stealth entries into homes, offices, and cars to photograph documents without anyone's knowing he was ever there. He'd always been quiet on his feet, and therefore he was so good at it that the Mossad offered him a full-time job. He turned it down to go to law school, but he never lost his touch. "What do you need?"

Before speaking, Abe glanced at the staircase to confirm that Hanna couldn't hear. "I believe that the bomb exploded in close proximity to an English-language Bible — an Old Testament for sure. Don't know whether it included a New Testament."

A look of comprehension appeared on Shimshon's face. "In other words, you don't know whether it was a Jewish or a Christian Bible."

"Right. And it could make a difference. But we do know it wasn't a Koran, and that's even more important."

"Is that all?" Shimshon asked this question as if answering it were the easiest thing in the world. "What else do you need?"

"Several things. First, we need evidence that fragments of the Bible were embedded in the bodies of the closest victims and that material from the Palestinian secretary of state's briefcase *wasn't*. Second, we need to know what other fragments might have hit the victims so we can confirm where the bomb was planted — in what kind of case or packaging."

"I get it. So if you find leather fragments, that points to a leather case. Plastic fragments to a plastic case, metal to a metal case, et cetera."

"Exactly."

Shimshon leaned back, the full scope of what Abe was asking him to do taking hold in his mind. "But where do you expect me to find out what fragments were in the bodies? That's pretty delicate stuff."

Abe exhaled. His cousin always did have a flair for the dramatic, especially when it came to spy games. He knew very well where to find out the information, but Abe obliged him by saying it aloud. "We need to see lab reports, autopsies, forensics — you know."

Shimshon rubbed his hands together. "Those are top secret. Sounds like at least a six on a scale of ten, but I'll get on it right away."

Abe stood and put his coat on. Before letting himself out of the apartment, he turned back to Shimshon and warned, "You can't use any of your old buddies." Shimshon nodded, and Abe continued, "You're on your own on this one. If anyone else finds out, they'll shut us down — or change the reports."

Shimshon clapped his cousin on the back. "I'm the lone wolf on this one, Abe. Blood keeps secrets."

XXXI

The Attempted Escape

A T FIRST EMMA HAD SLEPT well in captivity. The room was cool, thanks to a breeze that carried through the open window — she was four floors from the ground and assumed that her captors trusted she wouldn't risk crawling out of it. The mattress on the bed was lush and comfortable. And the smell of orange blossoms always soothed her as she drifted off to sleep.

But since Yassir's visit, Emma was constantly on edge. It didn't help that Mohammed and Nawal were jumpy when they were with her, and even the lazy guard was tense.

Now she slept with the beeper in her hand.

She was staring out the window at the moon, wondering what Abe was working on, when she heard it. A soft brushing against her closed door. She instantly jumped from her bed and searched the room for something, anything to use as a weapon. Of course there was nothing.

The sound continued, accompanied by whispers. Emma broke out in a sweat. She ran for the window, leaned out. It was a straight drop to the ground; the fall would surely kill her. There was no ledge, no nearby tree branch to grab hold of. Her throat tightened, and she looked anxiously, desperately over her shoulder at the door.

It opened, but only slightly. Emma tried to make herself disappear, pressing hard against the wall.

A small, slight figure slipped into the room, covered in shadow.

"Emma?" It was Nawal, dressed in black from head to toe.

Emma rushed forward, propelled by relief. But the expression on Nawal's face stopped her.

"Come quickly. Where is your black dress?"

"There," Emma mumbled, moving toward the clothing rack.

Nawal turned and shuffled through the clothes until she found what she was looking for. "Here. Quickly."

She reached for Emma's nightgown and pulled it up and off of her. Emma took the dress from her and stepped into it. "What's happening? Did the verdict come in?" Emma whispered.

Nawal clutched her hand and moved briskly to the door, peering out of it cautiously. "You won't last until the verdict comes in. So we're getting you out. Tonight." She grabbed a pair of shoes from the floor and thrust them at Emma. "Don't put them on yet. Not until we're out of the house."

"Rashid —" Emma said.

Nawal spun on her heel and clutched Emma's arm. "Rashid is not here. And they are planning to take you tonight. Now be quiet and let's go. Mohammed is waiting with a car."

Emma paused, remembering what Yassir had said: *Sometimes hostages try to escape.* The implication was clear — those who wanted to kill her might encourage her to "escape" so that they would have an excuse to shoot her. Was that what was happening now? Was she being set up?

Nawal, noting Emma's pause, hurried her along. "We only have seconds. There's no time to think. You have to trust me. You have to come now!"

Emma knew that her life could depend on the choice she was being forced to make. In an instant she decided. "I trust you, Nawal," she said as she followed the other woman, tiptoeing into the hallway. The ever-present gunman was sleeping in the corner. When they passed him, he snored loudly and shifted in his chair. Emma froze for a moment but hurried after Nawal, who was halfway down the hall.

When they rounded the corner, Nawal continued into an area of the house Emma wasn't familiar with. Behind a narrow door was a steep staircase. "Go!" Nawal commanded, whispering harshly into the dark. Emma began descending the steps, and Nawal followed, shutting the door behind her. Nawal kept her hand at the small of Emma's back, and Emma tripped over the bottom three steps before landing on her knees in the back entryway of the broad front room of the house, the room that led to the outdoor kitchen. Nawal unlocked one of the glass doors. "Come. We'll cross outside into the garage. Stay near the house."

Emma followed her out but was suddenly snatched from behind by her hair.

"What's this?" The sneer of the voice cut through the night, and Nawal lunged for Emma. Yassir pulled Emma into his body, so roughly she thought he must have ripped out a handful of her hair. The pain was searing.

For an instant, Emma thought she had been set up. This was the trap, and it was being sprung. But there was no time for thinking; action was needed.

Emma pulled her leg back and kicked her assailant in his groin and elbowed his stomach at the same time. Her women's self-defense class was serving her well, as it had nearly a decade earlier when she had used her martial arts to fight off an even larger man—a basketball player—who was trying to rape her. What also served her well was the element of surprise and Yassir's sexism. The last thing he expected was a physical attack from this demure Jewish girl. The excruciating pain in his groin caused him to let go of her hair, but he was seething with fury and offended machismo. Nawal attacked him with her fists, but Yassir lunged for Emma, knocking Nawal to the ground. Emma searched her pocket for Mohammed's beeper, but just as she found it, Yassir snatched the device out of her hand, threw it to the paving stones, and smashed it into pieces with his heavy boot. Emma began to cry. Nawal lay motionless in a heap.

Emma turned and ran right into Salma, who had a gun trained at her head. It was a setup—even if Nawal had not been a conscious part of it. The image of her grieving father flashed into Emma's mind.

XXXII

The Autopsy

SHIMSHON DECIDED that his easiest source of information would be the Palestinian Authority Security Service, which was notoriously sloppy and corrupt. He knew there would not have been a formal autopsy on Suri Chalaba, because cutting open a dead body is against Islamic law. But there would be a report on the condition of the body before it was buried. If he could see that report, he could find out what fragments, if any, had been embedded in the body of the prime minister of the Palestinian Authority.

Shimshon could bribe a member of the Palestinian Authority Security Service. They came fairly cheap. But he worried that it might get back to the Israeli security people, who, he knew from experience, were also bribing members of the security service. Abe had directed him to do it on his own, so the lone wolf had to devise a plan to break in to the place — or the computer — where the report might be kept.

These days you could break in to a computer without going anywhere near the actual machine. But the thought of hacking worried him. First, he'd have to hire somebody to do it; second, it was too easy to trace a hacker's source. So he planned an old-fashioned break-in.

Generally, his break-ins had been to homes, cars, businesses—easy targets, with little security. This one was different. The members of the Palestinian Authority Security Service were paranoid—and for good reason. The Israelis and the Americans—and who knew who else—were all over them. Every aspect of their work had been penetrated, from outside and inside. Information was money, and there was plenty of both to go around. So nobody trusted anybody, and everybody had someone else watching him. They weren't particularly good at it, but they were cautious. They were also ruthless, and anyone caught spying would be tortured and killed. No trial. No sentence. Just execution.

Shimshon decided on a bold daylight entry. He knew that the small building that housed the security service was near the al-Aqsa Mosque. Although it was formally closed on Fridays, a skeleton crew kept guard, taking turns going to the mosque for prayer. Shimshon also knew that on this Friday a particularly dynamic and popular imam would be preaching. He learned from his sources that on every fourth Friday a new group of guards would be rotated through and that the old guards might not know some of the new ones. This was that Friday. It was the optimal hour—the perfect storm of opportunity.

It was an especially hot and muggy day. The yellow residue of a khamsin lingered in the air. Shimshon simply walked through the front door at 11:30 A.M. just as the imam was beginning his sermon. Two guards sat glued to the television, watching the imam as he called for "death to the heathens." Everyone else was at the mosque. Shimshon mumbled a greeting in Arabic, which he both spoke passably and read, flashed a forged credential, and walked right into the records room. No one followed him. He knew he had only a few minutes before one of the guards might tire of the imam's repetitive rhetoric. Even charismatic firebrands grew boring after a while. He got to work immediately.

The records room was a mess, but he quickly located a drawer marked "American Colony." It was filled with papers, in Arabic, Hebrew, and English—as well as news clips and videos. He found one file with the name of the murdered prime minister of the Palestinian Authority. It contained six pages. Without pausing to read them, he took out his old Minox minicamera and photographed them.

As quickly as he had entered, he left, barely nodding to the television-watching guards. He had been in and out in less than five minutes. It was like the old days, but Shimshon suspected that the stakes were even higher.

XXXIII

The Photos

U NTIL THIS CASE Shimshon hadn't used his small darkroom much, and he'd thought about giving it to Mars and
Zara, who had begged him to turn it into a game room. As he
ran up the steps to his building, his old Minox in hand, he was
glad that he'd resisted their pleading.

When he opened the door, he saw Abe waiting for him at the
kitchen table, drinking a cup of coffee and reading through a
stack of legal pages.

Without a word Abe followed Shimshon into the darkroom.
"How long does it take to develop the film?"

"About ten minutes," Shimshon replied, shutting the door,
stripping off his coat, and rolling up his sleeves. "We have to be
careful not to expose it. I'm not going back there."

"Okay, okay." Abe consciously took a step back so that Shimshon had room to breathe. Abe didn't want to make him nervous. "Do it right," he said nervously.

Abe hated waiting. Lines were the bane of his existence. He was sure that his blood pressure actually rose when he had to wait in line. These ten minutes were a living hell, because he could only stand around and watch.

After a few minutes, images began to appear on the negatives, though it was impossible to tell what they were, since they were still sitting in tubs full of liquid. "They came out!" Abe shouted.

"Of course they did." Shimshon shot him a look. "What did you expect?"

"How soon before we can read them?" Abe reached his hand out, but Shimshon batted it away.

"*Savlanut,* Abe, *savlanut,*" Shimshon repeated. "Patience. A couple more minutes."

After a few more dips and dabs, Shimshon pulled the shots from their bath, opened the door, and brought the positives to the dining room. He laid them on the table. "Clean as can be," he said proudly.

Abe still couldn't make them out. "What are they?"

"There, precisely what you wanted." Shimshon pointed at one of the shots. "A report on the condition of the prime minister of the Palestinian Authority. No autopsy, but a description of the outside of his body. It's not pretty."

The text in the photo was in Arabic, a language that Abe didn't speak and definitely couldn't read. "What does it say?"

Shimshon read, "'The body of Prime Minister Chalaba was brought into the hospital by two paramedics. His head was severed from the torso, as was his right arm. There were flash burns all over his body. His clothing had been blown away, except for the middle of his left pant leg.'"

Shimshon paused and searched for the photo that contained the following page. "Is there more?" Abe demanded. "Anything about materials embedded in the body?"

Shimshon found the photo he was looking for and summarized what he was reading. "The body was prepared for burial by Imam Mohammed Zayid. All of the body parts were placed together in a cloth. Particles that had been embedded in the body by the explosion were removed and provided to the security service as evidence." Abe moved closer to Shimshon as soon as he said this. "These particles included what appear to be shards of metal, plastic, and pieces of paper with English writing." Shimshon and Abe exchanged excited glances. "There was also a piece of a round, plain, circular object with part of a number."

"Perfect!" Abe leaped from his chair and clapped his hands. "You got it."

"Got what?" Shimshon asked.

But without even explaining to his confused cousin how great his work had been, Abe gathered his papers and ran out the door. He was at the Pal-Watch offices before he had time to take a breath.

XXXIV

The Verdict

H ABASH HADN'T BEEN ABLE to get any information from his Palestinian contacts, but thanks to Shimshon's dirty work Abe didn't need it. Dennis Savage had told Rendi that the American football was made out of metal and that it had round plastic keys with code numbers. This was exactly what the Palestinian Authority Security Service said had been found impacted in the body of its prime minister. And thanks to Tom Ashe and a few of Danny's contacts in the Shin Bet, Abe was able to gather enough evidence that the paper fragments were from a Bible to prove that Faisal—and Dr. Avigdor—were lying about the location of the bomb.

Abe presented everything his team had found to the court in the form of a secret affidavit, with the photographs and other documentary evidence attached. The prosecution did not offer any countervailing affidavit, except for a one-paragraph statement from the head of the Shin Bet stating that Dr. Shai

Avigdor was on assignment out of the country and unavailable to submit to cross-examination. Abe's evidence wasn't conclusive, of course, because it was possible — as the prosecution had suggested — that Faisal had planted the bomb and then deliberately lied about where he had planted it, in order to improve his chances for an acquittal. Abe was confident, however, that Judge Shamgar would not believe this far-fetched theory and that he would reject Husseini's testimony. After all, how could Husseini have gotten access to the American nuclear trigger? That would leave the prosecutor's circumstantial case. Would Shamgar still convict Faisal based on the circumstantial evidence, even if he disregarded Husseini's self-incriminatory testimony?

Abe and Habash would learn the answer in just a few minutes, because they were gathered in the court awaiting Judge Shamgar's verdict, along with almost every major news organization from around the world, several prominent American and Israeli government officials, Rendi, Dennis Savage, and of course Faisal's mother. Rashid was nowhere to be seen.

The courtroom was tense as Justice Shamgar walked slowly to the bench. He looked directly at the defendant and said nothing for a very long moment. Faisal Husseini sat erect, eyes straight ahead. He refused to acknowledge Abe's presence. The judge took a few pages out of a file folder on his bench and began to read.

Abe peered over his shoulder and caught Rendi's eye. Her face was full of emotion. Emma was about to be sentenced, too, though of course Judge Shamgar didn't know that. By Rendi's side was Dennis Savage. His presence was notable; he was the handsomest man in the courtroom. He hadn't been to any of the trial, but he had shown up on this day for Abe and Rendi. Abe didn't even mind that one hand held on to Rendi's arm or the way she looked at Dennis with such affection; he knew his wife and knew that she needed the emotional support.

Judge Shamgar cleared his throat. "The State of Israel versus Faisal Husseini on charges of mass murder, conspiracy to murder, attempted murder (of those who survived their injuries), and mayhem. The state has presented two types of evidence, both of which I shall consider in turn. First is the corpus delicti. There is no dispute that many were killed and injured as the result of a powerful bomb, planted near the dignitaries on the stage outside the American Colony Hotel. I accept the state's forensic and medical evidence on corpus delicti. It has proved this element of the crime beyond a reasonable doubt.

"The state has also proved beyond a reasonable doubt the existence of a conspiracy. I am convinced that this crime could not have been carried out by one person acting alone. It required careful planning and execution by more than one person working together to achieve a common end by a common means. That is the definition of a conspiracy.

"I also agree with the state that all members of a conspiracy are equally and fully responsible for the criminal acts of all other members of the conspiracy. I agree as well that the government need not prove, or even know the names of, other members of the conspiracy. If it can prove that the defendant on trial here today, Faisal Husseini, played any role in the conspiracy, he would be guilty of the crimes charged. Although the government has alleged that he was the one who planted the bomb, that need not be proved. Even if he lied about having planted the bomb, I can and must find him guilty if the government has proved beyond a reasonable doubt that he played another role in the conspiracy, including taking the blame for something he did not himself do."

Abe was on his feet immediately. "That is not the law, Your Honor. A person who agrees to take the rap for another is not a co-conspirator in the actual crime. He may be an obstructor of justice or an accomplice *after* the fact, but not a co-conspirator."

The judge removed his reading glasses and sternly responded to Abe's challenge. "I am getting to that, Mr. Ringel. What you have said may be correct under American law, but under Israeli law a man who agrees to take responsibility for the crimes of others is a co-conspirator. This case is being tried under Israeli law, Mr. Ringel, not American law. Under Israeli law we do not charge defendants who lie with perjury or accessory-after-the-fact, but we can charge them with conspiracy under certain circumstances." Abe sat down, dejected, and the judge spoke to the courtroom. "I will now complete my judgment."

"Thank you, Your Honor," Abe said, with trepidation in his voice. Had the judge figured out a way to get around Husseini's false testimony — indeed even use it to convict him? At this point Abe wished he had confided in the judge the deal he had made to save Emma's life. If he had, Judge Shamgar would probably not have come up with a creative way to convict Husseini.

The judge resumed reading his judgment. "In order for a defendant to be convicted as a co-conspirator, he must have agreed with at least one person in the original conspiracy to take the blame. He is not part of the conspiracy if he decided on his own, or with others who were not part of the original conspiracy, to claim responsibility."

Abe let out a sigh of relief. But Husseini was still not off the hook. Maybe the judge would find that he had agreed with the conspirators to take the rap.

The judge continued. "Before Mr. Husseini testified, I found this a very close case. I thought it was likely either that he had planted the bomb or that he had agreed with those who had planted the bomb to take the blame. I was prepared to convict, because I believed, beyond a reasonable doubt, though not beyond all doubt, that he was part of the original conspiracy. Then he testified that he had planted the bomb in the leather briefcase of the Palestinian secretary of state. His lawyer has now proved, beyond all doubt, that this was a lie. The evidence proves that the bomb was not planted where the defendant swore he planted it. I am constrained by state secrecy not to disclose precisely where the bomb was planted, but I can say, having examined the new evidence provided in camera by the defense, that even the prosecution conceded it was not planted where the defendant swore he planted it. The fact that he had to lie in order to try to convince the court of his guilt raised a reasonable doubt in my mind about whether he had anything to do with the original conspiracy. If he did, he would probably know where the bomb was planted. It is more likely that after the bombing he conspired with people who had nothing to do with planting the bomb, in order falsely to claim responsibility for something that others did. He has not been charged with that crime. I must therefore, with great reluctance, find Faisal Husseini not guilty of the charges for which he has been charged." Then, turning to Faisal, Judge Shamgar announced in a firm voice, "You are free to leave, Mr. Husseini."

Pandemonium broke out in the courtroom, as spectators, including relatives of the victims, began shouting. Some tried to reach Husseini, who was quickly ushered out of the courthouse with his mother by security officers. Habash and Abe hugged, and Rendi ran to the front of the courtroom and threw herself into Abe's arms, leaving Dennis standing alone. If anyone thought it suspicious that the defense attorney's wife was so overcome with emotion, they didn't say anything.

XXXV

Emma

H ABASH RELUCTANTLY RETURNED to the Pal-Watch offices to celebrate with his staff, but only after Abe promised that he'd telephone as soon as he heard news about Emma. As he left them, Rendi gave him a long hug and a knowing look. Then she and Abe walked back to the King David Hotel, Abe holding his cell phone in his hand so that he'd hear and see as soon as a call came in.

But the phone never rang. Not once. Even after they made it the several blocks to the hotel, had ordered and eaten lunch, and watched an hour's worth of trial coverage on television.

Abe began to worry. For some reason he'd never doubted that the kidnappers would release her. Perhaps because Emma had sounded so confident that they would. Perhaps because he needed to believe it in order to motivate himself to do what he had to do to win the case. Abe had kept his word, even if he had to bend a few rules and employ some questionable tactics to secure Husseini's acquittal. Surely that wouldn't matter to Husseini's brother, who had observed most of Abe's performance from the back of the courtroom. He should be more than satisfied with the result Abe had achieved. But as he sat in his plush hotel suite, Abe couldn't help but remember that after all that had happened, Emma's kidnappers were a band of terrorists. They killed innocent people. Why should they be expected to keep their promises? His mind was a jumble of thoughts and confusion. Would he ever see Emma alive again? Why wasn't his phone ringing? The kidnappers knew that Husseini was acquitted. His brother had probably reached out to him by now, perhaps through their mother, who'd been taken out with Faisal after the acquittal. Maybe they were waiting to see whether he was safe. Maybe they wanted to see him in person, before they released her. Maybe...

Hours passed. Abe imagined the worst. He even began to have fantasies of revenge, in the event they reneged on the deal. Then, just before midnight, he heard a knock on the door. Was it the police coming to tell him the worst? Slowly he began to open the door, but even before he could see who was on the other side, he heard a soft voice.

"Daddy."

It was Emma. She stood in the doorway of Abe's suite, looking as if she were coming from a routine day at school or work. She wore a purple dress, tied at the back, and her hair hung beautifully around her face. The only sign that she'd been through any sort of ordeal was a bruise on her upper left forearm. It was in the shape of a human hand.

"Oh, my God, Emma." Abe moved toward his daughter. Rendi was just behind him. All three of them hugged and sobbed. After two minutes of this, Abe stepped back so that he could get a good look at her. "You look great. How do you feel?"

"Fine, Daddy." Emma smiled and held his hands. She looked as surprised as he felt. "I'm fine. I'm sorry I didn't call as soon as they let me go. They took away my cell phone. They dropped me off a few blocks away. They told me which room you were in and left me."

Abe and Emma hugged, a long hug, with more tears.

"Don't be upset, Daddy," she said when he finally stopped hugging her. "They treated me fine—mostly. Some of them were actually nice. And their place makes this room look like an unfurnished hut."

She deliberately withheld the information about the attempt by Yassir and Salma to kill her, and how Mohammed had suddenly appeared and insisted that it was Rashid's decision, not theirs, as to whether their prisoner should live or die. There was no reason Abe had to know how close she'd come to death.

Rendi and Abe shared a look. Emma smiled; she could read their minds. They were thinking about Stockholm syndrome— the phenomenon named after an incident in Sweden in which hostages began to identify with their kidnappers after a long time in captivity. Abe had been a consultant to the defense in the Patty Hearst case, in which many observers believed that the young heiress had been brainwashed into identifying with the Symbionese Liberation Army.

Emma sat on the chaise where Abe had spent many long hours hoping to hear news about his missing daughter. "I know what you're thinking, Daddy," she said glibly, looking for all the world as if she hadn't just been through such an ordeal. Except for the purple bruise that matched her dress. "Stockholm syndrome, right?"

Abe didn't answer. He and Rendi merely looked at her.

"No way," she went on. "I'm not about to join them or anything, but I don't hate them, at least not all of them. They kept their word, although some of them wanted to kill me even if you won the case. But the leaders made them keep their bargain. And by the way, Daddy, thank you for winning the case. You saved my life. They definitely would have killed me if you lost."

"I did what I had to do. The only important thing is that you're safe. Do you need a doctor or anything?"

Emma smiled broadly. "No. I'm fine. Let's have a drink to celebrate. But first I need to call Habash. He must be so worried."

XXXVI

Catch and Release

EMMA'S TIME IN CAPTIVITY had changed her. Not in physical ways, but emotionally. She felt stronger in her own con-
victions, more determined than ever to help change the political
situation in the Mideast, and resolute about going after what she
wanted.

When Habash picked up the Pal-Watch phone, Emma felt
this new resolution gather and intensify. Life was too short to be
circumspect. She was confident, too, because Rendi hinted that
Habash's concern over her had been more than that of a boss for
his employee.

"I want to see you right away," she said to him. "Take me to
the café with the strongest coffee in all of Israel."

"It's one o'clock in the morning, Emma. We don't have many
choices, but I know one that stays open until three. Meet me in
the café at the Ticho House."

Despite Abe's objections—he wanted her to pack her things

and board a plane to the States immediately—Emma left the King David Hotel an hour after she arrived. She walked to a Jewish café in a small museum that housed the art of a deceased Israeli artist named Anna Ticho. When she arrived, she found Habash at a table under a tree in the garden. She stopped in midstride when she saw him and couldn't repress a huge grin from spreading across her face. He stood awkwardly; he looked as if he wanted to approach her, but he stayed where he was. The garden was full of tables with couples out for a late-night coffee. Habash hadn't chosen only the place with the best coffee in Jerusalem but one of the most romantic date spots.

"Emma," he whispered when she reached the table. "Emma."

"I'm okay, Habash. Thanks to you and my father." She sat.

"It was all your father's doing. He was amazing."

Emma nodded. "Just a typical day in my father's life. Outsmarting the best lawyers a country has to offer, finding a smoking gun where nobody thinks to look, saving his daughter from certain death. It's all old hat to Abe." She tried to be as lighthearted as possible, because Habash's serious expression bordered on morose.

He didn't smile. He only stared at her.

So she soldiered on. "Order for me, Habash. Captivity did nothing to improve my Hebrew." Of the many things she admired about Habash, his ease in dealing with different cultures and his gift with languages were at the top of the list. "Tell them how much sugar to put in. And get me a munchie."

Habash appeared relieved to have a direct command to follow. He ordered a Turkish coffee—that's what the Israelis called it, at least for now—and a Lebanese pistachio and honey baklava.

The two of them sat there. There was no breeze, but the night temperature was cool. Habash looked around the garden, content to be outside. "Emma, I am so sorry."

"Don't. It's not your fault."

"It is. Adam was my contact."

Emma reached for his hand, but he pulled it away. "Habash, let's not spend our time together talking about this. I'm okay. I survived. And believe me when I tell you that Rashid would've found a way to get to me, Adam or no Adam. I've never been surer of anything, ever."

"I—"

"Habash, what do you do for fun?" she asked, breaking off a piece of the baklava and eating it with her fingers.

Habash looked stumped by the question and the abrupt change of topic. "Not much time for fun in this part of the world," he finally said, stumbling over the words.

"Think. There has to be *something*." She aimed for that light-hearted tone again. She realized that if Abe and Habash were going to stop regarding her as a wounded animal, she had to act as if nothing had happened to her.

After a moment he said, "Sometimes I go fishing in the north for a few days."

"I bet you throw them back."

"Mostly I don't catch anything, but you're right, I do throw back what I catch."

Emma saw her opening. "Catch and release, we call it in America. It's become a metaphor for certain types of relation-ships."

"You mean when men make a conquest and then release their prey after they finish with them?" Habash leaned back in his chair and peered at Emma with a cool, assessing gaze.

She knew exactly what he was trying to do. So she decided to tease him a bit, to make it a social argument. "You make it sound so exploitative and sexist. You know, some women do the same thing."

"It's so American." Finally a faint hint of humor out of him! For the first time since she arrived, he didn't look so serious.

Emma gestured around the garden, which was full of couples leaning close to each other. "We learned it from the Israelis, who are famous for their sexual openness."

"Infamous among my people. That's one of the reasons Islamic fundamentalism is growing so quickly. The imams preach that anything but strict adherence to Islam will lead to debauchery"—he pointed to a gay couple kissing over their coffee—"and prostitution and the end of the family."

"Sounds like the Christian right in America."

"It's more than that, Emma. Our traditions are so different. Your people are obsessed with the rule of law. My people are obsessed with the rule of God."

Emma realized that Habash was one sentence away from turning their reunion into a seminar on the roots of Muslim culture. "What about you, Habash? What kind of woman are you looking for? An Israeli type who's open about romance and sex or a burka babe?"

Now he laughed out loud. Quite an improvement! She liked the way he looked when he laughed, less as if the world were about to end.

"Certainly not a burka babe, though there are some babes underneath their burkas," he joked. "But not Lady Gaga either. Right now I have no time for a serious relationship." His mouth drew into a grim line, and his serious expression returned.

"So why don't you try some catch and release? There must be plenty of women who would nibble at your hook," Emma teased.

"I wouldn't be fun to date." He began to look around the café, and Emma understood that he was growing uncomfortable with the topic. She wondered if he really didn't know how attractive he was.

"That's ridiculous, Habash. You'd be a great date. A lot of women like serious types. You're dark and handsome," she said, more shyly than she expected to.

At the outright compliment, Habash's serious expression deepened. But then he smiled. "You left out the tall."

"Tall is overrated."

He appeared uncomfortable again suddenly, and his smile disappeared once more. "I don't like the gamesmanship inherent in dating. My fantasy is becoming close friends with a woman and letting it progress toward romance if both people feel something."

"What about work relationships?" Emma pressed. "Can they evolve into romance?"

"Hierarchy is not conducive to romance."

Emma thought for a moment before saying what she was thinking, but then she decided to let it out. "What if they were friends first, and then one worked for the other?"

"Is that a hypothetical?" Habash asked, smiling.

"Of course it is," Emma said coyly, placing her hand gently over Habash's. This time he didn't pull away. "What real person could I possibly be talking about?"

"Catch and release may be right for fishing, but I don't believe in it for friends," Habash said, withdrawing his hand from beneath hers. "Besides, you've been through an ordeal."

"No. We're not talking about that, remember? You said you didn't like gamesmanship? Then why don't we just cut to the chase and talk about us? I like you more than as my friend and boss."

This kind of directness took him by surprise. His mouth

formed an O, and he quickly looked around to see if anybody had heard. He was so unlike any American she had ever dated.

"I like you, too, but there are complications." Again shifting to serious mode.

"You have a girlfriend?" she asked evenly.

He pursed his lips, because she knew the answer to the question, and avoided eye contact as he answered. "No."

"A wife?"

Now he cocked his head and tried to converse with the table. "No. No."

"A boyfriend?"

That got him to look up at her. "That isn't even funny in this part of the world."

"Well, then? It's because I work for you?"

"Do you still work for me?"

"Of course. We have to find who bombed the American Colony. I'm not leaving Israel until we solve this crime, no matter what my father says. So what is it, then, if not another person or the fact that I work for you?"

He looked more uncomfortable than she'd ever seen him, and this was a man who had regular contact with terrorists. He took a deep breath and didn't raise his eyes from his lap. "There are two complications. You work for me. Also, you're American." Habash paused and then, looking away, added, "And Jewish."

This was the last thing that she expected to hear, and it made her angry. "Oh, my God! So, we're both lawyers, Yalies, human-rights advocates — human beings. It's so . . . so —"

"Jurassic?" he cut her off.

"Yes." She unfolded her arms and placed her palm flat on the table for emphasis. "It's Jurassic. It's yesterday. It's *racist*."

Some people at neighboring tables looked over at them. Emma's voice was carrying, but to Habash's credit he didn't try to silence her. Instead he replied calmly, thoughtfully. "Well, maybe I live in a world where differences still matter. Do you want your children to be Jewish?"

Emma shook her head and crossed her arms again. "Whoa, who's talking about children here? I thought we were discussing a little romance."

Habash looked disconcerted. "Catch and release?" he asked quietly.

She softened her tone. "No, nobody is catching anybody. We're just trying to have a bit of mutual fun. Life is too short not to enjoy every moment."

They didn't speak for a long time. Around them the café patrons returned to their coffees and food. Habash looked steadily at her and then said, "I'm not so good at fun. How do we start?"

"How about this?" Emma said, leaning over the table and kissing Habash gently on the lips.

He moved back ever so slightly. Realizing what he was doing, he moved forward a bit awkwardly and placed his hand over hers. She knew that public displays of affection were asking quite a bit of him, but he had made her too angry talking about her being Jewish for her to care much.

When the kiss ended, she sat back down in her seat. "We'll start slowly. See where it goes."

"If this is slowly, I would hate to think what fast is," Habash said self-consciously.

Emma laughed. She was happy that he was still sitting across from her, holding her hand.

XXXVII

The Blackboard

ABE HAD EVERY INTENTION of packing Emma up and taking her home to Boston the very next day. But as he feared and as Rendi cautioned she would, Emma refused to leave until the job was done, and in her mind the job was solving the entire mystery. She wasn't content with Faisal's acquittal. Now more than ever, she was determined to find out who the guilty party was.

More than that, she was convinced that only Abe could help her and Habash get to the bottom of the case. What Abe had done to save her just increased her admiration for his professional skills and reduced her ambivalence about his role in "her" big case. Abe begged her to drop it, but she was resolute. So the next day, Rendi and Abe met Emma and Habash at Pal-Watch. Rendi understood that there was more to the relationship between Emma and Habash than work, and this was all but confirmed when she and Abe walked into Habash's office and caught the pair standing a tad too close. Rendi uttered a surprised sound, and Abe stood in the doorway looking a bit unsupportive.

Habash guiltily sprang away from Emma and walked around to the other side of his desk.

"Glad to have her back?" Rendi asked knowingly.

"Of course. We need her if we're going to solve this case," Habash replied sheepishly, staring at the floor.

"Don't give him a hard time, Rendi," Emma joked, embracing her stepmother.

Any disapproval Abe felt evaporated when Emma kissed his cheek. He hugged her tightly, not wanting to let her go. Emma disentangled herself from his grip and trotted across to an overstuffed chair opposite Habash's desk. She flopped into it and stretched her legs. "Are you ready to get to work?" she asked. "The sooner we solve this thing, the sooner you can get me home, Daddy."

Abe smiled. "That's all the incentive I need."

Talking about work put Habash at ease. "I'm happy to take your help. You proved Faisal's innocence, so as far as I'm concerned you can do anything. Have you tried walking on water?"

"I'm Jewish. We don't do that. We learn to swim," Abe replied with a grin.

But his grin vanished almost as quickly as it appeared. Focusing on the task at hand, Abe took off his suit jacket, placed it over the back of a chair, and walked to the large gray blackboard that covered the near wall of Habash's office. "Let's start with what we now know that we didn't know before the trial," Abe suggested. He didn't want to waste time with further pleasantries. His primary goal was to get Emma home as soon as possible, and he knew he could achieve it only when the crime was solved. He also knew that the Israeli and American authorities were hiding something, though he had no idea why. His team seemed to be the only group interested in uncovering the truth — wherever it pointed. All others involved had an agenda and were looking to pin it on some group whose conviction would serve their interests.

"Okay," Emma began. "We know the bomb was planted in the nuclear football."

Abe wrote this information on the blackboard under the heading "Knowns."

"That eliminates the group that took me," Emma insisted. "A bunch of Marxist amateurs couldn't tamper with the case holding American nuclear codes. Besides, those guys don't believe in wholesale killing."

"Only retail," Abe said, shaking his head.

Emma shifted uncomfortably in her seat.

"Okay, let's put Rashid Husseini's group under the column of 'Didn't Do It,'" Habash said as he stood and took the chalk from Abe. "Who else?"

Nobody said anything at first, and then Emma spoke. "The Israeli government."

"Not so fast," Rendi interrupted. Habash's hand stilled, his piece of chalk dangling in midair. "We know the Shin Bet lied about where the bomb was planted," Rendi continued. "Why? Maybe to cover up something done by Israelis. I wouldn't put them on the board — at least not yet."

Abe nodded. "I agree that they're hiding something, though I doubt it was their own direct involvement."

Turning to Habash, Rendi asked, "Which Israelis would have a motive to kill their own prime minister, along with dozens of other Israelis who were in the crowd?"

"TNT," Emma interjected, not giving Habash a chance to answer.

Habash groaned, and Abe said, "No."

"Hear me out," Emma continued bravely. "That picture Mohammed gave me *did* incriminate TNT."

But Abe quickly dismissed this. "You're talking about the photo with the Star of David in the piles of rubble?"

Emma was dumbstruck. She looked at Abe with her mouth wide open. "He said you'd see it!"

"Who did?" Abe asked.

"Mohammed," she replied.

The room filled with tension, as Abe and Habash were angered at Emma's casual use of her abductor's name. Rendi placed a hand on Abe's arm, and so when he spoke, his voice sounded calm. "Emma, that photo proves nothing. TNT didn't do this. They'd never consciously kill the American president or the Israeli prime minister. Their goal is the elimination of a Palestinian state. Killing the heads of state of both their own country and their greatest ally's runs counter to their purposes. Not to mention that they'd never get access to the football."

"But what about the Star of David? It can't be a coincidence," Emma insisted.

"I hate to disappoint you and your buddy Mohammed," Abe replied, sarcasm coloring his tone, "but the picture was Photoshopped. I had a local expert check it out. It's a fake. A good fake, but a fake nonetheless."

Emma quieted. She hated being proved wrong, especially by her father. As Habash wrote the name "TNT" in the "Didn't Do It" column, she even sulked a little.

"The question is, who benefits from the death of all these leaders?" Rendi mused.

"Iran," Habash said matter-of-factly. "They have motive, but they could never get to the football."

"Let's keep to the plan. Listing those who *could* get to the football," Abe countered.

A silence descended upon the four of them. There was one logical suspect that nobody had focused on. Emma finally said what they were all thinking. "It could be an American. An American with high security clearance."

Habash didn't write this down. "Not necessarily. Though I agree with the high-security-clearance part. Any of the agencies that swept the room at the American Colony prior to the meeting might have been able to get to the football, as long as the agent in possession of it was willing to help."

"What if the Secret Service agent holding the football was a suicide terrorist?" Emma wondered. "What if he was al-Qaeda, or an Iranian agent, or just some kind of nut?"

"Unlikely. They screen those guys pretty carefully," Rendi noted.

"Who exactly *has* access to the football?" Abe asked Rendi. "Are there cryptographers who change the codes? Technical people who test the buttons?"

Rendi stood up and reached for her cell phone. "We should put Dennis on the payroll," she said jokingly. "I'll ask him. He'll know."

Two hours later the foursome split up. Rendi left to meet Savage for drinks, and despite threatening to join their "date" to make sure all was innocent, Abe went home to the King David Hotel to place a few phone calls of his own. He had to make arrangements for a longer stay in Israel, and now that he had a small idea of the size of their undertaking — proving who bombed the American Colony Hotel could take weeks, if not months — he needed people to cover for him in the States.

So Emma coerced Habash into walking her to Shimshon's apartment. It didn't take much effort, really. Habash was very happy that his feelings for Emma were now in the open. After their coffee date, all he could think about was when he could take her out again. So after one well-aimed jest about how she shouldn't walk by herself in the dangerous streets of Jerusalem, Habash grabbed her hand and escorted her.

When they got to the apartment, Emma asked, "Do you want to come in?"

Habash kissed her forehead. "Not now. You need to rest, and I should get back to the office."

Emma poked him in the ribs. "Haven't you learned anything from this ordeal? You can't work *all* the time!"

Habash's face grew serious. "Emma, I don't think Shimshon would like this very much."

Her puzzlement showed on her face. "What? Why not?"

Habash began to explain. "I was concerned about the differences between us, our religious differences, but I am not the only one in this country who feels that way. Shimshon does not like it when Jews date Arabs. I can tell."

At that moment the front door swung open. Habash immediately withdrew his arms from around Emma, and Shimshon stepped between them. Placing a protective arm around her shoulders, Shimshon guided Emma into the apartment.

Emma sputtered in surprise. "Habash! I'll see you tomorrow," she called out as Shimshon shut the door — politely but firmly — in Habash's face.

XXXVIII

Dennis Savage

S AVAGE AGREED TO TALK with Rendi about football protocol
on the condition that they meet for drinks. Rendi was happy
to oblige him; they hadn't had a chance to spend time together
as two old comrades since her arrival in Israel. But with Faisal's
acquittal and Emma's return, Rendi felt as if an iron yoke had
been removed from her shoulders. And she enjoyed this sort of
work. Investigations always stimulated her; she felt important
and alive and invincible.

It was midafternoon when she made her way to the coffee bar,
which was a cross between a fancy English tearoom and an Arab
café. It was nearly empty, as Rendi hoped it would be. She spot-
ted Savage sitting alone at a corner table, sipping Turkish coffee.
He was impossible to miss, with his blond hair and broad build.
He looked like a former college football player somewhat beyond
his playing years.

Rendi smiled as she saw him, approached his table, and kissed her good friend's cheek before sitting.

"You look beautiful today," Savage greeted her, with a teasing grin on his face.

"Cut the crap," Rendi scolded mockingly as she sat in the chair Dennis held out for her. "They teach you at spy school to flatter your contacts. I'm not a contact. I'm an old friend — and a peer."

Dennis's smile widened. His teeth were perfectly straight and gleaming white. "I know that, but you do look great. Especially considering everything you've been through." He squeezed her hand affectionately. "How is Emma doing? She must have gone through hell. I'll be honest with you. That morning at Pal-Watch, when I realized what happened, I wrote her off as a goner." A troubled look passed over his face.

"We didn't," Rendi said breezily. "I knew she was more valuable alive than dead."

Dennis shrugged and stretched his long legs in front of him. His pose was one of casual strength. "By any rational calculation, sure. But these bastards don't think rationally. They kill for fun."

"As distinguished from us good guys, who kill only for truth and justice. Speaking of the good guys, what's been the reaction to Faisal's acquittal?"

Intensity sparkled in Dennis's eyes. "Pandemonium. I think the American agencies were hoping Faisal would be found guilty so that this whole episode would go away. But now they're being forced to investigate and are worried about what they're going to find."

"You mean, worried that if a foreign government is behind the attack, there'll be serious, global consequences?"

"Exactly. They're worried about war. You know how certain

elements in the CIA are. They're already agitated that this case has gone unsolved for so long, and now that there's no solid suspect... well, public sentiment can be poked and prodded until the Americans are ready to duke it out with anyone. The Israelis wanted the fall guy to be found guilty because of his group's connection to Iran. Everybody has a favorite 'he done it.'"

Rendi remained thoughtful for a moment. "It sounds ridiculous to say, but I hope we discover that it was the work of a small fringe group."

Dennis nodded and retained his casual posture. "So what would you like to know now?" he teased.

Rendi opened a menu, though she didn't look at it for even a moment. "Now that the trial is over, Abe and Emma and I are asking the same question everyone else is: Whodunit?"

Dennis feigned shock. "Ah. You don't expect me to share all of my intel with you, do you?" he asked.

Rendi folded the menu and laid it over her place setting. "I just need some general information that isn't part of the current investigation, but rather from your past role as part of the presidential detail." Her tone was lighthearted. Truth be told, she was enjoying the banter with Dennis. She didn't always miss her spy days—there were many dangerous situations that she'd been lucky to live through, and at least one escape, thanks to Dennis. Going head-to-head with him always stimulated her intellect. He was one of her few contacts who would share information, though you might have to engage in a little gamesmanship to get it. After some back-and-forth, he'd tell her what she wanted to know; they had such a history together that Dennis trusted her to keep secrets, even from those closest to her.

Another truth Rendi couldn't deny was that she was beginning to find the entire investigation, in a word, fun. Especially since Emma's life was no longer at stake. She felt a twinge of guilt over enjoying the investigation of so tragic an event that had taken so many lives.

"I was the *head* of the detail," Savage proudly reminded Rendi. "I can only give you generalities. Nothing specific to this investigation."

"Right." Rendi batted her eyelashes at him, and he laughed. Rendi had always easily flirted with men like Dennis, men who were as cunning and lethal as they were smart and patriotic. "Who has access to the football?"

Dennis took her question in stride. He answered as if it were the most natural thing in the world for someone to inquire about the location of the American nuclear codes. "The president, of course."

Rendi nodded. "Who else? Are there technicians? Cryptographers? Anyone else?"

Dennis sat back up in his chair, crossing his long legs and quickly surveying the room while he drank. He was making sure nobody was listening to them. "Why are you interested in the football?" he asked casually. "It wasn't a nuclear explosion. The football wasn't involved."

"I can't tell you, but I need to know who had access to it."

"Silence begets silence," Savage said, smiling as he made the gesture for zipping his lips.

"All right, you win. If I tell you why we're interested in the football, will you stretch the definition of 'generalities' a bit?"

"Deal. Your turn."

Rendi leaned in. "We think the bomb may have been planted there."

There had been intensity in Dennis's expression, but as soon as Rendi spoke, it disappeared. He smiled broadly. "No way." When Rendi didn't laugh along with him, he regained his serious mien. "Rendi, it's not big enough to hold such a powerful bomb." As he said this, he folded his hands together and placed them in his lap.

"Would you like some more classified info?" she asked playfully, though seriously.

"Yes, please." He leaned forward, anxious to hear what she had to tell him.

"The explosion was caused by a special type of plastique that gets more bang for the buck than anything previously used. And surely you would know that President Moore's football was somewhat bigger than previous ones."

Dennis was deep in thought for a moment. "Do you know where the plastique came from? Was it American?"

Rendi shrugged. "We don't know. Anybody could have developed it: the Iranians, the Russians, the Chinese, the Pakistanis—any of them. It's not rocket science. Well, actually it is. It uses material developed in rocket and space engineering. The Israelis think it may have come from Iran."

"The Israelis would think that—or at least want us to think that. But we need more than thinking. We need proof."

"Do you have any?"

"Not yet, but you think the bomb was in the football because the football was big enough to hold it?"

"That's not all. There's the forensics," Rendi answered vaguely.

"We've seen the forensics, too," Savage said thoughtfully. "No one I work with thinks it was in the football."

"Maybe we're just better than you," she teased.

"Maybe." He made a gesture implying he was tipping his cap to her.

"Okay, I showed you mine. Now show me yours."

"Okay." Dennis shook his head slightly, as if to clear his

thoughts from the placement of the bomb. "The cryptographers never get near the football. Everything they do is remote."

"What about the guy who carries it around?"

"Poor Glenn." Dennis's voice became laced with sadness as he spoke about his fallen comrade. "Glenn Young. Mormon guy. Carried it for years before being blown to bits along with everyone else. Straight and loyal as they come. A real patriot."

Rendi hadn't expected to hear anything less. As she'd told Abe, the Secret Service's screening process was intense. It was unlikely that whoever held the football would have tampered with it. "Who else in addition to Young had access?"

"Roger Blakely is the name of Glenn's shadow. The guy who did the other shift. The 'quarterback'—that's what we call the guy who holds the football—works in two shifts, not the usual three," Dennis explained. "Twelve hours each."

"Where was this Roger Blakely when the bomb went off?"

"At the movies." Dennis shook his head, placing his clasped hands in his lap. "He's back in the States, with posttraumatic stress. He's not your man either. He's a born-again evangelical Christian and used to pray with the president. He's devastated."

Rendi leaned back in her chair and took a deep breath. "You're not helping."

Dennis chuckled. "Yes I am. It's the truth that isn't helping. A bomb in the football is a long shot. Too long for me. Keep investigating. You're not there yet."

XXXIX

The "Talk" and the "Story"

EMMA FOLLOWED SHIMSHON into the Regels' handsomely
furnished living room. Mars and Zara played video games
while Hanna cheered them on.

"What was that out there?" Emma demanded.

Shimshon sat next to Hanna and feigned innocence. "It's late.
I thought you should come inside."

Emma turned to Shimshon and said bluntly, "You were rude
to Habash."

Shimshon exhaled wearily. "Zara, Mars, go upstairs."

After two minutes of protests, the children left the room with
Hanna. Shimshon sat forward and folded his hands. "Emma, I
am looking out for you. Habash is a fine person, but he is different from you — different background, different culture."

"You mean he's an Arab," Emma said pointedly. In her mind she
noted that Shimshon had not mentioned religion as a difference.

"Yes," Shimshon insisted, "because he's Arab and this is Israel, where Arabs and Jews are in constant conflict."

Emma had sensed that Shimshon seemed uncomfortable with Habash, and she surmised the reason, but she was shocked at his directness. She couldn't believe that she was hearing such open prejudice from a man like Shimshon — educated, kindly, and loving. "Shimshon!"

"Just listen. I know you think it isn't a problem, but it is. It is not easy for people of different backgrounds to marry."

Emma's frustration got the best of her. "Why does everyone mention marriage? We're just dating."

Shimshon's face went white. "That is not a good idea. Especially in the Middle East."

Emma stood angrily. "I appreciate your concern, but I'm an adult and I can date whomever I choose."

"Yes, you can, and no one could stop you. But there's a reason that interfaith marriage and dating are so much more common in your country than in mine. It's not about religion alone. We're not particularly religious people on the whole. We are at war, and there are issues of loyalty and trust."

Emma thought for a moment, and then she blurted out, "You think Habash set me up, because both he and Adam — Mohammed — are Arab."

"I must admit the thought crossed my mind when I first heard what happened, but I became convinced I was wrong when I saw how Habash reacted to your kidnapping. It's clear that he really cares about you."

"Then why are you so opposed to us dating?"

"Just sit," he said gently. "Just sit and hear me out."

What she wanted to do was to storm out of the house, but she wasn't prone to such theatrics. Emma reminded herself that

Shimshon was a good person who cared deeply about her, if maybe a little out of touch with the times. "Okay. I'll listen."

Shimshon smiled appreciatively. "Let me tell you what happened to our ancestor Avi when he fell in love with a woman from a different culture — a Sephardic woman named Rachel Mizrachi."

"I'm not in love with anyone. We're just dating," Emma reminded Shimshon.

"That's how it started with Avi, too — he was just taking Hebrew lessons from Rachel."

"Then what happened?"

"As it turned out, Rachel was beautiful, smart, and very much engaged to another Sephardic Jew named Baruch."

"Habash isn't engaged to anyone," Emma insisted.

"That was only part of the problem, as you'll see."

"Okay, so what happened?"

Shimshon returned to storytelling mode as he recounted the romantic history of his ancestor Avi Regel. He told Emma how Avi had fallen (again on one leg) for his Hebrew teacher Rachel and how Akiba had warned his friend about the dangers of falling for a Sephardic woman, especially one who was spoken for.

"These are a different kind of people than you're used to. They'll sooner cut your balls off you than argue with you if they think you're messing with their traditions. And one of their traditions is arranged marriages to other Sephardim. You're out of bounds — a goy as far as they're concerned."

But Avi didn't listen to Akiba. Each week he made the trek to Jaffa for his lessons, and each week he fell more deeply in love with Rachel. To his mind the only obstacle was her fiancé, though Akiba cautioned that her family would never accept Avi. Avi didn't understand or believe this.

It soon became clear to both Avi and Akiba that Rachel was keenly interested in her new pupil, more than just as a teacher. One day Avi suggested that they go to a restaurant for their next lesson. "You can teach me how to order in Hebrew," he said with a wink.

"An engaged girl does not have lunch alone with a male student."

But Avi won the argument by promising to bring Akiba. Rachel knew what a wicked girl she was being by letting him win the argument. She wanted to go to lunch with him.

The following day Avi, accompanied by his chaperone, met Rachel at a Jewish-owned fish restaurant on the Jaffa waterfront, appropriately named Jonah's.

As soon as the waiter put down the plates, Avi started in. "This is a very nice restaurant. Does your fiancé bring you here?"

Rachel behaved as she always did. She pretended to be annoyed by his questions. "He doesn't like restaurants and especially fish restaurants. He's a couscous kind of guy. He loves his mother's cooking. I prefer lighter food. But she hates when I leave anything over, so I have to hide it," Rachel said, laughing.

"Where do you hide it?"

"In my purse — my very smelly purse." She grinned.

Avi met her gaze, and her face grew warm. "What does your fiancé think of that?" he asked.

"I hide it from him, too."

"Not a very good basis for a relationship," Akiba interjected.

"Secrets are the basis of every good relationship," Rachel mused, repeating something her mother and aunt said to each other often over tea.

"No, no, I don't agree," Avi insisted. "Secrets are poison. They create distrust. No more secrets. When I have a relationship, there won't be any secrets."

"Big talker, you," Rachel said, laughing. "Have you ever had a relationship?" She had been eager to learn the answer to this question.

"Not that kind," Avi said quickly. "But I had a wonderful relationship with Naftuli, my younger brother. We had no secrets. I miss him so much."

"That's different. Brothers are different from fiancés. And so are friends," she said, looking at Akiba. "If you had a girlfriend, you'd understand."

"But I want my wife to be my best friend, my sister, my confidant—and my lover," Avi said.

And then something in Rachel's heart made her ask a very inappropriate question. "Do you have any secrets from me?"

Akiba's fork clattered to the table. "Time to use the bathroom," he said, abruptly getting up and bolting away from them.

Avi's eyes grew serious. He moved forward in his chair. "Why would I? You're just my teacher. No, I don't."

"I don't believe you," Rachel said, looking into his eyes.

Avi looked away.

"See, you do. I knew it. You're a hypocrite, Avi."

"'Hypocrisy is the homage vice pays to virtue.'"

Something in Rachel snapped. Suddenly she had to hear him say what she suspected was true. That when he spoke of marrying a girl who would share his life, he was thinking of her. "You're admitting it. What's your secret? Are you afraid to tell me?"

"Yes, I am," he admitted. "If I told you, then you would stop being my teacher."

"You're a coward on top of being a hypocrite. Not a great combination," Rachel said with a smile. "But here's what I propose. I promise that if you tell me your secret, I won't stop being your teacher. But if you don't, or if I think you're lying, I won't be your teacher."

Avi sat glumly. Rachel felt as if she had just run a great distance. She could barely breathe. Avi looked over her shoulder, clearly hoping that Akiba was on his way back to the table. She could see him struggling with a decision. It was over, he thought. Nothing would ever be the same again, whatever answer he gave. If he revealed his secret, Rachel would be dishonored. If he lied, she would see through him. If he refused to answer, she would stop being his teacher. It was a trap. There was no escape. Avi wanted more than anything else to preserve what he had with Rachel. Her presence, her closeness, the banter, the flirtatiousness. He didn't want less. He couldn't bear having nothing. He couldn't have more. He knew that. She knew that.

Suddenly Avi realized there was only one way. He had to take her at her word. She had promised. If he told her the truth, she would remain his teacher. Quickly he made a decision—*al regel achat*—on one foot. Again. It was as important as his earlier decision.

"I love you. I can't live without you. I want to marry you. That's my secret. Now it's out. I won't hold you to your promise. You can stop being my teacher. But please don't."

Rachel heard a muffled sound—a controlled gasp—escape her lips. Then she looked at the floor. She had goaded this out of him, and now that he'd spoken the words, she hardly knew how to respond. Her own words came out in a stammer. "I...I have a secret too, Avi." She paused and looked directly into Avi's eyes. "I love you. You are the most interesting and decent man I have ever met. I want to marry you. More than anything in the world."

Avi reached to kiss her hands, but she pulled them away before they touched. All the joy of the previous moment turned instantly to grief. "But I can't," she said, hesitating for a moment. "I just can't. I would dishonor my family."

Avi's face made her feel ashamed of what she'd done. She had forced him to admit his feelings, when no good would come of it. "You can't marry a man you don't love, just because your parents want you to," he said, calmly but with great feeling. "You'll be ruining your life."

"There's more to marriage than love. Baruch is a good man."

It was the first time Rachel had pronounced her fiancé's name. Up until now it was always "my fiancé." Avi and Rachel both noticed the change. "You don't love Baruch," Avi insisted, picking up on her use of his name. "You can't let your parents do that to you. This is a new country. We need new ways. New rules. We have to break the old rules."

Now she began to panic. What if she were to do this? To tell her parents that she wanted to marry Avi. The weight of her obligations to them crushed her desires. "I can't. I just can't," she said with a tear forming in her eye.

"Then who's the hypocrite? Who's the coward?"

Rachel looked into his face, an adventurer's face, and knew the truth. "I am," she said, openly weeping.

It was at this moment that Akiba returned. He took one look at their faces and ungracefully tried to reverse back to the bathroom.

"No, stay," Rachel said to him. He appeared uncomfortable to have been caught coming back to the table. "Today is not a day for secrets," Rachel said.

Slowly, almost clinically, Rachel told Akiba what had happened. "And now I will tell my parents, and then Baruch. Enough. I don't know how they will respond. If they insist I marry Baruch, and Baruch will still have me, I must marry him. My family promised, on their honor. Baruch could have had many others. If I reject him, he will have difficulties. I must keep my family promise and honor."

"But why would Baruch want to marry you if you love Avi?" Akiba asked, scratching his head.

Rachel looked sadly at her two friends. They didn't understand the customs of their new country, and she hated having to teach them in such a heartbreaking way. "Because his father promised my father. And there's the dowry."

"It's business," Avi said contemptuously. "It's about money, damn it."

"Not for me."

Avi didn't hear these words. "I don't want your damn money. I want you. I want to have children with you. Poor children. Children who have to work with their hands. Not heirs to some merchant's fortune."

"Calm down," Akiba said. "I told you they wouldn't approve."

"It's not just about money — or business either," Rachel continued. "It's about tradition and honor and family and a promise. You don't understand."

"Don't patronize me, Rachel. I understand. I just don't agree. And neither do you."

"Even if I disagree, I have a responsibility."

"To whom? To yourself. To your future. To your children. Even to me, if you love me."

"I do love you."

"Maybe Chaim can help us," Avi said, referring to Rachel's uncle whom he had met on the boat and who had arranged for the Hebrew lessons.

"No," Rachel responded. "He's a man of the Old World. He speaks the language of the new. But he walks with a limp of the old. He will side with tradition."

She knew she was right, but Avi did not. It was as her mother and aunts often said to her: "You have to let the men decide for themselves what you already know to be true." She had no choice but to wait for him to be convinced.

So, with Akiba as chaperone, the pair of would-be lovers walked silently, somberly, in the direction of Chaim's house.

When they arrived, Chaim was wearing his customary afternoon suit. He embraced Rachel about the waist and kissed her cheek. "What can I do for you, you three wonderful youngsters? Are the lessons going well?"

Rachel squeezed his hand and said, "Too well, Uncle Chaim."

Chaim immediately understood. "We should summon your parents, Rachel. It is not appropriate to discuss such matters without them." His demeanor had changed from loving uncle to shrewd businessman in the blink of an eye. Rachel noticed that Avi and Akiba became instantly uncomfortable.

Rachel's grip on his hand intensified. "Uncle Chaim, I don't love Baruch. I love Avi," she confessed. She began to cry. Avi shuffled his feet awkwardly, and Akiba stared at the floor, absorbed by the sight of his sandals.

"I am not surprised." Chaim patted her on the head. "Baruch is like a brother to you. You grew up with him. Avi is an outsider — exciting, a bit mysterious. He's an adventure. Of course he is more interesting to you for now."

Rachel grew hopeful. "You understand!" she exclaimed.

"Yes," Chaim comforted. "But in ten years, who will you be more comfortable with? Who will be a better father for children of our heritage?"

"Excuse me, Chaim. But I'm right here. You're talking as if I were somewhere else," Avi said.

"With all due regard for you, Avi, this is not about you. It is about our family." His voice was coldly serious, as if he resented Avi's intrusion into his discussion with Rachel.

Avi placed his hat in his hand and stepped forward. "I want to be part of your family," he declared formally. "I love Rachel, and she loves me."

"I accept that, but there is the matter of family honor."

"Is that more important than Rachel's happiness?"

"If I thought you would make Rachel happier over her lifetime than Baruch, then that would be a difficult question to answer. But I have seen this before. Puppy love, lust—call it what you want. It doesn't last. The first time you have a fight, you will call her a dark-skinned Sephardic bitch. I know. I have seen it."

Rachel and Akiba recoiled at his harsh words, but Avi, her brave Avi, soldiered on. "You don't know me. I will always love Rachel and honor her and her family and her heritage. Please don't compare me to others."

"I'm sorry," Chaim said, looking at Avi. "I cannot agree. Your parents will not agree. Baruch's parents will not agree. I know that without even speaking to them. Baruch will not agree. That is our way. That is God's way. We cannot change it because two young people think they are in love. I'm truly sorry. I'm sorry that you feel the way you do about each other. But you must never see each other again. The Hebrew lessons are over. Akiba, take Avi home to Rishon L'Zion. Avi, have a good life, meet a nice Ashkenazi woman, marry her, have children. You will soon forget Rachel. And, Rachel, you must forget Avi. Baruch must never know of this conversation. Neither must anyone else, including your parents. That is the better way. We must keep this a secret. Secrets are the key to good relationships. You will marry Baruch after the holidays, and you will love him. I promise."

Rachel watched as Akiba gently led Avi out of the room, out

of the house, out of Jaffa, and out of her life. The last image she had of Avi was of him wiping angry tears. She thought she also saw a tear in Chaim's eye.

Shimshon looked directly at Emma, who was wiping a tear from *her* eye. He could see that she was angry at the message Shimshon was trying to send her by recounting this tale of unrequited love.

"Shimshon," she said, "that was over a hundred years ago. Don't you think people have evolved?"

"Emma, there are some traditions that cannot be broken. Habash is an attractive man, a decent man. But his people are at war with our people. He will always see you as a Jew. He was raised that way. Just as I will always see him as an Arab. I was raised that way. Maybe it will be different someday, but I'm afraid that it will not be in your lifetime. I'm sorry, but I must tell you the truth about how I feel."

Emma hated to disappoint her loved ones, and listening to her cousin campaign so emotionally against her relationship with Habash made her realize the source of Abe's discomfort earlier, during their blackboard session.

Her father did not approve either, though he would never say so directly.

XL

The Tell

THAT EVENING Abe ordered room service and looked forward to a cozy dinner with his two favorite women. At the very least, he hoped a nice meal would lighten Emma's mood. Since she'd come to the King David Hotel from Shimshon's, she'd been quiet and unresponsive to his queries about what was on her mind. He hoped that she wasn't reliving some kind of trauma from her abduction.

The food had been sitting in the room for twenty minutes before Rendi arrived. She kissed her husband and hugged her stepdaughter. After she kicked off her shoes and sat down at the table where the dinner was laid out, Abe asked her about her meeting.

"It was good," she said, smiling. "Dennis wasn't being entirely straight with me, though," Rendi announced. "He told me a few interesting things, but I'll have to work on him a bit to get everything he knows."

Emma sat on the chaise and surfed the Web on a laptop while Abe joined his wife at the table. "How do you know he didn't tell you everything already?" he asked.

Rendi dipped a bit of bread into a dish of olive oil. "Whenever he's hiding something, he folds his hands together and puts them in his lap. Almost as if he's protecting the family jewels. His hands were in his lap a lot."

Abe noticed a light in her eye — she loved the cat-and-mouse espionage game, even though she was happily retired.

"It could be usual spy crap," she said, clearly enjoying trying to solve this little puzzle. "The people he's working with want to break the case, or maybe they don't want anyone to break it. Maybe they want to prevent an international incident. Last thing they want is a bunch of amateurs like us beating them to the guys who did it."

Abe thought for a moment. "But he was very helpful to us through Emma's abduction."

Emma spoke without looking away from her computer. "Of course he was. He's always helpful. He's a good person. He'll do anything for Rendi."

Abe rolled his eyes. "You just think that because he's so handsome."

Emma raised her hands in the air, to show that she was guilty as charged.

Rendi began to twist the wedding ring on her finger, a tell of her own that meant she was trying to figure something out. "Emma, maybe he wasn't helping us only because of our friendship. He might have had an agenda. He works closely with American intelligence. *They* certainly have an agenda. He's probably carrying their water."

Emma didn't say anything. She resumed her research, clicking a few buttons on her computer keyboard and staring at the screen.

"But what is their water?" Abe asked. "Do you think he's about to break the case?"

"He doesn't need the glory of solving this case, Abe," Rendi said, alluding to his past as a hero. It was true. He was about as famous as a secret agent could comfortably be.

"How well do you really know him?" Emma asked. Rendi took a moment before speaking, and Abe waited expectantly, hoping she'd answer the question honestly. Abe had accepted Dennis as a fixture in their lives for so long, an "old friend" his wife was exceedingly fond of. There was a connection between the two that Abe didn't entirely understand, but then again there were so many things about Rendi's past that she wouldn't discuss. The exact nature of her relationship with Dennis was one of them.

"I know him." Rendi's voice was full of a gravity it didn't usually possess.

"Is he religious?" Emma asked innocently.

Rendi narrowed her eyes. "Why would you ask that?"

Emma shrugged her shoulders. "I don't know. It seems everybody here has some sort of interest in religion, whether as a spiritual system or a political stance."

Rendi smiled softly. "He's about as antireligion as you get. He's a fervent atheist. He reads all those books attacking God, religion, the whole works. He used to try to convert everyone around him away from religion. That's part of why he was always so effective when working on Mideast cases. He was completely objective when it came to religious issues. He hated them all!"

"It had to be hard being an atheist, growing up in his Irish Catholic family," Abe mused.

Rendi sat a tiny bit straighter in her chair. "I don't know. He didn't talk much about that. I think he might have been religious as a kid." She twisted her wedding ring.

Abe observed his wife. He sensed that they were venturing near one of those "It's a secret from our past" events that she wouldn't talk about.

Rendi continued, unaware of her husband's suspicions, "But that's typical of Denny. He doesn't even like to talk about his heroism — taking the bullet for the veep. You know, he nearly died. It was here in Israel. He was saved by Israeli doctors at the Hadassah Medical Center. He spends a lot of his free time here now; he never did before the shooting."

Emma jumped to her feet. "Oh, my God!"

Abe and Rendi were startled by her sudden outburst.

Emma gestured wildly with her hands as she spoke, clearly seized by an idea. "One of the first times you brought him to the house — Rendi, remember, I was thirteen or fourteen and gaga over him? — I asked him about the shooting, and he told me that it was a *miracle* he didn't die." Emma stared expectantly at Abe and Rendi, assuming they understood her point.

Neither of them did. "Where are you going with this?" Abe asked.

"Dad!" Emma said, frustrated. "Think about it. He's a fervent atheist, but he said it was a *miracle he didn't die.*"

A grin spread over Rendi's face, and she laughed out loud.

"What?" Emma asked defensively.

"Emma! I love you, but whatever you're trying to put together, it's not remotely possible." Rendi giggled. "It's just an expression. Like when the Red Sox won the World Series. How many times did your dad claim that was a 'miracle'? You can't read anything into his use of that overused word. I'm sorry."

"Does Dennis have any connection with TNT?" Emma asked boldly.

Abe shot her a look.

"Daddy, what if he developed sympathies with Israeli

extremists while he recuperated here? It's possible. Think about it. A doctor saves Dennis's life. That same doctor belongs to TNT, the group that planted the bomb. If the doctor is caught, he's finished. So Dennis covers for him and his group. It's possible."

Abe nodded reluctantly. "I guess it wouldn't hurt to look into his Israeli friends, the doctors who saved him."

"Abe!" Rendi admonished.

"Emma has a point, Rendi. He owes his life to them. Quite a debt. Could provide a motive for a cover-up. *We* have no agenda, other than solving the crime. If the finger points to Israelis, so be it." Then, looking meaningfully at his wife, he continued, "And if a finger points to your buddy Savage as being part of a cover-up, so be it, too."

"Maybe it's better to be amateurs." Emma smiled. "We're only interested in the truth, wherever it leads. We *can* 'handle the truth,'" she said, doing her best Jack Nicholson imitation.

Rendi sat quietly. She rarely found herself in disagreement with her husband, but her family was about to spend time investigating a complete dead end. And though her first loyalties were of course to Abe, she was irritated that he'd cast suspicion on her good friend Dennis.

XLI

The Truth

"I T WAS AN INTENSE WOUND," mused Dr. Eidelman, who had been in the emergency ward, trauma unit, when Savage was medevacked to Hadassah Medical Center in Jerusalem. "Artery in the leg. Lots of bleeding. He came in with a tourniquet that he himself had placed around his thigh. I think it was his tie. It saved his life. We stabilized him, but the bleeding continued intermittently. We kept pumping blood in, and he kept pumping it out."

Arthur Eidelman had been Abe's classmate in Boston, and the two men had run in the same circles; they were each passionate about social causes and supporting Israel in particular. Throughout their college careers, Arthur had spoken of leaving the States and settling in Israel. After medical school he made aliyah and became head of trauma at Hadassah. Abe and Artie had remained in touch over the years, meeting whenever they happened to be in the same city. They had similar political views, they both had children whom they loved very much, and they had both risen to the top of their respective fields. Normally when they got together, they exchanged photos and stories about their daughters. This time it was a professional visit.

The two men sat in the hospital cafeteria, drinking lukewarm coffee.

"I can't tell you any more about his medical history because of the confidentiality rules. I'm sure you understand," Arthur said.

"What I need to know isn't medical. It's more social," Abe said, ignoring a package of stale cookies.

"Social?"

"Could you tell me which of the doctors took care of him? I'm told Savage remained friendly with those who he believed saved his life."

Arthur chuckled. "He hated his doctors."

Abe had been taking notes, but upon hearing this he stopped. The pen dangled in the air as he waited for Arthur to continue.

"He believed we didn't do such a great job. And I can't blame him. He nearly died *after* we stabilized him."

Abe was disappointed. He wasn't sure what he'd been looking for, but he knew this wasn't it.

Arthur swirled the coffee around in his cup. "You should talk to Elizabeth Mitchell. She's a first responder emergency-room nurse. Earned her stripes in a combat unit. You'll like her. Great gal and a real beauty to boot."

Arthur winked at Abe, but Abe brushed off the implication. "I'm not interested in anything other than info about Savage, thank you."

Arthur was brave and reached for a cookie. "You should talk to her. Savage credits her with saving his life." He spit out his bite of cookie. "These are terrible. I miss American cookies."

"How did she save Savage's life, when the doctors couldn't?"

"Secret weapon."

"What do you mean?"

Artie replied, "She has a prayer group. They pray over people. Rub holy sand on their wounds. Do interventions. The hospital looks the other way, and she only brings her people in for cases that are beyond medical help. And sometimes it works. Psychosomatic, placebo. Who knows!"

"Do Jews believe in that crap?" Abe wondered.

"Some do, but Mitchell's not Jewish. She's a born-again Christian."

Abe shook his head. This didn't fit with what Rendi insisted about Savage. Abe always kept an open mind when working on a case, explored every possibility, no matter how extreme. But he hadn't really expected to find anything incriminating or suspicious about Dennis. Though Abe wasn't as close to him as Rendi was, they'd spent ample time together in Cambridge, debating political issues, discussing their favorite sports teams, and trading war stories about their jobs. Abe considered Dennis a friend, and he was growing more and more uneasy as Artie spoke.

Not to mention that he dreaded having to relay Artie's tale to Rendi. She was already annoyed at Abe for poking into Dennis's past; this news would definitely upset her. His wife had always been protective of her friends, Dennis especially.

Arthur saw that *his* friend was processing the story. "I know it sounds crazy. Just talk to her."

Abe drummed his pen against the legal pad in front of him. "Savage is an atheist. Why would he let people pray over him?" he asked, almost wishing that Artie wouldn't have an answer to his question.

"Savage *was* an atheist. He came into the hospital as a dying atheist. He left as a born-again evangelical Christian."

Abe dropped his pen. "I really wish you hadn't told me that," he said, thinking about his wife.

"Not many people know about this. He was very secretive. Concerned that it could affect his clearance or something. Swore everyone to secrecy. But I know that he went straight from here to the Kinneret. You know, what the Christians refer to as the Sea of Galilee. They baptized him right where Jesus was baptized. The whole schmear."

Abe was dumbstruck. There was another side to Dennis Savage, a side he was positive that his wife didn't know. As he sat there, he wondered what else they didn't know about their good friend Denny and his friends.

XLII

Elizabeth Mitchell

ABE LEFT THE HOSPITAL CAFETERIA and went to Pal-Watch, where he filled Habash and Emma in on what he had learned. Abe was surprised to find them in different offices. He'd expected the two to be working together, but there was a noticeable strain between them. He wondered what had happened to the blooming romance but decided it was a mystery best solved by Rendi. Besides, there were more important issues at hand — namely, Dennis Savage and Artie's information about his conversion.

Rendi was incredulous. "There's no way Dennis Savage is an evangelical Christian. We're talking about a man who thinks 'God bless you' is offensive!" She was so irritated that she couldn't sit still.

Abe knew that his wife had complete confidence in Dennis, but Arthur had no reason to lie. He was political, but not scheming. He was one of the most honest men Abe knew, which was why he hadn't become a lawyer, Abe always joked.

Emma, whose theories had been dismissed too many times for her liking during this investigation, immediately — and victoriously — set to proving that Dennis had connections with TNT. "Think about it, Daddy. He's saved by Israeli Christian extremists. They could have put him in touch with TNT, which also has a bunch of religious extremists. I checked it out. One of the surgeons at that hospital is a JDL member. I can't establish that they ever met, but it's a lead."

"Okay, TNT goes back on the 'Could Have Done It' list, but I'm still skeptical," Abe said.

Habash quickly threw together a dossier on Elizabeth Mitchell. Her family had been in Israel for over a hundred years. They were part of the original "German colony" of Christians who had moved to the Holy Land for religious reasons in the mid–nineteenth century. They had run Christian schools, missions, and medical clinics. They called themselves Christian Zionists and were fiercely patriotic to the Jewish state in which they lived as a religious minority. "We are the 'Jews' of the Jewish nation," Elizabeth was quoted in one newspaper article about Christians living in Israel. "Jews have lived as productive minorities in the Christian nations for centuries, so now we are living as a productive religious minority in the Jewish nation. We love Israel. And we love the land of the Bible, where Jesus walked."

There was personal information about her, too: She was fastidious and extremely neat. She was also tough as nails. As Arthur had told Abe, she had served as a combat nurse in the Israel Defense Forces and had risked her life on several occasions to get wounded soldiers out of harm's way. And recently she'd made news when several of the nurses at Hadassah Medical

Center had quit over a fear of biological terrorism — suicide martyrs were infecting themselves with the AIDS and mad cow viruses and targeting hospital workers for exposure. Elizabeth had spoken out against the nurses who quit, and she ended up recruiting a new staff, mostly women from the former Soviet Union.

Habash found nothing to suggest that Elizabeth was anything other than what she seemed: a pro-Israel evangelical Christian.

So Abe went to talk to her. He asked Rendi to accompany him, but she flatly refused. She announced that if he wanted to waste his time running down a dead-end lead, he could go ahead and do it without her.

One thing Arthur hadn't exaggerated about was Elizabeth Mitchell. When she walked out of the emergency room at midnight, she looked to Abe like a model in a television commercial about the perfect hospital in which to have cosmetic surgery. She was tall, lithe, and radiant, with long blond hair and deep blue eyes. Although she'd been through a typical rough day — several automobile accidents, a domestic stabbing, a number of sports injuries — she looked exactly as she must have looked when she'd arrived at the emergency room twelve hours earlier. Not a hair out of place, not a sign of perspiration, not even a stain on her neatly starched nurse's uniform.

Artie had set up the meeting, so Elizabeth was looking for Abe.

"Ms. Mitchell, over here. I'm Abe. Can we talk?" he inquired, walking toward her.

Elizabeth smiled broadly and reached out a manicured hand. "Hello, Mr. Ringel. Dr. Eidelman texted me about you. He said you were interested in talking about my prayer group. What can I do for you?"

"This will only take a few minutes. Can we have a drink?"

"I don't drink alcohol. How about some tea? The cafeteria is open all night."

As they walked to the cafeteria, Abe wondered who this smart, beautiful, and determined woman really was. Try as he had over the years, Abe could never get inside the minds of smart religious fundamentalists. It seemed such a contradiction. To him, intelligence meant questioning, doubting, changing, challenging — thinking. Justice Antonin Scalia, whom Abe knew casually, had once described himself as "a fool for Christ." Scalia was no fool for anyone, Abe thought. How could he totally suspend his critical faculties when it came to religion? How could this woman — this smart nurse — believe in faith healing, in prayer as cure? He was dying to ask her, but he had a different agenda that night. He had to find out everything he could about her patient, Dennis Savage.

When the two of them were sitting at the exact same table Abe had occupied with Artie the day before, Elizabeth said, "Nice job defending that terrorist, Mr. Ringel. I thought for sure he did it, but you changed my mind."

Abe was surprised at both the topic she chose and her willingness to admit a changed opinion. In his experience, devout religious fundamentalists were usually quite stubborn about their ideas. That's why he rarely picked them for juries. "Do you change your mind easily?"

"Depends on what we're talking about," she said softly.

Abe's first impression of her was that she was extremely secure and confident. She was also very warm. As they sat, nurses, doctors, orderlies all filed past them with their food, and she said hello to almost all of them. She had a way about her.

"When I'm working the emergency room, I change my mind all the time, as new data emerges. I'm a big fan of Bayesian theory."

Again, she surprised Abe. Thomas Bayes was an eighteenth-century mathematician and logician who was the personification of the skeptic, always changing as the facts changed. He had devised a mathematical approach—still used today—to deal with shifting probabilities.

"So am I," Abe responded. "Bayes is the patron saint of defense lawyers, because we always deal in probabilities—probable cause, reasonable doubt."

"He was also a Presbyterian minister," Elizabeth noted with a smile. "I don't use Bayes only in the emergency room. I also bring him to church with me," she said, tearing open a sugar packet and pouring the contents into her tea.

It was an opening, and Abe tried to sail through it. "You think about religion scientifically and skeptically?"

"Yes. I don't believe in living a dichotomous life the way some of my friends do. You know, scientist by day, religious fundamentalist by night. For me, the same kind of reason by which I live life from Monday to Friday at work has to operate on Sunday as well."

"Artie told me you were a Christian fundamentalist."

"Maybe by Dr. Eidelman's lights, because I believe in a God who answers prayers, who heals, who cures. But I'm no fundamentalist, if by that you mean someone who accepts religion on faith alone and does not subject it to the same intellectual standards as science."

"What scientific evidence do you have for faith healing?" Abe asked gently, without appearing to be challenging.

Elizabeth tilted her head. "I've seen it work—along with medicine, of course. I'm no Christian Scientist. I believe in medicine. I practice it." She gestured around her to the hospital. "But medicine alone sometimes fails. When it doesn't seem to be working by itself, I add a little prayer. Never as a substitute. God forbid. But only as a supplement. Can't hurt, can it?"

Abe couldn't help thinking of the old Jewish joke about the Yiddish theater star who collapsed on the stage. A doctor from the audience worked on him and after a few minutes declared, "It's no use. He's gone." From the audience came a shout with a thick Yiddish accent: "Gib 'im an enema!" The doctor replied, "You don't understand, he's dead. It won't help," to which the audience member shouted back, "It couldn't hoit!" Abe asked her, "No, it can't hurt if it's done in addition. But how can you be sure the prayer is helping?"

"I can't be sure. That's where Bayes and probability theory come in. But I've seen cases that have no medical explanation."

"Like Denny Savage?"

Elizabeth now straightened in her chair. Artie hadn't mentioned that Abe was interested in Dennis. "Yes, like Denny Savage. Why?"

It was Abe's turn to be charming. "I'm investigating something, and he's a friend. I know that your prayer group saved his life, and I wanted to know how."

Elizabeth appraised him with her eyes, taking his measure. He could tell that she didn't entirely believe him. At last she began to speak. "The bullet severed his femoral artery. He nearly bled to death several times. I've seen wounds like that on the battlefield. High mortality. Particularly high in terrorist attacks, because the bomb makers are now using rat poison, which is a blood thinner."

"How did you stop the bleeding?" Abe wondered.

"We kept giving him the blood-clotting medicine, and we also prayed. At first neither worked. Because he was a bleeder and an atheist. Bad combination."

"How did you get the prayer to work?"

"You mean how did we get the prayer and medicine to work together?"

"Yeah, together."

"It was a tough sell. We had to persuade him to open his heart and mind to the possibilities of prayer — of God."

"But he was a fervent atheist?"

"He was also a fervent believer in life."

"No atheists in foxholes?"

"Actually, I've seen atheists in foxholes. But Savage wanted so badly to live. He knew he was dying. I showed him the data I had compiled on the effectiveness of prayer and medicine working in tandem. He was skeptical in the beginning, but my data shook him. I appealed to his rational, his scientific side. It was a tough sell. Ultimately he opened his mind. He trusted me. He knew I wasn't interested in converting him solely for religious reasons. I wanted to save his life. Saving his soul was a natural consequence of saving his life," Elizabeth said, showing her first sign of emotion. She smiled shyly at Abe, reached for her tea, and crossed her arms in front of her chest.

Abe changed his tone from one of questioner to one of friend. "You healed him, converted him, and befriended him all at once. Quite an accomplishment."

"Yes, it was an accomplishment," she said proudly.

She went on to tell him more about Dennis. She was hesitant at first, apparently because of medical confidentiality and her promise of secrecy, but Abe was his friend and she was proud of her work with Dennis.

Abe was astounded by her story. Dennis's wound wasn't healing, even with prayer and medicine. So the leader of Elizabeth's church prepared some sand from al-Eizariya, the biblical town where Lazarus lived. Elizabeth sterilized the sand and applied it to Denny's wound, and shortly after that the bleeding stopped. When Dennis recovered, he demanded that Elizabeth introduce him to her leader, though he was an ascetic who lived simply and preferred minimal interaction with people. But Dennis got his way and eventually not only met him but moved in with him for several weeks. Elizabeth claimed that Dennis emerged from this time a changed man, that he became a believer and was committed to their church and at total peace with himself.

"Does the church have any connection to TNT or other Jewish extremists?" Abe asked.

"Not that I know of. We're not pacifists. We believe in our country's right to defend itself. But not in terrorism. That was not the way of Jesus, and it's not our way."

Abe thanked Elizabeth and left the hospital. He was fascinated by this smart, unusual woman, but his mind focused on what she'd told him about Dennis Savage. Something didn't click. A Secret Service agent. A convert to a religion whose leader lived like a hermit. The "tells" that Rendi had picked up.

Something was missing from the story. But what? The more Abe thought about it, the more he wondered why Dennis had been so interested in Faisal's innocence — why he'd offered help to Abe's legal team whenever Abe had asked for it. Abe wasn't convinced it was entirely because of his affection for Rendi. American intelligence had a strong interest in Faisal's trial and Abe's tactics. Abe had focused, during the trial, on what he could learn from Dennis. He did not focus on what Dennis was learning from him. It was a two-way street, and now Abe began to think hard about what Dennis had learned and why he needed that information.

Abe was anxious to get back to Rendi and share what he'd learned about her old friend, though he knew it would be difficult for her to accept. Maybe, if she could set aside her loyalty to Dennis, she could put it all together. Maybe she could figure out whom — if anyone — he was covering for, whom he was protecting.

XLIII

The Family Connection

"No way that could happen. Certainly not without me knowing." This was Rendi's obstinate response to Abe once he'd filled her in on his conversation with Nurse Elizabeth Mitchell.

Abe had returned from his meeting to find Rendi and Emma relaxing in the hotel suite. He ruined the quiet, happy scene with his news. While Emma booted up her laptop and researched Elizabeth's prayer group, Abe tried to make headway with his wife. "Rendi—"

"He's not an evangelical Christian. There's no way." She twisted her ring roughly. "Can you imagine me becoming a Hasidic Jew? Even if some Hasid saved my life? No way, no how."

"There're two accounts of this now, Rendi," Abe argued.

"I don't care if you find a hundred stories about Dennis converting. I *know* it's not true. I know it."

"How? How can you know for sure?" Abe demanded.

"I just do. He tells me everything. Especially personal stuff that he makes me promise not to tell anyone."

"Even me?"

"Even you, Abe. Personal stuff. He confides in me. Has for years. There is absolutely no way what Artie and this nurse are telling you is for real. *If* this happened, *if,* then he was infiltrating their group. That's it."

Abe didn't want to antagonize his wife any more than he already had. Emma was on his side on this one, though, and he set her to the task of finding out all she could about Elizabeth's church. What she found was intriguing.

It was called the Church of the Apocalypse. Emma couldn't locate the actual church, because there wasn't one. The closest thing the members had to an official meeting house was a small building in the town of Megiddo, in the north.

When Emma read this to her father, Rendi, and Habash, Habash's face went white.

Rendi saw it. "What's wrong now?" she asked.

"Megiddo," Habash said, as if it were plain to everyone.

Abe made the connection. "Armageddon!"

Pulling together some sketchy material from Internet sources, Emma concluded that there were about one hundred members of the church — fifty or so in Israel, a couple dozen in the United States, and a few scattered here and there. Their leader, Revelation Ruggles, was an ascetic man who wore rags, never cut his hair, and eschewed any pleasure of the body so that he could commune with God. Abe had a hard time marrying this image of the man with the pristine Elizabeth Mitchell or with the all-American Dennis Savage.

But then he remembered how many prominent Jews — actors, athletes, businessmen, academics — had been attracted to the Lubavitcher rebbe, also an ascetic religious figure. When it came

to religion, Abe concluded, there was no accounting for taste—
or belief. It was true, he acknowledged to himself, that his wife
could never become a Hasid, but then again she had never been
a fervent, radical atheist either. Perhaps, he speculated, extremist
disbelief and extremist belief were two sides of the same coin.

Abe remembered that Shimshon had once mentioned the
name Ruggles, when relating the history of his ancestor Avi. He
invited his cousin to join them for tea.

Shimshon was excited by the name of the leader: Revelation
Ruggles. He was a descendant of Deuteronomy Ruggles, who
had interacted with Avi Regel a century and a quarter earlier.
When Shimshon mentioned the connection to the past, Emma
asked him to fill in the details.

Shimshon related how Deuteronomy Ruggles was a fixture at
Rishon L'Zion. Standing six feet three inches tall, with a shock
of straight blond hair, the twenty-one-year-old Christian mis-
sionary cut a striking figure in a region of mostly short, dark
residents. His unusual name was always a source of humor. Each
of his siblings was named after a book of the Bible: The eldest,
a girl named Genesis, was called "Jen"; the youngest was Leviti-
cus, called "Cussy"; and the second-oldest, a boy, who was Exodus, called "X." Fortunately, there were no other siblings, since
Numbers would be hard to nickname. The parents, Gustav and
Catherine, purposely gave their children unusual names in order
to encourage them to pursue the family calling of spreading the
Gospel of Jesus.

Gustav's family had been German Templars, a messianic
Christian group from Württemberg in southern Germany. The
Templars had come to Palestine in the 1860s.

Catherine's father and grandfather had been British mission-
aries. Her father had written a widely read travel book in which
he traced every step walked by Jesus during his brief ministry

in the Galilee and Jerusalem. Their mission was to save the Jews, whom they loved because of the Old Testament, and the Arabs, whom they pitied because of what they regarded as their "silly" Koran, a pale imitation of the "real" Bible.

Shimshon described how every Friday at the crack of dawn, Deuteronomy — known as "Deut" — would appear on the dusty streets of Rishon, handing out his evangelical Christian conversion tracts, in Hebrew, to anyone who would take them. Although his religious handouts threatened fire and brimstone — "the destruction of Sodom is nothing compared with how those who reject Jesus will be treated in Hell" — Deut himself was the epitome of gentility and reason. He always came bearing small gifts — chocolates, candles, and, of course, Christian trinkets (*"goyisher tchotchkes,"* as Akiba referred to them).

Everyone in Rishon liked Deut, because no one worried that he would ever convert anybody. One of the religious residents of Rishon said that Deut's visits even made some of the townsfolk feel "more appreciative of their Jewishness," because Judaism wasn't "so scary."

Deut also liked the Jews of Rishon, because they were always polite to him and some even seemed to listen. Occasionally a former Yeshiva student would engage him in a debate about some interpretation of a biblical story. *Who knows,* Deut thought, *maybe some of it seeps in, and someday one of them will see the light and save himself from eternal damnation. It doesn't hurt to try.*

After lunch, which he usually spent at the Rishon dining room where the local women made a daily feast, Deut walked down the road to Beit Dijan. He waited outside the town mosque until the service was over and then attempted to hand out the same religious pamphlets, but in Arabic, to the exiting Muslims. They, too, treated him kindly but no one would stop to listen or talk, beyond a polite salaam alaikum, because their imam forbade it.

After two hours Deut would leave, with his backpack still filled with the Arabic pamphlets and the *goyisher tchotchkes*.

Shimshon explained that Revelation Ruggles was from the same family of devout Christians that had been trying to convert people since their arrival in the Holy Land. For several years before he turned to his ascetic ways—the ways of Jesus, as he put it—he was the leader of the Christian Zionist movement in Israel. There was plenty of information about him from this period. He had been very involved in politics and the media but had since given that up as too worldly. Now his brother Ecclesiastes was the public face of the church.

But, to Rendi's relief, any further investigation into the Ruggles family and their modern-day connection to Dennis Savage had to be put on hold, because that same night Rashid Husseini was arrested for kidnapping Emma.

Faisal Husseini—now a free man, but still a widely reviled figure—brazenly showed up at Pal-Watch. He came as a messenger for his brother. Rashid was now calling in his chip. He wanted Abe to be his lawyer.

XLIV

Rashid Redux

Prior to Emma's kidnapping, Rashid rarely left the comfortable Jericho safe house. It was a relatively secure place. The Israelis occasionally conducted raids in that ancient biblical town, and there was virtually no Hamas presence there. Rashid was as fearful of Hamas as he was of the Israelis. As a Marxist Arab, he was anathema to the religious zealots of Hamas.

Once he decided to release Emma — to keep his deal with Abe Ringel — Rashid knew there was no going back to Jericho, at least not for a while. He couldn't count on Emma's keeping her promise not to disclose the location of her kidnappers. Nor could he rely on her having been adequately blindfolded during her trips to and from Mohammed's home. When his brother Faisal was freed by the Israeli court, their mother took him to a prearranged rendezvous point. Rashid worked on him for days in an effort to persuade him to change his ways and join Rashid's group. He told Faisal he had been poisoned by his own group because they were afraid he would either deliberately or inadvertently admit the group's innocence. It was a work in progress, but at least Faisal was losing interest in the Martyrs of Jihad, believing that they had used him and didn't trust him. He was still a long way from becoming a Marxist, but he liked the members of Rashid's group, especially Mohammed, and agreed to stay with them for a while.

With his family situation stabilized, Rashid decided to travel to Belarus, where an international conference of Marxist organizations was being held. He couldn't chance being identified and captured by Israeli security at Ben Gurion Airport, so he decided to fly out of Amman Airport in Jordan, where security was far more lax. Except first he had to make it into Jordan. Rather than risk being stopped at the Allenby Bridge border crossing, Rashid decided to cross into Jordan illegally, by simply traversing a narrow, isolated bank of the shallow Jordan River in the dead of night. Except the Israelis had been tipped off by a double agent who was a member of Hamas but also informed against Hamas enemies. Rashid was captured by Israeli soldiers and brought to Shin Bet headquarters, where he was identified by intelligence officials as the head of the Marxist organization that had kidnapped the American woman.

Rashid remained silent when interrogated, asking only for a lawyer, by name—Abe Ringel. The investigators denied his request and continued to question him, not only about the kidnapping but also about the assassination bombing. He refused to answer, alternately remaining silent and repeating his demand for Abe Ringel.

After twenty-four hours of continuous but futile questioning, the Shin Bet finally decided to notify Rashid's family of his capture and his request to be represented by the American lawyer. When Faisal delivered the request, Emma insisted on accompanying her father, but Abe and Habash wouldn't let her. Making sure she was safely shut in at Shimshon's, Abe took a taxi to the Shin Bet's interrogation center outside Tel Aviv. Habash remained in Jerusalem; they didn't think Rashid would talk if Habash were present.

When Abe got to the center, he had to pass through three layers of security. Frisked, questioned, and annoyed, he was led into a small room with no windows and no discernible ventilation system. It was stuffy and dim, with one table in the middle of the room, flanked by two plastic chairs. Abe waited for five minutes before Rashid was led in by a pair of armed men in three-piece suits. The men left Abe with Rashid, and then the two of them were alone.

"I see you are a man of your word, Mr. Ringel," Rashid began. Though he'd been through an ordeal, he was composed. Wearing a prisoner jumpsuit made most men scared and vulnerable, but this man was in complete command of his emotions. His accent was slight, and Abe could see what Emma meant about him. He was a terrorist, but he was gentlemanly.

"You kept your word. I will keep mine." Abe didn't feel so gentlemanly. This was, after all, the man who had orchestrated and perpetrated a heinous crime against his family.

"It must be strange to be sitting across the table from—"

"Be quiet now!" Abe shouted. "Do not complete that sentence. We are being recorded." He pointed above him, to the wall where a camera was mounted.

"It is not necessary that I complete the sentence," Rashid said evenly. "You know what I was about to say." He nodded deferentially.

"And so do they," Abe said. "If you want me to defend you, you will have to listen to everything I tell you. No improvising. Speak only in specific response to my questions. Is that understood?"

Rashid breathed in. "Clearly."

"Now, do you want me to represent you?" Abe retrieved a notepad from his briefcase and wrote down a quick summary of where Rashid was being held and what the charges were. While he wrote, he asked his questions.

Rashid nodded again. "Yes."

"Do you want me to try to free you?"

"Of course."

"Did you speak to anyone who questioned you?"

"Only to ask for you."

Abe liked this answer. "Nothing else?" he asked hopefully.

"Nothing else."

Abe exhaled and sat back in his chair. This man was far easier to work with than his brother had been. "Good. Now please tell me precisely what they asked you."

Rashid placed his hands, which were cuffed, upon the table and joined them into a fist. "They asked me why I kidnapped your daughter. Then they asked me why I released her. Were we paid money? Were we made any promises? They wanted details of the kidnapping: how? who? where? They asked about the group. Our ideology, our means, our connection to other groups and acts."

"Anything else?"

He gestured at Abe's pad, to let him know to write down what he was about to say. "Yes, they asked about the bombing and whether my group was involved. Did I know who might be involved? They offered me a reward if I could point them to the perpetrators. They threatened to arrest my mother if I didn't."

Abe raised his eyes to Rashid's and said very slowly, leadingly, "But you couldn't."

Rashid's eyes were shrewd. "I didn't say that."

"Or you wouldn't." Abe felt as if he were playing chess with a very skilled opponent.

"That is correct."

Abe sensed that perhaps Rashid was trying to tell him something, even with the tape recorder going. Abe decided to put it in his memory bank but to let it pass for now. He would certainly want to pursue it if and when he secured Rashid's freedom and could talk to him without being overheard by Israeli intelligence. But first he had to figure out how to defend a man he knew had kidnapped and threatened to kill his daughter.

Faisal Husseini watched as the American lawyer Abe Ringel emerged from the prison where the Israeli authorities were holding his brother Rashid. He had to make his move now.

He bounded around the building that bordered the alley where he'd been waiting for Abe to appear. He walked slowly and steadily toward the man, who stood on the edge of traffic, trying in vain to hail a taxi.

Abe's back was turned. He didn't see Faisal approaching. It was just as well. Had he seen him, he'd likely have run.

Just as Faisal reached Abe, a cab came to a standstill beside him. Abe opened the rear door, and Faisal grabbed at him. Abe swung around defensively. "What are you doing?" he demanded, fear apparent in his voice.

Faisal stepped away from him. "Don't worry. I am not here to hurt you. I...I am a man of honor. And men of honor acknowledge those who have helped them. Thank you for helping me."

Abe stared at him, stupefied. "I don't know what to say. I was surprised when you came to Pal-Watch to get help for your brother."

Faisal's stern expression didn't change. But he spoke more during this hot afternoon than he ever had before. "Blood is thick. This I have learned. Who I thought were my brothers were not. Rashid may not understand me, but he would never try to kill me."

Abe understood that Faisal was speaking of the Martyrs of Jihad and of what he believed were their unsuccessful attempts to poison him. "You must not approve of Rashid's politics either."

Faisal shook his head. "His politics involve a lot of reading. So many books they say I should try. I don't think I'll ever understand his cause, but he is my brother. I don't want to see him go to jail. I know you will do for him what you did for me." And then Faisal extended his hand. Abe shook it, still in disbelief, as he climbed into the waiting taxi.

XLV

The Promise

"THE GOVERNMENT CALLS as its first witness: the victim, Emma Ringel," prosecutor Dafna Rabinovitz announced.

The trial began only two weeks after the authorities caught Rashid. This was because after the acquittal of Faisal the Israeli government wanted to show that it wasted no time dealing with suspected terrorists. Abe had also requested a quick turnaround. The media was being even more brutal: "Is there anyone this guy won't defend? Even the terrorist who kidnapped his daughter!" He didn't want to be in Israel longer than he had to be, and Rashid was eager to get the trial over with.

Abe knew that the prosecution was going to call Emma as its chief witness. Though he'd warned the state that Emma wouldn't identify Rashid as her kidnapper, Dafna Rabinovitz seemed to believe that she'd change her mind once she was under the scrutiny of a judge.

"Objection, Your Honor. Ms. Rabinovitz knows that Emma Ringel has refused to testify," Abe responded. He thought it ironic that he'd represented both brothers. That was about the only similarity to the two cases. Where Faisal had been obstinate and rude, Rashid was calm and polite. He answered any question Abe asked; some of his answers were deliberately obtuse, but Abe found it refreshing to deal with a client who wasn't always going on about not trusting Jews.

The judge in this case, a man named Levin, squinted through his glasses at Abe. "Yes, I know her preference, but this is an obligation. She has been subpoenaed. She must testify, or else…"

"Or else what?" Abe asked. He was standing behind his desk; Rashid sat next to him in his prisoner's clothes. "Are you going to put the victim of a kidnapping in jail because she promised not to testify against her kidnappers if she was released?"

Dafna Rabinovitz couldn't believe her ears. She was on her feet immediately, ready to pounce on Abe's words. "Your Honor, it sounds like Mr. Ringel is admitting that his client was in fact the kidnapper."

"It does sound like that, Mr. Ringel," Judge Levin said, smiling.

"Perhaps," Abe acknowledged, sitting back down casually. "Except that I have no direct knowledge about who kidnapped my daughter. Any so-called admission I may be making is nothing more than hearsay, which is inadmissible under Israeli law." He folded his hands serenely and laid them on the desk. Unbeknownst to the judge and prosecution, he had very carefully chosen his words and was watching to see that they fell into his trap.

The prosecutor certainly seemed worked up. She paced back and forth in front of his table, the sun glinting off the gold buttons of her suit jacket and her heels clicking against the floor. "But your daughter's refusal to testify is also an implicit admission that your client was the kidnapper. And her admission is based on direct eyewitness evidence. She actually saw him."

Abe spoke only loudly enough for the judge to hear. He continued to keep calm. "But she won't testify. So you have no direct, admissible evidence from her either. You can't convict my client based on an inference you seek to draw from my daughter's refusal to testify, especially because she herself has not given any reason for her refusal."

"Pretty clever, Mr. Ringel," Judge Levin said angrily. He glowered and pointed his gavel at Abe. "Let's see how long she chooses to remain silent after I send her to jail for contempt of court. Bring Ms. Ringel into the courtroom," he commanded the officers of the court.

Abe, Rashid, and everyone else in the room turned to the double doors behind them. They were opened with a high-pitched squeal, and Emma appeared in the doorway. She seemed smaller and younger than she actually was, dressed in a prim outfit. She walked in defiantly, her head held high. She passed Habash and Rendi in the small spectator area, and that was the only time that she shifted her focus from the judge.

When she arrived at the front of the room, the judge gestured for her to walk to the stand, which consisted of a plastic chair to her left. After administering the oath, the judge looked directly at her and issued his order. "Ms. Ringel, I direct you to take the witness stand and answer Ms. Rabinovitz's questions."

Emma took her time situating herself in the chair. She did not look at Abe or Rashid. The prosecutor stalked over to her. "What is your name?" she spit.

"Emma Ringel."

"Did this man" — Ms. Rabinovitz pointed to Rashid — "kidnap you?"

"I respectfully refuse to answer," Emma said politely.

Ms. Rabinovitz slammed her hands down on the ledge cordoning off the witness stand. "You have no privilege. You did nothing that could incriminate you. Why do you refuse to answer?"

Emma's chin rose a bit in what was a clear mark of defiance. "I can't tell you."

Ms. Rabinovitz stepped back and changed her tone of voice. The next question came out less angrily. Abe continued to sit with his hands folded. He wasn't concerned about Emma; he'd spent hours coaching her on how to answer any questions the prosecution might throw at her. "Why can't you tell me?"

Emma shook her head. "I can't tell you that either." Abe quickly sneaked a look at Rendi. She nodded at him to show her support.

"What *can* you tell me?" Ms. Rabinovitz asked snidely.

"Nothing about this case," Emma replied, matching her tone and then holding a hand up to stop the stream of questions. "Let me help you here. I won't tell you why I can't answer, and I'm aware that I'm under legal obligation to testify."

Ms. Rabinovitz crossed her arms. "Then I assume that you are aware that refusal to answer constitutes contempt of court?"

Emma smiled. "Yes, I am."

"Are you aware that the judge can order you to jail until you agree to testify?"

"It will do no good. I will never testify, even if I have to spend my whole life in jail. Believe me. I will never testify, no matter what you do to me." Emma said this quite calmly. Abe was so proud of how she handled herself that he had to keep himself from smiling.

At last the judged interceded, not only to silence the murmuring crowd but to move matters along. "I do believe you, Ms.

Ringel, but believe me, too!" he shouted, and used his gavel to point at his second Ringel that morning. "You will remain in jail until you testify. Officer, take her away and put her in the cell downstairs."

Now it was Abe's turn. He stood suddenly and said, "Wait one minute, Your Honor. Before you order her to jail, she is entitled to a hearing. Although I'm not her lawyer in this case, I have standing to be heard because she was called as a witness against my client. Will you order the court stenographer to read back what Your Honor just said?"

"What *I* said?" the judge asked incredulously. It was clear from his demeanor that he'd had enough of this family. Rashid seemed to be enjoying himself; he looked up at Abe with an almost-smile on his face.

"Yes, Your Honor, what you said. You will see why it's relevant."

"Fine," the judge snapped. "Read it back."

The court stenographer began to read the judge's last statement. "'I do believe you, Ms. Ringel, but—'"

"That's enough," Abe cut her off. "You can't order her to jail under Israeli law." Abe held up an Israeli law book. Habash had proved most helpful, researching the statutes and cases that Abe thought he might need.

The judge's face turned bright red, and he looked as if he wanted to strangle Abe. "What are you talking about, Mr. Ringel? I know Israeli law. I've been a judge for twenty years. When a witness refuses to answer, the judge may order her to jail until she agrees to answer."

"That is generally correct," Abe acknowledged. "With one important exception." He opened the book. "Let me read from the Israeli Supreme Court decision in *Siegel v. Israel*. In that case a rabbi refused to testify against another rabbi in a corruption case. The court ordered him to testify and threatened him with jail. The rabbi swore that he would never testify against the other rabbi, because the chief rabbi of his sect had ordered him not to. Here is what the Supreme Court ruled:

"'The sole purpose of the civil contempt power is to coerce the witness into testifying. When it is clear that the witness will not be coerced because of strongly held religious, moral, family or other considerations, then jailing the witness does not serve that purpose and may not be employed.' The Supreme Court ordered the rabbi to be released from jail," Abe said triumphantly.

Behind him Habash clapped his hands. He loved being able to observe Abe in action.

The judge wasn't as impressed. "What does that have to do with this case? Ms. Ringel is not a rabbi, and she is not invoking any religious objection to testify."

"That case is controlling, Your Honor. Remember, you made a finding of fact. My daughter testified under oath — swore — that she will never testify even if you were to send her to jail for the rest of her life. And you replied — let me quote — 'I do believe you, Ms. Ringel.' In other words, you found her testimony credible. You believe that she will never agree to testify. Under the *Siegel* precedent, you can't send her to jail if you believe she won't change her mind."

Ms. Rabinovitz stood openmouthed, and for a moment the judge was stymied. Then he reached for the book angrily. "Give me the case," he insisted. After reading the passage, he rose hastily, banged his gavel, said, "Fifteen-minute recess," and stormed out of the stunned courtroom.

"Will it work, Daddy?" Emma asked as she quietly approached her father.

Ms. Rabinovitz glared at them, furious that her chief witness was clearly conspiring with the defense attorney—even though he was her father.

"I think so," Abe said softly, ushering Emma away from Ms. Rabinovitz's stare. "Habash says that Judge Levin is a tough judge but an honest one. He believes you. Everyone believes you. I certainly believe you really would stay in jail."

"Yes, I would," Emma said, dropping her voice so that Rashid couldn't hear. "I made a promise. I can't break it."

Abe gestured to his client, who was eavesdropping and had heard every word. "Even to a kidnapper who might have killed you."

Rashid laughed ironically at this.

"That's the point," Emma said to both of them. "He didn't kill me. He released me. He kept his promise. I have to keep mine."

"I know that," Abe said. "You are a woman of your word—for better or worse."

Five minutes after he bolted out of the courtroom, Judge Levin returned.

"I've read the case," he announced, standing behind his table. The entire courtroom waited for his ruling. "Regrettably, Mr. Ringel, you are correct. I'm not sure I agree with their decision, but I am bound by it. I will not order your daughter to jail." Then, changing the tone of his voice, he turned to Emma. "Even before reading the *Siegel* case, I had qualms about jailing the victim. We never do that in rape cases when the victims won't testify. I thought I was bound by law to jail her, but this case says no."

"But, Your Honor." Ms. Rabinovitz jumped to her feet in a fury. "Without Ms. Ringel's testimony, we have no admissible evidence against a terrorist who we all know kidnapped this woman."

Rashid looked at her blankly.

Judge Levin replied in a stern voice, "That is the way the law works, Ms. Rabinovitz. It has worked that way since the Bible required two witnesses for a conviction. If there was only one witness — even the most credible witness possible — the guilty criminal went free."

Abe now rose to his feet, and asked politely, "Do I take that to mean, Your Honor, that the case against Rashid is dropped?"

The judge turned a sardonic eye on him. "Yes, Mr. Ringel, you get another guilty client off. Does that make you feel good?"

"It's my job, Your Honor. Just like it's your job to apply the law."

"Mr. Ringel, I'm reminded of a conversation between your great Justice Oliver Wendell Holmes and one of his law clerks, who criticized one of the justice's decisions as 'unjust.' Holmes replied, 'Young man, we are in the law business, not the justice business.' Maybe someday, Mr. Ringel, the law business will become the justice business. Court is adjourned."

Everyone stood. The judge left the room, the prosecutor gathered her files and departed in a huff, and Emma ran from the witness stand to Rendi and Habash, who were sitting behind Abe.

Abe watched as the officers of the court approached Rashid. He stood for them and raised his hands so that they could remove the cuffs. They were going to escort him to the jail, where he'd be given his clothes and his personal belongings and then released.

Before they led him away, Abe grabbed Rashid by the arm. "Now we're even. No more promises to keep. Next time you're on your own. We're finished here, except for one thing."

"What's that?" Rashid was as civil as he'd been throughout the trial. Abe noted the command he had of his emotions.

"When we talked in jail and you told me that your interrogators had offered you a reward for telling them who did the bombing, I said that you couldn't and you said, 'I didn't say that.' What exactly did you mean?"

Rashid smiled cryptically. "I meant that I think I could tell them who might be involved, if I wanted to, but I didn't want to help the Israelis."

Abe's grip on Rashid's arm tightened. "You mean you know."

"I have some ideas." Rashid looked at his arm, and Abe let him go.

"Ideas?"

"Information." Rashid nodded his head. "Nothing absolutely conclusive, but I know some things."

"Share them with me. I am not the Israelis. I helped you twice. You took my daughter. I think you owe me."

Rashid hesitated a moment and then caught a glimpse of Emma. She stood just behind Abe, not close enough to hear their conversation. "I will tell you this." He lowered his head. "They were not Arabs."

"Were they Jews?"

"They were not Jews."

"Christians?" Abe said, running out of options.

"They were not Christians. They were not Americans. More I will not tell you. I have paid my debt," Rashid said, gesturing to the guards that he was ready to go. Without a word, he left Abe standing there.

Abe related to Emma, Habash, and Rendi what Rashid had said.

"Who's left?" Rendi wondered, hoping that this new clue would finally dissuade Abe and Emma from again focusing their attention on Dennis Savage.

Emma shrugged. "I don't know. Maybe Martians," she quipped.

"I think I know," Habash said with a smile.

XLVI

The Hunch

HE SAID IT WASN'T ARABS. He didn't say it wasn't Muslims. The Iranians and the Pakistanis are Muslims but not Arabs, and they're both involved with sophisticated explosives," Habash whispered as they all walked away from the courthouse.

"It's not the Pakistanis. They limit their terrorism to India. Sure, they don't much like Israel, or Jews for that matter, but they would never endanger their relationship with the United States by killing an American president," Rendi said with the assurance of a former intelligence agent who had spent some time in Pakistan.

"The Iranians are involved with nuclear explosives, but this explosion was plastique, not nuclear," Abe said, slowing down about a block away from the courthouse. There was an outdoor park with tables and chairs set up. Abe sat, and the others gathered around him.

"But they are also developing other sophisticated explosives. Remember that a nuclear bomb needs a nonnuclear trigger, especially a dirty nuclear bomb," Habash said.

"So what do you think?" Abe asked.

Habash thought for a moment and then said, "Look, if it was a group that had any connection to the development of nuclear weapons, then it couldn't be Palestinians, because we have no nuclear program. But if we're looking at the Iranians, the attack could be religiously motivated. The Iranian leadership believes in the coming of the twelfth imam." Abe, Rendi, and Emma looked at him blankly. They weren't getting the connection he was making, so he elaborated. "They are apocalyptic. They believe that widespread death will hasten his coming."

"Like some Christian extremists who want to hasten the second coming of Christ," Emma volunteered.

"Yes." Habash nodded at her. "The theology is quite different, but the outcome is similar."

"So the Iranians are non-Arab Muslims, their leadership is apocalyptic, they know how to make sophisticated explosives. They have motive and means." Emma took off the light jacket she was wearing and placed it behind her chair as she sat down next to her father.

"But no opportunity," Abe mused. "How the heck could Iranians get close to the nuclear football?"

"There's no way. Maybe it wasn't *in* the football but right near it," Rendi said.

"Even so. How could Iranians get anywhere near the president with an explosive?" Abe wondered.

"Maybe they bribed someone in the security detail," Habash suggested.

"There were overlapping security details. Americans, Israelis, Palestinian Authority, Hamas. It wouldn't be easy," Rendi said, growing perturbed. Habash was merely thinking out possibilities, but Rendi feared that any suspicion about the security details would reignite Abe's suspicions of Dennis. This was still a sore point between the two of them, though Rendi had set aside her displeasure for the duration of Rashid's trial.

"Wait a minute," Emma interjected. "If the Iranians did it, why would the Mossad cover for them? They're Israel's worst enemies."

"Maybe they bribed an Israeli security person," Habash surmised.

"Or maybe they weren't covering for them. Maybe they wanted Faisal convicted *because* of his group's connection to Iran," Rendi surmised.

The four of them lounged for a while in the sun, until Abe felt he was beginning to burn. All he wanted was to solve this case and get his daughter on a plane back to Boston. "Look," he said, "so far we have only a lead—a speculative one to be sure. In the first place, I don't know whether to believe anything Rashid told us. But the Iranian angle is one we haven't fully explored. We do know that Faisal Husseini's imam has connections to some radical Iranian mullahs, but that seems like a dead end if Faisal's group wasn't involved."

"But if they were involved," Emma speculated, "that could explain how Faisal's brother would know of an Iranian connection." She paused, then added, "Just because you got him off doesn't mean he didn't do it."

Abe understood her unspoken subtext. A decade earlier, Abe had secured an acquittal for a famous basketball player who'd been charged with rape. It later turned out that he in fact was guilty. He subsequently tried to rape Emma. It was a horrible experience for the then high-school senior.

"I know that, Emma," Abe said softly. Glancing around at

his team, he instructed them, "Look, we're back in the realm of speculation, which is no substitute for hard research. Let's get to work. Rendi, check out everyone in the security detail. Particularly those who survived. If someone did it for money, he wasn't a suicide bomber. Habash, you check out the Iranians, through your sources, with an eye on whether Faisal's group had any connections with them. Emma, I want you in the library. Away from danger. You've been kidnapped, threatened with jail. Enough. Stay out of harm's way."

"Oh, Daddy, I can take care of myself," she scoffed.

"Need I remind you who got you freed from the kidnappers and from jail? You may be running out of luck. The library work is important. First you can research more about Dennis Savage's weird friend in Megiddo. Does he have any connections to Iran? Stranger things have happened. Then I want you to find out everything you can about this twelfth-imam business and what these zealots believe is needed to help him come back. It's important. It may hold the key."

"I'll help Emma and keep an eye on her," Habash volunteered.

Emma smiled shyly and lowered her head. Their eyes met, and Rendi nudged Abe to see if he saw the lovebirds as she did. Apparently he didn't — he still felt that there was some tension between them.

"That's fine, but I need you to do something else, too. I need you to snoop around the Shia rumor mills. Find out what they're saying to each other. See if they're talking about any Iranian connections. You must have Shia friends."

"More like acquaintances, but my family has some connections. I'll find out what I can."

"And everyone be careful. No one seems to want us to get the truth here. Everyone seems to be covering for someone. The closer we get, the more dangerous it will be."

XLVII

The Rest of Avi's Story

THE PAST COUPLE OF WEEKS had been torture for Habash Ein. Emma was back, and they were dating casually — afternoon coffees, walks after work — but she was distant. She wasn't her usual vibrant self.

At first Habash suspected that it was the aftereffects of her kidnapping. She deflected the topic whenever he broached it, and Habash decided it was the rift with Rendi over Dennis Savage that was weighing on her. And then Rashid was arrested, and Abe took the case. Emma's mind was on the possibility she might go to prison for not testifying.

So as the two of them walked through Independence Park, Habash realized that since that first date Emma had never let him take her to Shimshon's. And while they worked during the day, Emma kept a respectable distance from him, especially if Abe and Rendi were present.

All at once it clicked into place.

Her family didn't approve.

He felt suddenly bereft, but he understood. He himself hadn't told his parents or brothers about his new relationship. And he recalled his own initial hesitancy about getting involved with a Jewish woman.

"Let's sit," he said.

Emma followed him to a row of benches situated in front of a garden walk. The scent of flowers filled the dusk air, and she reached for Habash's hand. "This is a beautiful place," she said wistfully.

"A garden in the desert," he concurred.

"Like us."

"What do you mean?" He turned toward her and placed one knee on the bench between them.

She smiled. "I mean, with all the intrigue and suspicions and danger here, this"—she pointed back and forth between the two of them—"has been a refuge."

Habash released her hand and stretched his arm across the top of the bench, behind Emma's shoulders. "I wanted to talk to you about that."

Emma groaned. "Oh, no. You're not going to try to back out of this again, are you?"

Habash looked at her intently. "Do you want me to?"

A blush overtook her face. "Of course not."

"You don't bring me to Shimshon's anymore."

Now the red color deepened. "You were right. He doesn't approve. He keeps telling me stories about his great-great-grandfather Avi and his troubled romance with a local girl named Rachel."

"I know that story. It's in a book that's well known in Israel. Remember that Avi and Rachel were both Jews," Habash stated. "So what does it have to do with us?"

"Avi was an Ashkenazi Jew and Rachel was a Sephardic Jew, and her family was adamantly opposed to them being together."

Habash's arm dropped to her shoulder. "The history of this place, of your family, has affected you more than you expected, I think."

Emma nodded. "It really has. Before I came here, I laughed whenever my father preached about the family history and its relevance. But now I see that a person's history directly affects his or her present."

Her voice was melancholy. It wasn't an emotion Habash often heard from her. "Do you want to stop seeing me?" He asked the question quickly, and it came out more bluntly than he intended.

She looked shocked and surprised. "No! You're my garden in the desert, even though I know that Shimshon is adamant that our relationship is doomed the way Avi and Rachel's relationship was doomed."

"Doomed? No way. Shimshon probably told you only the beginning of the story, because he wanted you to know about the difficulties of intercultural relationships. But there was more to the story. I know, because it involved my family as well. You need to hear how it eventually turned out."

Now Emma was really annoyed at Shimshon. He had told her only part of the story—a half-truth. She was anxious to hear the good parts that he'd left out. "Tell me," she said, moving a bit closer to Habash.

He held Emma's hand as he told her how Avi had learned of the stabbing of a Jewish merchant in Jaffa by two radical Arabs. The victim was Baruch Ezratti, the man to whom Rachel was engaged. His death, a week later from his wounds, left Rachel unattached.

After he learned of the man's death, Avi spent day and night in deep contemplation. Baruch had been killed by two Arabs in retaliation for the murder of Ali Barakit by Gershon Kahana. Everything was so closely connected in the history of this tiny but explosive part of the world, Emma thought as she listened to Habash recount the story of Avi and Rachel.

It pained Avi greatly that his first thought was not sadness over the death of Baruch, whom he had never met, but rather excitement about what Baruch's death might portend for Rachel — and for them. Then he quickly realized there could still be no "them." He was still an Ashkenazi "goy" to Rachel's family. He imagined Rachel's pain over the loss of her fiancé and then fantasized about the guilt her ambivalence over losing a man she didn't love must have caused her. But it was not an ambivalence she could act on. Only after that realization set in could Avi begin to consider the implications of Baruch's murder for the Jews of Palestine and for relations with their Arab neighbors.

Days later Chaim Mizrachi arrived at Rishon L'Zion looking for Avi. They had not been in communication since that fateful day when Chaim told Avi never to see Rachel again. The two men silently embraced as Avi whispered the Jewish words of condolence for a departed relative.

"I'm here on a mission," Chaim said. "A mission on which no one sent me."

Chaim had a look of sorrow in his eyes as he described his mission. "I have spoken neither to Rachel nor to her parents, but I want you to visit Rachel and try to comfort her."

"That will be difficult for me if I know that I still can't be with her."

"I cannot speak for Rachel or for her parents, but I can speak for myself, Avi," the older man said, gently placing an arm around the younger man's shoulder. "If Rachel will have you as her husband, your marriage will have my blessing. Baruch's death has convinced me of two things. It was not God's will that Rachel marry Baruch. Why else was Baruch picked to die? This is a new world in which we must work together. Your marriage to Rachel will symbolize the breaking down of old walls."

Avi was ecstatic, but he tried to keep his feelings under control as he responded to the older man. "I don't know about the God part, Chaim, but I do know that I love Rachel. I'm sorry that Baruch was killed. I don't want to see Rachel unhappy."

Chaim bent his head and instructed Avi, "Go not as a suitor, but as a friend offering solace. As far as God is concerned, He works in mysterious ways. Usually a young woman like Rachel who loses her betrothed remains unmarried, because all the men from good families have been spoken for. So now God has sent new men — good men like you and Akiba — from faraway places. God sent you for Rachel. I was His unknowing messenger sent to meet you on the ship. It is God's will."

"As long as it's Rachel's will and has your blessing, I will go to her."

"The rest is in God's hands."

Avi smiled, thinking that God had already done His part of the job. The rest was now up to Avi.

"So what happened?" Emma asked anxiously.

Habash smiled as he told her about Avi's trip to Jaffa. Rachel was at home with her mother and sisters, greeting visitors who were stopping to pay their respects to the family. After hours of listening to people's condolences, she felt ready to scream.

Just then Avi walked in. He was dressed as she'd never seen him. Gone were his khaki shorts and linen shirts. In their place were a dark suit and a hat. His eyes were full of sadness. He didn't approach her. Rather he stood in the doorframe and spoke softly. "I came to pay my condolences to my teacher, Rachel."

She said nothing. A fresh set of tears streamed down her face.

"It makes me sick to see you so unhappy." Still he stood in the doorway.

She dried her face with one of Baruch's handkerchiefs and found her voice after a moment. "Thank you, Avi. I was hoping you might come, but I couldn't be certain they would let you in."

"Chaim knows I am here," he told her soberly.

Suddenly Rachel's grief lifted. Her quick mind figured it all out, but she was not certain enough to speak the words she felt in her heart.

Avi's gaze never wavered. He trained his eyes on hers as if he were trying to assure her that they were going to be together. His eyes were all he could rely on; it was too soon to speak the words.

"Baruch was like a brother to me." Rachel gestured him toward two upholstered chairs, and they sat.

"Baruch was a good man. Everybody says so," Avi said lamely.

"He was so happy. He was looking forward to our wedding. He even learned how to dance."

Their conversation progressed with difficulty. Rachel yearned to hear Avi express his feelings, to repeat what he'd said those weeks before in the restaurant on the water: that he wanted to marry her. But they both knew it was too soon. She wished for time to pass quickly so that their hearts could speak. For now she turned away modestly whenever he looked into her eyes. It was her proper role. She was a mourner, not the object of a suitor's affections. She also knew that her eyes were a window to her heart—a window she could not close as easily as she could her mouth. Avi understood. They each showed their love by discreetly concealing it. There was a place for secrets, as she had always suspected.

Avi returned to Rachel's home every day for the next week.

When the thirty days of mourning were over, Rachel stopped wearing black. There were still a few tears, but also a few smiles. On the first visit after the mourning period, Avi softly reached for her hand. It was the first time they had ever touched. Rachel pulled away, not because she resisted his touch, or even because she thought it inappropriate. It was a purely physical reaction to the electricity of the touch itself. It was a touch at once so tender and so powerful that it left nothing in doubt. Rachel threw herself at Avi, kissing him fiercely. It was her first passionate kiss, as it was his. They both felt it in their hearts as well as their loins. It was a kiss of love and passion. The kind of kiss Rachel had believed she would never experience.

"I cannot spend my entire life staring out windows. I will marry you," Rachel said insistently. "Even if my parents don't approve. I want to have children with you. Live with you. Die with you. Be buried next to you."

Avi's heart was entirely too full. "I love you, Rachel." They kissed each other again and stopped only when Rachel's maid entered the room. After a shriek from the maid and a quick bribe from Avi, he whispered feverishly in Rachel's ear, "When can we be married?"

"In a year." She pushed him away from her so that there was a decent distance between them. The maid pointedly looked the other way. "Any sooner would not be proper. You must ask my father. But I will lay the foundation first. I will speak to Chaim. He will know what to say."

Avi kissed each of her fingers. "As far as I'm concerned, you already said it. You will marry me. That's all I need to know. I hope your parents will approve. I want our children to know their grandparents. They will have no grandfather on my side and may never see their grandmother in Poland. They will need your parents."

"Where will we live, Avi?" Rachel asked with joy in her voice. She couldn't keep herself from giggling.

"That depends on where we want our children to grow up," Avi replied.

"I want our children to work the land, to be the new kind of Jews this country can produce. I don't want them to be merchants," Rachel insisted.

Avi remained silent. He understood what Rachel was saying. She didn't want her children to be like Baruch or Chaim or the rest of her family. She wanted them to be like him, a *chalutz*—a pioneer. Avi did not want to appear to be overanxious to agree. It would look self-serving. But it was also what he wanted for his children. It was important to Avi that Rachel was not simply trying to please him. There was no need for that. This was really what she wanted. It all made sense: her love of teaching, of meeting new people, especially new immigrants. A part of her always wanted to break away from her past and move to the future. He was her vehicle. He was also her true love. It was all too good to be true, Avi thought. "Too good to be true," he mused aloud. "That's the old way, the Polish way, the Yiddish way. We were always worried about giving an *ayin hara*—an evil eye—to any good news. Here things are different. Nothing is too good to be true."

When Habash completed his tale, Emma couldn't speak. It was incredible to think that such a love story was a part of her own history. "How do you know all this?" she asked.

"Avi and Rachel wrote to each other every day between the time they agreed to marry and their wedding day. After they died, their grandchildren found their letters and published them. It was a bestseller, because it told an important part of Israel's early history." Then, pausing, Habash continued, "It also had implications for my own family."

"How so?"

"Remember Avi's Muslim partner, Ali? After his murder, his wife, Leila, had had enough of her brother Mustafa and those who breathed hatred. So she moved to Nazareth, to live among the community of Christian Arabs there."

Suddenly something connected in Emma's mind. "No!" She smiled broadly and touched Habash on the arm. "So?"

"That's right. Leila met and married Marcus Ein, my great-great-grandparents. My great-grandfather's name was Ali."

"After her murdered husband," Emma supplied. "What happened to Mustafa?"

Habash shook his head. "He became a leader of the local Muslim Brotherhood and eventually was killed in a shootout with a Jewish defense group from a kibbutz near Jaffa, but not before he had the blood of dozens of Jews on his hands. His two sons became followers of the grand mufti and participated in the Hebron Pogroms of 1929 in which nearly one hundred Jews were murdered. The grand mufti, Hajj al-Husayni, was a great-uncle of Faisal and Rashid. Small world, no?"

"What happened to Avi and Rachel?" Emma wondered.

"They had a relatively happy life together. Shimshon didn't want to tell you that part of the story." Habash pulled her close to him. "Now do you think we can have a happy ending?"

Emma leaned in and kissed his cheek. "I'm more interested in beginnings than in endings," she said. "I just want to respect my family's attitudes unless we become more serious."

Habash was thrilled. "Then let's get more serious," he said, just before kissing her passionately.

XLVIII

The Discovery

I TOLD YOU IT WASN'T in the football." Denny smiled at Rendi over coffee in a Jerusalem café. Rendi had called him and asked to meet for coffee; she hadn't seen or spoken with him since Abe had discovered the information about him and the Church of the Apocalypse. During Rashid Husseini's trial, the Ringel family had been focused on other things. But now that their investigation of the American Colony had resumed full bore, Rendi wanted to clear Dennis's name once and for all. She was sure that if Dennis had met with Ruggles, it had been a covert operation, not a conversion. She assumed that he'd been on a mission, though for which agency she could only guess. And the best way to get to the bottom of the Savage mystery was by direct contact.

When she saw Dennis at the restaurant, she was consumed with an overprotective feeling. Here was one of her dearest friends, and he had no idea that he was being investigated by her husband. She felt, oddly, that she was betraying Dennis's faith in her. She thought about immediately coming clean, about telling him what Abe had uncovered, but she didn't want to put him on the defensive or make him feel unjustly persecuted. And maybe — just maybe — Abe was onto something. So when she was done with small talk, she told Dennis that she and Abe were focusing on Iran.

He crossed his ankle over his knee casually and leaned back, his broad athlete's build making it seem as if he were about to break his chair. He looked just as he always did — relaxed, open, and friendly. Rendi realized with a sudden shock that she was relieved. Abe had gotten her so turned around; she was half expecting Dennis to whip out a Bible or something.

"We're focusing on the Iranians, too. They fit the profile, and I had my people analyze the explosive," Dennis said.

"And?" Rendi asked, curious.

"It's consistent with possible origination in Iran. We know they're working on a small plastique nuclear trigger that would fit in their Shahab missile."

Rendi understood the term "consistent with." It was an intel fudge. More than guesswork, less than hard evidence. She decided not to press the issue, at least not directly. For her this was good news. If there was proof that Iran had created the plastique involved in the explosion, then the focus would move away from the Church of the Apocalypse and Denny's relationship to it.

Now all she had to do was find out what the Americans really knew about the execution of the crime. She put her chin in her hand and glanced at him. "How do you think they got the bomb past security?"

"We haven't figured that out yet. There are ways. Bribery,

false-flag operations. Deep moles. Good intelligence agencies can figure out ways to breach security."

She ignored a tiny voice in the back of her mind telling her that if anyone could get past multiple security agencies, Dennis could. He was as good as they got. Instead she returned the conversation to Iran. "And the Iranians are good."

Dennis smiled. His dimples danced on his face. "Good as any of the bad guys get. And they are all over Hamas. They could have gotten a Hamas security agent to become a suicide bomber and carry the bomb to the stage. What else did Rashid tell you?"

"Not much." Rendi shrugged. "He was evasive."

"Was he sure it wasn't Palestinians of any persuasion?"

"Positive. Also not Americans, Israelis, or Christians."

Denny looked pleased. Rendi noted that he placed his folded hands in his lap. "That's what we think."

"What have you come up with for motive?"

Dennis didn't answer; he merely looked at her expectantly, so she continued, "We're looking into the twelfth-imam business."

This was as comfortable as she felt broaching the topic of the Church of the Apocalypse, and yet her comment landed between them like a small bomb. Dennis's eyes widened ever so slightly, and his posture slowly straightened. "The Americans haven't gotten that far."

All of Rendi's senses became instantly more alert. "So you haven't investigated any like-minded groups? Religious sects with an apocalyptic bent?"

Dennis raised her slight smile with a full-on grin. "Not that I know of." Rendi quickly noted his hands. They were in his lap. "Rendi, not many people know me the way you do."

Her heart began to beat quickly, but she was careful to

maintain a placid demeanor. With all sincerity she responded, "Me, too, Dennis. You're one of the people I trust the most."

He covered her hand with one of his own. "So I'm going to tell you something."

Rendi breathed purposefully, hoping to keep calm.

Dennis picked up his head and leveled a steady gaze at her. "We have more than just 'consistent with.' We have an actual chemical match between the plastique used in the explosion and a secret lab in Tehran."

Out of the corner of her eye, Rendi once more noted Dennis's hands. They were again in his lap. She couldn't make heads or tails of it. Denny never deliberately misled her.

"What kind of chemical match?" she asked. "Narrow or broad? What possibility of a false positive?"

Dennis said, "There's always a possibility with these kinds of tests, especially with chemicals degraded by an explosion like that."

"So...what? Ten percent probability of a match? Fifty percent? What?"

"More than ten, less than fifty, but not much less. It's a pretty good match."

Rendi was quiet. If the Americans were able to prove that the Iranians had killed their president, there'd be a demand for retaliation from the public and perhaps from intelligence agencies.

"What are you waiting for? Why not announce your findings and take action against Iran?" she said at last.

Dennis stretched his legs. "You know why. We have to be one hundred percent sure on this, especially after the WMD fiasco in Iraq. And it could be a false flag—maybe another group has set it up to look like it was Iran. Maybe even the Israelis. They'd love to see us bomb Iran and destroy its nuclear program. Maybe they're setting up the Iranians. Anyway, before we'd act, we would coordinate with Israel, if they weren't trying to pull the wool over our eyes. I'm sure you know that your husband's client Faisal's group has some Iranian connections through their imam. That's why the Israelis were so anxious to convict him. Anything that connects the bombing to Iran, even indirectly, helps their cause. Still, the Israelis have great intel on Iran, particularly on the ground. They believe Iran had a hand in it, and they're trying to convince us of that. I think they may be right, but we're in no rush. The Iranians aren't going anywhere anytime soon."

"Unfortunately," Rendi added.

Before they could continue, a call came through to Denny's cell phone. He checked the incoming number, chose not to answer, and stood. Kissing Rendi's cheek, he explained that he had business to take care of. She watched him leave the café, her mind processing everything he'd said—and *not* said. She'd hoped to be able to leave this coffee date with definitive answers, even though in the world she and Dennis occupied, definite answers weren't easy to come by.

She felt certain that Denny wasn't telling her everything. This in itself wasn't an indicator of his being complicit in anything illegal. Her infiltration theory was still a strong possibility—far more consistent with what she knew about him than Abe's conversion theory was. Rendi knew that in her and Dennis's kind of work not everything could always be shared, especially not an infiltration, but she wasn't sure Abe or Emma would accept that. She was just going to have to investigate the Megiddo connection herself. Without telling Abe.

XLIX

Armageddon

THE NEXT MORNING Rendi woke early, kissed Abe's forehead, and told her groggy husband that she'd be out all day. Then, arming herself with printouts of Emma's research into Revelation Ruggles and his church, she rented an SUV and drove north toward the biblical town of Megiddo, known in English as Armageddon — a corruption of the Hebrew *Har Megiddo*, the Mountain of Megiddo. She was determined to learn more about the religious group that had allegedly saved Denny's life and to clear him of the unfounded suspicion that Abe seemed to have of him. Who was the strange man named Revelation Ruggles? What did his family's history — going back to Avi Regel and before — tell us about his motives? Did he have any connection to Iran — was that the angle Dennis had been working on when he'd infiltrated them?

Megiddo, in biblical times a bustling center of activity, was now a kibbutz in the Jezreel Valley with a tiny population of under five hundred people. Tel Megiddo, a small hill, had become a center of archaeological excavation and was a major tourist attraction. In 2005, Israeli archaeologists discovered the remains of an ancient Christian church there, thought to be the oldest in the world.

Christian fundamentalists flocked to the ruins of the church. Since there were few hotels in the area, it had become a favorite spot for camping. Squatters put up a few shacks in wooded areas not too far from the Tel. One of these shacks served as the Church of the Apocalypse, where Revelation Ruggles lived in ascetic simplicity.

Rendi checked in to the modest guesthouse in Kibbutz Megiddo, posing as a journalist—a cover she'd used successfully in the past. She didn't intend to stay the night but thought the staff at the guesthouse would be a good source of local information. Upon checking in, she was given a pamphlet about the history of the kibbutz, which was established after World War II by Holocaust survivors.

"Aren't you afraid to live in the place where the final battle is supposed to be fought before the End of Days?" she asked the old man who checked her in. She was tired from the long drive and anxious for human contact. But also, she knew from her spy days that information often came from the unlikeliest of sources. Striking up innocent conversations sometimes led to important bits of information.

The man handed her a key and showed her the number tattooed on his arm. "We've lived through the End of Days. The future doesn't frighten us."

Rendi paused. The man pulled his arm away and returned to his business behind the desk. She looked around the guesthouse's main room, hoping to find pamphlets about the Church of the Apocalypse. There weren't any.

"Excuse me, sir?" she asked the man. He looked up from

the book he was reading. "Could you tell me about Revelation Ruggles?"

"I know who he is. There are several so-called prophets who moved in around here after they found the old church. It's good for business. They don't hurt anyone. We leave them alone. They leave us alone."

"Does anyone in the kibbutz have any direct contact with Ruggles?"

"What are you? A tax collector? He doesn't have any money. That's for sure."

Rendi shook her head and smiled at the crotchety old man. He was impervious to charm. "No. I'm thinking of writing something about the Church of the Apocalypse."

The man peered at her, scratched his head, and returned his attention to his book. "There's a man in the kibbutz, Sali Gibon, who has spoken to him. Fourth house down the street."

"Thank you," Rendi said, but she needn't have bothered. The man was absorbed in his reading.

She walked up the stairs to her small room. Sitting on the bed, she spread Emma's research out on the coverlet, quickly rereading each page. Then she called Abe.

"Where are you?" he asked immediately, without even a proper greeting.

"Hello to you, too," Rendi joked. "I'm checking on a few things. Nothing to worry about."

Abe made a disappointed sound. "This is about Dennis, isn't it? I want us to be on the same side, you know."

"We *are* on the same side, Abe. I'm doing research, just as you asked."

Her evasive answers didn't fool her husband in the least. "You know I hate it when you're so secretive."

"Then it's a good thing we met after my spy days," she replied dryly.

"Rendi, just be careful, and be in contact. I can't take any more danger to the people I love," he said, ending the call.

Rendi felt a pang of guilt. She hated to be in conflict with Abe, especially now, after the ordeal with Emma's abduction. But she knew that he was wrong about Dennis, and this was the only way to prove it.

After splashing some cold water onto her face and freshening up, Rendi walked down the block to a small wood-frame house. A young man answered her knock. He wasn't more than twenty-five, and, judging from his tan skin, he spent a lot of time outside. Rendi looked past him into his house, searching for religious articles on the walls or tables. She couldn't see much, though. "Hi, my name is Rendi," she said, extending her hand. She smiled her most dazzling smile at him. In her experience she'd found that a little bit of beauty and a lot of flirting often softened the tersest of informants. Especially those who didn't know they were informing. "Can I ask you something?"

The man shook her hand absentmindedly, staring at her while he did. She guessed he must not come into contact with many women, because he was all but drooling. He didn't appear to be very bright, and he was unconcerned that a stranger had appeared at his door. She saw that his hands were dirty. "Sure. Ask away." His attempt at a flirtatious grin was deplorable. He was missing three teeth.

But his open manner inspired Rendi to be forthcoming. "What can you tell me about Mr. Ruggles?"

The man leaned against the side of his door and crossed his arms over a ratty T-shirt. "You mean the old guy in the shack" — he gestured down the street — "or his son?"

Rendi followed his gesture with her eyes but didn't see anything of note. "I didn't know he had a son. Let's start with the old guy."

"Revelation. Weird name, huh? He's some kind of religious figure. People come to see him. Not too many. And not too often. Mostly he stays to himself."

"The man who owns the guesthouse down the street told me that you'd met him."

He shook his head and smiled his toothless smile. "I sell fertilizer, among other things. He needed some. You need some?"

Rendi schooled her expression, but her heart started beating rapidly. This was a lead. "No, thank you. Was it for his garden?"

"I guess, though he has only a tiny garden and he ordered a lot. I was out there on deliveries four or five times. He always paid in cash. Maybe he has another garden somewhere in the woods."

Rendi took a breath. "I'm writing an article on his church. What can you tell me about it?"

"He wouldn't let me in. He said only believers could enter. I didn't want to go in anyway. I could see inside, and it was weird. There were calendars all over the wall. Dozens of them. Marked in different colors. It didn't look like a church, although there was a crucifix with a very bloody Jesus. It grossed me out."

Rendi said a silent prayer of thanks. If only all her witnesses were this helpful. The poor man hadn't even asked her who she was. "Did you ever see any of his followers?"

"Once, when I came to deliver the fertilizer. I think he was an American. Tall, blond, crew cut. Looked American. Could have been Swedish. I'm not sure. Another time his son pulled up with a truck as I was leaving."

Tall. Blond. Crew cut. That matched Denny. Again her heart picked up speed. Logic told her there weren't too many Swedish-looking Americans in this part of the world. This didn't prove

that Dennis had become a worshipper or a believer. It only indicated that he'd met with Ruggles. Perhaps the American agencies had learned about the fertilizer purchase and sent Denny to
investigate? But how to explain his first meeting with Ruggles,
after he'd been shot? That had been years before....

The man, not realizing he was interrupting the dozens of
thoughts racing through Rendi's mind, asked, "Why don't you
write something about the kibbutz? It's a lot more interesting
than a church in a shack with calendars on the wall."

"Maybe I will," Rendi said as she shook Sali's hand and
thanked him. He leered at her once again, told her to come by
anytime she needed fertilizer, and then disappeared into his
house.

Rendi considered calling Abe to tell him what she'd found out
about the fertilizer, but she didn't want to worry him. Nor did
she relish another argument with him about Denny. She decided
that she'd contact Abe once she'd spoken with Revelation.

Revelation Ruggles's shack was only a few miles away. Getting
into her car, she followed a map the owner of the guesthouse
gave her and passed the path to the small shack several times in
an effort to get a good look. There was a truck parked near the
shack; she wondered if it was the same truck that Sali had mentioned. If it was, then it belonged to his son.

Rendi parked her SUV about a mile from the path to the
church and walked the remaining distance to the shack. She
checked her cell phone on the way to see if Abe had called her;
he'd promised he would if he, Habash, or Emma came up with
any information on the security details and their possible connection to Iran. There were no messages. She continued to hike,
remembering how she hated the heat of the desert. *If I decided
to chuck civilization and live in a shack, I'd do it on a lake,* she
thought.

Fifteen minutes later she knocked on the door of the Church of the Apocalypse. The truck was gone, some dusty tire tracks in its place. The man who answered was rail thin and had a long, dirty beard. His hair was down to his waist, covering the ribs that poked out through his yellowed skin. He wore pants and nothing else: no shirt, no hat, no shoes.

"Hello, Reverend." She didn't offer her hand, mostly because he looked so dirty that she didn't want to touch him. "I was hoping to talk to you about your church."

"Are you a Christian?" Ruggles asked suspiciously.

"No, I'm not," Rendi answered.

Revelation stepped outside the shack and closed the door. "I'm sorry, then, but you cannot enter the church. How did you hear about us?"

"I came because my husband heard about you from Elizabeth Mitchell."

Revelation's eyes softened, and he warmed up to Rendi instantly. "A fine woman. I've known her family for years."

"I'm thinking of writing something about your church."

Revelation stepped back into his shack, speaking as he went. Rendi had to run to catch his words. "We do not want to be written about. People will not understand us. We do not want people to understand us. We are a small church of believers."

"How many are you?" she asked quickly, moving closer to him.

"I cannot continue the conversation. I do not want to be rude, but you must go now. I want to be alone."

He tried to shut the door in her face, but she jammed a foot inside the doorframe. "Can you tell me about your son?"

"We are private people. Good day," he said, kicking her in the shin so that she'd move her foot. He closed the door quickly, but not before Rendi caught a glimpse of the calendars and the bloody crucifix.

She stood staring at the closed door for several moments and then set off for her car. When she returned to the guesthouse, she placed a call to a friend who worked in the Israeli telephone company — at least that was his cover. He was a Mossad operative who could find anyone. He told her that there were only six Ruggleses in all of Israel: Ecclesiastes in Tel Aviv, Job in Eilat, Revelation in Megiddo, Romans in Jerusalem, and Kings in Ashkalon. Lamentations was the only other Ruggles. He lived in Haifa, at 12 Palmach Street. This was Revelation's son — the son with the truck.

Armed with an address and a phone number, Rendi got into the SUV and drove to Haifa, headed toward Lamentations' house. She found the street with no trouble and walked to number 12. She knocked. No answer. She knocked again. This time she thought she heard a slight noise from inside. Maybe a dog or cat. She tried to look inside through the window, but the drapes were shut tight. She went around the back to see if there were any windows through which she could take a peek inside, but every one was covered tightly with drapes, curtains, or shades. Then Rendi smelled something peculiar. She couldn't immediately identify the smell, but it was familiar. She sniffed again. Then she remembered. *Fertilizer.* She bent down and dug up a small sample of dirt from the ground and put it in her handkerchief. Again she heard a slight noise. She looked up just in time to see the window shade move ever so slightly in an upstairs room. She was being watched. She returned to her car and drove back to the guesthouse in Megiddo.

She walked quickly over to Sali's house and knocked on the door.

When he saw her, he opened his door wider so that she could enter. "You've decided to write about the kibbutz? Come in."

She stayed where she was, on the stoop. "No, not yet, but I

have a question for you. Does this sample of earth contain fertilizer?" she asked, opening her handkerchief.

The man bent over her open hand and inhaled. "Sure does. Where is it from?"

"It doesn't matter. Can you tell whether this is the fertilizer that you sold?"

Sali picked up a bit of fertilizer on his finger. "I can't, but somebody can. The government makes everyone tag their fertilizer with a chemical ID. They did that after the Oklahoma City bombing in the United States."

Rendi didn't respond to him—her mind was racing too quickly. She carefully rewrapped her handkerchief around the sample, placed it in her bag, and began to walk away. As she did, she heard Sali call after her, "You're not really a writer, are you?"

As she headed for her car, she left Abe a message saying that she wouldn't be home until the next day.

L

God's Work

I CAME AS SOON AS I COULD," Denny said to Revelation Ruggles as he sat down at a small table in Lamentations' home in Haifa. The old man sat on a chair, balanced on its very edge. His spine was completely erect, and his hands were folded at his knee. Denny noted that his hands shook ever so slightly, and the old man hardly ever showed emotion. A knot of dread settled in Denny's stomach. "What does she know?"

"Too much," the old man said. "She knows about Lamentations. And we think she knows about the fertilizer."

Dennis inhaled slowly.

"She was sneaking around my yard," Lamentations complained. He looked nothing like his father. His hair was cropped close to his head, and he wore fashionable clothes. He worked for an insurance agency in Haifa and looked every inch the part of a conservative businessman. The truth about him was more elusive. He'd gone to school in Macedonia, where he'd studied chemistry.

"Did she find the laboratory?" Dennis asked.

"I don't think so," Lamentations replied begrudgingly. "But she took some dirt samples. They could contain some traces of chemicals in addition to fertilizer."

"Has *anyone* been near the new lab?" Now Dennis was agitated. He rose to his feet and walked back and forth between Lamentations and Revelation. He'd never been comfortable with the idea of operating their lab at Lamentations' home—were anyone ever to suspect them, it would be too easy to locate.

When the elder Ruggles had called him to say that a woman had been asking questions, he knew that it was Rendi before Ruggles even described her. They'd known each other too long. Then, when Revelation mentioned that the woman's husband had spoken with Elizabeth, it was only a matter of time before Dennis discovered Abe's connection to Arthur Eidelman. Dennis hadn't been surprised. He didn't like Dr. Eidelman.

"No," Lamentations answered Dennis's question about their lab. "We have it booby-trapped and wired. And only the initiated know about it."

"Is there any way Elizabeth could have found out?"

"She knows nothing," Revelation said calmly. "Only the ten initiated know, and only we know who among the believers are initiated. I trust them all. The six of us here in Israel, the two in America, the one in Iran, and the one in Russia. But now this woman suspects something."

"What should we do?" Lamentations beseeched his father.

"She must be silenced before she tells what she knows," the old man ordered, his eyes meeting Denny's. "Is she still here?"

"Yes," Denny sighed. Ceasing his pacing, he turned to his spiritual leader. "Since you told me about her visiting Lamentations' house, I've monitored her calls and bugged her room and car. She hasn't said anything to anybody, only left her husband uninformative messages. She doesn't trust the Mossad not to be listening to her calls. But I know she's planning to drive back first thing tomorrow and meet Abe."

Revelation raised his hand. "You must stop her and silence her."

It was an instruction that Dennis both expected and dreaded. He had carefully rehearsed his answer so as not to arouse suspicions from his leader that he would have any reservations about doing what he knew he had to. "I know," he said resolutely. "You can count on me."

"I hope so. You failed me once. Your first plan was too complicated. The new plan we are about to implement is elegant in its simplicity." Revelation extended his hand to Dennis, and Dennis knelt next to him.

"This one is going to work," Dennis assured the old man. "And I will stop those who are trying to thwart us," he said, turning his face away so as to hide his sadness.

"Go, my son, do God's work, with my blessing." Ruggles touched Dennis's head, then stood and left the room.

Denny left Lamentations' home with a heavy heart. He knew what he had to do, and it pained him. Rendi had been a friend to him, though she was a nonbeliever. But Dennis recalled his conversation with Revelation after he'd approved Dennis's plan for the bombing of the American Colony, and later when he ordered the poisoning of Faisal Husseini. The master refused to kill a fly or a worm, but he was willing to kill hundreds and, if necessary, thousands of human beings. Denny had respectfully asked him why. The old man looked at Denny and explained.

"These soulless creatures have no life after death. There is no heaven or hell for them. Only the end of all life. They have no fault, no blame. To end their only life is a sin.

"Human beings have souls and free will. Their life here on

earth is a mere prelude to eternity. To believing Christians, death, other than suicide, is of no matter. If they have lived a good life and accepted the Lord, they will live in heaven eternally. If they end up in hell, it is because they exercised free will. A human death is no tragedy. Nor is it a sin to cause it in the name of God."

Denny, who was skeptical about nearly everything and everyone in his professional life, believed in the old man who had miraculously saved his life, and he believed that by following his orders he was killing for the sake of their God and for a higher purpose. He had killed before, to protect his country. Now he was being told to kill someone he loved in order to save the world by destroying it. Rendi had been one of the best friends he'd ever had. She was loyal, discreet, and trustworthy. He knew what his duty was to his master and to his God. He knew he had promised his master that he would fulfill his painful duty. What he did not know — what he could not know until the moment of truth — was whether he could go through with it, whether he could actually end the life of his dear friend Rendi.

LI

The Explosion

W HEN RENDI WOKE the next morning, she reached for her cell phone so that she could tell Abe she was returning home. Sitting up in bed, she saw what she'd seen the night before. No service. She tapped on the monitor of her phone, but it did no good. She was a bit surprised, because in a country as small as Israel there was generally pretty good service. But this was a fairly out-of-the-way place, so she chalked it up to a dysfunctional cell tower. Hopefully, the house phone would be working; last evening it'd been out of order. She got out of bed and ran the shower.

Fertilizer. This didn't connect the Church of the Apocalypse with the American Colony bombing—no trace of fertilizer had been found at that crime scene. But the amount of fertilizer bought from Sali indicated that the church might be planning something new. Rendi hoped that Dennis was aware of this and was working to stop it. But a contrary voice in her head cautioned that if Dennis were a member of the church and wanted to plant a bomb somewhere, it'd be easy. He had connections, money, fame—he could walk into any embassy, state building, or media outlet and do pretty much what he wanted.

She couldn't decide whether her best next step was to get back to Abe so they could plan their next move or to track down Dennis and confront him with what she knew. Either way she was headed back to Jerusalem. After her shower she packed her things, checked out, and walked toward her car. Her cell phone still had no signal. A few feet from her, she saw a man jabbering away on *his* cell phone. Suddenly she began to wonder. She reached into her purse for her car keys. She had rented the SUV from the rental company that serviced the Mossad. They always provided remote ignition keys that started the engine from a distance of fifty feet. Something led her to press the button. As she did, the car exploded in a ball of flame.

She fell to the ground. The man on his cell phone was also thrown to his knees. Rendi dragged herself up, stumbled over to the man, and saw that he wasn't seriously injured. Neither was she—her knees were scraped, and there was a small cut on her cheek, but she was fine. Somebody had planted a bomb in her car. She ran to the guesthouse parking lot, broke the driver's-side window of the first car she saw, threw her luggage in the back, and used the tools she always carried to start the car. She drove away as the guesthouse operator chased after her screaming, "That's my car! Bring it back!"

She drove at breakneck speed, hoping to be stopped by the police so that she could talk them into escorting her to Jerusalem. Someone was trying to kill her! It might be the members of the Church of the Apocalypse, but she couldn't rule out other suspects. Ignition bombs were used by intelligence agencies as well as terrorists and the Mafia. Besides, from what she'd seen of Revelation

Ruggles, he wasn't familiar with sophisticated explosives. Again the nagging voice in her head: *But Dennis Savage sure was.*

No one stopped Rendi. She hit the steering wheel, cursing her bad luck: Israeli drivers were notorious speeders. In fact, several drivers passed her. She looked nervously at each of them, wondering whether they were trying to harm her. After what seemed like a lifetime but was only a bit more than an hour, she arrived in Jerusalem and drove straight to the King David Hotel, where she found Abe sipping coffee with Emma and Habash on the veranda overlooking the old city.

At the sight of her — battered, slightly bloody, and definitely frenzied — Abe and Emma leaped to their feet.

Rendi held up a hand. "Not here. Quick, upstairs to our room."

As the four walked silently through the busy lobby of the hotel to the elevators, Rendi's condition drew gaping looks. Abe couldn't hide his concern, yet she wouldn't let him touch her. She was all business.

When they got to their suite, Rendi stood in the middle of the room and announced, "Someone tried to kill me."

"Oh, my God," Abe replied, putting his arms around her.

She shook off his hug. She didn't want to be tempted by her own emotions, and if she thought about what had happened, she feared she'd be too upset to think rationally.

Abe instinctively understood this. He stepped away from her and asked calmly, "What happened?"

"Abe, I was in Megiddo —"

"Megiddo!" Abe cried.

"Yes, I'm sorry that I didn't tell you, but I was trying to get to the bottom of this Dennis business, and I wanted to do it alone."

Abe's face was a mask of surprise. Rendi had never withheld anything of this magnitude from him before; she'd been cagey about her past, but never about anything in the present day. He was too concerned about her condition to argue with her now. Calmly, he sat on the edge of the bed. "I understand. Now tell me, what happened to you?"

Rendi took an uneven breath before recounting her brush with death and the discoveries that had precipitated it. She showed them the dirt sample and said that it had to be analyzed immediately.

"Who can we give it to, without increasing the danger?" Abe wondered.

"I have a friend," Rendi said shakily. "A guy who specializes in analyzing chemicals. He teaches in the biochemistry department at Hebrew University."

"Can we trust him?" Habash asked.

"I think so. We were very close," Rendi said mysteriously. "Not that way, Abe," she added quickly. "I saved his life once when we were in the field. He was about to come into contact with anthrax, and I tackled him. I'll take the sample over to him this afternoon."

"No," Abe said. "Not you. If Denny is involved in this—and even you have to acknowledge now that he's become a prime suspect—then it stands to reason that he's got the phones here bugged."

"I still don't think it was Denny!" Rendi shouted.

Emma and Habash looked at each other nervously.

Abe stepped to his wife and spoke calmly. "Rendi, you have to accept what's happening here. You said yourself that you asked Dennis about investigating apocalyptic groups. You're telling me that in the course of one day Ruggles could have disabled your phone and rigged your car with explosives? He obviously has the help of a highly skilled operative, Rendi."

She merely shook her head and said quietly, "I know. I know. But still…"

Abe hugged his wife.

"I just can't believe it," she sobbed into Abe's shoulder. "I've known Dennis for years! I know him about as well as I know anybody and I just can't…I *don't* believe it. Maybe someone is trying to frame him," she offered. At her expression of such anguish, Emma and Habash looked away.

Abe rubbed her back in an attempt to soothe her. "Right now the important thing is to get that fertilizer sample to your friend."

"I'll do it," Habash said. "I'll take the sample to him. I've got colleagues at Hebrew University, too, so it'll be easy for me to find him."

Rendi left Abe's embrace and tried to pull herself together. Raising a hand to stop the three of them from jumping into action, she said, "This isn't only about me. We're all in danger. All of us. Whoever blew up my car was trying to stop me from telling you what I found. When they realize I didn't die, they'll assume I've told you my suspicions. We're all in danger."

Emma's face went white, and Habash put an arm around her.

"First, let's get out of this hotel. We're sitting ducks here. Let's go to my cousin's until we sort this out," Abe insisted. "We go by taxi, not any of our cars. No phones. And we'll have to keep away from Pal-Watch for the time being."

They quickly packed their things and took a cab to Shimshon Regel's house. At Regel's, Abe, Rendi, and Emma got out of the cab while Habash sped along to Hebrew University, the dirt sample in his case.

Shimshon opened his door in a welcoming manner, face broad with a smile and eyes shining. That is, until he saw Rendi's condition and Abe's scowl. They hadn't called ahead because they didn't trust their phones, so Shimshon didn't learn what had happened until the Ringels were huddled in his foyer.

"You're safe here," he assured them. "I don't think anybody knows where I live."

Rendi, who knew very well how easy it would be for any intelligence service to track down Shimshon's location, said nothing. It was nice of him, of course, to try to set their minds at ease, but she knew that the four of them couldn't linger at his home. Inevitably it would be found and targeted. "Let's hope not," she said. "The last thing I want to do is endanger your family."

Hanna insisted that Rendi wash her wounds. Rendi initially resisted, but Hanna's maternal manner won out, and she led Rendi gently to an upstairs guest room, where she showered, changed, and allowed herself two minutes to weep. Meanwhile Shimshon brought Emma and Abe into the kitchen, where he made them eat. Emma placed her cell phone on Shimshon's table, so that she'd see immediately if Habash called.

"We told him not to use his phone, remember?" Abe warned.

"I know, Daddy, but I can't stand not knowing where he is. What if Dennis got to him?" Emma was working herself up into a state.

Abe didn't answer. He himself was shocked at the entire turn of events: that Rendi had felt so strongly about Dennis's innocence that she'd gone to Megiddo without telling him, that Abe's suspicions about Dennis were seeming more and more likely to be true, and that his wife had narrowly escaped an attempt on her life.

Just then Habash walked into the kitchen. His face was grim and his posture full of tension. Abe could tell from his expression that his news wasn't good.

"Well?" Rendi asked, entering the kitchen wrapped in a plush purple bathrobe. Other than a few scratches along the side of her face, she looked absolutely fine.

"The sample of earth contains more than fertilizer," Habash announced. "It has traces of ammonium nitrate, which when combined with diesel fuel makes a powerful explosive. Worse yet, it has traces of enriched uranium as well as residue from other chemicals that could be used in making a dirty bomb."

Hanna stifled a noise, and Emma tried to be brave. But Abe and Rendi didn't bother hiding their concern.

"What else did he say?" Rendi referred to her old friend Kobi, the man whose life she had once saved.

"He said that the sample suggested that there was some leakage in their transportation system. He suggested that experts with the right equipment might be able to track the leaked residue to where they're assembling the bomb."

Everyone in the kitchen was quiet. Finally Hanna asked, "Where did you find this dirt?"

"In Israel, not far from Megiddo. In the backyard of Revelation Ruggles's son," Rendi answered. "Someone is making a dirty bomb to be detonated in Megiddo."

"It makes perverse sense," Shimshon commented. "The final battle, the End of Days."

"Or the twelfth imam," Habash added. Rendi and Abe looked to Habash. He continued, "I know you found this in the backyard of a member of a Christian sect, but that's not a smoking gun. It could still be a false-flag operation, involving the Iranians. And the Ruggles family is just a convenient cover."

"The Ruggles family!" Hanna exclaimed.

Emma nodded at Shimshon. "You kept saying that history would solve the mystery," she said sadly.

Abe spoke up. "Maybe Revelation was coerced or bribed into helping the Iranians, though that seems unlikely. Or maybe this is their own plot. Whatever the answer, we've got to stop it. And we've got to answer the sixty-four-thousand-dollar question: How is this connected to the attack at the American Colony Hotel?"

LII

Arish Sopher

THE IRANIANS ARE WORKING on dirty-bomb technology. Actually, they're closer to a dirty suitcase bomb than to a deliverable nuclear warhead."

Abe and Rendi sat in the office of Arish Sopher, an Iranian Jew and the Mossad's main man on the Iranian nuclear program. Arish was a nuclear physicist who had worked for the shah. When Khomeini took over, the Mossad got him out. Then they smuggled him back in with a new Muslim identity. He knew everything there was to know about Iran's nuclear program.

When Rendi first proposed asking him if the Iranians could have been behind the dirty-bomb materials found in the soil behind Lamentations Ruggles's home, Abe balked.

"Can we trust him?" he asked Rendi. When she nodded, he said, "Why? Did you save his life, too?"

"No," she replied. "The other thing. We were an item once. He still cares about me."

And so Abe found himself sitting across from his wife's ex-boyfriend. Normally he'd feel a bit uncomfortable, but the stakes were too high and Rendi insisted that Arish could assist them. Abe was all for asking for help. His only goal was to protect his family, and they were in over their ears in trying to prevent a future crime—nuclear mass murder. He knew they—Team Ringel—weren't capable of stopping it alone. They needed all the help they could get.

Arish sat in a large, overstuffed desk chair. His face was lined with wrinkles, and his skin was ashen, but Abe could see that he was a charming person, if a little messy. His office was crammed full of papers; they were falling out of drawers, teetering in tall piles on his desk, and crowding the floors. He wasn't neat, but he knew his stuff.

"And they're not even working on a World War II 'Fat Man'–type bomb to be dropped from the air, since their air force is incapable of making it past Israel or other air defenses."

"So what do you think?" Rendi pressed, leaning forward and trying not to topple any of the mountains of paperwork between her and Arish.

"There are only five possible sources for the nuclear material you found traces of near Megiddo," he said, reading from the report the scientist at Hebrew University had given Habash. "The first and most likely is Iran. They could have smuggled it in through Syria or Jordan. The second possible source is Pakistan—the Khan network. We know they have sold to Iran. It's possible they have sold to Iran's surrogates. The third is the former Soviet Union. Ukrainian generals have all kinds of nuclear material for sale to the highest bidder. They'll do business with anyone. Fortunately, their biggest customer is the United States, which conducts false-flag operations all over Eastern Europe, buying nuclear material on behalf of 'bad guys' whom their intel operatives pretend to be representing. Fourth is the United States itself—unlikely. American nukes are quite secure."

"And fifth?" Abe asked.

"You won't believe this, but fifth is Israel. A few right-wing fanatics have managed to get jobs in Israel's nuclear facility at Dimona. We're a bit worried that someday one of them might steal some material and give it to fanatical settlers who will use it to prevent being evacuated from the West Bank. Unlikely, but possible. We check very carefully, but we can never be sure of the ideological bent of all our nuclear workers. Remember that traitor Mordechai Vanunu."

"No one is above suspicion here," Abe explained.

"There's only one way to be sure." Arish shrugged, closed the file, and handed it to Rendi. "We'll take possession of the sample and follow its nuclear trail. It's unlikely to lead anywhere. The leakage may not be continuous, but we'll try. More important, we need to get our hands on this Dennis Savage character. He seems to be able to connect all the dots—the American Colony, Megiddo, Iran, Ruggles. Where is he?"

"Last I saw him was in Jerusalem," Rendi said tensely.

"It's possible—probable—that he was in Megiddo yesterday," Abe volunteered. At his side, Rendi stiffened.

Her former boyfriend noticed, too. "You don't think he can help us figure out what is going on?"

Rendi reluctantly admitted, "I think he probably can. I just need to know for sure which side of the law he's operating on with this."

"Or maybe you don't want to know," Abe said, a bit snidely.

Arish waited a moment before speaking. "Then perhaps he won't answer our questions willingly. We'll need to set a trap to get him to surface."

"I don't think that's necessary," Rendi countered.

Abe snapped—he'd finally had it with his wife's obstinate refusal to admit the truth. "You don't think it's necessary! Why don't you pick up the phone and call him, then!"

Rendi stared at her husband helplessly. A long moment passed. Finally she said, in a small, defeated voice, "He wouldn't answer."

Abe breathed heavily and turned to Arish, who had sat with averted eyes during the exchange. His wife had capitulated, he knew, and so now the next thing to do was come up with a plan for getting Dennis into custody. "What do we use as bait?" he asked.

"You," replied Arish, pointing in the general direction of Team Ringel.

"Me?" Abe asked rhetorically. Then quickly he answered his own question. "Okay, I'll be the bait."

"No. It has to be the whole family," Arish insisted. "Savage knows that all of you are aware of what Rendi found. He will bite only if he can get all of you at once."

"No way," Abe retorted. "I'm not putting Emma and Rendi at risk again. No way."

"You have no choice. He will not go after you alone. You must be together."

Abe knew that Arish was right. He also knew that Rendi and Emma would insist on going along with him.

Rendi and Abe left Arish and walked the three blocks from his lab to Mossad headquarters. There the agent in charge cooked up a scheme to lure Savage into action, using the entire Ringel family as bait. Abe agreed to this only once he was assured that a crack Mossad protective squad would always be near them.

Over her cell phone—which had begun to work soon after she'd survived the car bombing—Rendi arranged for a family dinner at the Pomegranate Restaurant, a small natural-foods café on the outskirts of Jerusalem. She suspected that Denny would be monitoring her phone. All the "waiters" were Mossad operatives, as were the "parking attendants," the "chefs," and the other customers. As Team Ringel sat down at an outdoor table to enjoy a dinner of food grown on a local kibbutz, the trap was set. The food was terrible, having been prepared by Mossad "chefs," but the group pretended to be enjoying themselves, wondering if Denny would appear.

After the main course — artichokes in a pomegranate vinaigrette — a car drove up to the front of the restaurant, and a man with a bald head and black goatee got out of it and walked away from the restaurant. Rendi observed this and nudged Abe under the table. When the man was about one hundred feet away, he pressed a button and began to run toward another car, parked around the corner. Mossad agents were waiting for him. They had prepared for a remotely detonated car bomb and had electronically done what they had to do to prevent the bomb from detonating. Abe and Rendi stood as they watched five Mossad agents descend upon the waiting car in front of the restaurant. Rendi gasped as they pulled Denny from the driver's seat.

Abe couldn't stop his wife from running to him. "Please tell me!" she screamed. "Please tell me you're working a job!" Abe, who followed her, desperately trying to corral her, understood what she was saying. She was pleading with him to admit that he was working an undercover assignment.

"Stay back, ma'am," one of the agents commanded Rendi. She didn't heed the order and rushed to where the men had subdued Dennis.

"How? How could you do this?" She was agitated, her fury boiling over.

At first it appeared that Dennis wouldn't say anything, but after a moment of tense silence he spoke softly. "Rendi, I'm sorry.

I had no choice. You could never understand." The Mossad agents dragged him into an unmarked police car.

Rendi felt as if she'd been slapped across the face. She stood on the sidewalk dumbfounded, watching as the car sped away.

There was nothing but silence as a cab drove the four of them back to the King David Hotel. Two undercover policemen escorted Team Ringel and took up residence outside their hotel door. Rendi didn't seem to notice anything, not her husband's attempts to console her or Emma's exclamations of disbelief or Habash's quiet contemplation about what could have caused such a complete transformation in Denny.

They entered the hotel room, and Rendi lay down on the bed.

"Is there anything we should do?" Emma whispered to her father.

"I don't know," replied Abe sadly. He'd never seen his wife take something this hard.

A knock sounded at the door, and Habash went to see who it was. A short, muscular man with pockmarked skin and a tough demeanor entered. He introduced himself as Natan, the chief inspector assigned to Dennis's case.

"Where is he?" Habash asked, accustomed to dealing with the authorities in matters involving the many detainees he had represented over the years.

"Mr. Savage was taken to a secret Mossad interrogation center."

Habash knew what this meant. He translated the man's terse language for Abe. "I know where many of their 'secret' locations are. This is probably the one beneath the cellar of an old British jail near an abandoned Arab village on the outskirts of Jerusalem."

Abe sighed and glanced at Rendi through the door of their

suite. He assumed she could hear their conversation. His wife always heard everything.

"Are you going to torture him?" Abe asked, not wanting to be complicit in any illegalities.

"Not physically," the chief interrogator assured him. "There are better ways, I can assure you, especially for a trained agent like Savage."

"When they're finished with him, he'll *wish* they had used physical torture," Habash said angrily.

"What will you do?" Abe asked.

"We cannot tell you, and you do not want to know. All I can say is that everyone has demons in his past, and we know how to bring the demons back. Our methods require extensive knowledge of our subject. One size does not fit all when it comes to interrogation techniques. But that is why I am here. I want to talk to your wife. We understand she knows him better than anyone. I need to know everything I can about Mr. Savage's past — about his demons."

"I'm not telling you anything," Rendi announced from the doorway between the front room of the hotel and the bedroom. Nobody had heard her approach, and all four of them jumped at the sound of her voice.

"Please, Mrs. Ringel. There are many lives at stake," the inspector pleaded.

But Rendi stepped back into the bedroom and shut the door.

The chief inspector looked helplessly at Abe.

"Give me a minute," Abe said before following Rendi into the bedroom.

When he opened the door, he found Rendi in tears on the bed. The sight stopped him in his tracks. He and his wife had been through so much together, and she almost never cried.

"Rendi," he said gently, approaching her and sitting by her side. "Rendi—"

She took a deep breath and dried the tears from her face.

"I know you care for Dennis—"

Rendi looked at Abe sharply, but he soldiered on.

"I know you care about him, but, Rendi, he may be complicit in the planning of a nuclear attack. Anything you know that could stop it...You have to tell them."

She shook her head sadly. "That man today in the street, who tried to kill us, that's not the Dennis I know and love."

"No," agreed Abe somberly. "He's not the man I've known these years. I can't imagine what could have happened to change him so completely, but I think *you* know."

They met each other's gaze, and Abe saw that he was right. Rendi did know something.

She averted her eyes in an attempt to control her emotions. "In the field, if you can't trust your partner, you're dead. He's trusted me with his secrets for decades, and I've kept them."

Abe tenderly put his hand on her knee. "Rendi, the right thing to do is to help the investigators get information from him. With what's at stake, anything is fair game."

She covered her husband's hand with hers. "I know. I know." Her voice broke.

After they emerged from the bedroom, Rendi sat down next to Natan and looked into his eyes. "I will tell you what you need to know. You may use it to interrogate him. But I need you to promise that you will never publicly disclose it."

"You have my promise," Natan said, putting a hand over his heart.

Rendi then told the interrogators what she knew about Denny's past. As she related the information Denny had confided to her years earlier, Emma's eyes grew wide with shock. Abe then related his conversations with Dr. Eidelman and Nurse Mitchell. The interrogator took notes and then placed several phone calls, speaking in coded language that Team Ringel had difficulty following. Rendi managed to distinguish the word *galech,* which is a Yiddish colloquialism for "priest."

Though she knew she'd done the right thing, she felt terribly guilty for spilling Dennis's sordid secrets. The old Dennis, the Dennis who'd been her friend and saved her life, deserved better than this. But the man who'd tried to kill her and her family did not.

LIII

The Interrogation

D ENNY WAS BROUGHT to the underground interrogation unit blindfolded, gagged, and shackled. After languishing for hours in a small, quiet cell, he was hustled down the narrow stairs to the cellar, and then, after a trapdoor in the floor was opened, he was lowered into a new cell. He was placed in a chair, and the blindfold, gag, and shackles were removed.

"It's no use torturing me. I'm a trained intelligence operative. Your tactics won't work on me. You can torture me, kill me, threaten my family. I won't talk," Denny said with cocky assurance.

"Why would we torture you?" the chief interrogator asked, smiling. "We know that such primitive methods would never work. We just want to ask you two or three questions."

"What are they?" Dennis demanded. He'd been in tight spots before and rarely allowed himself to give in to fear. He was completely confident in his ability to withstand the Israelis' questioning; he believed in the righteousness of his actions, and he trusted that God would come to his aid.

"Where is your nuclear laboratory?" the chief interrogator demanded, looming above Dennis. "What are your plans? Who are you working for or with? Iran? Pakistan? What was your role in the American Colony bombing?"

Dennis smiled calmly, in complete control of his emotions. "I won't tell you anything. I don't fear you. I have my God."

They'd heard that before!

The interrogator stood over Dennis, appraising him. He'd questioned many men and used different tactics for different sorts. This kind of person, an agent of another government who believed that God was on his side, could only be broken emotionally. Physical torture was useless on a man such as Dennis Savage, who was inured to pain or threats. Fortunately for the investigator, Rendi had been thorough with her information. "I want to introduce you to someone from your past," the interrogator said slowly.

"Rendi? Fine," Dennis spit cavalierly. "Bring her in. I can handle her."

"No, not her. Someone from your far more distant past."

Denny was taken off guard by the interrogator's reference and frantically tried to determine who it could be. He didn't have long to puzzle over it. Instantly the door to the cell opened, the lights were lowered somewhat, a strange smell began to spread through the room, and a shadowy figure appeared.

Dennis couldn't see who it was in the darkness.

"Hello, Dennis," the man said. Dennis immediately recognized that working-class Boston accent. "Do you remember me? I'm Father Bulger."

At the mention of that name, Denny tried to stand but couldn't. The room grew darker, and the smell — which he recognized as incense, a smell he was very familiar with from his childhood in the Catholic Church—wafted toward him and mingled with the strong odor of alcohol on Father Bulger's breath. Suddenly he felt a jab in his buttocks, as the interrogator injected him with a drug.

"This will help you relax," the interrogator said in a soothing voice. The effects of the drug were near immediate. Denny grew disoriented; it became difficult for him to remember where he was. He tried to fight it. *This is now. Father Bulger was back then. This is now. It's a trick. Don't fall for it.* Then gradually his mind and his emotions went back to the time when he was a thirteen-year-old altar boy, when Father Bulger would take him to the dark, dank basement of his church.

Denny was transported back to those terror-filled years as he heard Father Bulger issue his frequent demand: "Lower your pants, and we will continue where we left off." As the priest moved closer, young Denny pulled down his own pants. "I know you enjoyed it, as I did. That's why you never told your parents. You didn't want it to stop. But you were afraid. Don't be afraid. I will be gentle, as I always have been with you."

"Get away from me, you pervert!" Denny screamed.

The interrogators forced Savage facedown onto what looked like a massage table. They shackled his hands to the sides of the table, pulled his pants and underpants down, spread his legs and chained them to the sides of the table. As Denny screamed at the top of his lungs, "Father Bulger" walked slowly toward the foot of the table and put his hand on Denny's leg. The disorienting drug was coursing through his veins and making it difficult to distinguish past from present.

"There is nobody here to help you," the priest intoned. "You are alone with me. Your parents know. Yet they do nothing. My superiors know. The police know. They will not help you. Only

I can help you. I am your only true friend. Put your trust in me. Put your trust in me. Tell me what I need to know to save you. Tell me. Tell me."

Denny's disorientation got worse. His mind was a jumble of confusion. The drug increased its effect on his brain, making him drowsy and confused. Was this a dream? Was it real? Was it back then? *Is it now? Is Father Bulger really here?* His emotions took control of his mind. He let out an animalistic scream. Then he blacked out, but only for what seemed like a moment. Unconsciousness would not save him from this descent to a hell that had been the source of his secret nightmares for decades.

Denny continued to scream, loudly at first, as if to drown out the priest's importuning, and then, when it became clear no one was listening, lower. Finally his scream became whimpers. Then acquiescing silence, and ultimately a flow of words and information.

LIV

The Whole Truth

W E GOT WHAT WE NEED, thanks to you," the interrogator said to Rendi as he entered the room where Team Ringel was ensconced. Unwilling to sit in their hotel room waiting anxiously for the interrogators to tell them what they'd learned, Rendi had insisted that the agents take them to the interrogation unit.

They had spent several tense hours in a cold room with only stale coffee to warm them. The mood in the room was heavy. Emma was adamantly opposed to rough interrogation of any kind, and instead of being thrilled to be alive, to have her family alive, she'd been arguing with Abe.

"It's not pleasant, but it will save lives! Thousands, perhaps!" Abe thundered. "Maybe even ours."

Emma refused to see his point. Even when Habash tried to comfort her, she remained angry. Rendi said little throughout.

Her mind was on Dennis, on her former friend. She still felt empathy for him, maybe for the man she'd thought she knew. She felt guilty about revealing the secret of his sexual abuse at the hands of Father Bulger—a secret he'd long ago confided in her because his nightmares were becoming unbearable and because he trusted her never to reveal it. But trust had to be mutual, Rendi had reluctantly concluded when she realized that he'd tried to kill her and had been preparing to kill so many more.

"We know where the lab is located, and we have a nuclear team on the way," the interrogator continued. "It is Iran. You were right, Rendi. Savage told us that. Lamentations Ruggles had met with Iranian agents at an insurance convention in Istanbul. We checked his travel documents, and they confirm the trip. They smuggled the enriched uranium into Haifa in a ship's container from the Republic of Georgia. He also told us that Iranian agents planted the bomb, made from plastique manufactured in Tehran, at the American Colony. They compromised one of the American security people, a Secret Service agent named Roger Blakely, whom Savage had converted to his cause. He planted the bomb in the football, then went to a movie. We've notified the FBI in the United States. The circle is closing."

Abe, Rendi, Emma, and Habash received this news solemnly. Habash removed his glasses and rubbed his eyes. "I was hoping it wasn't Iran. You know that the Israeli government and maybe the Americans will have to retaliate against them, don't you?" he asked the group. "This could cause a major war," he said despondently.

Abe looked at Emma and Rendi. His only thought was to get them out of Israel before Iran could retaliate against an attack, whether with a nuclear-tipped rocket or a dirty bomb. He also worried that the Israeli nuclear team that was on its way to the lab might not make it in time—surely Dennis's people knew that he'd been captured. What if they made a move before he could talk?

Then, suddenly, Abe's skeptical defense lawyer's mind clicked into gear. "Wait a minute!" he shouted. "How can you be sure Denny is telling the truth about Iran? Is there any corroboration for *that* part of his story?"

"He was tortured," Emma said. "He would say anything. Of course he told you what he thought you wanted to hear."

The interrogator put his hands on his hips. "Our methods are infallible. He described the precise location and dimensions of their lab, and we were able to identify a match by satellite photography. It was self-proving. So was the trip to Istanbul and the Iranian source of the plastique. We don't rely on his word, especially because he's a trained agent. We corroborate everything by indisputable physical evidence that can't lie. He also told us about the nature of the upcoming plot. He said that the Iranians had contacted Revelation Ruggles again after the American Colony bombing and that they agreed to work together on detonating a dirty bomb. And he gave us the money guy behind all of it. His name is Bob Buchanan. He's an American. Bankrolled the whole thing."

"If Iran was involved in it, why did Buchanan have to bankroll it? It doesn't make sense," Abe insisted. "My gut is telling me Denny may be telling the truth about the dirty bomb and the plastique in the football but lying about Iran." He turned to Habash. "Hear me out. What if Denny's real purpose is to ignite a war between Israel and Iran? He's a disciple of an apocalyptic religious leader who lives in Megiddo and who is trying to bring about the End of Days."

"Go ahead," the interrogator said, looking warily at Abe. Abe understood that the interrogator would be insulted by any suggestion that Denny had successfully lied to him even about part of his account, but he also knew that the interrogator had to learn the whole truth.

"Okay," Abe began. "Here's what I think happened. It all fits together. Occam's razor."

"Whose razor?" the intelligence officer scoffed.

"Occam's. William of Occam postulated that the simplest explanation — for our purposes the one involving the fewest people — is probably right."

"Well, what is the simplest explanation?" Emma wondered.

"That the Christian cult, funded by the like-minded American, did all this on their own and are trying to bring the Iranians in — to frame them. It's like 9/11," Abe pronounced. He was speaking to his family, Habash, and the investigator as if they were his jury.

"You had me until you said it's like 9/11," Emma countered. "How, exactly?"

"The evil geniuses who planned 9/11 figured out how to use American airplanes as weapons against America. These guys are trying to use America and Israel as weapons to attack Iran as a beginning to the End of Days. Their first attempt at sparking Armageddon was the mass assassination at the American Colony. It failed."

"What do you mean, failed? It killed the president, the prime minister, and so many others," Emma answered.

"Yes." Abe wagged his finger as he made his point. "But it didn't produce the kind of massive retaliation against Iran that they were hoping for. Somehow they managed to get plastique explosives that were 'consistent with' — a fudge — those manufactured in Iran, but that alone didn't prove that Iran planted the bomb. They might have gotten the plastique from Hezbollah, who got it from Iran for use against Israel. The plot was too complicated. It required too many leaps to involve Iran. They left too few clues. It wasn't clear enough to justify a full-scale attack on Iran, certainly not after the WMD fiasco in Iraq."

"They were probably hoping that Husseini's conviction would be enough," Habash speculated. "But your father ruined that approach by proving that his client was innocent."

"That's why they tried to poison Faisal—to protect against the possibility of an acquittal. Everyone believed that Faisal's group did it, but they were wrong," Abe continued.

Emma shook her head. "It may have failed in that sense, but it certainly had an impact on the world."

"Yes, but not the impact they were seeking," Habash said quietly. He quickly understood Abe's theory and was inclined to believe that the defense attorney was right.

Abe smiled at him. "Their End of Days scenario required massive retaliation, hopefully nuclear retaliation, by Israel and/or the United States, which would lead to further retaliation, again hopefully nuclear, against Israel. And remember that the United States has promised to regard a nuclear attack on Israel as an attack on the United States and has pledged massive retaliation."

"The final battle," Rendi added. "Beginning at Megiddo."

"Exactly. The small cult was emboldened by how easy it was for them to kill so many leaders with one blow. Since they were on no one's radar screen, they weren't even suspected. This encouraged them to take it to the next level: a nuclear attack on Israel with even more and clearer Iranian fingerprints. Israel would have no choice but to attack Iran."

"Where did they get nukes?"

"We'll know that as soon as Arish's team gets to the lab," Rendi said.

"Wait a minute," the interrogator interjected. "We know that Denny told us the truth about the lab. Why would he lie about Iran?"

"Because he *could*," Abe replied. "He couldn't lie about the lab. It's either there or it's not. It's self-proving. If you didn't find it where he said it was, he was fearful that you guys would continue whatever you were doing to him — whatever opened his mouth in the first place. But the Iran stuff couldn't be proved or disproved. He knew that if his information about the lab turned out to be true, you would probably believe the Iran accusation, because it seemed so connected and so plausible. He also told you about the trip to Istanbul, which was true and helped to confirm his story. But it doesn't prove that Lamentations actually made a deal with Iranian agents. It does, however, point yet another finger at Iran. It was enough to lead you to believe that Iran was the guilty party."

Abe paused to see if his argument was succeeding. It was, so he continued to its conclusion. "And if you believe the accusation against Iran, the United States would be bound to retaliate against Iran. Israel would urge an attack by the United States against Iran. They've been pressuring the United States already. At the very least, Israel would be forced to attack Iran, and Iran would retaliate against Israel."

"The End of Days. The Apocalypse. The biblical prophecy fulfilled. It all makes sense — at least to them," Rendi chimed in.

"It was their best chance to bring the Second Coming."

Emma sat silently. It all made sense. Rendi only hoped that the Mossad agents got to the lab before Denny's cohorts had a chance to strike.

LV

The Lab

LAMENTATIONS RUGGLES WAS at the lab in the woods of
Megiddo, under a building that had been used as part of an
abandoned garbage dump. The lab had been constructed in the
cellar of the building. When Revelation lost cell-phone contact
with Denny, he'd directed his son to try to detonate the material they had assembled. They'd previously agreed that if contact were lost, they should assume that Denny was captured and
that it would be only a matter of time before the plot was discovered. They had hoped for more time, in order to smuggle in
more nuclear material, but they already had enough for one dirty
bomb. They also had enough conventional explosives — a combination of fertilizer, ammonium-nitrate fuel, and PETN — to
detonate the nuclear material. Lamentations would not live to
see the End of Days, but he would know he was responsible for
bringing them about, and he would be rewarded with the only
reward that mattered.

They had gotten the nuclear material through contacts in the Khan network. It was part of a shipment destined for Iran and had the same characteristics—the same chemical signature—as nuclear material identified in Tehran by American and Israeli agents. When detonated, it would leave unambiguous Iranian fingerprints. The man in the United States had paid a fortune for it, more than he would have had to pay for Ukrainian nuclear material. But it was worth the extra money to get the material from the Khan people, who believed they were selling to an Iranian intelligence operative—their initiate in Tehran. A false-flag operation, as Rendi had suspected. By purchasing the material in this way, it was far more likely that the Israelis and Americans would see Iranian fingerprints, even though they were planted prints. This would set off a series of retaliatory attacks and counterattacks, which would culminate in a nuclear exchange, the final battle and the End of Days. It was a good plan. It could work. If only Lamentations were able to detonate the dirty bomb before the Israelis found it and stopped him.

Lamentations knew exactly what he had to do. He didn't worry about contamination. If things worked out, he would lose his mortal coil within hours. So what did a little nuclear contamination matter? In heaven there were no bodies, only incorporeal souls. He took the priceless uranium from the lead boxes in which it was stored and began his process. His research on nuclear technology had paid off. His father knew what he was doing when he'd sent him abroad to learn this esoteric science of destruction.

In the meantime an Israeli commando unit, trained to find and disassemble nuclear bombs, was rushing by helicopter to find the lab. Using sophisticated Geiger counters and other highly classified technologies—technologies that had been developed for possible use in an attack on Iran's nuclear facilities—the unit zeroed in on the area in which the lab was hidden. Suddenly the Geiger counters spiked, indicating that nuclear material had been exposed to the air.

"They've taken the nuclear material out of the lead cases," Uzi Ramon, the head of the unit, announced.

"Everyone put on your nuclear shields. You're exposed."

The commandos placed their protective garments around their bodies as their helicopters circled over the small building from which the nuclear signals were emanating.

"It may be booby-trapped. Take all precautions," Uzi warned. "We can't attack by bombing the lab from the air. It will risk detonating the nuclear material. We have to come in from on top of the house, which is less likely to be wired. Lower the ladder," Uzi ordered. *"Acharai."*

Acharai was the battle cry of the IDF. It meant "after me." The leaders of Israeli elite units — and there was no unit more elite than Uzi's — prided themselves on always being the first into battle, on leading their soldiers into harm's way rather than commanding from the rear. That's why casualties were always so high among Israeli commanders and officers.

Uzi lowered himself down the ladder, followed by the other commandos. They landed on the sloped roof of the house and quickly found a small attic window, which they opened and crawled through. They raced downstairs, with stun guns drawn, expecting to meet armed resistance. What they saw shocked them.

Lamentations Ruggles — a small, bespectacled man, dressed in a suit and tie — looked like a pharmacist filling a prescription. He kept working, ignoring the commandos, even as they ordered him to back away from the table. The explosive trigger was neatly arranged and ready to start the chain reaction that would disperse radiation into the windy air. Uzi shot him with his stun gun, and he fell to the floor.

Uzi rushed to the table and saw that the man on the floor had been just minutes away from detonating the nuclear material on the table. Uzi made sure there were no timers, booby traps, or other materials capable of causing a detonation. Then he ordered everyone out and back to the copter, to reduce the risk of nuclear contamination.

"Take this guy with us. He's contaminated. Treat him accordingly. Then secure the premises and call in the ground team. Make sure to disable any explosives, if you find anything I might have missed. Tell them to gather up the material and put it in lead boxes. Then we're out of here. Job well done," Uzi commended his unit as he ascended the ladder back to the hovering helicopter.

The Gulfstream

"Wow, a private plane. I've never flown in one of those," Emma gushed, looking around the posh Gulfstream V. "How did you score this, Daddy?"

Abe reclined in the tan leather seat opposite his daughter and poured himself a glass of water. "Anything to get you home," he joked. "We have some appreciative friends in high places. Don't get used to it. Back in Boston you fly coach."

"Or frequent flier, on your account." Emma grinned. She, too, was sitting in a large leather seat, looking as if she hadn't a care in the world. She was young, in love, and had just helped solve one of the most infamous mass murders in global history while preventing an even worse one.

It had been five days since Lamentations Ruggles was captured in his lab. He was in the hospital being tested for radiation poisoning, and the Israeli and U.S. governments were fighting over who had first crack at prosecution. With the arrest in

Israel of Revelation and the arrests in the States of Roger Blakely, the compromised Secret Service agent, and Bob Buchanan, the bankroller, all the perpetrators of the American Colony bombing were behind bars. The only loose thread was Denny, because of the way they got him to make statements. No Israeli or American court would allow a conviction to be based on the methods used by the interrogators. Rendi was convinced, however, that the Israeli authorities could convict him of his attempt to murder her without his coerced statements. In any event, his career as an intelligence resource was certainly over.

After the plot was aborted, Abe reached out to his former client Rashid Husseini and asked him why he had pointed them in the direction of Iran. Rashid told Abe that he truly believed that the American Colony bombing had been orchestrated by the Iranians, because of their apocalyptic mind-set. "I was wrong," he admitted sheepishly to Abe. "So were a lot of other people, including the Israelis. Wishful thinking perhaps. Because I do not believe in religion, I was hoping it was religious fanatics, but not my brother. I was wrong. Please accept my apology."

The entire story had caused a sensation in Israel, and the authorities were only too happy to fly the Ringels home in high style if that meant less media time for Abe.

Abe was as relaxed as he'd felt in a long time. Knowing that his daughter would be taking a job in the capital until her clerkship started, put him at ease. With Habash's help, Emma had been convinced that Israel was too dangerous for her. At least for now. "I still have more than a million miles accumulated. You can use them to visit your father whenever you want," Abe offered.

"Better yet, you come visit me. Washington isn't that far from Cambridge, and I'm going to be busy in my new job."

"Human-rights division of the State Department. Could there be a more perfect place for you?" Rendi said proudly.

Emma smiled. She was excited about the job, which she had applied for and been offered via e-mail within days after the story of Dennis Savage and the Ruggles men broke. She decided to take it, because she couldn't stand to be stationed so far away from Abe and Rendi. "I'll be traveling a lot! Africa, Eastern Europe, Asia, the Middle East. I can visit the Regels."

"And Habash," Rendi said knowingly.

The night before Emma left, Habash had confided that he'd been offered a gig teaching a four-week seminar at the Kennedy School in Cambridge. He'd turned it down three times, but since Emma would be in the States for the foreseeable future, he had reconsidered and accepted.

They agreed to keep open the possibility of intensifying their romance, but Emma turned down Habash's request for an exclusive relationship. Life was too unpredictable for an adventurous young woman to become tied down to one man. Moreover, the events of the past weeks had pained her into wondering whether her attraction was more toward the excitement and challenge Habash represented than to the man himself. She wasn't sure whether she loved him or admired what he stood for and did. Perhaps both. Time would tell, and Emma had plenty of time.

"No more Lone Ranger stuff," Abe insisted. "No more following anonymous leads. No more kidnappers. I don't know if I can win any more cases. I'm getting a little old for that sort of stuff."

"Don't worry, Daddy. The State Department won't let me go anywhere on my own. They'll be keeping an eye on me."

"They'd better. You never know where the enemy lurks. Who would have imagined, when this all began at the American Colony, that it would end with a tiny pro-Israel Christian sect—a sect that traced its roots back to our ancestor Avi—that wanted to bring about the destruction of the world? Who could have imagined?"

"Shimshon told us that history would solve the mystery," Emma mused.

"But what he didn't warn us was that history would also provide false leads," Rendi added.

"They weren't even on our list," Emma observed.

"That's why they came so close to pulling it off," Abe asserted. "The smaller, more tight-knit, and obscure the group, the harder to find."

"Who knows what other self-appointed crazies are out there right now plotting our destruction! We live in apocalyptic times," Rendi said, shaking her head.

"It's a frightening time," Abe agreed.

"But what a challenge! It's a great time to be alive. I can't wait for my next adventure," Emma said, hugging them both, as the Gulfstream carrying the Ringel family made its way back to the United States.

ACKNOWLEDGMENTS

I want to express great appreciation to Melanie Downing for her perceptive editing and substantive contributions to this book, and to Les Pockell, who helped to shape my thinking about its structure and content. My agent, Helen Rees; my assistant, Sarah Neely; and my family and friends all encouraged me. A special note of appreciation to my son, Elon, whose insights improve everything I write. My wife, Carolyn Cohen, painstakingly read through drafts and gently pushed me to make constructive changes. Even more important, she encouraged me with her love.